THE GHOST WHO WALKED IN THE GARDEN

Dolores Stewart Riccio

This is a work of fiction. All the characters and events portrayed in this novel are either products of the author's imagination or used fictionally.

ISBN-13: 9781523429165
ISBN-10: 152342916X

Also by Dolores Stewart Riccio

The Cass Shipton Adventures:

Circle of Five

Charmed Circle

The Divine Circle of Ladies Courting Trouble

The Divine Circle of Ladies Making Mischief

The Divine Circle of Ladies Playing with Fire

The Divine Circle of Ladies Rocking the Boat

The Divine Circle of Ladies Tipping the Scales

The Divine Circle of Ladies Painting the Town

The Divine Circle of Ladies Digging the Dirt

The Divine Circle of Ladies Burning Their Bridges

Spirit, a novel of past and present lives

The Ghost Who Came Home from the Auction

My First Murder

Poetry

Doors to the Universe

The Nature of Things

(Anthology) Feast: Poetry & Recipes for a Full Seating at Dinner

Cookbooks

Superfoods: 300 Recipes for Foods That Heal Body and Mind

Superfoods for Women

Superfoods for Life

Nonfiction (with Joan Bingham)

Haunted Houses U.S.A.

More Haunted Houses

In memory of my dear friend, Ginger—
Virginia Saunders-Wyler

ACKNOWLEDGMENTS

With eternal thanks to all those who contributed their interest, enthusiasm, and expertise to this book:

my dedicated copy-editor and kibitzer, Joan Bingham;

the several good friends who have read and commented on this novel in manuscript: Pam Aieta, Nancy Brady Cunningham, Linda Courtiss, Jonnie Garstka, Lois Karfunkel, and to Jennifer Caven for her inestimable editing skills.

Tis the last rose of summer
Left blooming alone,
All her lovely companions
Are faded and gone.
No flower of her kindred,
No rose-bud is nigh
To reflect back her blushes
Or give sigh for sigh.

I'll not leave thee, thou lone one,
to pine on the stem!
Since the lovely are sleeping,
Go, sleep thou with them.
Thus kindly I scatter
Thy leaves o'er the bed,
Where thy mates of the garden
Lie scentless and dead…

- Thomas Moore -

The Berwinds

Hugh Belmont Berwind 1864-1919 m. 1888 to Edna Delano Pell 1870 -1930

Hugh Delano Berwind 1890-1918 m. 1917 to Rose Redford 1893-1918

Hugh Redford Persey Berwind 1918-1978

[adopted by William Alfred Rafferty and his wife Mabel O'Neill Rafferty

name changed to William Martin Rafferty m.1951to Jennifer Higgins 1925-1985

also known as Billy Martin, famous World War II poet]

Gerard Rafferty (Gerry) 1956 - m.1990 to Stella Razanno 1960-

Anna Gloria Rafferty 1993-

George Victor Berwind 1893-1956 m.1925 to Flora Belle Amory 1900-2002

George Amory Berwind 1928-1938

Paul David Berwind 1930-1938

The Amory Sisters

Flora Belle Amory 1900-2002- m.1925 to George Victor Berwind 1893-1956

George Amory Berwind 1928-1938

Paul David Berwind 1930-1938

Eleanor May Amory 1905-1975 m.1925 to Henry James Swett 1890-1960

Henry James Swett Jr. 1930-2000 m. 1965 to Carolyn Brewster Cabot 1945 – 1998

Henry James Swett III 1967-

Paul Francis Swett 1970-

Jane Cabot Swett (Lady Jane Gamble)1972-

m. 1992 to Lord Terrance Gamble divorced 2000.

Hon. Robyn Gamble 1993-

The Burns Sisters

Mary Margaret Burns 1873- 1948 worked for Berwinds from 1890 to 1938

Sister Mary Joseph Burns 1870-1940 (formerly Patty) Augustinian nun at St. Rita's Mission

JUNE 1

Things to Do Today

Call Jamie re: auction
Don't forget magnet, magnifying glass, notebook, sandwiches
Buy with yr head not heart—no portraits or letters!!
Mix up non-lethal-to-dogs spray for roses, garlic powder. Also buy ladybugs.
Libr. return How to Talk to Your Teen*, borrow* Stress Management for Stepmoms
Pick up cardamom for Moira, draw the line at saffron

"Fine items from the estate of Flora Amory Berwind with selected additions"

Holding the catalog she'd received in the mail last week, Olivia moved slowly around the room, viewing the antiques, collectibles, and box lot jumbles with a practiced eye. She jotted notes on "possibles" with prices beyond which she would not bid, as was her rule. One of Bill Byatt's classier auctions, she decided, even though it was being held in the Elks Lodge. Some lovely Art Deco pieces: lamps, vases, objets d'art, and furniture.

Olivia could see Jamie's cloud of red hair bent over a rack displaying dresses and furs in the slim "flapper" style that her zaftig friend would never in this lifetime fit into, but there was always the jewelry, some stunning geometric designs. Jamie was devoted to vintage jewelry, but Olivia was more interested in some of the marquetry pieces, and one delicate table lamp with stained glass shade, red roses and vivid green leaves. Olivia didn't know why she was so obsessed with roses lately, unless it was simply because the roses she'd planted at her new husband Dave's place, her home now, were just coming into full bloom. She suspected that most of her choices would bring bids far beyond her own modest assessments, but the exciting thing about auctions was, you never could tell when some prize might be scooped up for a song. A good auction, as Jamie often said, was a combination of theater and gambling in one addictive package. But Olivia, who prided herself on prudence and fiscal restraint, was more attracted by the thought of buying unique pieces at bargain prices.

Bill Byatt, the auctioneer, set a glass of ice water and a cup of hot coffee on a small table beside the podium, and rapped his gavel loudly to bring the buyers back to their chairs. "Ladies and Gentlemen, welcome to the Roaring Twenties! Tonight we're selling many museum quality items from the estate of Flora Amory Berwind, Art Deco masterpieces by named artists, as well as a variety of other desirable collectibles of the Jazz Age. Everything you see on display here must be sold tonight. And by the time we've emptied this room, many of you will be taking home a real treasure. So … let's have an auction!"

Jamie slipped into her chair and handed Olivia one of the gin and tonics she had hastily purchased at the Elks Lodge bar. "I've got my eye on an emerald ring that I probably can't afford, but buyers are unpredictable. I'm keeping the good thought."

Olivia was intent on Googling the life of Flora Amory Berwind. Her curiosity had been aroused, and she must have immediate answers. "Didn't we go to a Berwind estate auction last Christmas? I just can't figure where all this 1920s stuff came from," she said. "It doesn't make sense. Flora couldn't have been *that* old."

"What difference does it make?" Jamie whispered as brisk bidding began on the first lot, always a showy item to concentrate the attention of buyers. An Art Deco stained glass panel was being held up by two brawny young runners. "I heard the sellers are distant relatives. Or in-laws. Or something like that."

"Sounds about right." Olivia skimmed the Flora Amory Berwind entries on her iPhone. "Flora, noted philanthropist, benefactor of the SPCA, lived to be 102. Died in 2002. But her estate was held up in probate for ages. Apparently, there was a dispute among family members that dragged on and on. Finally settled in 2012. By then the attorneys must have taken a sizeable share, such a waste. That probably explains the auction we went to last year—court costs and legal fees. Now the winning heir is ready to cash in on the rest. Some of the more valuable pieces were sent to Sotheby's months ago, the rest parceled off to Byatt, possibly because the Berwind summer estate was in Duxbury. Must have been an Art Deco showplace. There was also an apartment at the Dakota on the Upper West Side in Manhattan. Oh, well—you're right. *Makes no difference now*. There a gentleman's marquetry case I've got my eye on. The kind of thing that might be set on a highboy, to hold cuff links, watches, and the like."

"For Dave?" Jamie asked.

"Not necessarily." Dave owned one waterproof digital watch, no cufflinks. As a detective with the State Police Unit of Plymouth County and the foster father of three teenage kids, male jewelry was not even visible on his radar. Olivia, on the other hand, liked subtle gold pieces, pearls, and opals, but nothing too showy. "I've check marked that rose lamp, too, but I'm afraid it will go too high."

"Maybe. Let's just hope that whatever you bring home is safe."

"Safe?"

"You know what I mean." Jamie hummed a few bars of the Twilight Zone theme music.

"Don't even go there, Jamie," Her friend's sly dig was a warning not to buy anything with otherworldly vibes, as Olivia had done in the past. But there was a little good in every mischance. That incident had led to her meeting the love of her life, Dave.

Bidding went along briskly for most of an hour. Olivia won the marquetry case for ten dollars more than she had been prepared to spend. Next, she found herself outbidding a dealer in the front row for a Lalique Oceania paperweight that she hadn't even noted in her catalog. She vowed to exercise more restraint when the lamp came up.

After about an hour, some buyers wandered outside for a smoke or to the rest rooms or to the bar for a beer. Olivia and Jamie ate the kasseri cheese sandwiches Olivia had packed.

A Tiffany black dahlia vase went to the single bidder during a few moments of mass inattention. But the hiatus soon passed; buyers settled down again to spirited bidding. Bill Byatt never troubled himself to sell by lot numbers—76 might be followed by 14. Olivia waited until almost 9:00 PM to bid on the Tiffany lamp. By the time it came up, however, the lamp sold for three times the amount she'd jotted down in her catalog. The emerald ring, as well, was quickly bid up to $750, and Jamie sat on her hands, scowling. She did buy a lady's silver watch with the characteristic Art Deco "exploded"

Roman numerals, and a short black "speakeasy" dress with a tiered, beaded fringe.

"I think I can let out those seams," Jamie said. Olivia smiled but did not reply.

The next item was a box lot of cookbooks that Olivia had glanced at earlier, noting a fine 1922 edition of *Fanny Farmer's Boston Cooking School Cook Book* and a 1946 edition of *The Joy of Cooking* among a number of ephemeral church and school "fundraiser" cookbooks. Another unplanned buy, but when no one would bid over $20, Olivia couldn't resist, knowing those two alone were worth at least $200. Not that she would sell them. Perhaps a peace offering to Dave's foster-daughter, Moira, whose passion for all things culinary was so amazing in a teenager. Her hand shot up of its own volition. $25, and the lot was hers.

They left long before the last of the items was sold. Jamie, a private nurse, was starting a new live-in assignment on Monday morning (her favorite kind of patient, a rich old fellow, John Peter Whelan, with a mansion in Dover) and she had a million things to do tomorrow, Sunday. "I've had enough excitement and frustration for one evening," she declared. They picked up their purchases at the desk and left in Olivia's Honda minivan, always their preferred transport to auctions, rather than Jamie's silver Mustang convertible, in case they fell victim to some bulky item such as an armoire. It had been known.

While Olivia drove, Jamie examined the marquetry case admiringly. "Nice wood grain. Maybe Dave would like it for guy stuff, coins and such. He could always remove the brass plaque."

"What brass plaque?"

"The one inside the box. Didn't you look under the tack red velvet lining?" Jaime asked.

"Oh. No. That's not like me, is it?"

"No, it's not. You don't miss much, usually."

"Is the plaque engraved?"

"Yes."

"Well?"

"To my lovely boy Hugh Delano Berwind on his twelfth birthday," Jamie read the inscription. "Beautiful lettering. Probably kept his jackknife and slingshot in it. Maybe a dried toad skin."

"Hugh?"

"Hugh," Jamie affirmed.

"Couldn't be the same one."

"You mean 'To Hugh from his Rose, *I shall but love thee better after death*'? That Hugh, whose name is in the flat silver locket with no chain you bought at Byatt's last year? With the curl of dark hair tied with a pinkish ribbon?"

"It's just a weird coincidence. And besides, I've never had any eerie vibes from that locket."

"Not yet," Jamie closed the marquetry case. She picked up her flapper dress and stroked the extravagant jet beading. "I wouldn't have minded living in the twenties. Those gals really knew how to party."

~

Whoever had lined the marquetry case with red velvet had not been very skilled. It fit badly and had loosened over the years. The cloth came away readily when Olivia lifted it. Underneath was a decorative paper lining, a dignified gray pattern surrounding the Phillips Exeter oval seal depicting a beehive at sunrise. *Finis Origine Pendet*. "The end depends upon the beginning." Olivia liked the paper better than the velvet, which was, as Jamie had pointed out, cheap and ordinary. When she ran her finger over the engraved brass plaque inside the box, she noticed that one tiny end of the paper was coming unglued. She thought she would cement that in place as well, but she forgot to make a note of it.

The Lalique paperweight gave a pleasing touch of elegance to Olivia's oak desk. She moved it from place to place until she found the perfect arrangement. *There!*

The box of books she left in the kitchen without remark and was gratified later that day to find Moira seated on a high stool paging through Fanny Farmer. "Wow, this old lady was sure into candies. I could do the penuche fudge. Oh, and there's a recipe for watermelon pickle in *that* one that I might try. Mom made some the year before..." Moira let the sentence dangle and pointed to a stained red booklet: *The Book of Pickles and Preserves by the Ladies League of St. Rita Parish.* When Olivia picked it up, a bookmark fell out. No, not a bookmark, a Mass card, a pretty thing decorated with bouquet of pastel blue flowers. *Mary Margaret Burns is enrolled for a continuing Holy Sacrifice of the Mass at the Church of Saint Rita by her loving sister, Mary Joseph, A.A.* Olivia touched the silvery edge, still bright and delicate. There was something appealing about the card. It would make a lovely bookmark. Olivia put it in her pocket.

~

In the whirlwind of her love affair with Dave and the perils they'd faced together last year, Olivia's orderly life and careful habits had been scattered like confetti. She'd had to weather the turmoil of selling her cottage in Scituate, the furor of organizing their wedding, and the personal upheaval of moving into Dave's home.

Located in Marshfield, the sprawling farmhouse was a faded Colonial red. It had probably begun small but had been continually enlarged through the generations. Nevertheless, Dave had added a new wing to the first floor, which was theirs alone. Olivia loved the view across the street, an expanse of marsh, awash with delicate pastels and alive with a noisy population of birds. Beyond the marsh, separated by a row of cottages and an old inn, was the Atantic shore.

As a self-employed Archives/Records Management Consultant, Olivia could and did postpone assignments during these life changes. Still, she felt that only her methodical routines and firm control of events had kept her from being overwhelmed. And once she'd really settled into Dave's world (perhaps "settled" was the wrong word—it was more like being flung into a battle of wits, a test of her strength and resolve), she was naturally relegated to the role of stepmom to Dave's foster family of three teenagers. Although she'd resigned herself to this—there being no way to have Dave and not take on the kids—Olivia's managerial skills had been strained to the utmost. She clung to her list-making with renewed devotion to detail, if only to enjoy the fantasy of controlling family life rather than having it control her.

Dave's first partner in the State Police, Detective Tom O'Hara, had been shot to death in front of his own home on the orders of a Boston crime boss. This tragedy had left his three children essentially orphans, because their mother, Alice, was serving eight to fifteen years in the federal prison in Danbury for her involvement in an urban terrorist gang when she was sixteen. She'd fled the gang after a bank robbery gone wrong, changed her name from Teresa to Alice, and become a nurse, which was how she had met Tom. Almost believing in her own fictional rebirth as a new and different woman, Alice had never revealed this deception and the reason for it to Tom. After they'd married and started a family, she'd felt safe at last, but the FBI had tracked her down a few years ago, delivering a killing blow to the O'Hara family.

Then the second disaster struck, Tom's murder. Dave, who knew and loved the O'Hara children, couldn't bear to see them separated and parceled out to foster families. He'd arranged with Alice to become their legal guardian.

Surly Kevin, now fifteen, still refused to give his mom a break, after what he considered to be her ultimate betrayal of their family. His emotional outlet and saving grace was Celtic music, and Olivia could usually read his moods (ranging from angry to mournful) by the rhythm of the bodhrán he played every day in his room.

Moira, fourteen, an accomplished cook, was not about to give up the role she'd assumed in Dave's bachelor home to Olivia, the mom-come-lately. Although Olivia herself loved to cook, especially dishes based on her Greek heritage, she realized the advantages of allowing glowering, sassy Moira to reign supreme in the kitchen—some of the time. *Blessed are the peacemakers* for they shall not have to make the meatloaf every single Thursday night.

Danny, eleven, was a computer whiz who disappeared for days at a time into a bedroom that resembled a giant spider web of power cords. He seemed to have few friends, with the exception of Olivia's two rescue dogs, Sadie and Bruno. Bruno, the Shepherd mix, was Danny's devoted companion, while Sadie, the big-headed white Pit Bull Terrier, divided her time between Danny and Moira (with the undeniable benefits of special treats in the kitchen).

Olivia was not put out by this seeming desertion; her dogs' inability to dissemble was somehow endearing. Sadie would still leap onto the bed with Olivia and Dave if the bedroom door was left ajar, and Bruno still preferred rides in Olivia's Honda to any delight on earth. No matter how softly keys were taken up off the hall table, Bruno would hear them jingle and abandon all other posts to come running.

Sometimes Olivia felt she must have been mad to take on this menagerie, but in her heart she knew there was no way she could have given up her passionate connection to strong, smart, sexy Dave with his soft, kind brown eyes and inviting mouth—and marriage was an all-or-nothing-at-all deal. Dave's total commitment to those he loved was part and parcel of who he was, as well as a reassuring quality in a husband. Possibly peace and sanity are greatly over-rated anyway. But just to keep a rein on the utter chaos, Olivia relied even more on her daily list. She favored small moleskin notebooks in a variety of colors, with lined paper and ribbon markers.

Almost by accident, while researching the storage of original probate court documents, Olivia happened upon a report in *The New York Times* of the family scandal that had been central to the settlement of the Berwind estate. She could hardly wait to show Jamie the article she'd printed out. Jamie now occupied a well-appointed room at the Whelan mansion in Dover but was relieved by another nurse from Friday through Sunday, so she spent the weekends in her own townhouse at The Willows.

"Lunch tomorrow at that new place on the Green Harbor? The Cedar Point Inn?" Olivia called Jamie on Friday night. "I hear their cocktails are fantastic." As Olivia knew she would, Jamie snapped up the lure. She was devoted to gin martinis made "just so." Stirred, *not* shaken. One didn't want the gin diluted by melting ice.

"One small hitch. Mike. I can't leave Mike to hang out on his own." Jamie's son spent most weekends at her condo.

"Bring him to our house. Dave's got some follow-up interviews on a fraud case, but the kids will all be home, even Kevin, and more importantly, the doggies," Olivia promised. The grinning hospitality of Sadie and Bruno would be a bonus. Mike, a thirteen-year-old traveler between parents, grandparents, and private school, had never had a dog of his own.

"That should work. As long as Kevin doesn't give Mike the usual cold shoulder, and Moira, the little minx, refrains from hanging all over him," Jamie agreed.

"Good. I've found some background on the Berwind story that I'm dying to share,"

"Uh-oh," Jamie sighed. "Couldn't we just let poor Flora rest in peace?"

"Of course. Just a little follow-up gossip. I'm curious about Hugh and Rose, of course, but that's all. I've got my hands full with my own family right now. No time to pursue the past," Olivia said, and thought she meant it.

JUNE 15

Things to Do Today

Lunch with Jamie Cedar Point, bring NY Times *print-out*
Plan weekly menus with Moira. Straighten out schedule.
Libr. return Stress Management for Stepmoms,
borrow Negotiation for Dummies & Boston Red Sox 101
Call agency—new job? specify easy hours
Portfolio, check daily, catch up on research

"Did you ever read the whole story of the Berwind scandal?" Olivia had the grace to allow Jamie to take the first beatific sip of her exquisite martini before she launched into this new enthusiasm.

"Now that you mention it, I faintly remember something. Didn't one of the nephews go to jail? Stealing from his demented old aunt?"

"Great-aunt. Yes, that's the story. Sentence, one to three years. Got off with time served when he agreed to settle with his siblings, Paul and Jane, who'd been left out entirely. They claimed that Flora's last will had been obtained by the trickery or forgery or both of their older brother, Henry James Swett III, who had got himself appointed Flora's live-in caretaker. Also that Henry had been systematically selling off the family treasures while abusing his great-aunt Flora, shutting off the heat in her room and feeding her scraps. Can you imagine? The original will had divided her millions evenly between the three surviving Swetts. Except for a couple of million in trust for the care of her dachshunds. She'd been quoted as preferring the company of her dogs to that of her only living family, her sister's grandchildren, but then the dogs mysteriously died. Talk about elder abuse!" Olivia handed Jamie a copy of the article on the Berwind case that she'd printed out from *The New York Times* website.

Jamie stuffed it into her copious handbag unread. "I can see that you're rather worked up about this, so I ask you again, what difference does this make, now, to us? Caring for the elderly is not a walk in the park, you know." Jamie gazed at the harbor view and took another sip. "What a perfect afternoon! And you can see the lighthouse from here."

"Hugh Delano Berwind would have been Flora's brother-in-law if he hadn't died in 1918 on the Western Front," Olivia persisted. "So, after the death of their parents, Hugh's younger brother, George, inherited the entire Berwind fortune. George married Flora in 1925, and they became the parents of two boys who died young of typhoid fever. When George passed on, his wife inherited the whole shebang. The present heirs are the grandchildren of Flora's sister, Eleanor. They're not even Berwinds. They're Swetts."

Jamie sighed. "Families evolve over time, not necessarily the survival of the fittest. How's your cosmo? I'm having another. You?"

"It's perfect. But no thanks. It wouldn't do for the Lowenstein stepmom to stagger home in an inebriated state. Kevin would scowl at me and slam into his room. Moria would take notes to report to Dave later. And poor Danny would simply spill the beans unintentionally."

"Better you than me, girlfriend. When I marry again, it's going to be a rich old duffer whose children are all grown and scattered to the ends of the earth. Take John Peter Whelan, for instance. No progeny of his own, two brothers he rarely sees, a favorite grandniece who's constantly in and out of rehab, and a bunch of rapacious cousins he won't even let in the door. And he's got all that beautiful money."

"What about marrying for love?" Olivia was suffused with a soft glow just thinking about the new pleasures and prospects love had brought into her life, the whole world opening like a blossom. But explaining that to Jamie would be like describing a rainbow to someone who was color-blind. And besides, Jamie would giggle.

"I tried that—twice." Jamie signaled the waitress and pointed to her nearly empty glass. "And the only good thing that came out of my first marriage to Moody was Mike. My second to Finch was simply a total loss."

"I wonder what became of Rose after Hugh died?"

"Well, obviously they never married. So his brother George became the sole heir, so what?" Jamie was not yet on board with Olivia's latest craze.

"Flora outlived her only sibling, sister Eleanor. And outlived Eleanor's son, Henry James Swett Jr. as well. The only family members left to inherit the Berwind fortune were Eleanor's three grandchildren. Although Flora apparently preferred her two dachshunds. But the very last will, the one that was hotly disputed, left everything to her so-called caretaker, Henry III."

"So, what's the problem with that?"

"I don't think you've been listening, Jamie. When there are many millions involved, there are always relatives who will do anything to get their hands on the family fortune. And they won't be crazy about sharing with one another, or anyone else.

It may be that the dachshunds died of natural causes, but I wonder. And how do you suppose Henry III got the courts to appoint him sole caretaker to his senile, rich great-auntie?"

"A clever lawyer, a friendly judge," Jamie looked around for their waitress to re-appear.

"We'd better order as soon as she brings your *second* cocktail. I'm having the 'award-winning' chowder with fried clam garnish and the lobster salad." Olivia took another cautious sip of her cosmo.

"Make that two. I've always thought that a younger wife is better off with a prenup. Once a gal has a well-drawn, generous prenup in place, the greedy family has no cause to sue and will have to be satisfied with whatever other cards have been dealt them."

"You haven't read enough about wills of the rich and famous, Jamie. It's not unusual for the battling to go on for a decade while law firms gobble up the estate. The Berwinds are a case in point."

"*The first thing we do, let's kill all the lawyers.* That's Shakespeare, you know." A hint of worry dimmed Jamie's usual exuberance. "Just as I feared, you're becoming obsessed with past wrongs again. I don't have a good feeling about this."

"Okay, okay. At least I'm not being *haunted* by some vexatious ghost."

~

After that seafood banquet at Cedar Point, Olivia was not thrilled to find Moira, wearing her customary wrap-around chef's apron, already embarked on slathering a slab of fresh salmon with Dijon mustard for their supper. Dave, whose fraud case had taken him to downtown Plymouth, had stopped by the Town Pier fish mart on his way home at Moira's request. Then a murder suspect had been arrested in Kingston, and Dave had rushed away to interrogate him before a lawyer got into the picture.

Meanwhile, a family melee had erupted. Olivia reflected that investigating a murder (particularly a cold case, as this one was) might be a lot less stressful than refereeing another O'Hara dust-up. Her attempts to restore good will were usually met with strenuous resistance. After all, who asked her to interfere? Hadn't they been managing perfectly well on their own before she moved in and wanted to change everything?

She found Danny fighting back tears, Bruno trying to comfort him, and Moira screaming at Kevin.

"This retard needs his head examined," Kevin insisted.

"Well, you don't have to be calling him names, you dumbhead!" Moira shook a wooden spoon at her older brother, her pale blue eyes flashing fire.

"Look at that wanker! He's going to cry like a baby." Kevin scowled in disgust.

Bruno barked indignantly, placing his body between Danny and his two battling siblings. Sadie came rushing from the master bedroom, where she had been napping in luxurious comfort, anxious that one of her charges might need safeguarding. Her big white head swiveled back and forth among the combatants, sniffing up news.

Danny had plastered himself against the kitchen wall near the back door. The long fair hair that almost covered his outstanding ears appeared drenched with sweat. He was small for his age, and Olivia thought he was emotionally fragile as well.

Feeling the mellow glow of that relaxed luncheon with Jamie swiftly evaporating, Olivia laid a protective hand on

Danny's shoulder, shutting off Kevin's scornful glare. "What's the matter, honey? Is there anything I can do?"

"I know what I saw, I don't care what anyone says." Dannycrossed his arms and glowered back at Kevin.

Olivia had a moment of apprehension. Still, she pursued the source of Danny's distress. "What did you see, Danny? Did something frighten you?"

"There was, too, a lady, because I saw her with my own eyes. She was in those rose bushes *you* planted. And I could see right through her. But no one believes me." Danny fought manfully against a sob.

Uh-oh. Instantly, Olivia realized that no good would come out of Danny's encounter, whatever it was. Best thing would be to discover the truth of what happened as gently as possible. "Okay, I believe you. You saw something. But it's not there now, right?"

"That's it!" Kevin hit the door frame with the flat of his hand in a gesture that exuded disgust. "Humor the little freak."

"Name-calling is the last resort of the unintelligent. Whatever happened, it was real to Danny." Olivia put a guiding hand on Danny's shoulder. "Come on, honey, why don't you show me where?"

Feeling sorry that she had spoken so sharply to Kevin, Olivia thought a trip to the garden might break up the conflict. Bruno and Sadie agreed enthusiastically and rushed out the front door as soon as Olivia opened it.

Olivia was proud of the rose garden, her own inspiration. The backyard was shaded by big, old maples with outdoor furniture arranged comfortably underneath. Dave's wrought iron sculptures added a whimsical touch. But not much in the way of flowers, except impatiens, would grow there. The front of the old farmhouse, however, faced southeast and got brilliant sunlight from dawn through early afternoon. There was a full-length porch where old-fashioned rocking chairs were lined up in an inviting row, a perfect place to enjoy the riot of roses. They cascaded over a picket fence, twined on trellises, and climbed the new arbor at the front gate. She had plans for more, gradually replacing most of the lawn with an artful, romantic garden.

"Good heavens!" Jamie had exclaimed when she'd seen Olivia's garden burst forth in glory practically on the first day of June. "Aren't you overdoing the rose-covered honeymoon cottage a bit? What do the kids say?"

"They hate it," Olivia had confessed. "But as Moira kindly put it, better I should play in the dirt outdoors than mess around with her kitchen, which she's got arranged just the way she likes it."

"Too many cooks?"

"*You think?*"

Now as Danny and Olivia stepped onto the porch, she took a deep breath of pure rose perfume and sweet grass. (The scent of garlic spray had evaporated, she was glad to notice.) In the gradually deepening shadows of late afternoon, the fragrance of June seemed even more delightful. For a moment, she almost forgot why she was here with a hiccupping, fearful boy by her side.

Both dogs took the opportunity to relieve themselves, despite Olivia's shout, "No, no, not here, *get out back!*"

"She was right there!" Danny pointed a trembling finger at a group of four trellised roses, pale to deep pink, grouped around a white wrought iron bench.

"Are you sure, honey? Might it have been sunlight slanting through the lattice work?"

Danny swallowed back another sob and wiped his nose on the end of his Boston Celtics T-shirt. "She walked right through them."

"What did she look like? Was she pretty? Or scary?" Olivia was almost afraid to ask.

"Sort of pretty, I guess. And really, really thin."

"Thin? You mean, like a skeleton?"

"No, no, I'm telling you, she was a real person. Only see-through, like the holograms at Disney World. Bruno was there with me. He saw her, too, and he didn't like her at all."

"Did you see her face?"

"She was wearing a light dress. Sort of like the sky, only paler. Her hair was dark and soft-looking. I don't know about her face. I don't remember it." Danny had stopped sniffling, his tone bordering on the belligerent now. Olivia knew how stupid someone felt, trying to explain a vision, if that's what this was.

"I believe you, Danny. I've seen a lady like that myself. Misty, was she?"

"I guess. Are you going to tell Uncle Dave? He won't believe me, either." Danny kicked a stone lying in the path onto the grass. Bruno ran to see if it would turn into a ball, but when he got near the bench among the roses, he sniffed the air, backed up rapidly, and whimpered.

Sadie, who'd settled herself down where the last remaining ray of afternoon sunshine was warming a patch of grass, got up stiffly. Heading toward the stairs, she barked twice, sharply. An order given, and received. Bruno followed her onto the porch, where both dogs stood with their heads turned toward Olivia, waiting with the impatient patience of canines for the door to be opened.

It wasn't the first time that Danny had seen a ghost. The same was true for Sadie and Bruno, who'd been spooked plenty of times last year at Olivia's cottage in Scituate.

This can't be happening again. Time to change the subject, Olivia decided. She put her arm around Danny, moving him toward the porch. "Let's go inside and forget about that weird lady.

Let's just be glad she's gone. And think about going to Duxbury beach for a picnic tomorrow, instead." Dave had promised that Sunday would be family day, although he never really knew if he would be called in for some emergency. Still, the South Shore was hardly a high crime area, and there was every chance that their Sunday outing would go ahead as planned.

"Okay, Aunt Liv." Danny was the only O'Hara who gave Olivia a family rank. He took her hand now, and they went back into the house. His fingers were sticky and damp, but Olivia appreciated his trust. "She wasn't old, you know. She was lots younger than you."

As soon as Olivia opened the front door, the dogs barreled inside and bolted upstairs. Danny hurried up after them. Olivia went to offer to help with supper, which help Moira would refuse, she knew. But Sunday would be Olivia's. Sunday through Wednesday, Olivia had insisted, would be her days to cook dinner, and that was that. Moira needed to focus more on teen activities. Olivia had decided to make a devil's food cake for the picnic. But when she opened the refrigerator door to check on eggs and milk, she found that Moira had been there ahead of her. A perfect cake stood on the top shelf, shimmering yellow frosting garnished with paper-thin slices of lemon.

"It's for the picnic, Dave's favorite." Moira turned away with a half-hidden smirk. "But you can do the sandwiches, if you want. I made chicken salad. It's in that blue bowl."

Olivia sighed. She'd have to get up pretty early in the morning, literally, to beat Moira to the stove. What would Jamie advise? *Count your blessings*, probably.

"That cake looks elegant, dear. But how about your book report? *Kidnapped*, was it?"

"Oh, I did that at school. Danny's going to print it out for me this weekend," Moira said. "Want to set the table for supper?" She handed a stack of plates to Olivia, who stifled the temptation to throw a few.

"*Kidnapped* was made into a movie. Would you like me to see if it's on Netflix?" Olivia offered.

Moira brightened from her usual scowl. "Who's in that, anyway?"

Olivia thought the Michael Caine remake was the best. Moira had never heard of Michael Caine, but she graciously acceded. Olivia was tempted to chalk that up on the kitchen wall, but she took the plates and dutifully began to arrange them on the long oak table.

"Hey, Liv—is Danny sick in the head or anything?" Moira asked.

"No, dear, he is not sick. He saw a girl in the garden, that's all. Or he imagined her. Doesn't matter now. Kevin worries too much."

"Oh, that's good then. I need him to print out my book report."

"Don't you have your own printer?" The O'Haras each had a private bedroom now that she and Dave had moved downstairs into the new addition. Computers were *de rigueur* for school work, but neither Moira nor Kevin had the elaborate set-up that dominated Danny's kingdom.

"Mine needs toner." Moira checked the salmon with a cooking fork. "Not done yet." She slid it back into the oven.

"Wow! That's so impressive." Olivia hoped her words didn't sound as phony as they felt. "You're an amazing cook, dear, but wouldn't it be better if you concentrated on your schoolwork?"

"Hey, Liv—school's out next week, in case you don't remember. And I'm going to Johnson & Wales, anyway, not some artsy-fartsy liberal college. Who wants to read those dumb books about pirates, anyway?" Moira began to mash potatoes with a vengeance. "And by the way, Liv—Danny never saw queer stuff until Dave brought you here, you know."

Olivia poured herself a glass of chardonnay from the open bottle in the refrigerator. If she didn't get a handle on this family thing, she'd find herself at AA confessing her frustrations to a roomful of strangers. *Hi, my name is Olivia Andreas, I mean, Lowenstein, and I'm a stepmother.*

~

The weather on Sunday afternoon had been perfection for picnics. Predictably, the water was still frigid, though. Olivia hadn't even worn her bathing suit, though the rest of the family had. How youngsters endured that bone-chilling temperature was a mystery to her. Dave, of course, was required to jump in bravely, if briefly. Being a woman, Olivia reflected, means never having to show off one's physical prowess. A good thing.

They'd driven far down the dunes to the third crossover in Dave's dark red Bronco. Giving new meaning to the term "hangdogs," Sadie and Bruno had been left behind to press their noses mournfully against the living room windows. Dogs were not allowed to roam free near protected beach grass and bird habitats, and Olivia's were too rambunctious to manage on leash. Kevin had been missing from their party, as well, having preferred to spend Sunday with his buddies, a rock group calling themselves the Celtic Storm, in which Kevin's Bodhrán was the heartbeat. But he'd been home by the time they'd returned, sandy and exhausted.

No one had told Dave yet about Danny's sighting. Olivia guessed it was up to her to give a clear, concise account before her stepkids could embroider the incident. Enclosed in the privacy of the master suite to change before supper, she broached the subject.

"Danny thought he saw something that disturbed him in the rose garden yesterday," she began. Cautiously, she described the boy's vision of the girl in a light dress, in the least alarmist language possible.

Dave looked up from stepping out of his sandy bathing shorts. "He's an imaginative kid. Lives in an otherworldly place of zombies, aliens, vampires, and evil slugs. I suspect that all those computer games are addling his brain."

Olivia rummaged in her closet to find something warmer than she'd worn to the beach. Also, to offer no expression of belief or disbelief to Dave's assessment of the incident. The sudden warmth she felt traveling from her neck down her back was Dave moving closer. Perhaps Olivia didn't believe in auras, but she could always feel the attraction of Dave's energy whenever he came near, as if she would be compelled to lean toward him. He slipped the sundress straps off her shoulders. "Let's take a shower together," he suggested, his voice low and husky.

Olivia turned toward him, and those smooth, hard arms immediately pulled her close. His neck smelled deliciously of brine, seaweed, and himself.

So that ended the discussion of ghost sightings for the time being.

~

Leave it to Moira to keep the pot boiling! "We never had ghost ladies in the old days," she declared on Monday night, pushing a piece of Olivia's moussaka around her plate. "Is this lamb? I hate lamb."

"No, dear. It's grass-fed ground beef," Olivia said.

"You know what I think? I think we should have this whole place exorcised." Moira assumed a pious expression. The carroty hair stood up around her freckled face like a halo. "The Church has special priests for that. I saw one on YouTube who will exorcise by Skype. It only costs $299. We could all chip in. Lay Olivia's ghosts to rest for all eternity."

Danny kicked the table leg. "It wasn't a ghost. It was a hologram, I told you."

"Oh, sure. A hologram wandering around our front yard. *Space Invaders* or *Zombie Apocalypse*?" Kevin helped himself to another huge slab of moussaka. Olivia marveled at how much food he could shovel in and still remain as skinny as one of the sticks he used to play the Bodhrán

"Cut that out, all of you," Dave said. "Let's keep our minds on enjoying the good new days, especially this delicious casserole."

"Have you ever seen *The Amityville Horror*?" Moira persisted. "I think the rose lady will be back some night when we're all asleep in our beds, and…"

"Is there any of that delicious lemon cake left from the picnic?" Dave interrupted, and was rewarded by the girl's satisfied smile and a change of subject.

Although Olivia was thankful that Dave always knew just how to manage his wards, she was uneasy, as well. Maybe she should just get rid of the silver locket and the marquetry box. The locket didn't even have a chain; it was a thin, flat oval inscribed with a design that might have been elaborate, unreadable initials. Cleverly hinged, opening it risked breaking a fingernail. Inside, two frames with real glass. Under one, the portrait of a lovely girl; under the other, a lock of dark hair. She believed it was meant to be slipped into a man's pocket as a keepsake. Maybe she could sell them on eBay. Or the Duxbury consignment shop.

On the other hand, Olivia knew there was a hidden story there, somewhere between the two evocative mementoes. A mystery meant for her to unravel. Why? Because she could. She'd done it before.

Jamie was right, Olivia thought. This was crazy. She was obsessed. Perhaps she was suffering from an undiagnosed case of OCD.

Still, after the kitchen was cleared up (by Kevin and Danny, another tribute to Dave's management skills), she thought she'd have another look at the marquetry box, on top of her bureau now, home to the few pieces of jewelry she wore most often. The family would be totally absorbed in the Red Sox game, an enthusiasm she was being taught to share.

~

What a handsome box it was! Olivia ran her fingers over the intricate design of inlaid wood, as smooth as skin. Was it Hugh's mother who'd given her boy this grown-up birthday gift? Olivia knew her curiosity about a total stranger, long dead, was being aroused, and this was not a good sign. Perhaps the best solution would be to give this obviously masculine trinket box to Dave, as Jamie had suggested in the first place. He might not be the jewelry type, but he'd find some use for it, she was sure. She'd seen three or four versions of the Swiss Army knife thrown into his top drawer, from the Explorer model to the Huntsman.

Opening the box, Olivia took out the string of pearls, an opal pendant, a gold rope chain, and some earrings that she wore often. Also that silver locket she'd bought at Byatt's last year, which seemed somehow to belong there. She would put these pieces back into her jewelry case. She touched the brass plaque, still bright as if someone had just polished it. She wondered what Hugh Delano Berwind, aged twelve, had kept in there when he went away to Phillips Exeter, as she assumed he had from the heavy paper lining with the school's insignia. Preparation for all those qualities of leadership and integrity that would get him killed in World War I, a beautiful young man in his prime. How did she know he was good-looking? A vague recollection tugged at her mind. Almost as if she were being haunted by a face she'd never seen. Or had she?

Snap out of it, Olivia! She gave herself a mental slap.

Olivia fingered the loose seam she'd noticed before in the box's lining. She should paste that back into place before giving the box to Dave. Carefully, she lifted the unglued edge. It was longer than she had thought. Her index finger slipped along the wood underneath.

That was strange! There seemed to be a thin folded paper under the lining. A letter? Olivia wondered how long it had been hidden underneath. Her index finger seemed to have a will of its own, as it opened the lining a bit more, like slitting the flap of an envelope. Now she could just reach the folded paper and slide it toward the opening. Slowly, intently, she pulled it forward, through the open seam.

The wonder of auctions was the forgotten treasure a chest or a desk might have kept secret for years, only to be discovered by a stranger curious enough to investigate its hiding places. Olivia unfolded the thin creased paper and read what was on it with some difficulty but much experience. She'd been employed on a number of records management projects that involved barely legible original documents.

It appeared to be a handwritten will.

Lieutenant Hugh Delano Berwind, declaring himself to be sound of mind and body, bequeathed all his worldly possessions to his wife, Rose Redford Berwind, in trust for their unborn child. Dated August 24, 1918. Witnessed by Sargeant Joseph Lennon.

His wife, Rose!

As the import of such a document dawned on Olivia, she began to feel light-headed. She sat down on the bed and studied the paper in her hand. It certainly looked genuine. She pictured a patched canvas tent, a fold-out table, an oil lantern, a young man looking reverently at the portrait in a locket, writing this last testament to protect the ones he loved most in the world. Asking his sergeant to witness the signature. A witness who would be long dead now, if he hadn't been killed in the war.

Moira was wrong. It wasn't their pleasant home that needed an exorcism. It was Olivia herself. She might not be possessed by the Devil (in whom she didn't believe anyway), but she was certainly possessed by certain spirits from the past. Mrs. Mitchell, that wise woman of the Wampanoag, had told Olivia that she might be a natural medium, or channeler as those adepts were sometimes called. A listener to whom spirits can communicate their unfinished business—the deceits, damages, debts, and untimely deaths. Wrongs that have kept them bound to earth, that have turned them into ghosts condemned to walk on the midnight stairways and rattle in the cobwebby attics of the living.

She was just like a radio tuned to one damned station that was not only foreign, it was not even of this world. Who asked for that!

The last time this had happened, there had been murders and danger. Olivia shuddered.

She guessed she wouldn't pass the Berwind box on to Dave after all. Placing her few pieces of jewelry and the locket back inside, she closed the lid. Then she took the handwritten will into the pleasant office that had been added to the master suite so that she could work at home whenever possible. It was furnished with an oak desk and swivel chair, a rocker with a needlepoint-covered footstool (rose design), and a leaf-green wing chair. The Lalique Oceania paperweight she'd bought at the Berwind auction was on her desk next to the computer. She laid the still folded will under this with other current research projects. The paper seemed almost to shimmer, but that was probably caused by a reflection from the knobby glass starfish. She turned out the light and left the room. *Tomorrow*, she thought.

What had happened to Rose? And the child? Olivia wondered. Why had Hugh's brother inherited everything? The Berwind family should have welcomed into their home and hearts the mother of the only child Hugh would ever have. And that child would have been an heir, possibly to a share equal to George's. What had the Berwind estate been worth? Hundreds of millions.

Could Dave help to unearth records as far back as World War I? He would have better contacts than she. On the other hand, she had more experience in accessing and evaluating old papers. Also, if she consulted him, would she be setting herself up for a lecture on the dangers of getting involved in other people's business? Much as she loved Dave, the subtle changes in her autonomy that marriage had brought sometimes chafed a bit. After all, she'd been single and answered to no one for several years before deciding to marry this man and his family. Opening up the Berwind can of worms might lead to a conflict, or even a quarrel between the two of them. Really, the more loving thing to do would to spare Dave the worry at this early stage of the investigation.

Investigation? Sometimes a person just has to listen to herself to figure out what she's up to. Maybe she should rethink this, before her own compulsive nature got the upper hand.

There was a roar of pure joy from the living room. Some Red Sox batter must have hit a home run. Olivia went to join the cheering crowd and allow everyone to tell her at once just what had happened, and who had triumphed, and why, and how it compared to the records of others, and so on back unto the dawn of baseball.

JUNE 18

Things to Do Today

What happened to Rose Redford? Baby? Birth records?
Hawthorne Library
Find another groomer for S &B.
Take Moira shopping & lunch, girl stuff

Sometimes Olivia missed the no-nonsense glasses she'd worn in the old days, that slight barrier between her feelings and the observing world. But two years ago the ophthalmologist had declared her vision to be perfectly normal—whatever slight myopia she'd had was now outgrown. She'd started, then, putting aside the glasses on some occasions, especially occasions that involved the attractive detective she'd begun dating. And besides, Dave had declared himself in danger of drowning in her sea-green eyes, so what was a girl to do? She'd stashed those glasses somewhere for safekeeping, but after the wedding and her move to Dave's, they were never found again. *Safekeeping*, Olivia had concluded, was the place where things got lost.

Now, looking from their bedroom window at the marshes across the street, she wondered if her distance vision was as good as it might be with glasses. Olivia didn't like to miss anything. As if on cue, a snowy egret rose from the reeds and soared in a splendid arc that her gaze followed far into the summer sky. She wished it were that easy to follow the lives of a couple who had died a hundred years ago. Ordinary people left very little trace of their passions, their losses, their griefs. That was why accurate record-keeping was so vital.

For days, she spent hour after hour crouched over her computer, trying to find a trace of Rose Redford, and a notice of her marriage to Hugh Berwind, possibly only a few weeks before he had been sent to the front to be killed. "Unborn child" his will had said, but that might only mean that he knew Rose was pregnant. But if they had married before she was enceinte, why was there no record of Rose's existence in the Berwind newspaper archives? The Berwinds were a noteworthy and occasionally notorious family whose doings had been constantly reported —and still were, if you counted that last scandal about Flora Berwind's estate and the wretched care she'd been given during the last months of her life.

Probably a shot in the dark, but Olivia thought she would just have a talk with the clever reference librarian she'd encountered at the Hawthorne Library in Scituate. In the past, that gracious gray stone building had been a refuge of peace and privilege for Olivia. It would be a comfort just to wander through those pleasant old rooms on a weekday morning. Admonishing herself that she really must return to the working world soon, before that placement service lost interest in her excellent references, she grabbed her car keys off the hall table.

Uh-oh. Bruno came bounding down the stairs from Danny's room, a tongue-lolling grin plastered across his black snout. "Sorry, fella," she said. "It's too warm this time of year to leave you in the van. You understand, don't you?"

Bruno did not understand. In his own clumsy fashion, he gamboled about her as she tried to get out the door, expressing infinite joy in the ride he knew would be forthcoming. In the end, Olivia just gave in to the inevitable. Bruno would get a short jaunt around the marsh before Olivia took off for Scituate. The instant she'd made this wimpy decision, Sadie strolled in from her favorite lounge under the kitchen table, followed by Moira who wanted Olivia to buy two pounds of truly sweet, tree-ripened peaches, or if not peaches, small strawberries because the big ones were tasteless. On second thought, Moira had better pick them out herself.

Olivia sighed and complied with everyone's wishes—waiting with the dogs and running the AC while Moira felt, smelled, and ultimately rejecting peaches in favor of strawberries—before dropping them all back home and continuing on her primary errand.

Although the Hawthorne was as soothing as ever, the helpful reference librarian was on vacation. But the assistant at the circulation desk, Madeline Tremble, who remembered Olivia's dedication to research projects in the past, suggested something that intrigued her. "Have you ever been to the Black Hill branch library in South Plymouth? I shouldn't admit this, but..." she looked over her shoulder, clearly not wanting to be overheard, "there's a librarian at Black Hill whom I would consult in a heartbeat if I had hit a stone wall in my research, such as you describe. Her name is Fiona Ritchie, and she's rumored to work absolute *magic* when it comes to finding obscure or missing information." She jotted down the library's address and librarian's name on a slip of paper, adding a few words introducing Olivia as a researcher, and handed it to her. Then Maddy (incomprehensibly) winked at Olivia and turned away to serve another patron.

Olivia glanced at her watch. Noon. Moira wouldn't miss her, in fact would welcome her absence from the kitchen while she prepared lunch for herself and Danny. She consulted the note Maddy had given her and headed for Black Hill.

~

The Black Hill Branch Library was 1920s bungalow, the Winona model that had once been sold by Sears for $1,998. A decade later it had been bought by the Plymouth Woman's Cooperative for Folk Arts; they still had a quilting room in the basement. The library was located across the street from the bluffs, but Olivia thought that the upstairs dormer would provide a pleasing glimpse of the ocean. She approved of the exterior which had been painted one of the original Sears' colors, Sunrise, with white trim and a brown roof. She approved of the interior even more. It was furnished like an old schoolhouse. You could almost hear the whispers of long-gone children in its shadowed recesses. Rather than circulation desk units, there was a single "teacher's" desk for the librarian, a padded swivel chair, sturdy bookcases, cozy reading nooks, round tables for study groups, and even the obsolete catalog file—all made of warm aged oak. A small computer on the desk hummed and buzzed alongside a Tiffany dragonfly lamp and a dish of butterscotch candies.

There was no one in sight except an imperious Persian cat who hissed malevolently at Olivia from its cushion on top of the catalog. She wondered where the librarian could have gone in this small place. Three rooms of the original first floor had been converted into one big room now, with a small kitchen at the back of the bungalow, but no one was in sight. Olivia rang the service bell on the desk.

A low, musical, but commanding voice said, "Omar, you mind your manners!" A plump older woman popped up from behind a low bookcase of picture books. She had a round face, gray eyes, and a straggly crown of once-red braids stuck with two yellow pencils. When she hauled herself up off the floor where she had been sitting, the many silver bangles she wore tinkled softly. The sound was actually soothing. Nevertheless, Olivia was beginning to wonder if she hadn't been sent on a fool's errand. What had Maddy Tremble been thinking?

"May I help you? I'm Fiona Richie, and this is my companion, Omar Khayyám." The librarian waved a multi-ringed hand toward the irascible cat, studying Olivia above half-frame glasses perched on the end of her nose.

Olivia proffered the introductory note from Maddy and explained her interest in a young couple named Hugh Berwind and Rose Redford, that he had been an Army Lieutenant killed in World War I, and Rose may have been his wife. Olivia had been unable, however, to verify their marriage, and Madeline Tremble had suggested that Mrs. Ritchie might be able to help.

"And you haven't been able to find any trace of the marriage? How interesting. I assume you have reason to believe it existed, and if so, it must be recorded somewhere. Also their deaths. I would want to go there as well. There's always a great deal to be learned from death, dear. *O sting, where is thy death?* Hers, of course, since we already know that Hugh Berwind was a casualty of war." Mrs. Ritchie sighed sadly. Then she drew out a crystal pendant on a silver chain from somewhere beneath a mossy green T-shirt imprinted with the legend *Nemo me impune lacessit.* She polished it on the hem of her tartan skirt and began to swing the pendant in haphazard circles.

Olivia felt as if she were swinging off-balance herself. She reached back into her memory of Latin I and II to translate "No one provokes me with impunity."

"Scots. Order of the Thistle," Mrs. Ritchie said, just as if she knew exactly what was going through Olivia's mind.

Mrs. Ritchie lowered herself heavily into the swivel chair and hooked the crystal onto the monitor. Olivia noticed a copious green suede bag was propped within reach. A walking stick with a distinctive silver handle, an animal's head, leaned against the librarian's chair. Something intimidating about it. Olivia hoped she wasn't developing a fanciful streak.

Mrs. Ritchie began punching keys and humming to herself, not a tune exactly—more a meditative phrase, like *Ommmmm*. "Kettle's on in the kitchen." She waved toward the back of the bungalow, those bangles jingling again. "Why don't you make us a cup of tea while I delve, dear." The tone of her voice was pleasing but also compelling. A cup of tea was a fine idea, Olivia decided at once.

In the little kitchen with its charming 1920s décor, even a Hoosier cabinet, she found a thistle-painted tea set, a jar of lapsang souchong, and a cookie tin. The kettle was indeed bubbling, and in short order, Olivia had everything arranged on a tray, which she carried back to the main room. She set this on one of the round tables. The resident cat immediately swooped down from the catalog onto the table and curled his tail around the cookie tin.

Mrs. Ritchie joined her, beaming. "Omar is so very fond of my shortbread." She gave him a cookie crumb and an admonitory shove off the table. "Now, I have found one little snippet of information. A woman named Rose Berwind is buried in St. Rita's churchyard in the town of Harvard. Have you ever driven through there in the springtime? So lovely, all those apple orchards, don't you think, dear? Her dates are 1893 to 1918, so I think this may be your girl. Now as it happens, there also used to be a convent next to the church, and also a home for women in need of assistance, run by the Sisters of St. Rita, who were Augustinian nuns. Many unmarried pregnant girls found sanctuary there when they were abandoned by others."

"Good heavens!" Olivia exclaimed. "I was only in the kitchen for a few minutes. I've been on this project for ten days, and nothing…nothing has surfaced. You must be some kind of genius at this sort of thing."

Mrs. Ritchie, still beaming, shrugged in a self-deprecating way. "Oh, *find and ye shall seek*, as the scripture teaches us. But now, I would wonder, wouldn't you, dear, what became of the child? Because I'm guessing that our Rose died at the home giving birth, and that's why she was buried in St. Rita's churchyard and not somewhere in Boston."

"Boston?"

"Just a guess. Hugh Berwind, who appears to have been a graduate of Harvard University, probably met Rose Redford somewhere in Cambridge or Boston. She may have worked as a waitress at one of the restaurant chains, like Schrafft's or Childs. Everyone ate there. Very genteel. Because if she'd been a girl he'd met among the Berwinds' social set, your search would have turned up her name in society news of the time. Now, to tell you the truth, I'm making up a story here, but there has to be a story, doesn't there? I'm guessing Rose herself had no family, or only distant family, either in affection or location, since she ended up in the care of the Sisters of St. Rita's. And what would the Sisters have done with the child, do you suppose?"

Olivia felt like a great white light had suddenly illuminated her brain. "*Adoption!* That would explain everything. I've been trying to imagine why Rose and her child were never embraced by the Berwinds, why Hugh's child never inherited his share of all that money."

"So you find this scenario plausible, then? Good. You seem like a determined young lady, dear, and you'll find what you're looking for eventually. When you figure out what that is." Mrs. Ritchie refilled their tea mugs.

Olivia made a number of quick notes in her moleskin notebook. But this was all so tenuous. Olivia could feel the certainty of a moment ago fading away like the images of a dream. So much depended on whether Hugh and Rose had been legally married. "You're right, Mrs. Ritchie. I'm not completely sure what I'm doing."

"Shortbread?" Mrs. Ritchie held out the open tin to Olivia, who shook her head. "The Sisters of St. Rita knew her as Rose Berwind, meaning she was representing herself as married, or perhaps as a recent widow. Poor little thing! St. Rita's church will have baptism records, for surely it would have been a sin not to baptize the infant, even if they did arrange an adoption soon after Rose passed on to Summerland."

"Summerland?"

"Some call it Heaven."

"But what I need most is to prove they were married!" Olivia still felt this information was central to her search, although she was not clear on what she was actually searching for. Nor why she just didn't let the whole history of that young couple remain in "the cloud of unknowing."

"Hmmm. I confess that I couldn't find that information. Perhaps we have to think outside the possible, so to speak. Yet I do feel that St. Rita's holds the key to the child." Mrs. Ritchie looked thoughtful. "There are insistent spiritual forces around you, dear—surely you are aware? And those forces are interested in justice for the living, because that is what brings peace to the dead."

"Oh, I rather wish those forces would leave me to get on with my own life," Olivia confessed ruefully. "I'm not comfortable with this kind of craziness."

"Karma is *la belle dame sans merci*, dear." Mrs. Richie patted her hand. "Now I must warn you that the home was closed in 1949, so its files may now be in the cellars of the church, and adoption records from those days were firmly sealed. If you keep running into a stone wall, do come back, and we'll see where the cracks are, so to speak."

With many thanks and a few personal reservations, Olivia said goodbye to the Black Hill librarian. Although the woman's skills were awesome, Olivia rather hoped that she would not be impelled to return, that she would give up this questionable quest to unearth a hundred-year-old love affair.

~

Olivia spent the rest of the afternoon at her computer, trying not to research St. Rita's in Harvard. Surprisingly, she'd found the Holy Mass card for Mary Margaret Burns stuck under the Lalique paperweight, although she was sure she'd tucked that card into a book she was reading, *The Great War, a definitive history of World War I, with 400 Illustrations*. Olivia enjoyed big solid histories and biographies, nothing sensational or ephemeral, titles that might be found on a short list for the Pulitzer. She was not a fan of mysteries, in literature or in life.

Then there was the mysterious presence of rose petals drying on her desk, especially disconcerting, despite the pleasing fragrance. She'd placed vases of cut roses in the living and dining rooms, but there was no way they could have shed their petals in her office. She wondered if Danny had been poking around in here, although why and how he would have brought in petals was another mystery. She typed "Computer Camps" and "Tech Camps" into the Google search engine. There was a summer program at MIT—somewhat inappropriate for sub-teens, she decided. Not that she wanted to get rid of Danny, just to give him something else to focus on besides ghost sightings.

Another focus—maybe that was what she needed, too. Olivia checked for consultant openings at the placement service with which she was listed. While waiting for the computer to divulge relevant material, she picked up the browning, curling petals, and dumped them in her wastebasket. They were still velvety to the touch.

The placement service offered no consultant positions that met Olivia's requirements (possibly because she really wanted some easy project that wouldn't interfere with her new family life).

Her next search was for a new dog groomer, one who had never met her dogs before. The nearest one was Happy Tails, some distance away in Barnstable. It was possible to make an appointment online, but Olivia hesitated. She hoped pet groomers did not share information about difficult dogs. It wouldn't do for the incident of Sadie biting the hand that clipped her nails to come to light. Sadie hadn't drawn blood, though; it had just been a warning. And then there was the time that Bruno had taken ear-cleaning as a bodily insult.

Olivia even considered learning the art of pet grooming herself—courses were offered. Yes, that would probably be best, especially now that the weather was warm and the whole messy business could take place in the backyard. Nail-clipping might still be a problem, though. Olivia remembered that there had been one sweet little assistant vet at the Wee Angels Animal Hospital, who routinely snipped Sadie's nails without a single growl. Even though Sadie's medical records warned that the pit bull was "very nervous." What was her name? *Dr. Wu! Lian Wu.*

Olivia would do the baths herself—Danny would be glad to help—and save the nail-clipping for the next scheduled shots at Wee Angels. She would ask for Dr. Wu.

She'd already checked her portfolio, as she did every morning. A longish stint with a brokerage firm had introduced Olivia to that high stakes, real life game, stock trading. To her great satisfaction, she'd found that her meticulous research habits, analytical mind, and even her caution consistently paid off in a most rewarding way.

After the financial disaster of her first marriage—all those debts Hank Robb had left her to clear up—Olivia had learned to keep her own counsel, and her own bank account. Dave had no idea of what she'd actually spent on Ethan Allen furnishings and Vera Wang linens for their wing of the farmhouse. Olivia figured he had enough financial worries, with those three foster kids. Moira was already planning on Johnson & Wales, and Danny's skills could very well lead him to MIT or some similar high tech college. Kevin was still a wild card. His musical talent and dark temperament might take him in any direction.

Her fingers idle on the keyboard, Olivia admitted that the Rose problem was still nagging her. With a sigh, she returned to the archives site where, for a small monthly fee, she had unlimited access to birth, marriage, and death records. She typed in the search space: "Marriages: Rose Redford and Hugh Berwind." The answer flashed back in moments: "No exact matches, 25,487 possible matches." How could there be no exact matches? She resisted the impulse to begin reading the entire list of possibles. Life was too short for this sort of compulsive pursuit.

NANNY BURNS

If you think being a ghost is just a bedtime story, you've got another think coming. But don't look for me in the closet or under the bed. I'm not there, dearie. In fact I'm not anywhere.

I'd like to move along, really I would. I've been told there's a place even more heavenly than Cornwall by the sea, where women like me, the ones who did the real mothering, get a chance to put up their feet and drink perfectly-brewed Orange Pekoe on the Porch of All Sunsets, while we decide if we want to have another go at it, maybe take that cruise to the Isle of Rebirth. But I never could abide a thief or a bully getting away with his wickedness, not on my watch, especially not perpetuating a mischief that upset my Hugh's last wishes, and everything after that. I've been looking down at that legacy of thievery and wrongdoing for who knows how long, there being no time or tide in this place. Could I possibly make things right for my lovely boy and his Rose?

Well, I could say I'd die trying, but I don't hold with foolish talk. And besides, that dying part is still a little hazy. I know I did it already, but I don't recall the particulars.

Hugh must be here somewhere. I've seen those Specters of the Western Front wandering in Perpetual No Man's Land, the young men who've not been able to make peace with what was done to them. And life was doubly unfair to my boy. His beautiful girl, lost to him, wandering in her Garden of Regret, sometimes on this plane, and sometimes reaching into the past, even though we're supposed to be timeless now. Something mighty sad keeps drawing her back there. If only I could remember more of the story, I'd have a clearer notion of what to do.

They tell me that true lovers will always find each other again, eventually, when they're free to release the tragic past. You wouldn't think an old nanny like me would be such a romantic, but I was, I am (after all, I've had my moments, too), and I feel somehow responsible, if only I knew why.

I remember this for sure. Even when he was still in nursery, that George was never satisfied. He wanted Hugh's toys, and if he couldn't have them, he'd find some way to break them. The Lord knows I tried to teach him better.

He certainly married up when he wed that beautiful Flora, so full of life, and generous, too. A shame about their children, although it served George right. I remember how the typhoid took both their little ones. Never got a wink of sleep the whole time they were ill. Then their mother Flora just about went off her head—nervous breakdown, they called it. She got gently escorted to a sanitarium in Switzerland, while I got rudely hustled out the back door. All those years of caring for Berwind youngsters, and a few old ones, too, and I was just dumped out with the trash, too old to find another nanny position. That's just not right, and I know you'll agree with me, dearie. As I used to tell little George, "The Dark Angel is going to get you for that, Georgie!"

Someone took me in, though. Wait. I'll remember who in a minute. A friend? A cousin? Then Flora, the dear soul, recovered her wits and provided me with a small pension, unbeknown to Himself.

It's like a picture puzzle with half the pieces missing. I know there's something I have to do, but what is it? Something to do with Rose. Trouble is, I have a hard time collecting my wits these days.

There's a woman I met here, she calls herself Ayah Bharata, rattles on about the Raj or some such nonsense. The Lord knows she is one burnt up brown lady. I mean, literally. When the babe in her care died of cholera, the old lady grandmother poured cooking oil on Ayah Bharata and lit a match. And Ayah Bharata's not going anywhere until she gets even with that family. All she's waiting for now, she tells me, is for the sons of their sons to open that grand hotel in New Delhi.

Ayah Bharata swore to me that, if I want to make things right, I need to contact someone on the Other Side.

So I told her, it's not that easy, Ayah Bharata. The Guardians keep crooning, let go, let go, Nanny Burns, if you ever want to leave behind all that sorrow and get on with your own ascendance. (Whatever that means!) And I say, I'll do what my heart tells me is right, thank you very much, and no backtalk, please.

I remember when Hugh was twelve, and they sent him away to school, I thought that heart of mine would just break in two pieces. But I still had George to raise for three more years. My work was cut out for me there, all right. I used to say to myself, Mary Margaret Burns, just you stop moping. Put on your red stockings, fix yourself a hot toddy, and make the best of a piss-poor situation.

And I'm still saying it. (They make a nice hot toddy here, and a body never gets the wobbles after.) Now, where's that inlaid box I gave Hugh when he went away to the academy? His treasure box. Even took it with him when he went to war. Ayah Bharata says she would follow that box, if she were me.

And Rose. What did George do to Rose? Small wonder I can't rest.

JUNE 22

Things to Do Today

Moira, wear new dress for Danbury
Where does Kevin go? Check.
Call Mrs. Mitchell – séance? Jamie?
Start keeping journal, weird stuff?
Where is my list of life goals? Poss. revise.

Olivia always tried to tread a fine line between helpful confidante and interfering interloper with Dave's foster children. Which side of the line she fell on differed from day to day, but she'd managed to steer Moira to a really flattering Ralph Lauren striped dress (blue and white) that Moira actually liked. Olivia had ordered it from Lord & Taylor online, and it had arrived in time for Moira's forthcoming Danbury visit. Although Moira tried hard to suppress her pleasure, a small smile came and went as she shook out the reality that had only been a postage stamp image online. Olivia thought this might be the first time the girl had ever received a package meant for her alone.

She wondered if Alice would approve. Although Olivia had once offered to go to Danbury with Dave and the youngsters, they'd all looked so horrified, she'd hastily backed down. Dave had taken her in his arms and kissed her in apology (a move that easily won her over, bemusing her senses), explaining that only immediate relatives were allowed to visit, and she'd have had to wait in the car for who knows how long. He'd had to pull some official strings himself, just to be added to Alice's visitors' list, because the children could only go in to see their mother if accompanied by an adult.

∾

Moira had noticed that some of the other kids dressed up like for church when they visited Danbury, and she hoped the new dress would please her mother. But she didn't want to give Liv any ideas about being great pals in future, so she'd stayed cool.

Even when Moira had encountered something ghostly in the rose garden herself, she'd kept quiet about it. She hadn't wanted to give Liv the satisfaction.

Like the vision of a fairy tale princess, a figure had moved between the rose bushes without ever touching the ground. Moira thought the girl might be crying. It made her shaky, just thinking about it. But it was Liv who was to blame, whose fault it was that everything was going to crap around here. Still, that weird business kept bothering Moira like a splinter in her finger. Maybe she should just squeeze it out.

While she was thinking this over, Moira occupied herself with whipping up an angel food cake, taking out her nervous energy on the placid egg whites, which she vigorously whisked by hand to an upstanding fluff that could hold a spatula upright. Moira felt a pleasing sense of control, over the cake batter if not that disturbing event. Spooning the airy batter into the tube pan, Moira decided it would serve Olivia right to be hit with this new disturbance.

Just as Moira was sliding the pan into a pre-heated oven, Liv wandered into Moira's domain. She'd smiled at Moira, that fake smile, like a teacher who thought she knew everything, and asked about the cake. Perfect with strawberries, she'd said, as she filled the electric kettle and turned it on. Moira watched with disgust as Liv selected an herbal tea bag. Some wacky herb called kava-kava.

Moira felt a direct attack would work best. "Say, Liv, I think you ought to dig out all those roses you planted in front of our house and take them straight to the dump. There's something weird about them. A devil's out there, all sweet-smelling and evil, knocking on our door." Moira turned her back to grab a coke out of the refrigerator. She didn't want to see Liv's expression. Probably mad as hell.

"Weird in what sense, Moira?" Liv proceeded calmly to make her tea, but that didn't fool Moira, who knew when she'd drawn blood.

"Well, you know how Danny saw a queer girl out there that spooked him real bad. A ghost or some other evil being. Maybe it was a vampire. Bride of Satan. Whatever."

Liv looked at Moira, in that hateful knowing way of hers, and sat down at the table with her cup. She removed the teabag, squeezed it against the spoon, disposed of it neatly in the saucer, and took a sip. "You saw her yourself, didn't you? Why don't you tell me about it, honey. Maybe then we can have a clearer idea of what to do. Because I will never believe that our roses are to blame."

Moira's eyes burned, as if she might cry or something. She opened her Coke and took a long swig, leaning against the refrigerator. Cold and sweet. Too sweet really. To tell the truth, she wasn't all that fond of Coke, but sometimes the syrupy stuff made her feel better.

"Yeah, well...there sure is some zombie creature floating around out there. Filmy. A filmy figure, like a girl in a painting. I only saw it for a minute, but I know something was there, because it gave Sadie the creeps, too. She took off like a streak of lightning. Found her under the hammock out back, shaking. So, what I think is, it's all the fault of those roses you planted. Never happened before."

"I'm sorry, honey. That must have been really scary. I don't know how to explain it, because I've never seen anything out of the ordinary out there myself. But whatever's going on, it's not the fault of the garden. That's just plants, and beautiful ones. So before we go off the deep end about roses, let's just see if it happens again. Maybe it's just a summer anomaly. I mean, a one-of-a-kind experience."

"I know what anomaly means, Liv. And I wouldn't bet on it."

~

On the morning of the O'Haras' monthly trip to Danbury to visit their mother, Alice (formerly Teresa), in Federal prison, Kevin once again disappeared. Having practically ordered the boy to join the party this time, Dave looked white-lipped and grim as he packed Moira's picnic basket in the Bronco. But he didn't forget to compliment her on the new outfit—even though Moira was slumped over as if to hide her budding breasts, gently outlined under a girly dress. It was a drastic change from her usual jeans or shorts and tank top, in odd color combinations such as orange and pink.

Olivia saw them off with a jolly wave. Danny waved back cheerfully enough, although relegated to the back seat of the Bronco. Moira had asserted her right as the elder of the two to ride in front, where she barely glanced out the passenger window, raising her hand in a sullen salute. It was just as well, Olivia thought, that Dave had put her off accompanying them. She didn't envy him.

So there she was, alone for the day with only two disconsolate dogs for company. She poured herself another cup of coffee and sat in one of the farmhouse rockers on the front porch, admiring her garden. If there was a ghost, she was absent from the scene today. Nothing but sunshine and vivid shades from blushing pink to gorgeous red, with glossy green leaves. And the sensuous fragrance! Olivia had chosen to plant English roses specifically bred for scent. *Exquisite.*

Sadie and Bruno napped together in a tree-shaded spot on the side lawn, right at the edge of the garden, occasionally opening one eye to gaze at Olivia morosely.

Olivia rocked and thought about Kevin. On Danbury days, he usually made himself scarce until evening. Lately, he'd been acting even more secretive, uncooperative, and unsociable, all signs that Olivia associated with trouble. Sex or drugs. She hoped the former, as it was much less damaging. Had Dave given him the safe-sex talk? A stern warning about drug dealers targeting teens on the South Shore? She decided to check around his room, in case. She'd recently read an article, "How to Tell if Your Teen Is Using Drugs", and she knew what to look for. Bruno followed her curiously as she went upstairs; he slumped down in the hall right outside Kevin's bedroom door.

But Kevin's room was as clean and neat as a Marine barracks—no contraband in the pockets of his clothes, no gummy mirrors or sticky CD covers, no deodorizing spray or eye-drops, not even any prurient magazines. On the wall, a Dropkick Murphys poster leered at her with knowing grins. In the obvious absence of any evidence, Olivia began to feel terrible about her suspicions. She had no business being here.

Even worse, she was heartily sorry to be caught snooping when Kevin appeared unexpectedly at the door of his room, closely followed by a willowy young girl. Fine-boned angular features in a thin face. Long hair of pale gold. Nearly as tall as Kevin.

He scowled at Olivia accusingly. "What are *you* doing in here?"

Invention favors the trapped step-parent. "I'm on my way to the dry cleaners. Thought that jacket you wear all the time might need freshening."

"I'll take care of my own stuff, *thanks very much*. No need for you to go poking around when I'm out, Liv."

"I'd have asked you, but I didn't expect to see you until dinner, or even later. Aren't you going to introduce me to your friend?"

The girl reddened. Olivia hoped she wasn't blushing, too. Her excuse for going through Kevin's things had sounded pretty lame, even to her own ears.

Kevin mumbled, "Norah" and something unintelligible. "She's going to give me lessons."

"How do you do, Norah. I'm Olivia Lowenstein, Kevin's foster father's wife. Lessons in what, Kev?"

He gestured toward the fiddle in the corner, which had remained in its case untouched since Olivia had purchased the instrument for him at auction last Christmas. A pricey fiddle that had once belonged to Liam O'Leary.

"Norah's from South Carolina, but she's with us now. With Celtic Storm. The other fiddler's gone to classical at Julliard."

"Fine. Sounds like a fun challenge. I'll call you when lunch is ready. Would you like to eat out back at the picnic table?"

Olivia thought Kevin might refuse lunch, just to make a point. But he simply nodded and turned away. He pulled out his desk chair for Norah and picked up the fiddle case. Olivia departed for her office downstairs, ostentatiously leaving the bedroom door even wider open.

Soon she was listening to music, some of it toe-tapping Irish folk music, some of it ineptly imitated by Kevin, screeching and discordant. *For my sins*, she thought. Even Bruno ran away downstairs, not to Olivia's office but to find Sadie where she reposed in the bedroom. The pit bull never allowed Bruno to join her on the king-size bed, but he had learned to be content with the Persian carpets that adorned the wide pine floors.

When even the dog deserts you, it's time to reevaluate your life. Olivia made a note on her To-Do list. *Time to give up buying haunted artifacts. New interests!! Check out Centre for Study of Ancient Docs at Oxford, online course?* With more and even smaller companies installing sophisticated computer programs, records management was fast becoming an obsolete skill. Olivia thought she'd like to specialize in something more esoteric, such as verifying ancient original documents. A good outlet for her natural investigative skills.

She went into the bedroom to get her handbag in case she needed a credit card to order a course. As an obsessively tidy person, she noticed instantly that the lid of the marquetry case on her dresser, always left closed and latched, was now open. Her pearl necklace was draped half in and half out of the box. For a moment, she wondered if Kevin was paying her back, but then she realized that the fiddle had never stopped playing all morning.

Olivia restored the pearl necklace to its paper-lined nest. Then she saw something impossible to fathom. She picked it up wonderingly. The card of the Holy Mass for Mary Margaret Burns, last seen under the Lalique paperweight next to her computer, seemed somehow to have transported itself to the marquetry case. The blood drained away from Olivia's head; she thought she might faint at any moment. Sitting down quickly on the etched roses duvet, she put her head between her knees. Sadie nosed her solicitously. Bruno sniffed her shoes.

I do not believe this. I do not believe this.

Olivia thought of the Red Queen in *Through the Looking Glass*, a book she had never enjoyed as a child. Too surreal and unsettling. But she remembered the Red Queen had advised Alice to practice believing the impossible. "When I was younger, I always did it for half an hour a day. Why, sometimes I've believed as many as six impossible things before breakfast."

One impossible thing was difficult enough.

Although Olivia still felt rather sick to her stomach, the new discipline of jotting down weird stuff that happened in a new moleskin notebook, dove gray (which seemed like an appropriate ghostly color) steadied her. Added to Danny's ghost in the garden, the rose petals on her desk, and Moira's sighting, she noted the open marquetry case, the spilled pearls, the traveling Mass card. She wanted to describe each incident to Mrs. Mitchell, who had been such a fund of practical wisdom in the past.

By lunchtime, Olivia had pulled herself together. She brought out tuna sandwiches, melon, cookies, and lemonade for the three of them. The maple-shaded backyard was idyllic. An eastern breeze brought the cool scent of ocean and pine trees across the marshes, mingled with the essence of algae thriving in thick reeds.

But there seemed to be some vow of silence in effect. Every conversation Olivia initiated was met with either monosyllabic replies or simple silence, punctuated by disdainful smiles.

How are the fiddle lessons progressing? *Okay*. Are you two in the same year at school? *Nope*. Do you have any plans for college or some other school after you graduate? *Shrug*. Finally, Norah said she'd have to go home now. Where? *Strawberry Hill.* Kevin went with her, both youngsters on their bikes, pedaling joyously toward freedom from adult prying.

When the rest of the family returned at five, a hushed gloom still prevailed. Danny was red-eyed, and Moira unusually quiet. She'd not been allowed to bring the angel food cake into the visitors' area. So Moira, in a fit of fury, had dumped the whole thing in a rubbish barrel. The rest of the sad tale was revealed in monosyllables. Alice didn't look like herself anymore. Her dark wavy hair had been cut short and was showing more gray. She didn't remember that Danny was in the sixth grade now. She wanted Uncle Dave to formally adopt the O'Haras, even though that meant she'd have to give up parental rights.

Olivia served Greek grilled chicken, orzo with feta, sliced tomato salad, and garlic bread without one negative comment from Moira. Dave talked about the several horse farms they'd passed where the stop signs said "Whoa!" He said that Alice looked well and was still working as a chef in the kitchen. She thought she might take up that career full-time when she was released (*in ten or fifteen years,* was the unsaid phrase).

Kenny did not return at all until nine, the O'Haras' usual curfew. He went straight to his room and slammed the door.

What a relief when Dave and Olivia were finally alone in their suite—now to share the real news of their day. Olivia told Dave about Kevin's friend, Norah, and his new interest in the fiddle, omitting the detail about being found going through drawers in the boy's bedroom. Dave said Alice's parole hearing had not gone well. It was really too soon. Driving home, Moira had hinted that she'd seen something strange in the rose garden—what was that all about? Danny sniffled all the way home and would not be comforted. Dave was beginning to dread these monthly visits, which so often left everyone out-of-sorts.

Finally they just lay together on the bed, watching TCM, *The Uninvited*, which seemed to Olivia almost too intuitive. She switched it off and moved over into Dave's arms, which were always waiting for her.

"Are you sorry you married a man with a ready-made, angst-ridden family? You probably never figured on being the stepmom, sort of, to three teenagers with issues."

"Sometimes it *is* a bit like being thrown into the deep end of the pool. Are you sorry that you married a woman who attracts ghosts and other weird happenings, like flies to pie?"

But soon it was apparent that they weren't all that sorry.

They ousted the dogs, locked the bedroom door, and turned out the light. A perfect summer night for love-making. They knew each other well now, the tracings of skin that would drive the other wild, the fierce concentration that knew its way home.

The next morning, Monday, Olivia texted Jamie: "Something bizarre with Mass card. Also, Moira saw the resident ghost in garden. Setting up a séance with Mrs. M, this weekend, Sat night. You'll come? Need morale support."

Jamie texted back: "Don't we all. OK. I'll bring my exorcism kit."

"You have exorcism kit?"

"Blue Sapphire gimlets."

"Last time you made pitcher of those, you had to drive me home."

"LOL. We'll be at your house, so no prob. You just roll into bed. I can crash on your sofa."

"Mike?"

"Grandparents' weekend."

"Good thing. Kevin's learning to play fiddle."

"WTF did you do in your past life?"

"Don't believe in all that stuff."

"Ha ha ha. See you at the séance, sister."

JUNE 29

Things to Do Today

Check Jamie re: séance tonight
Check O'Hs plans still on:
    Kev at gig, Danny, game with Vinny, Moira sleepover
Where are adoption records for St. R's Refuge?
Paleography, Univ. London, Institute Historical Research, free online course
    sign up, add to resume

Olivia phoned Mrs. Mitchell and made arrangements for the Wampanoag shaman and channeler to help her contact the ghost in the garden that both Danny and Moira had witnessed. There was a time when Olivia wouldn't have been caught dead at a séance, but recent events in her life had revealed that the well-ordered secular world she preferred might be only a small part of some vast unimaginable universe of limitless dimensions.

Mrs. Mitchell, proprietor of a gift shop called the Moon Deer in Plymouth Center, answered her phone in a voice that was musical and reassuring with its broad Harvard accent. She agreed at once to conduct a séance at Olivia's new home, just as if she'd been expecting the call. Olivia mentioned that Jamie Finch would be joining them, and Mrs. M. said that she remembered Jamie warmly as the nurse who had cared for her elderly mother.

Olivia was pleased that this was a business deal; she was, in effect, hiring Mrs. M. for her unusual expertise in such matters. It put the evening's plan on a down-to-earth footing, however far out of this world it might actually be.

Dave said he'd be out in the garage working on his wrought iron sculptures if needed and reminded Olivia how her foray into the supernatural last year had not ended well. Olivia promised that this gentle ghost from long ago and far away couldn't possibly pose a danger to anyone now living. Everyone connected to her must be gone by now. Although Dave smiled and kissed her, the expression in his eyes was skeptical, which caused her a slight uneasiness.

As always, Mrs. M. was almost a half hour late. Meanwhile, Jamie suggested mixing up a pitcher of gimlets to get them in the mood, but Olivia insisted that only tea would be served until after the séance. Clear heads must prevail, Olivia asserted, while Jamie merely chuckled.

Olivia had nearly forgotten Mrs. M.'s magical way with animals. Sadie and Bruno rushed to meet her, bowing like slavish devotees greeting their guru. The channeler crouched down to their level and murmured to them while they whimpered back, as if exchanging all the news since their last encounter.

"Sadie has a slight tremor. She may have been upset by those ghostly vibrations in the garden," Mrs. M. commented as she rose to her feet again and readjusted her turquoise shawl. "Otherwise, she seems quite content living here with you and the children. And Bruno—if anything, he loves family life even more than she. He's feeling a bit of stiffness and pain in his hips, though. You might look into one of those nutritional supplements that seem to help canine arthritis. Now, where have you set up our table?"

Olivia ushered Mrs. M. into the large, comfortable living room that smelled of cinnamon from Moira's latest baking foray, essence of rose from a bouquet Olivia had arranged, and a hint of dog. A little round table and three straight chairs had been placed in front of the fireplace, the hearth decorated with pots of ivy. A single candle on the table and several more on the mantel would be their only lighting. Olivia brought in a tray from the kitchen with a steaming pot of kava-kava tea, which she laid on the coffee table. They sat on the sofa and cushioned chairs, drinking tea and talking.

"Before we begin the séance, why don't you tell me more about the two manifestations and whatever other incidents have occurred." Mrs. M. sipped tea and waited. Sadie and Bruno lay contentedly at her feet.

"First it was Danny, our youngest, who saw a girl wafting about in the garden. He described her as looking transparent, like a hologram. Naturally, his siblings didn't believe him. But then, Moira, who's fourteen, saw the girl in the garden as well, although she was loathe to admit it. Blamed me and my roses. I haven't seen anything myself, but there have been some incidents." Olivia explained about buying the locket last year and the marquetry case this year, the link she suspected between the two items. She mentioned finding the handwritten will and its surprising contents, the rose petals appearing on her desk, and the strange incident of the traveling Holy Mass card.

"Hey, Liv. You never told me about that Mass card." Jamie tasted her tea and made a face.

"Oh, sorry. Kava-kava may be an acquired taste." Olivia passed the honey to Jamie. "When something eerie like that happens, you're tempted to blame your own faulty memory before you will admit to yourself that the damn card moved its own self."

Mrs. M. suggested that Olivia bring in the marquetry case and the locket, and she did so. Then she lit the candles and turned out the other lights. They seated themselves around the round table that now held one candle and the two artifacts. Placing their hands on the table, they touched little fingers and waited.

"We invite the spirit who walks in this garden to speak to us." Mrs. M.'s voice was low and rhythmic. They waited quietly, realizing that silence is not that silent after all. An AC hummed, the kitchen clock (wild birds) trilled the hour, and the dogs stirred restlessly. From time to time, Bruno snored lightly.

After a while, perhaps twenty minutes, the atmosphere in the living room abruptly changed. It seemed as if a cool breeze blew through, causing the candle on the table to flicker. The marquetry case slid an inch or so closer to Olivia. Bruno woke with a start and shook his head. Sadie jumped up and ran from the room, up to the second floor where the youngsters had their bedrooms. Bruno lumbered upstairs right behind her. Olivia felt dizzy, and then faint. She closed her eyes, just for a moment, and heard someone crying softly.

"My darling boy, my darling boy killed in the war. What happened to his Rose? Why did no one take care of her?"

As if from a long distance, Olivia heard Mrs. Ms's inviting tone. "We welcome you, spirit, and we're here to help you to find the answers you seek. Are you not the girl, Rose?"

The crying stopped. A brisk elderly voice announced, "Don't be daft, dearie. I'm Nanny Burns. And you can take it from me, if there's trouble in the family, it'll be that George. I raised those two boys, so I should know."

And that was the end of it. Olivia became aware that Jamie was holding her upright.

"Let go! What are you trying to do?" She struggled free from her friend's grip.

"I'm trying to revive you, Liv. You just went off the deep end and began talking in tongues, or something. What *was* that, Mrs. M?"

"Olivia is a natural trance medium, although that's never been part of her belief system. Spirits search her out. What you heard tonight was a spirit speaking through her. Although it may have been the girl in the garden who was crying. I wonder…is it possible that you're being haunted by two spirits this time?" Mrs. M. asked.

"*Two* ghosts, you say? Oh, good grief! I'm going to get a cold cloth for Liv. Maybe one for me, too." Jamie gazed Heavenward, then hurried into the kitchen.

"Are you saying it was I who spoke? You heard me? Because I heard me, too." Olivia felt nauseous and confused.

"Yes, Olivia, it was you and only you. Channeling someone called Nanny Burns. Do you suppose she is also the Mary Margaret Burns for whom a Holy Mass was said? You … she … mentioned a George in the family. Some kind of trouble-maker."

Jamie came back with a well-wrung cold cloth. Steering Olivia to the couch, she draped it across her forehead. "I suppose we'd better skip the gin, girlfriend. You look as pale as if you'd seen a ghost. Ha ha."

"Oh, that does feel good." Olivia pressed the cloth over her eyes gratefully. "For goodness sake, don't tell Dave what happened here. He'll think I'm bonkers."

"Too late," Jamie said.

For Dave had just appeared in the door that led to the kitchen. "Don't tell me *what*?" He snapped on the lights and immediately sat down on the edge of the sofa next to Olivia. "What the hell is this, Juliet's tomb?"

"Dave, I don't know if you've met Mrs. Mitchell?" Jamie introduced the American Indian woman, who had moved to one of the cushioned chairs and was sitting quietly with her elegant hands in her lap. The large diamond ring she wore flashed in the electric light.

"How do you do?" Her serene smile was reassuring, and her dark eyes shone with sympathy. She leaned forward to where Dave was sitting and extended her hand. "Don't be alarmed, Mr. Lowenstein. Your wife will be quite all right in a few moments. There has been some interesting activity here this evening, about which she will certainly want to tell you, but perhaps a little later. May I suggest a cup of strong coffee for your wife?" Mrs. M. rose, rearranged her scarf, and picked up her deerskin handbag. "Liv, dear, let's talk tomorrow. Do you still have that bear fetish I gave you? Keep it close for a while. Bear people like you are strong and caring seekers after deeper knowledge. Bear will give you his protection. Good night now, Liv."

"Yes. Thank you, Mrs. M. Definitely, talk tomorrow. Dave?" While Dave showed their guest out the front door, Olivia murmured. "I'm going to have to look into the Berwind family. I need to know who's who. Like a family tree or something."

"Nannies like that one don't grow on trees." Jamie said. "I'll make the coffee."

ROSE

Is this what it's like to be a spirit?

I feel as if I'm trapped in an eternal dream. In my dream, I am always in a garden. A rose garden. Hugh loved roses, and he loved me. Sometimes that's about all I can remember. I've been wandering in this maze of fog for I don't know how long...misty stuff that clings to my shoes and fingers like weightless cotton candy.

Lately, though, I've begun to remember other things, sad things. I remember holding an infant, how my heart embraced him—rocking him in my arms before he was taken away from me, but I don't know why that happened. I remember the sweet smell of his skin, his mouth so like Hugh's. My own dear baby.

I remember our April wedding, just a simple service in Christ Church at Deer Park, where my father lived. His name...different from my mother's. But she was in Boston. No, she was gone. I think I remember her funeral. Is that why I went to my father? Hugh was being sent to France on a White Star *ship. When I told him I was with child, he wanted us to be married at once. I remember Hugh beside me, holding me, so reassuring, so handsome in his officer's uniform. He would make everything right. My husband now.*

I remember my father insisted I call myself by his name, Persey. I, Rose Redford Persey, take thee, Hugh Delano Berwind.

I can see Hugh waving goodbye from the train window. He would come back to me, he promised me that. We would be a family someday.

My father would take care of me until he returned. But then my father died suddenly a few months later. The flu. Hugh had made me promise, if I ever needed help, I must go to his parents in New York. They didn't know about us yet, I would need to bring our wedding certificate. By then I was big and awkward. And when I got there, his parents were still at their Massachusetts place.

And I remember being met by Hugh's brother George, who screamed at me that Hugh was dead. Killed in action in some dreadful place. Belleau Wood. Waving the telegram in my face. He knocked me to the floor in a rage, grabbed my certificate, and called his man to drag me into that car. I hardly know how long we drove, I was out of my mind with grief. But I wasn't being taken to Hugh's parents. I remember being handed over to the nuns at St. Rita's. After that, all I knew was waves of pain. Broken body, broken heart. My love was dead—could that be true?

I don't remember what happened after that … what happened to my son. Baptized, the nun said. Save his soul. But I feel sure that I can find my son if I just follow the locket, the one I gave Hugh with my picture. He kept it with him always. "Rose in my pocket," he called it.

Hugh used to say that true love has no beginning and no end, that we meet and recognize each other as true lovers—and for a time, we are together. Even if he died, Hugh said, he would go on searching for me and would find me in any existence where I happened to be. Will he find me again here, or will I have to move on, as I am told, out of this dream, to a place where we can be reunited?

There are Guardians here, whispering to me to come out of the shadow garden, to move away from the past, to let go, and go…where? Somewhere filled with love and light. But I can't leave yet. There's something…what happened to my beloved baby, our boy?

JULY 1

Things to Do Today

Berwind family tree?
What about the Swetts?
Lunch Jamie Wed., ask J. Whelan, Irish Catholic?
5-year goals inc. martial arts
Libr. return Negotiation for Dummies & Boston Red Sox 101, *pay fine, borrow OCD self-help*

Olivia was grateful that she lived in a time when instant retrieval of data was so quick and reliable. Even though computer programs were rapidly making her records management skills nearly obsolete. She wondered why she hadn't Googled the Berwind family right at the beginning, when she had found Hugh Berwind's handwritten will. But never mind now, for here was the decline of the Berwind dynasty neatly outlined in tree form online.

Hugh Belmont Berwind 1864-1919 married 1888 to Edna Delano Pell 1870-1930

Hugh Delano Berwind 1890-1918

George Victor Berwind 1894-1957 married 1925 to Flora Belle Amory 1900-2002

George Amory Berwind 1928-1938
Paul David Berwind 1930-1938

Hugh Belmont Berwind, Hugh and George's father, had been an only child, the sole beneficiary of the Berwind fortune in iron, copper, coal, and banking. He'd died in 1919, perhaps heartbroken after the death of his eldest son. Although his surviving son George had sired two boys, both of them died very young in 1938. The flu or typhus, Olivia imagined. What a terrible tragedy that must have been. But what of Hugh's mother, Edna? Had the existence of Rose Redford been hidden from Hugh's parents? If Rose had actually given birth to the child mentioned in Hugh's will, wouldn't Edna have welcomed her dead son's child with eager arms? But that might have screwed up brother George's inheritance. As it was, he got the whole lot. Olivia clicked a few more links. In excess of 200 million. And for what? The Berwind money had eventually gone to the Swetts, Flora's sister's children. There was no Swett family tree conveniently printed online, but with a few clicks here and there, Olivia managed to construct a fair imitation.

Henry James Swett 1890-1960 married 1925 to (Flora's sister) Eleanor May Amory 1905-1975

Henry James Swett, Jr. 1935-2000 married 1965 to Carolyn Brewster Cabot 1945-1998

Henry James Swett, III, 1967-
Paul Francis Swett 1970-
Jane Cabot Swett (Lady Jane Gamble)1972-
married 1992 Lord Terrance Gamble divorced. 2000.

Hon. Robyn Gamble 1993-

And there they were, the three living Berwind-Swett heirs. Henry III had tried to grab the entire fortune for himself, but he'd been legally forced to share. A little family blackmail. If his siblings had pressed charges for the surreptitious sale of his elderly great-aunt's art works, Henry III would have gone to jail. Nice bunch of kids, Olivia thought, comparing them in her mind to the O'Haras, who might tease and bicker but would stand by one another, especially that feisty Moira, who had once come home from school with a black eye after a tussle with a bully who'd been taking Danny's lunch money. And they were generous with each other. Danny's losses had been made up from the others' allowances. (Which had only served to make Moira madder.)

Olivia wondered if any of the Swett heirs knew that Hugh may have fathered a legitimate child. It might have been one of those guarded family legends, relatives who are never mentioned to outsiders: the horse thief who was hanged, the socialite who ran away with an Italian gigolo, the bastard raised by a tenant family. *The lost child of Hugh Berwind.* If she were to ask one of the living Swetts about that possibility, which would she choose? Jane, probably. Women were more sympathetic to such romantic stories. *Lady Jane Gamble.* Divorced the bloke, kept the title.

But before she approached Jane, Olivia needed to find a record of Hugh and Rose's marriage. Although she'd never stopped looking, using every bit of her considerable reference experience, no documentation had surfaced. Olivia wondered...that librarian over at Black Hill had shown a rather miraculous grasp of finding relevant material. It was she who had suggested looking up Rose's death record when a wedding record failed to surface.

Which led to the second big question: what happened to Rose's child? Adoption had made sense, but those records, especially since they were Catholic records, would be tightly sealed.

A small voice inside Olivia's consciousness asked her why she was pursuing Rose's story so obsessively. *Good question*, Olivia told herself. And she hadn't even seen the ghost in the garden with her own eyes, even though she had deliberately toured her rose garden at twilight, a time of mysterious shadows, and by moonlight, when white ladies were wont to wander. She was beginning to feel left out.

~

"Now, why have you suddenly become curious about my patient? Of course Whelan is an Irish name. I don't suppose you ever read Forbes magazine? His is one of the five richest Irish families in the world, pharmaceuticals." Jamie smiled smugly, sipped her martini, and gazed out at the ocean with a blissful expression. Jamie's patient was spending the week with his cardiologist, a family friend, on Martha's Vineyard, an unexpected holiday for his nurse.

They were lunching at Cedar Point again, and the seaside place had lost none of its culinary luster. Their cocktails were accompanied by an appetizer platter of lightly battered, fried oysters with a piquant sauce.

"I thought you said his family had dwindled down to an unpleasant few."

"His adored grandniece Harper—how he dotes on that little hussy!—and some spurious second cousins. I did mention two brothers, as well, although neither of them seems to be particularly close to my patient. Maybe they're just too busy to call. Geoffrey, the Earl of Ballybane, runs their pharmaceutical interests in the UK. He's grandfather to darling Harper, whom he has disowned. And Patrick Whelan, who's the Bishop of the Diocese of Worcester. No kids there, of course. That we know of."

"A bishop!" Olivia breathed the word with a reverence due only to Popes.

"Forget it, Liv. I am not—I repeat, *not*—getting into one of your harebrained crusades to bring justice to some poor dead soul."

~

Lunch had been an oasis of quiet refreshment in Olivia's day, compared to the chaos that awaited her at home. Come to think of it, there was never any serious expectation of peace and order in a house where three teenagers resided, but this problem was considerably graver. Kevin, whose license was only a few weeks old, had been picked up by the police in Brockton for driving his friend's car under the influence. Dave had gone to Brockton immediately to find out what was going on with his ward and what could be done about it.

"Uncle Dave sure is pissed." Moira relayed the news to Olivia with an air of pious satisfaction. She continued browning beef for stew as she talked, stirring the pot with a long-handled wooden spoon "I think it's that girl Kevin's been hooking up with, that Norah Slattery. *Slattery,* all right. I knew she was trouble."

"Give her a break, Moira. She's teaching him to play the Irish fiddle." Olivia sighed; she got herself a cup and a kava-kava teabag.

"And a few other things, too, I bet." Moira added beef broth to the hot pan in a mighty sizzle. She began to slice carrots. Olivia reflected that Moira was always looking elsewhere when she delivered these little zingers.

"What do you mean, exactly?" Olivia plugged in the electric kettle.

"No one's home at Sean Brady's during the day. So that's where Kev and herself go to 'practice.' Okay by me. Who needs to listen to that screeching? But if Norah's brothers get riled up about it..."

"Have you talked to Uncle Dave about any of your suspicions?"

Moira slid the carrots from the cutting board into the pot. She rummaged in the spice cabinet for thyme. "Didn't want to grass on Kev."

"But you're telling me."

"That's okay. You don't really count. I mean it's not like telling the boss."

Olivia finished making her tea and took the cup in their bedroom. She curled up on the chaise lounge with a sigh and gazed out at the marsh across the street. *How did I get myself into this swamp of emotional conflict?* Because Dave had come into her life—the smart, sexy man of her dreams—and he'd been single! (She might have the O'Haras to thank for that.) She couldn't resist him, and now look! He'd be in one of his gray-faced, implacably stern moods when he returned with Kevin. She hoped the boy would meet his foster-parent's wrath with chastened compliance, but she doubted it.

Finishing the last of her herbal tea, which didn't seem to be as calming lately as it had in the past, Olivia went into her office to check for emails, maybe even an offer of employment. But she found herself idly perusing old news about the Berwinds and the Swetts instead. She zeroed in on Lady Jane Gamble nèe Swett. She'd be in her early forties now. The most recent photo, shown at a fund-raising gala in *South Shore Living*, revealed a gamine face that could have been ten years younger except for a certain hard canniness about the eyes. Olivia, who had herself gone through a demoralizing divorce, attributed that air of toughness to whatever Lady Jane had suffered in the process of shedding Lord Terrance. She just knew this woman would be her most sympathetic entrée to solving the Berwind conundrum.

JULY 5

Things to Do Today

Spec. effort: Kevin
Deadhead roses
Poss. Black Hill
Write mission statement for this year:
  be a friend to O'Haras
  yoga for stress or tai chi
  no more ghosts—does this mean no more auctions?

Shouting matches and bouts of sulking continued at the Lowenstein household through the following days. Kevin was grounded, never mind what important gigs had been promised to the Celtic Storm. His cell phone and laptop were confiscated, and he was forewarned that his presence at the next family outing to see Mom at federal prison would be compulsory. Behind the closed door of Kevin's room, the angry rhythm of his Bodhrán, plainly audible throughout the house, was beginning to get on Olivia's last nerve.

After the July 4th enforced family excursion (enforced for Kevin—Moira and Danny were delighted) to watch the fireworks over Plymouth Bay, Dave had escaped to work, and she supposed he was counting on her to play warden, but enough was enough.

She picked up her car keys and found herself facing two eager dogs panting with anticipation. "Sorry, guys. It's too hot to leave you in the car." Then with a sudden inexplicable change of heart, she hurried upstairs and knocked on Kevin's door. "I'm going for ride to Black Hill in Plymouth. Why don't you come with me? Sadie and Bruno are so disappointed that I can't take them, but leaving them in a hot car is out of the question. Maybe you'd enjoy a change of scene. My errand is at the branch library. Probably about a half hour or so. You could keep the car running for the AC while I'm inside."

What a surprise when Kevin actually came out of his retreat and gave her an expressionless nod. He was wearing a black T-shirt with cut-off sleeves, black jeans, and black boots, a back pack dangling from one hand. He shrugged it on. His dark blond hair was jelled darker, and the wallet in his pocket was attached to his belt by a heavy chain. He wore a linked identity bracelet engraved with *The Celtic Storm*. "Where's the kids?"

"Moira and Danny took their bikes to the library to borrow a few of the books on their summer reading lists. Also I believe there will be a PG movie shown after lunch. Moira packed sandwiches." She pushed away Bruno and Sadie who were whining and attempting to nose her back down the stairs.

"Sounds about right. Okay, let's go."

Would this be an opportunity for Olivia to test some of those communication do's and don'ts she'd read about in *How to Talk to Your Teen*? She began as soon as they were all settled into the Honda, delighted dogs drooling on the cracked-open back windows.

(*Talk to your teen about whatever interests him.*) "How are the fiddle lessons with Norah progressing?"

"Okay."

(*Notice your teen's feelings.*) "You must be feeling upset about the loss of your license."

"Nope."

(*Offer your opinion without lecturing or judging.*) "Your Uncle Dave only wants you to be healthy and happy. Drinking will make you sick and miserable. And you'll want to get your license back, and keep it."

"You think?"

(*Answer questions directly.*) Yes, I do think that.

(*Offer assistance.*) "And I'd really like to help."

"Listen, Liv. Don't try to get around me, okay?"

After riding the rest of the way in strained silence, the library looked as quaint and inviting as Olivia remembered. Now that they were there, though, she wondered what Kevin would think of her going so far out of her usual route to this Plymouth branch. She turned from Shawmut St. onto Beach Plum Rd., following the little library sign, the silhouette of a reader with an arrow pointing the way. There was only one other car parked in front of the cottage library. "You'll run the motor from time to time for the AC?"

"Thanks, but no thanks. I'll take Sadie and Bruno down to the beach, if there is one." Kevin took a package of cigarettes out of his back pack. "Don't rush on my account."

"I'll leave the keys here, in case. Are those cigarettes? Does Dave know you're smoking?"

"Nope. Unless you're going to rat me out."

"I wouldn't call it that. I'd call it saving your life." Olivia gathered her handbag and got out of the car. Kevin followed with the two dogs, dancing with excitement on leash; he headed straight for a little path that looked like it would lead down to the water.

"Nice chatting with you, *Mom*." Kevin's tone was bitingly sarcastic.

(*Share your feelings openly and honestly.*) "Listen, Kevin, I'm not trying to replace your mom. But I would like to be your friend, if you'll let me."

"Sure. See you later." He strode off with the two deliriously joyful dogs. *A walk! A walk!*

"I don't know how long I'll be. Less than an hour, I guess." Olivia realized she was speaking to the back of Kevin's head. Directly and honestly, of course. She wondered if the author of *How to Talk to Your Teen*, Gladys Piffin, had ever actually tried to converse with a brooding fifteen-year-old.

But her feelings of frustration and inadequacy somehow lifted when she entered the sunny room with its golden oak furnishings burnished by time. A woman and two small children were just leaving with a canvas tote bag that overflowed with picture books. This time Mrs. Ritchie was sitting at her desk instead of on the floor behind a bookcase. She looked up from the book she was perusing, half-frames perched on the tip of her nose. It was a rather decrepit volume, perhaps an old cookbook. Her irascible cat, Omar, sat like a suspicious sentinel on the oak file catalog. His glittering green eyes spoke volumes of distrust.

Three yellow pencils stuck at crazy angles in the librarian's coronet of braids, giving her a slightly tipsy appearance, but her smile was cheerful and welcoming. "Hello again, Olivia! How can I help you today, dear? Hit another stone wall, did you?"

"Without going into a lot of detail, let me just say that it's become increasingly important to find some record of that young couple—the ones I told you about last time—their marriage, you know."

"Yes, indeed, I remember. I see that you are troubled. And I don't think we'll find a record through the computer's search engine, or you would have got there yourself already. What we need to know first is where the marriage took place, don't you think?"

"Yes, of course. But how?"

"Have you ever heard of dowsing, dear?"

"But we're not trying to find water, Mrs. Ritchie."

The librarian laughed, a deeply infectious laugh that Olivia couldn't resist joining, although nothing seemed funny to her. "And I'm not going to use a forked stick. Although I do have one in my reticule. Witch Hazel is the best wood for that, you know. But for searches like this one, when the computer fails, there's nothing like real crystal."

Mrs. Ritchie pulled the tear-shaped crystal pendant from underneath her blouse, some kind of bright plaid cotton. She rolled her swivel chair over to a nearby shelf and rolled back holding an enormous atlas, which she opened on her desk. Turning to a map of the United States, she gave the pendant a brisk rub between her hands. "Best not to let it get cold. Very sensitive, these divining crystals. That's why I keep it close to my body at all times."

Holding the pendant by its silver chain, she allowed the teardrop to dangle over the map. As Olivia watched with disbelief, it moved a little erratically and even swung wildly outside the borders of the book, and yet she could have sworn that Mrs. Ritchie held her be-ringed hand perfectly still the entire time.

"Dear, dear, no wonder."

"No wonder what?" Olivia was thoroughly confused by the procedure she was witnessing.

"No wonder you couldn't find any record. That marriage didn't take place in the United States. I'd bet my best rowan wand on it."

"Then where?"

"That's what we're going to find out. Roll that big globe over here, will you dear?"

The large handsome globe was set on a low wooden stand with wheels. It moved quite easily. But what was bothering

Olivia about this whole performance was the niggling suspicion that she was watching some kind of witchcraft. Could this be? In *Plymouth?*

Mrs. Ritchie began again, the same rigmarole with the pendant, slowly turning the globe with her other hand. In a very short time the pendant began to swing in a smooth, deliberate arc over the North American continent. "I think I've got it," she said with a small smile of satisfaction. Then it was back to the Atlas for another go, this time turning the page to Canada.

More decorous swinging until the pendant finally came to a still point. Olivia looked over the librarian's shoulder. "Is that crystal pointing to Toronto?"

"Yes, Olivia, I believe it is. And *believing is seeing*, that's what I always say. You should be able to search out the rest yourself. I just bet you're eager to get back to your computer right this minute. But how about a nice cup of tea first?"

"My stepson, my husband's ward actually, will be waiting for me outside. Impatiently, I don't doubt. But I may have an even more difficult search later." Olivia paused, not sure of how much she wanted to reveal right now.

"Let me guess." Mrs. Ritchie looked at her keenly over her half-frames. "It's that child you're after. Rose Berwind died in childbirth, so we discovered last time. This young couple were parents, and you want to know what happened to the baby—was he adopted, and if so, by whom?"

"Good guess, Mrs. Ritchie. Yes. But the problem is, a Catholic adoption in the early 20th century might be almost impossible to trace."

"Oh, no, dear. Anything is possible. We must remember that *all things wait for those who come.*"

Another screwed-up proverb. As Olivia had noticed before, Mrs. Ritchie was a regular Mrs. Malaprop, and yet somehow the librarian's peculiar twists made a different kind of sense. "I'll try to keep that in mind."

"You may need to put your question to the Divine Cosmos, of course. I could help you there."

Divine Cosmos, indeed. Some kind of a weird cult, Olivia thought. Wasn't it upsetting enough to be driven by a ghost (or two!) into all kinds of uncharacteristic pursuits, like actually hosting a séance? Still, if she did find that a marriage between Hugh and Rose had taken place in Canada—of all places!—she would have to give credit where credit was due.

None of this was what she said, of course. She thanked the plump librarian sincerely and promised to get in touch if she needed any more help with her queries.

"Till the next time, then. And if you need more expertise than I can offer, I have some friends..." Mrs. Ritchie laughed again, that hypnotic laugh that made Olivia chuckle, too.

She was still chuckling when she got back to her Honda and discovered that the dogs were stowed in it, the windows still cracked open, and the AC running full blast. But not a sign of Kevin. She turned off the motor, checked Sadie and Bruno's leashes, and opened the car door. "Okay, you guys. Let's go find Kevin." An assignment they would be much better at than she, with her poor human senses.

Sadie and Bruno, eager for action, practically pulled Olivia off her feet, not in the direction of the path to the beach, but back to Shawmut St., and there they halted, milling about in the perplexed fashion of dogs who have lost the scent.

Kevin must have caught a ride, Olivia thought. But he didn't have his cell phone, so he couldn't have called anyone. How could anyone know they had made this impromptu trip to the library? Unless he hitched. Yes, that must be it. Dangerous mode of travel. Not to mention, Dave would be wild. And it would be all her fault. Although he hadn't *specifically* told her not to invite Kevin to leave the house, possibly he'd taken that restriction for granted.

Olivia trudged back to her car to find Mrs. Ritchie in the library's front yard clipping purple coneflowers and laying them in an old-fashioned flower basket. "Echinacea, the cure-all herb. Although I'm only an amateur herbalist, but I have a friend… Oh, my dear, you look worried. What ever happened? Where's the boy?" The librarian put down her basket so that she could greet Sadie and Bruno, who were gently nosing her striped skirt.

"Sadie and Bruno led me up to Shawmut St, but the track ended there. He's not carrying his cell phone, so the only explanation is that he hitched a ride somewhere. My husband will not be best pleased. I wish I knew where he's gone so that I could get him back to the house before Dave gets home."

"In that case, come back inside, dear. Yes, yes…of course it's okay to bring the pups. There's no one else here now but ourselves, and Omar's at home today. I believe I can find your boy for you."

Olivia followed numbly with Sadie and Bruno eagerly leading the way. Mrs. Ritchie filled a stainless steel bowl with water and put it down for them in the tiny kitchen. Apparently, they were quite thirsty; they slobbered noisily.

"Let's try a bit of local dowsing, dear." Mrs. Ritchie took a map of Plymouth and Surrounding Towns out of her desk and laid it down, smoothing it flat with a flash of rings. The many silver bangles she wore on her wrists tinkled softly. Olivia felt inexplicably soothed and hopeful.

The librarian pulled the crystal pendant out from between her breasts as she had done before, rubbed it between her hands, and held it over the map. A few moments later, it began to circle lazily, moving toward Pembroke. It came to rest over an area called Strawberry Hill.

"Oh, I know exactly where he must be, that wretch." Olivia snatched up the dogs' leashes and pulled impatiently. Sadie and Bruno got up reluctantly from their cool nap between the stacks. *A dog's work is never done* implicit in their sighs. "He's got a girlfriend who lives there. Norah Slattery. I remember now that she mentioned Strawberry Hill. Later, when I asked Kevin about the place, he said some Irish travelers from South Carolina are stopping there. I thought it must be an inn."

"Strawberry Hill is a camping ground. *The* Irish Travellers? May I suggest that you Google that name and do a bit of research? Double l, usually."

"Yes, yes…" Olivia hustled the dogs out the door with a hasty "thank you."

"Come back any time, dear."

Olivia thought she had all she needed, for now anyway. She waved gratefully at the plump little figure in the doorway. Through a trick of the light, she almost thought the woman had become taller and was wearing a coronet of those crazy purple blossoms.

Once Olivia had located Kevin, surprisingly, it had not been all that difficult to persuade him to get into the van and come home with her. Bruno and Sadie sniffed every part of him that their wet noses could reach from the back seat, taking in new scents from that wretched camp. The dogs had not thought much of the place, either, and had growled protectively at anyone who came close to Olivia's Honda while she was out talking to Kevin and Norah. Talking *at* was perhaps closer to the truth. All she ever got back were those infuriating monosyllabic answers.

Olivia had never believed in intuition, even though she'd often been afflicted with that so-called "gut feeling." Right now the notion came to her strongly that Norah was thinking of running away and wanted Kevin to go with her. The girl had given her father a look that spoke volumes to Olivia. Should she tell Dave? Based on no evidence but a hateful stare?

Cian Slattery's tall broad frame filled the doorway of their trailer, which bore a South Carolina license plate. He had the same fair coloring and pointed chin as Norah, but not her paleness. Broken veins stained his cheeks, and the beginnings of a beer gut leaned over his wide leather belt. When Olivia had glanced at his silver buckle—a wolf?—he'd leered at her. Did he imagine that she fancied him? *In your dreams, Buster.* But in that instant when they'd locked eyes, Olivia had seen quite plainly that Cian Slattery thought there might be some advantage to his daughter's friendship with Kevin. *What could he be up to?* She didn't quite know *how* she was aware of his thoughts, but in fact, she felt as if she knew this man's nature. Maybe some latent ability to read micro-expressions of the face and body language; there had to be a logical explanation.

Olivia and Kevin didn't talk much on the way home. She'd rather given up on *How to Talk to Your Teen* anyway. Let him brood all he wanted; at least, he'd be present and accounted for when Dave returned tonight. Olivia considered suggesting that Kevin not mention his escape from house arrest, and her part in it, but then she decided that would be cowardly. There was something troublesome about the milieu in which Norah lived, and Dave needed to know at least that much, if not the full measure of her suspicions.

~

Kevin admitted to himself being surprised as hell that Olivia had found him in such short order. He even wondered if she'd snuck a GPS into his backpack. A quick search revealed nothing but his own stuff, however; maybe he'd been watching too many cop shows.

Olivia was a real pain in the butt, even if she was kinda hot for an old lady, those long legs, and that smooth little ass when she was leaning over her friggin' roses. Always trying to be good buddies with him and the sibs. The only reason he'd headed home from the camp without kicking up a hell of a fuss was because he was uncertain himself whether he wanted to try Dave's patience even further. Dave had always been okay, a real friend stepping up to the plate when Kevin's dad was shot down, taking in Moira and Danny. And him. Although he could have done for himself perfectly fine. Got a job, crashed with a friend. But he'd gone along with Dave's plan to keep them all together just so's he could keep an eye on the sibs.

Probably it had been a dumb idea to drive his buddy Sean's Chevy truck when they'd both been wasted on his dad's whiskey. There was always plenty of liquor, and everything else, at Sean Brady's house. Sean's instrument was a very fine Irish bouzouki imported from Australia. The back and sides were Tasmanian Blackwood, with an ebony board. Liam, the fourth member of their band, played a classy Fender guitar. If it weren't for Norah, Kevin would have felt out of his element. But like Kevin, Norah had to depend on her own talent, never mind what her folks could hand out.

That was another thing that bugged him. Their parents never bothered to keep tabs on Sean and Liam the way he was hounded by Dave. Guess it was because Dave was a cop. But no matter what Dave ordered him to do, there was one rule Kevin would not obey. Kevin would never agree to visit that woman

Alice who called herself his mom. He'd heard how she was eager to give up her parental rights. What was that all about? Dave had said Alice wanted to clear the way for him to adopt Kevin and the sibs legally, but Kevin thought Alice just didn't care to be saddled with kids when, or if, she ever got out of jail.

Norah was so cool. She even thought it was awesome to have a mother locked up by the Feds, like it was some kind of status symbol. Maybe because she didn't know where her own mom was. That's one thing about Alice; Kevin was always going to know just where she was for the next ten years. Big deal.

Norah lived with her dad and two older brothers, Ray and Kyle. They'd been friendly enough, even though Norah said he should watch out, they could be rough and mean when they were crossed. Kevin wondered if that was why she kept an Irish knife strapped under her shirt. So far she'd never been caught with it at school. Too smart for them all, that was Norah. Moira called Norah a "ho," but that was just Moira; she'd never liked any girl he fancied.

NANNY BURNS LOOKS IN AGAIN

Boys will be boys, dearie. And no one knows better than I the difficulty of getting someone else's offspring to tow the mark. A body needs good old-fashioned resolve and perseverance to take on someone else's youngsters. Even then, it will probably be a thankless task.

I've propelled myself (my spirit or something) back to find that marquetry case I gave my dear Hugh, just as Anya Bharata advised me to do, and, frankly, that exercise was much like trying to bundle oneself into a tight corset. (No corsets where I am now!) But Anya Bharata was right. My pursuit of justice is on the right track now. I feel it in my bones (if I still have them).

I moved a few things around—those pearls, that Mass card my sister sent me—simply to bring attention to Hugh's cause, not intending to bring on an attack of the vapors, dearie.

And now there's the added worry of that rascally ward who ran off without a word! Just out of curiosity, I followed the young master O'Hara when he hitched a ride, just like any low-class bum. Flying after that rascal was rather an awkward exercise for someone who's used to traveling on her own sturdy feet. As a matter of fact, I landed on a tree branch (a fairly smooth and strong one, fortunately). This big old oak was looming over a disreputable outdoor habitat. Tents, trailers, cooking pits, and an ugly block building for washing up and privies. People sitting around drinking and singing. Strictly lower class amusements, if you ask me.

But that's where the scallywag went, right into that nest of ne'er-do-wells, looking for a girl, of course. A thin blonde creature who plays the violin like a mad person. I wonder if I can cramp her fingers? Never tried that sort of trick, but I hear tell of it from my companions.

I watched her father looking out from the trailer door, not at all unhappy with his daughter's new suitor—the sweet scent of money, I don't doubt. The whole lot of them squatting in this part of the camp—they look like a bunch of tinkers to me. Up to no good.

JULY 10

Things to Do Today

5-year goals, inc. study of antique docs, intro to new field
Libr. borrow A Skeptic's Guide to Ghosts
Google: Irish Travellers
Google: finding adopted child
Google: St. Rita's Refuge for Women

Moira was making dinner again, happily dicing and chopping ingredients for some kind of magnificent salad. "Grilled tuna on a bed of greens and things," Moira said with a superior little smile, her smattering of freckles gleaming from the kitchen's heat. A fresh cornbread stood on the counter. Alice O'Hara's handwritten cookbook lay open on the kitchen table.

Olivia could detect the pungent odor of raw red onions, which would certainly give her heartburn. But she'd just count her blessings on a hot night like this. Still, she wondered why the girl persisted in taking on all this work, when she could be strolling through some air-conditioned mall with her girlfriends, texting their way from store to store just in case one of them got lost in jewelry or shoes.

Truth be told, Moira didn't really have many friends; family seemed to take the place of friends in her world. Immune to peer pressure, her outfits bore no resemblance to the reigning teen fashions, and she professed no interest in boys and sex. Moira might have been the perfect target for bullies, Olivia reflected, if she had not been quite so quick to pay back worse than she got. Olivia wondered if there was anything she could do to help Moira make friends. Probably not. A kid was basically on her own in navigating the currents of school social life, sink or swim.

Only it would mean so much if Moira just had one really good buddy. Olivia knew this because she'd had Jamie. All through the miseries of high school and a cold, bleak homelife, Olivia had been warmed and cheered by Jamie and her family. The Andrews had treated her as if she were one of their own, and indeed, she'd spent enough time at their house to qualify. Moira needed a friend like that, the kind you kept for a lifetime.

Unexpected free time ought always to be used to advantage, Olivia thought. She retired to the peace of her office and systematically Googled all references to the Travellers. Depending on which articles you read, they were a tribe of fun-loving, free-wheeling Irish gypsies who preferred to live unencumbered by middle-class mores and values—or they were a gang of toughs and thieves preying on the honest citizens of whatever place they infested, mostly the southern states. Olivia thought both views were probably exaggerated, although the term "gypsies" might be closer to the mark. "Hippies" would have done as well, except that the Travellers were quite clannish and tended to marry within a few closely-knit families.

So, why then was Norah's father so cordial to Kevin? Was he planning to adopt him into the family? Or blackmail Dave into rescuing Kevin from the Slattery clutches? The situation would bear watching. She closed down all the Travellers links without making any notes. It wouldn't do for Kevin to find her researching his new friends.

She turned then to St. Rita's Refuge for Women.

St. Rita's Refuge for Women was established in 1892 as a place where poor, unmarried, pregnant females could learn fine sewing skills while receiving free room, board, and medical care, up to and including the birth of the child, as well as adoption services afterward. Girls could elect to stay on and work as seamstresses, or a stipend would be offered to those who wished to reenter the outside world. The refuge was closed in 1949 after a fire destroyed most of the clinic and the workrooms, as well as extensively damaging the offices. Although the case was determined to be arson, it remained unsolved.

"Shit, there go the birth records," Olivia exclaimed to Wikipedia. Wondering about the fate of those poor pregnant girls working in the sewing sweatshop—the ones who stayed on probably had no other place else to go but the streets—some choice! Olivia continued clicking informative sites and news accounts.

The fire erupted just after midnight. Seven girls, two newborn babies, and one nurse had been in residence at the time, and all escaped with only minor injuries. The staff and a few full-time seamstresses, housed separately at the nearby convent, were unharmed. The single fatality was the death of Mother Perpetua who ran back into the building to rescue some valuable patterns and succumbed to the smoke. The refuge had been renowned for its delicate hand-made wedding veils and christening robes. Its linen and lace creations were sought after by prominent families and even royalty throughout Europe and America.

Spared from the conflagration was the charming St. Rita's Chapel of Roses. The diminutive house of worship is situated on a hill above the refuge with a lovely view of surrounding hills and orchards. The original Italian edifice had been imported from St. Rita's native province of Cascia, stone by stone, as a gift from the William A. Haggerty family.

The chapel is still visited by thousands every year, to view its famous The Stigma of St. Rita *stained glass window (a thorn that pierced her forehead bled for fifteen years). The Christmas roses in the chapel's garden have been known to blossom even in winter.*

"Chapel of Roses! Christ, this is beyond irony." Olivia closed down her laptop. Tomorrow she would find her way through the maze of Canadian marriage records with fresh energy. After a blissfully refreshing shower, she put on a new yellow sundress that showed her well-toned arms and tanned olive skin to advantage. Maybe Moira would allow her to set the table for dinner.

Moira had already set the table, *thank you very much,* in the dining room, away from the heat of the kitchen. Finding a pitcher of iced tea in the refrigerator; Olivia helped herself to a glass, feeling somewhat like a slacker. The sun had retreated from the front porch for the day, so this was the perfect time to let go of the problems of step-parenting and obsessing about long-ago love affairs and just enjoy her rose garden. On impulse, she sidetracked to her bedroom and took the silver locket with Rose's portrait out of the marquetry case, slipping it into the pocket of her sundress. *How whimsical I'm becoming.* The thought made her smile.

The scent from the garden was subtle and lulling, the shadows long and cool. Olivia loved her roses, the lush colors, the glossy leaves, even the thorns, like duennas guarding their lovelies. She closed her eyes, rocking gently back and forth in an antique oak-and-cane chair where countless women had rocked before she was born. She may even have drifted off for a few minutes.

When she sat up with a start, she felt a slight chill like a cold hand caressing her bare shoulders. She looked out at the ornate white iron bench and the arbor. Rubbed her eyes and looked again. Something like a sheer scarf seemed to be blowing…no!

Not a scarf! It was the figure of a girl in a summer dress, chiffon perhaps. A brush stroke of dark hair curling about her beautiful translucent face. A girl who wasn't quite all there.

"Rose," Olivia said aloud in wonder.

As if oblivious to this other dimension, Olivia's dimension, the girl trailed a hand over the blossoms that surrounded her. She began to cry silently, traces of tears running down her nearly invisible cheeks. *She is weeping for her husband, and her son. How do I know it's a son?* Olivia could read the spirit's thoughts, or believed she could. "Tell me what became of him, Rose. Who took your boy when you left this life?" Olivia didn't know if she were speaking aloud or merely thinking the words, but the answer came to her quite plainly, in a clear, musical voice that was not her own.

"The priest…I told him I wasn't a Catholic. He said I was dying, and even though I had refused the last rites, he would baptize my son so that he would be saved. Mother Opportuna offered to be his godmother. I wanted my baby to be named Hugh, his father—and for my father, too. Hugh Redford Persey Berwind. But the nuns gave my Hugh away. The priest knew…the priest knew."

From her silvery feet to the wispy waves of hair, the vision faded away, until there was nothing but the empty bench with the roses cascading around it. Olivia startled out of her reverie. Had she been dreaming, after all? She didn't think so, because the girl she'd seen matched Danny's sighting—the sad lovely girl, the garden bench, her vague form fading into emptiness.

Hugh Redford Persey Berwind. Where did the Persey come from? And why did the vision say "the priest knew" in a voice of such anguish and betrayal. Olivia would think about that.

Mrs. Mitchell had told Olivia to ask herself questions just as she was falling asleep at night. "Invoke the Great Spirit to guide you. And keep the fetish I gave you under your pillow. Bear will search for an answer while you are sleeping." The Wampanoag believed in dreams, Mrs. M. had said. As a shaman herself, she set great store in answers that came to mind as she woke. "And Google. Sometimes Google can be as inspirational as a vision quest."

Olivia thought she would start with Google and then work her way up to the Great Spirit and the bear fetish. But still she didn't move. It felt as if she were still in a daze. She was even thinking of herself in the third person. *Let Olivia be quiet for a while and absorb the experience.* It wasn't every day that a ghost gave advice on a research project.

She was still sitting there, rocking and musing, when Dave drove into the driveway a little while later. He smiled broadly, strode up the stairs, and pulled her right out of her bemused state, kissing her soundly. There was nothing like Dave's tender mouth and firm embrace to bring Olivia back to earth. And earth was the right place for love—as well as for sensible reflection.

ROSE

How did I get here in this garden again? Before this moment, everything around me was mist and fog. And voices, soft comforting voices, whispering that the haziness would lift and my way would become clear, that Hugh was waiting for me. I wanted with all my heart and soul to follow those voices, but I can't leave this limbo I'm in until I know what happened to our child. How long have I been waiting for someone to hear me? There doesn't seem to be any sense of time passing where I am now. Once in a while I think I glimpse another grieving young mother, unless it's only my own reflection.

And now I've fallen into a place where everything is roses, Hugh's favorite flower. I can sense that there's someone nearby who is listening, but she seems to be on the other side of a veil that shimmers like heat waves you could walk through and yet is impenetrable. How strange it is to come back, to find there is someone who holds in her hand that silver locket, the one I gave to Hugh when he went off to war, never to come home again.

I'm trying to tell her that Father Damian knows where my baby was taken. I understand now that I had to leave him. I was a broken vessel, life drained out of me like water. But if only Hugh's parents could have known there was a child for them to love. Maybe this young woman will find out where he is and tell them. Unless it's too late.

The voices whisper that nothing is too late or too soon in the place where I am a wanderer now. Before I return there, I will lay my quest in this stranger's path. I believe she is someone who will take it up for me.

If I try very hard, I can almost remember that name, that family. I want to tell the woman who holds our locket the name I heard the priest say to Mother Opportuna. They thought I had gone somewhere. They said that. Mother said, "The Berwind girl is gone, Father." And he said that there was an important donation promised if they could find a healthy, handsome boy of good stock for a certain senator and his wife. "And thanks be to God, Who has sent to our care one more inconvenient young woman and her unwanted infant, like a gift from Heaven. Two families blessed on this one night. One family needing to see the last of her, and one who will welcome the infant with joy and patronage. You must expedite the paper work, Mother Opportuna. Never mind the waiting list this time."

I was up on the ceiling watching Mother when she made a telephone call from her office. No official forms. Just a chauffeur at the back door, and she handed my baby out into the night.

What was the name of that chapel, the name of its donors?

I'll remember. I know I will.

JULY 11
Things to Do Today

Marriage records Ontario circa 1916
Poss. take Moira to mall. New clothes, Danbury visit?
Irish Travellers? What does Dave know?
Jamie: Whelan and St. Rita's Refuge.

Ontario had a searchable online data base of marriages and other vital statistics, but it dated from 1927 to the present century. What to do if you wanted records prior to 1927? The Mormons, of course, who trained volunteers to gather genealogy records from everywhere in the world, and then made those records available to all seekers. Family histories were assembled and safeguarded because of the Mormon belief in the Eternal Family, linked throughout time.

Eureka! A fully digitalized data base of marriages in Ontario from 1869 up to the present century was available online from FamilySearch.org.

God bless the information age and the Mormon obsession with family ties! Still in her summer silk robe, fortified by an oversized mug of coffee, Olivia clicked and scrolled with a growing sense of hopeful accomplishment. The criteria required that she note the town or city in Ontario in which the marriage had occurred. Adelaide to Zorro, it would have been a formidable list, but she had been pointed toward Toronto, the capital.

In the midst of her gleeful self-congratulation, Olivia did pause to remember that she would never have thought to look at records in Ontario, Canada, if it hadn't been for that quirky little librarian at Black Hill with her crazy crystal. That resource was definitely a keeper. And besides, she'd rather liked the woman, something so comforting and motherly about her. Olivia hoped she didn't turn out to be something weird, like a witch. It had been quite enough to have sought out the help of an American Indian shaman.

Olivia began her search of Toronto marriages circa 1916-1918.: *Hugh Delano Berwind and Rose Redford.*

And hit that proverbial stone wall she'd collided with so many times before. Olivia was still in her robe tapping keys when eleven-thirty rolled around. Such a lapse in her orderly morning habits was beyond belief. She closed down the laptop and headed for the shower.

A half hour later, showered and dressed, Olivia noted the squeezing sensation in her stomach was signaling that she had completely forgotten breakfast—brunch it would have to be at this hour. For once, she had found the spacious kitchen (with cheery green cabinets of the shade she deplored but Moira adored) unoccupied. Looking through the window while she made herself a slice of toast, she saw Moira in the backyard hammock reading, with Sadie snoozing underneath. Moira was wearing lime green shorts and a purple tank top, both too small. An idea occurred.

Consuming the toast in a few famished bites, Olive called out to the girl from the back door. "Hey, Moira—would you like to go to the mall with me? After-the-fourth summer sales are on!"

Moira looked up from *The Hunger Games* with her usual scowl. "Can I get some decent sneakers?"

"Okay."

"Adidas?"

"Sure."

"All right, then."

Leaving the two disconsolate dogs with Danny and Kevin, Olivia and Moira took off in a rare moment of mutual rapport.

"Are you hungry?" Olivia had ditched the notion of a full brunch and settled for the single slice of toast.

"We haven't had lunch," Moira pointed out. "How about Persy's Place? We're going right by there. They only serve breakfast stuff, but it's way better than MacDonald's or the Food Court. I don't eat that junk."

Persy! The name reverberated in Olivia's brain like the bells of St. Timothy's.

Persy's Place was a Plymouth favorite, serving breakfast fare all day. Olivia's dream or vision in the garden had included the name Persy or Persey. Its connection to Rose was unknown, but perhaps it was an unexplored link to her search. *Serendipity!* With or without the e? She would try it both ways.

With this latest inspiration on her mind, Olivia practically sleep-walked through her brunch with a surprisingly affable Moira, but she came back to life for her mission to supervise some decent shorts and T-shirts, in colors that they both could agree upon. And the Adidas sneakers, too, of course. Plus a pretty little yellow dress for her next trip to Danbury. Moira wore dresses only under duress, but she liked to please Dave. She and Olivia had that in common, if little else.

Moira quickly whisked the new clothes up to her room, thus avoiding any possibility of teasing from her brothers, for whom matching outfits, subdued colors, and—horrors!—a dress would signal a severe breakdown of Moira's tomboy ethic.

Olivia hurried into her office to boot up the laptop and return to the Toronto, Ontario, Marriage Index. She tried all combinations of Persy/Persey added to Hugh Delano Berwind. Then she tried Rose Persy/ Persey Redwood. Really, this was too much! Tears of frustration filled her eyes. Sliding a hand into the pocket of her white cropped pants for a tissue, she suddenly remembered the locket she'd never retrieved from yesterday's sundress, now in the hamper. Good Lord, what if she'd thrown it into the washing machine! She jumped up, ran into the bathroom, and retrieved the locket from the hamper. Polishing the smooth silver lightly on her blouse, she slipped it into the breast pocket.

One more combination: Hugh Delano Berwind and Rose Redford Persey.

Bingo!

How awesome was that! Married in Toronto, Canada, July, 1917. Making a quick note, she looked for and found a copy of the marriage certificate and printed it out. Christ Church, Deer Park. She would have to get her hands on a notarized copy of the original from the church's archives.

There! Flushed with success, she needed *to tell someone immediately*. Glancing at the on-screen time, she noted it was five o'clock—maybe Jamie would be on her supper break. Texting would not do it—she simply must spill the whole success story on the phone.

But Jamie's cell phone, skipping the musical rendition of "Diamonds Are a Girl's Best Friend," went immediately to voice mail. "Call me on your break!" Olivia begged urgently.

She began to reflect again on the name Persey added by Rose to her wedding certificate, meaning it was her legal name. It occurred to Olivia that Rose's parents may have been separated or divorced at the time she married Hugh.

~

"No, I will not ask Mr. Whelan if he knows anything about St. Rita's Refuge and the babies who were adopted out of there." Jamie had kept her phone off until almost six, and now on her supper break had listened critically to Olivia's tale of triumph—and her latest request. "Why would he know anything about a place that, as you have told me, burned down in 1949? Stop and consider for a moment how long ago that was. You and I weren't even born yet. Give up on this one, my friend. Talk about *Mission Impossible*!"

"John Peter Whelan was born in 1931. I looked him up. He might have heard *something*. Well, anyway, I have Rose's death certificate, which does give "complications due to childbirth" as the cause, and I'll soon have the marriage certificate." Olivia was not about to abandon her mission when she had come so far, but she had to admit that Whelan was the longest of long shots. "I guess I've got enough to bring up the possible existence of an unrecorded Berwind baby to Lady Jane Gamble."

"Oh, good God in Heaven, I wouldn't do that if I were you."

But Olivia didn't have time to argue the matter right then. It was, for a change, her turn to cook, and she had 14-ingredient Greek meatballs and rice pilaf in various stages of preparation.

"I don't see what harm it will do. But I have to go now and get dinner ready. We must talk later, though. How about coming over for breakfast on Sunday? Bring Mike. Kevin will be here because he's grounded until further notice."

Jamie groaned. Olivia couldn't tell whether it was because Kevin would probably be in a filthy mood, or because she had not given up her quest to find Rose's child, and probably never would.

"See you Sunday, then. Dave usually brings Danny and Moira back from catechism class around ten-thirty, and by then everyone is starved. Come at ten so that we can talk while I prepare the feast. And by the way, not a word of this to Dave."

~

Olivia's first attempt to contact Lady Jane Gamble was a handwritten letter on classy monogrammed stationery, citing some matters of importance to the Swett family that she had recently learned during her research into St. Rita's Refuge in Harvard, Massachusetts. She included her cell phone and land line numbers, and her email address, and she marked the envelope "Personal."

Nevertheless, it was Lady Jane's secretary who answered, with a crisp note thanking Ms. Lowenstein for her interest but declining an interview.

Olivia wanted to follow up with a phone call, but Lady Jane's phone number was unlisted as either Gamble, Jane S., or Swett, Jane C.

It did seem like another drop-dead end, but Olivia's dogged nature would not allow her to give in so easily to the rich and obdurate. She wrote another letter, this time dropping a few hints as to the matter she wished to bring to the Swetts' attention. A child born at St. Rita's Refuge in 1918 might be an undiscovered heir to the Berwind legacy, which had been eventually inherited by the Swetts.

"If you expect the Swetts to welcome this news, you're even more deluded than I feared," Jamie had said when apprised of Olivia's non-progress.

Olivia had to admit that Jamie might be right when her next communication from the Swetts came by way of the law firm of Hatchett, Hammer, and Cleaves, signed by the senior partner, Aaron Hatchett, Esq., demanding that Olivia Andreas Lowenstein cease and desist from contacting Lady Jane Gamble by any means whatsoever with nuisance claims concerning the Berwind estate, to avoid subsequent legal action.

~

"Golly, I think you may have hit a nerve there." It was late afternoon on another Sunday. Jamie was lounging on the rocker in Olivia's office, shaking her head over the file her friend had laid in her lap. It was a deep pink folder, labeled *Rose and Hugh*. "Legal action does sound rather serious. Will you quit with the Swetts now? Before you get smacked with a restraining order and have to explain the whole story to Dave. Not to mention your ghost in the garden. You'll be lucky if he doesn't have you committed."

"I should never have told you about the ghost. No matter. Dave will believe I saw what I say I saw, I'm sure of that. I just haven't wanted to worry him while he's so busy at work."

Jamie snorted. "Just don't look to me for a character witness. I'm sure you're bonkers."

"Anyway, I'm thinking of trying Henry James Swett III next," Olivia confessed. "I had thought it would be easier to spark a woman's interest in a lost child, but I see I was wrong."

"*Let me tell you about the very rich. They are different from you and me*," Jamie quoted F. Scott Fitzgerald, her favorite author. "For one thing, they frequently get away with murder. And when they get caught, they don't do much jail time, if any. Henry III is a case in point, starving and swindling his own great-aunt, and getting away with it scot-free. A crook like that is not going to take kindly to another heir popping out of St. Rita's woodwork."

"Come on into the kitchen while I make you a martini. I think you need an attitude adjustment." Olivia swung around on her office swivel chair.

"Okay. Two olives, stirred not shaken. But you, dear Liv, need a guardian angel, not a ghostly apparition."

"It's shady on the front porch now. Let's take our drinks outdoors, and you can admire my roses."

"You mean, you expect me to relax in Ghostland?"

"I don't think Rose will show up for a non-believer, and the rocking chairs are very comfortable." Olivia never thought she'd feel at home discussing ghosts, just as if they were people.

"That's it. You probably fell asleep and dreamed the whole thing."

~

At first, communication with Henry James Swett III appeared to be more promising than the exchange with his sister. About a week after Olivia sent Swett a duplicate of her letter to Lady Jane Gamble, she got a call on her cell phone from Henry III himself. She was in her rose garden pulling weeds at the time, sweat stinging her eyes with salt. Yanking off her gardening gloves, she went up to the porch and collapsed on a rocker in welcome shade to take the call.

Swett said he was responding to her letter, which had piqued his curiosity. He had an actor's voice, a rich dramatic baritone that drew in the listener. "What possible interest could our family have in this, what did you call it? St. Rita's Home—for wayward girls, I assume."

Olivia wiped her brow with the edge of her T-shirt, wishing she had a glass of iced tea in hand. "*Refuge.* I said 'Refuge,' and I did not say 'wayward girls,' Mr. Swett. I thought you ought to know that my research has uncovered the possible existence of a son to the late Hugh Delano Berwind, an infant born at the Refuge and subsequently adopted by another family."

"And what in hell, Madam, were you doing researching the Berwinds?" he demanded with Shakespearean resonance.

"I wasn't." Olivia lied without compunction. "I was researching the history of the refuge for an article I might write, and I came across the death of a girl named Rose Berwind from complications of childbirth."

"So? However did you connect those spastic dots, Mrs. Lowenstein? And what was your interest, exactly?"

"The name rang a bell." Olivia found herself telling this man with the mesmerizing voice about her auction purchase of the marquetry case that had once belonged to Hugh Delano Berwind. She did not, however, mention the handwritten will she'd found under the lining. "…and when I checked, I found that Hugh Delano Berwind had married Rose Redford Persey in 1917, not long before he was killed in the war."

"No such marriage was ever acknowledged by the Berwind family. At the very least, it would have been noted in the Berwind Bible, Mrs. Lowenstein. That Bible is now part of my own library. Surely, if there has been such a union, it would have been part of the family's history. A child put out for adoption from a Catholic refuge sounds very much like the illegitimate offspring of a unsanctioned liaison."

"What if Hugh Berwind referred to his marriage in his own handwritten papers sent home by the War Office?" Olivia was still leery of using the word "will."

"If you have papers of that nature, you'll have to turn them over to my attorneys for verification. Are you prepared to do so?"

"No. Not yet." Olivia felt the quicksand beneath her feet.

"Until you are paid some vast sum, I presume. How much did you think you could scam us for?"

"I don't want any money. All I want is to trace the child of Hugh Berwind and Rose Redford Persey. And his descendants."

"Because?"

"Because they are entitled to a share in the Berwind legacy."

"And your interest is what?"

"It's a long story."

Henry James Swett III laughed. It was a deep, attractive, and moneyed laugh. "I imagine so. I'll discuss this wild story you're not telling me with my brother, my sister, and my attorney, Gretchen Weinhardt. You'll be hearing from us."

Olivia wondered if that were true. Henry III would get back to her, but how? She thought it was just as well that she hadn't mentioned the ghost of Rose in the garden.

Now she had two high-powered lawyers to worry about. Olivia wondered if Ms. Weinhardt was the attorney who had managed to settle the claims of his siblings and keep Henry III out of jail. Should she contact legal representation on her own behalf?

Or should she just trust in the otherworldly forces that had led her this far.

THE REGRETS OF HENRY JAMES SWETT III

Women have always disappointed me, Henry reflected morosely, as he slouched on the library's leather sofa in the Berwind apartment at the Dakota in New York, nursing a tumbler of single malt Glenfiddich. He was haunted by the empty places on the walls where masterpieces had once hung, not because he worshipped great art, but because they'd had to be sold to satisfy various nefarious legal and gambling debts before the estate had been properly settled.

His disillusionment with what he thought of as *the unfair sex* had begun with his mother, Carolyn Cabot Brewster Swett, bluest blood on the East Coast, who had been as cold to him as a mama shark, before she'd slipped away into the briny deep. Literally. After a night of quaffing magnums of champagne, the Brewster family's reunion had not been going well when his mother had fallen off the Brewster yacht with barely a splash. Or so her cousins declared at the inquest. Personally, Henry thought that spiteful Bebe Brewster may have given Mama a push. Two years later, his father, the feckless Henry Jr., had dropped off the twig, leaving Henry III head of the family, all that was left of it, just Paul, Jane, and himself.

As the eldest, although only 33, it had fallen on Henry's shoulders to guide the family fortunes (which at the time consisted mainly of their father's losses and debts) and to cope with crazy Great-Aunt Flora Belle, who was richer than Croesus, sole heir of the Berwind fortune in iron, copper, coal, and banking—over 200 million. She had already outlasted most of her family and seemed determined to live forever. The young Swetts were her nearest relatives, and they had "Great Expectations." Until Auntie Flora (another disappointment) began talking about leaving a chunk of her assets to her two dachshunds and their caretakers, ex-Flamenco dancers, Ricardo and Marielena Villalobos.

There ought to be a law, but there isn't, Henry griped. Beloved pets with brains the size of walnuts could inherit a world of luxury in which they had no interest—while their caretakers enjoyed the lavish life style for them. What can one do when the law fails to deliver justice?

Right! Someone has to give justice a hand. But Henry preferred his hands to remain unsoiled, so he had begun to cast around for a professional. At the Class of '89 dinner, a fellow Princeton alumni, who'd recently solved a division of assets problem with his ex, had put Henry onto an unusual detective. *Melissa Hyde, Private Investigator with Benefits.*

Henry had given her a call, using good old Budgy as a reference, and they'd arranged to meet at this out-of-the-way Asian place in Cranston, Rhode Island, with a clientele that valued privacy. Shrouded windows, dim lights, background music loud enough to drown out conversation, and screened booths.

At first, Henry had been taken aback by this woman's appearance. She'd looked more like his cleaning lady, complete with an umbrella and a bulging tote bag from which Henry had expected her to haul out torn rags and polish. But she'd come highly recommended, so he'd outlined his problems, his prospects, and his hopes. She'd been easy to talk to, like an elderly cousin who appears to be listening intently, but with a little half-smile that suggests borderline dementia should not be ruled out. Still dubious, Henry had wondered if he was making an awful mistake.

But while they'd been talking, an upsetting incident had occurred, very unusual for the Golden Dragon. Two young Asians had pushed in the door, shot an older Asian who'd been having a quiet drink at the bar, and then appeared to be looking around for any possible witnesses. Before Henry could turn his brain onto *Help!* Ms. Hyde had the two of them crouched down behind an upturned table. Holding a compact Sig Sauer in a steady grip, she'd appeared to be just waiting for one of the assassins to poke his head around their partly open partition. Henry had immediately revised his assessment of her abilities.

At this early stage of the game, Ms. Hyde hadn't yet disappointed Henry. In fact, she'd had some ideas for creative solutions to his situation. If all went as she was prepared to arrange, Great-Aunt Flora would end up in Henry's conservancy, giving him free access to her impressive art collection. The daschunds and their sleazy keepers would cease to be a problem, Ms. Hyde assured him. It was his own sister Jane (Lady Jane *la-de-da* Gamble) the PI advised him to watch out for. His brother Paul, a devotee of Eastern mysticism, did not concern himself with worldly possessions as long as he could continue to support his ashram and his guru, Swami Bijoy Krishna, but Lady Jane ran with an expensive crowd who summered in Newport, wintered in West Palm, and spent "Autumn in New York" in multi-million dollar apartments. She had her own place on Park Avenue, courtesy of Lord Terrance Gamble's eagerness to be rid of her.

Missy Hyde had been right there. Dear Jane had turned out to be another disappointment. Instead of being grateful that

Henry had taken over the insalubrious task of elder care, she'd sicced Hatchett, Hammer, and Cleaves onto him, demanding a full inventory of Auntie Flora's possessions, which his avaricious sibling viewed as part of her inevitable inheritance.

The resulting unpleasantness had nearly landed Henry in some minimum security Club Fed. He'd had to agree to an inequitable three-way split, an unavoidable loss to Henry. At least he'd been able to negotiate possession of Auntie Flora's apartment in New York, while Sister Jane got the Duxbury "cottage" on Powder Point, which she'd promptly sold for 2.5 million. Paul had been quite satisfied with the Sanibel condo, where he frequently welcomed his Eastern friends and the Swami.

But then, adding fresh coals to the fires of injustice, along had come this *gadfly* from the boondocks of Marshfield with some fantasy rightful heir to make a claim on the Berwind estate. *Now I ask you*, Henry asked the Modigliani dame over the library mantel (a first-rate copy of the original that had hung there in Auntie Flora's heyday), *if I balked at sharing with Paul and Jane, my own flesh and blood, is it likely that I'd let some Berwind imposter rock my yacht? Will no one rid me of this mercenary meddler?*

Henry had already paid off Missy Hyde for the business with Auntie Flora's will, the additional difficulty of the daschunds and their Flamenco caretakers, and now he had to call back the PI at considerable expense to deal with this improbable busybody, Olivia Somebody.

He simply wanted her and her "missing heir" fiction to disappear from his life forever. Was that asking too much?

JULY 20

Things to Do Today

Picnic on Sunday! Dux Beach, Jamie & Mike
Check Dave, any suitable males?
Warn Moira, Jamie will bring deviled eggs
Extra cooler, extra ice, room for eggs
Confer Whelan? What about bro the Bishop?

With his grounding restriction finally lifted, his cell phone back in his possession, and the computer returned to his room, Kevin had practically disappeared into Norah Slattery's orbit and the Strawberry Hill mélange. The curfew was still in effect and his freedom tenuous, so Kevin managed to slam into the house on or about 9:00 PM, but the rest of his time was unsupervised, which made Olivia uneasy. Dave had strongly recommended that his oldest ward look for summer employment but accepted Kevin's explanation that jobs were scarce and besides, the Celtic Storm did earn a few bucks on the occasional gig—for which he needed time to practice with the band. So Kevin had managed to remain a free agent this summer. The few times he'd been observed coming home dusted with sawdust, he'd muttered something about helping Norah's father with repairs. This did not set Olivia's mind at rest.

She and Dave had discussed the issue of Kevin's hanging with the Travellers a number of times. Dave said that, since there had been no complaints about whatever home repairs the Slatterys had contracted, they would just have to trust in Kevin's good sense not to be party to anything illegal. Olivia admired Dave for the trust he showed in those he loved, but she didn't share it.

Also, Dave reminded her, Kevin had showed good faith and a willingness to change by at last visiting his mother in Federal prison on their last family trip to Danbury. Moira and Danny had been thrilled, of course, although the drive home had been even more subdued than usual. Kevin had been surly and uncommunicative with his mother, present in the flesh but visibly absent in spirit. Alice had cried over Kevin's coldness, while Moira's new yellow dress had gone unadmired, and Danny's summer reading list with eleven books checked off, unpraised.

"Do you think Kevin is her favorite? The Prodigal Son?" Olivia asked. After a grim, silent supper with Moira and Danny (Kevin had immediately bolted for Strawberry Hill), Olivia and Dave were alone now, sitting close together in the backyard glider as he told her about their trip to Danbury. The sweet odor of decaying reeds drifted off the marsh, along with the pungent presence of resin from the tall pines surrounding the backyard. A new moon had just risen, and the clear night sky was vivid with stars. An owl hooted twice, then there was only the whisper of evening breezes. A peaceful conclusion to a gloomy day.

"Hard to tell. At least he came with us. I look at it as a promising start." Dave's arm around her back pulled her closer.

"Your glass is always half full. I do like that about you." Olivia reached for the wine bottle on the picnic table and filled both their glasses.

"Correction. My glass is now completely full."

"But doesn't your good nature interfere with your job?"

"That's why I'm happy to stay here on the South Shore. Low crime rate. Although no longer free of big city drugs. That's becoming an escalating problem, even in the schools. Kids only 15 and 16 are dying of overdoses. Heroin's become too damn cheap and accessible." Dave sighed, "So tell me, how's your search for the Berwind heir proceeding?"

How wonderful it was that Dave was so tolerant of her latest obsession. Or how clever. Because now she felt free to share the latest developments, which at heart she wished to do. So Olivia told him that she'd heard nothing since her last phone conversation with Henry III. "Maybe he's just written off my query as a load of nonsense. There's been no follow-up, such as another legal threat from another attorney."

"And you call me an optimist! Did you really expect that the Swetts would help you find a missing heir?"

"I don't know. Jamie says I just like to poke a stick into the hornet's nest and see what happens. You remember that she and Mike are coming with us to Duxbury tomorrow? We'll have to take both cars. What a shame we can't take Sadie and Bruno, too!"

"Maybe they'll enjoy a cool and peaceful Sunday at home, quietly snoozing in our bedroom09."

But that turned out not to be the case.

MISSY HYDE ENCOUNTERS A PROBLEM

I like dogs. I really do. But I'm not fond of the way they screw up my work. That's why I've started carrying a little pouch of "doggie deterrent." A few hot dogs laced with a fast-acting knock-out drug I got from a vet whose wife I was surveilling, a woman who never left home without her Rottweiler. That mutt would spend hours sitting at attention outside a motel room, as *semper fi* as any battle-ready Marine.

Suffice to say, the smoky treat proved irresistible, and I got the photographic evidence for which I am handsomely paid. Because, yes, that is my profession, I'm a PI with an extensive repertoire of services. Or as I have it printed on my business cards, *Melissa Hyde, Private Investigator with Benefits.* The benefits are these: if investigation doesn't solve your problem, I have other solutions on offer, some of them final. One-stop shopping for your troubled situation, whatever it might be.

My profession usually comes as a surprise—in fact, a double-take—to those I encounter in the course of my work. Wearing my straw hat and pink Nikes, carrying a paisley handbag and an umbrella, I look much more like a bemused tourist than your worst nightmare. *Walk softly and carry.*

I've done a few jobs for Henry James Swett III in recent years, some that might have stretched the definition of "investigation" beyond its normal limits. It was I who "assembled" evidence to declare Swett's elderly and extremely wealthy great-aunt mentally incompetent in order to exercise a probate conservatorship. And it was I who convinced a wayward judge to appoint Swett as guardian of all matters, financial and personal, pertaining to Flora Berwind—before Swett's two younger siblings, Paul and Jane, realized what had just hit their fond hopes. Although Paul wasn't the swiftest arrow in the quiver, chic Jane, a Givenchy devotee, was every bit as cunning and vicious as her big brother Henry. The Chanel 5 hit the fan when Jane discovered that Henry was financing his gambling addiction with the private sale of his great-aunt's art works, treasures that should have been part of the estate all three would share when Auntie Flora finally died of despair and neglect. (I had to admire the old lady, though, for the tenacious way she hung on to life in that cold room, gumming up one boiled potato a day, as if she knew how sorely she was thwarting her jailer. I was almost sorry about the dachshunds.)

With a little help from me, Auntie Flora had been convinced to draw up a new will in favor of her favorite nephew, Henry. I'd warned him not to cut out Paul and Jane entirely, but he was too greedy and needy to listen. After Auntie finally shuffled off this mortal coil, a major scandal and lawsuit ensued, of course. It was all I could do to keep Swett's bespoke ass out of jail while all parties agreed on a compromise. But they did, and at last it was time for me to take a vacation somewhere tropical and make some quite satisfying deposits in my off-shore accounts.

Back to the dog problem. Just as I thought I had the Swett affair all settled, I got the panic call to meet Henry III at that cheap Asian restaurant in Somerville where none of his friends and associates would be caught dead. Some woman named Olivia Lowenstein had been making unsettling inquiries about a long dead heir whose descendants might have a claim on the Berwind millions. Swett needed to know if she had actually located those descendants and who they were.

When I Googled the Lowenstein woman, I found that she freelanced as a professional records manager and the husband was a detective with the Plymouth County State Police Detective Unit. So, not your average unwary subjects. Next, I drove to Marshfield in a late 1980s Dodge, my favorite surveillance car, and sniffed around the Lowenstein place. It seemed to be crawling with teen kids and two surly dogs. On the other side of the big ugly marsh that separated their house from the shore, there was an old inn, The Harborside. The inn's lot gave me an unobtrusive place to park. Using high-powered binoculars, I staked out the house for days. Impatience was rewarded, finally, on Sunday morning, when the entire family took off with picnic baskets and umbrellas stowed in the husband's Bronco. But they had left the two mutts closed up in the house.

I picked the back door lock quite easily and immediately threw a few treats toward the menacing duo who seemed to want nothing so much as to go for my throat. The hot dogs usually work fine, but the female, a homely white pit bull, not only wouldn't touch them herself, she growled and pushed away the other big bruiser as well. Using my umbrella to fend off the snarling pair, I just about made it out the door unscathed.

Obviously, I would have to come up with a Plan B.

JULY 21
Things to Do Today

Just relax and have good time for once!
Life is good.

It had been another perfect picnic Sunday, even though Dave had not been able to provide a single male friend for Jamie to scorn. *Maybe next time.* Olivia was determined to get Jamie off the rich old duffer track and back into real life. She would think of something. Still, Jamie, her curvy body encased in an attractive plus-size black swim suit and her red hair carelessly pinned atop her head, attracted plenty of attention from others who had driven far out on the dunes like us—without any help from her friends. She'd even gone off for a brief ride on a board boat with a muscular guy who looked like the model for a romance novel. But then she'd run back with barely a backward wave at the guy.

Mike had scowled at his mom, and she'd ruffled his hair. When the scowl hung on, Olivia had suggested that Mike teach her the one-handed, ear-piercing whistle she'd seen him use to call Sadie and Bruno to his side. Might come in handy sometime. They'd washed their sandy fingers in the waves, and after many tries, with Danny joining in, Olivia finally got it. The gloom had lifted, but Moira had clapped her hands over her ears and insisted they quit torturing her and the other beachgoers.

It was a soggy, gritty, skin-reddened lot who'd spilled out of the two cars around four that afternoon. Sadie's anxiety was apparent from the moment the youngsters rushed into the house, carrying coolers and sandy towels. Bruno, on the other hand, had such a hangdog guilty look that Olivia sent Danny to scout around and clean up any "accidents" that may have occurred in their absence. But Danny reported no messes anywhere upstairs. By then the dogs were outdoors taking care of business, but the aura of agitation in Sadie was far from relieved. She hurried back into the house, followed by Bruno who was noticeably limping. Olivia was glad she'd bought those supplements that Mrs. Mitchell had recommended.

"I think Sadie's trying to tell us something," Moira said. She was tempting their canine palates with a leftover ham and cheese sandwich, but Sadie wasn't haven't any. Bruno, however, was gratefully devouring his share and hers.

As if in confirmation of Moira's concern, Sadie began to bark, running around the kitchen table in a frantic fashion, sounding the alarm for some pressing peril no one else could perceive. Olivia had seen this kind of canine behavior before, when there had indeed been real danger. It was completely different from the reaction her dogs exhibited when a ghostly incident occurred. No barking then, just skedaddling to a safe place with nervous panting and tails between their legs.

"Do you think Sadie could provide us with a few details?" Jamie was checking the refrigerator to see if the gin was suitably chilled. Mike strolled into the kitchen looking for his mother and was immediately cornered by Moira and Bruno. It was painfully clear that Mike preferred the dog's devotion to the girl's.

"I'm inclined to pay attention to Sadie's warnings. I'll be right back." Olivia went into the bedroom to find Dave, who was just coming out of the shower wrapped in a towel, looking tanned and gorgeous. She shook off that thought, however sweet. "Dave, would you just go around the grounds to make certain everything is in order? Sadie is behaving strangely. You know what a good nose she has for trouble."

A few minutes later, Dave appeared, hastily dressed. He crouched down at Sadie's level. "What's all this, girl? You've got everyone on edge. Come on, let's go check out the property." He jumped up, shooed the dogs out the back door, and jogged around the whole area, not only his own half-acre but also across the street, the grassy shoulder of the marsh. Danny and Mike rushed to share in what seemed like a jolly good adventure, and Bruno joined in the fun at a dignified trot, working out the arthritic kinks of hanging around the house all day. But Sadie hung back near the kitchen door, sniffing the outside doormat.

Olivia called Mrs. Mitchell at the Moon Deer. She had a customer and would call back later. "Always listen to what Sadie tells you," she said before she ended the call abruptly. Olivia thought about that while she showered off salt and sand. Mrs. M. seemed to believe that dogs could talk, as apparently they could, to her.

Jamie had disappeared to shower and change in Moira's room upstairs by the time Dave jogged back. He was puzzled but good-natured about finding nothing amiss. "Maybe Sadie needs Prozac. A guy at work said Prozac worked well for his old boxer who had some real behavioral issues. Inappropriate barking, doggie paranoia."

Olivia, who'd held the kitchen door open for the returning search party, felt herself becoming annoyed and defensive. "There is *nothing* wrong with Sadie, honey. Mrs. M., who's a genius with animals, says we ought to listen to whatever Sadie tells us, and she's definitely trying to give us a message. I'm convinced that someone was here while we were at the beach. Someone Sadie did not like. Look at her!" Sadie had remained outside, stubbornly snuffling up the scent on the mat. "I bet she sets out to track whoever it was."

As if she'd heard, Sadie looked up and howled once, then trotted across the street, nose to the ground, running back and forth in a distracted fashion right to the edge of the marsh. It seemed as if the scent had been lost, overwhelmed by the odor of swampy reeds. Watching this performance, Dave said, "I wonder if someone came across the marsh. Rather a soggy trek, although I've seen plenty of birdwatchers out that way, overflow from the Daniel Webster wildlife preserve. And even some guests from the Harborside Inn."

Dave turned abruptly from watching Sadie's frustrated ramble and examined the screen door more carefully. "No marks, but that doesn't mean anything. All anyone needs is a good set of lock picks. Why don't you look around and see if anything is missing?"

"I will, but I doubt it. If someone got in here and met our crime-control unit, I bet they left in an almighty hurry. Maybe didn't even take time to re-lock the door."

"Who came in first? Moira?"

Moira looked up from the counter where she was wrapping up leftover brownies. "The back door? I was carrying a cooler, couldn't reach my key. Told Danny to open the door for me, and he did."

"Did you use your key, Danny?"

Danny puzzled this out with a deep frown. Finally he said, "No, I just turned the knob. I thought Moira or somebody must have unlocked it."

Olivia and Dave looked at each other. *Was it possible?* She called Sadie back into the house.

Jamie appeared, now wearing a short, colorful peasant dress. "I need a pitcher to mix up a batch of gimlets. Say, what's the matter with you two. You look like you've seen a ghost, if you'll excuse the expression."

Moira dragged over the step stool, opened a cabinet door, and reached into the top shelf for a tall cocktail pitcher with a glass mixing rod. Olivia hadn't even known they owned such a thing. She really must get a handle on this kitchen.

"Rose's Lime Juice?" Jamie addressed this question to Moira, the queen of all she surveyed.

"In the dining room liquor cabinet. I'll get it." Moira dashed off, a willing helper.

Jamie winked at her. "The chatelaine in charge. So, tell me, what do you believe went on here while we were sunning and funning today? Sadie's spooked, so now you think you've been burglarized?"

"Sadie *is* behaving oddly. We locked the back door when we left this morning, and it was unlocked when we came home."

Dave got a bottle of Stella Artois out of the refrigerator and opened it. "If someone did get in here, I wonder what kind of reception he got from Sadie and Bruno. Must have been some amateur. Should have known we were guarded by canines. A professional criminal would have checked that out."

"Not to mention, he wouldn't have broken into a cop's house in the first place." Jamie busied herself pouring Blue Sapphire gin over ice and adding a jigger of lime juice that Moira handed to her. She stirred the mixture in the cocktail pitcher thoughtfully, then topped it up with a splash of soda. "Do you suppose this could have anything—anything at all—to do with the Swetts?"

"What for? I haven't given them any grief, merely asked a few questions. If only I could trace the child," Olivia said. "Do you suppose Whelan's brother, the bishop…?"

"No, no, a thousand times no," Jamie said. "Moira, dear, could you bring me a couple of cocktail glasses from the china cabinet? Do you know which ones are they are?"

Giving Jamie a scornful glance, Moira ducked into the dining room again and brought back two 1930s cocktail glasses that were perhaps smaller than Jamie had in mind.

Bruno was scraping at something under the cabinet, and Sadie growled at him. Danny got down on all fours to see what it was. "Oh, look at this, Uncle Dave. There's a couple of old pieces of hot dog under there. Moira must have dropped them."

"We haven't had hot dogs since last week, dumbass. And I did not *ever* leave food on the floor," Moira declared indignantly. She grabbed the offending pieces of meat away from her brother and tossed them into the garbage disposal.

"*Moira! No!*" Dave had taken a plastic sandwich bag out of the drawer and was reaching toward the sink, but Moira had already turned on the motor.

"Too late," Jamie said. "What did you think, Dave? Poisoned hot dogs? That's a bit bizarre, isn't it?"

"Moira, you and Danny go into the lav and scrub your hands thoroughly with soap and hot water." Dave was not pleased. "Moira never leaves so much as a crumb on the floor. I would have liked to check out those tidbits at the lab."

A thoughtful silence descended, full of unspoken misgivings. Dave sighed. "Maybe not amateurs."

"But what could they possibly be after?" As soon as Olivia posed the question, she thought of her office and the various notes she'd made on scraps of paper, now held under the Lalique paperweight beside the computer. And, of course, the Holy

Mass card for Mary Margaret Burns, although how that might be connected, she couldn't imagine. "I'll just go look around my office again. Danny, did you check all the bedrooms when you went upstairs? The computers?"

Danny looked anguished at the very thought. "My stuff was all there. The other rooms looked like they always do."

"Everything was just as I left it in my office, too," Olivia said. "We must have a zillion computers in this house, and yet everything appears to be undisturbed."

"Here's one scenario." Dave took a long swallow of beer. "Someone observed all of us leaving this morning. He then picked the lock and entered the house, prepared to slip the dogs a drugged treat to knock them out. But for some reason, Sadie and Bruno wouldn't take the bait and behaved aggressively enough to frighten off the intruder, who left without relocking the back door."

Jamie poured drinks for herself and Olivia. "If only dogs could talk...what great witnesses they would be. Sniffing their way down a line-up. Testifying in court."

"And she hasn't even had a drink yet," Olivia said.

NANNY BURNS REMEMBERS PAST GRIEFS

It's like a hole in my heart, remembering how I missed my sister Patty when she disappeared into the Augustinian order. Patty and I had both been trained as nurse's aides, and she was talking about going for her nurse's cap, if only she could get the money together, when she changed her mind—overnight, it seemed to me—and applied to become a novitiate. She may as well have dropped off the face of the earth. My best friend in all the world, gone for good.

Sister Mary Joseph she was named then, and any contact with her family was discouraged by those grudging martinets. I barely saw Patty once a year, and then under such formal circumstances a real conversation was impossible. She did seem radiant, though—I'll give them that.

Another good thing, the Augustinians continued Patty's training, and she became a full-fledged nurse as she had always wanted to be. Then when she was posted to St. Rita's Refuge in Harvard, we did get to see each other occasionally. Not so radiant then, with all the meanness and misery she witnessed as a charity nurse, but still she seemed content to have achieved a profession.

Time has no meaning here, so I don't know how long I drifted around before I starting looking for Patty. But Patty had Gone Ahead, I was told, so all the sadness of losing her companionship hit me again. More memories, disturbing ones, came to mind. Patty had seen some bad things happen to those poor, friendless young women who were her charges.

It's coming back to me that Patty told me about George abandoning the girl who claimed to be Hugh's wife at St. Rita's. Patty said Rose was sick with grief and about to give birth when the driver dumped her at their door. I knew at the time I should have done something, but what? Rose died of childbed fever, George's wife, Flora, was still in Switzerland recovering her wits, and Hugh's mother Edna was rumored to be suffering from dementia, although some of the maids whispered that it was the drinking.

Still, Patty had an idea with whom Hugh's son had been placed. And she told me, but I did nothing. The Berwinds had chucked me out like so much trash, and it was only later that Miss Flora made things right.

But I'm haunted by the most awful sense of guilt.

Me, haunted! That's irony for you, dearie.

I've been following Hugh's treasure box (well, that's what he called it when he was twelve) and the girl who keeps it on her dresser now. There's something about her—different from most people on the Other Side. It's like there's a channel open to her thoughts. I believe I can find a way to tell her what happened to Hugh's son.

Guess I'll wheedle my way into that world again. Like being whisked through a wind tunnel. One big whoosh. Think I'll wear my red stockings. They always did give me courage.

JULY 25

Things to Do Today

Libr. Stop Thief! How to Safeguard Your Home, *also* Trading Options for Dummies
Mrs. Ritchie, other sources adoptions?
Appt. Moira, Vision Center
Dave, check Slattery, complaints?
Saturday, Music Cir., green dress?
5-year goals inc. reinvent career, internship in antique docs?
Google Jamie's new guy, age?

Olivia now had two impossible things to accomplish before breakfast. (Well, not really *before* breakfast. She was not the Red Queen, after all. But to accomplish *soon.*) She had to find the names of the couple who had adopted Rose's baby. And she had to figure out who was trying to break into their house, and why. As she sat dawdling over another cup of coffee at the kitchen table, amid the remains of breakfast, she considered her options and made a note on her To Do list.

Before Dave had kissed her goodbye this morning, he'd mentioned looking into an alarm system. His new partner, Jimmy Kidd, had recently installed something he recommended; Dave would find out the details. Olivia reminded him that it would have to be an alarm that his wards could manage without setting it off every time they let themselves into the house, and that it must not have a motion sensor that could be triggered by dogs.

Then he'd asked her if it could possibly be true, as Jamie had suggested, that the Swetts were involved. Olivia said no, that was just Jamie's vivid imagination. Millionaires employ attorneys, not thugs, to eliminate possible threats. Nevertheless, she promised not to contact any member of that family again, a promise she immediately regretted.

After breakfast, she went outside to spray the roses, which had begun to get that dilapidated late summer look; they would be gorgeous again as soon as September rolled around. The August humidity would dissipate, and the dry, sunny fall weather would restore the roses' will to bloom. Moira and Danny would be back in school. Olivia would be beginning her new courses. *Western Manuscripts & Documents 1500-2000* offered an exciting bibliography, including works on identifying handwriting and authenticating official documents Yes, at this time of year when summer begins to pall, Olivia looked forward the brisk incentives of fall. Maybe September would get her mind off her failure to solve the mystery of the Berwind baby.

Working in the rose garden was now a more guarded activity than it had been before she'd seen the girl's ghost with her own eyes. Olivia glanced around nervously for the specter of Rose, but any shimmering effect was strictly the result of the July heat. She thought about going for a ride in her air-conditioned car, listening to some cool jazz; maybe she would head over to Black Hill and have another chat with Mrs. Ritchie.

Where was everyone? She'd better check first.

Moira was found prone in the backyard hammock, squinting in a disconcerting way at a book from her second summer list,

Anne of Green Gables. Olivia made a note to have Moira's vision checked before school started. "I'm going to the library—will you keep tabs on Sadie and Bruno?" Sadie at that moment was lolling on the shaded back patio. Olivia assumed Bruno would be found wherever Danny was. She'd been very careful not to jingle her car keys.

"Okay. See if they've got *The Coming-to-America Cookbook*. Or maybe, *Black Potatoes*. That's the story of the great Irish famine."

"Sure." But Olivia doubted those rather specialized subjects would be found at the small branch library. She routinely ordered her library books via computer from the Marshfield Library. "Where's Danny?"

"Playing Velocity 2X. Vinny T.'s coming over. I'll keep an eye on them, don't worry."

"Right. Thanks, honey. I'll just go turn off my computer and I'll be on my way."

Olivia found her office surprisingly cold and wondered if the AC was set properly. She tapped the Power Down icon, and suddenly everything went crazy. The monitor seemed to be scrolling random images from some website Olivia must have forgotten to close, although she didn't remember Googling stone chapels, so why were those photos and sketches flashing across the monitor? Finally the PC closed out, and Olivia left her office.

Diana Krall's *Quiet Nights* accompanied Olivia to the library, the smooth contralto voice cool and relaxing, just the antidote for sizzling summer. There was something to be said for going off on one's own, away from the angst of parental concerns which she had never sought for herself. That Kevin, for instance. Olivia was not easy in her mind about his newest associations. She would ask Dave to check again for complaints against Cian Slattery and his construction team.

Olivia was glad to see other cars at the little bungalow library. She worried that the town of Plymouth might decide to close a branch that was underused. She parked between a green Rav4 and a blue Mazda wagon. Inside, the library was for once crowded with children who, judging by their varieties of fair coloring, all seemed to belong to the petite blonde curled up on a cushioned window seat, intent upon some kind of needlework. The youngsters, supervised by their older sister, were filling a basket with books, oblivious to the Persian cat hissing at them maliciously from atop the oak file.

Silver bangles tinkling, Mrs. Ritchie waved Olivia over to one of the round tables where she was talking to an attractive older woman with unruly sandy hair and a captivating smile. Some kind of energy radiated from her. Olivia resisted its pull even while the woman's warmth reached out to her.

"Olivia! Come and meet my friend Cassandra Shipton. She may be able to help you. Cass, this is Olivia Lowenstein—you remember that I mentioned meeting her? A gal on a Mission Impossible? *The impossible we do at once, the difficult takes a little longer*. Motto of the US Corp of Army Engineers."

Wasn't that backwards? Olivia was beginning to feel a bit dazed, as sometimes happened when conversing with Mrs. Ritchie. "Well, I really don't think..."

"And this is Deidre Ryan and her family. Cass and Dee are two of the talented friends I told you about. Deidre is an expert on ghost sightings, aren't you, Dee?"

The little mother did not look best pleased with this label, but she grinned impishly. "Not willingly. But you know—ghosts happen."

"Mrs. Ritchie, I wasn't planning..." Olivia was reluctant to spill the details of her Berwind search to total strangers.

"Olivia has set herself the task of finding the adoption records for a child who was born in 1918, when all such documents were sealed." Mrs. Ritchie smiled at her encouragingly. Olivia supposed she had to find help somewhere, more likely with Mrs. Ritchie's friends than the Bishop of Worchester. Perhaps they had some special expertise in adoption records.

"I admit I could use some help. Oh, I did find the marriage certificate through the Ontario site, thanks to you. The couple was married at Christ Church in Deer Park, but now I have that other matter still to resolve. From what I've been able to find out, also thanks to you, the child was born at St. Rita's Refuge, which was closed after a fire in 1949. The church is still there in Harvard, though. The town, not the college."

"Holy Mother, if it's the Catholics, you'll never find out through regular channels." The blonde spread her work out on the windowseat and examined it critically. The embroidered legend read *Trust Your Inner Faery.*

"You'll probably have better luck with irregular channels." Cass Shipton smiled enigmatically. Olivia noticed her unusual eyes, green as were Olivia's, but a darker shade, quite smoky and magnetic. She wondered if this woman also claimed to be an expert in ghosts.

"No, I don't see dead people." Cass Shipton spoke as if replying to something Olivia had said aloud, which was very unsettling. "I see the living, but I see a little clearer than other people. Just glimpses now and then."

"Cass is a clairvoyant," Mrs. Ritchie explained. "When you come up against something as impenetrable as the adoption records of a last-century Catholic institution, Google alone won't get you there—what you need is a magic wand, so to speak."

How weird is that! "I'm not comfortable with magic wands or magic anything." Olivia was becoming terribly uneasy in this strange company. An image of the three witches of Macbeth came to mind, but she shook it away. "Look, Mrs. Ritchie, I do appreciate the thought, but I think I'd just muddle along on my own. But while I'm here, my husband's ward would like me to borrow either *The Coming-to-America Cookbook* or *Black Potatoes*. I suppose I'd better look for those at a main library?"

"Just a minute, dear." Using her swivel chair like a power scooter, Mrs. Ritchie zoomed her way around the stacks and came back with two books. "How old is the young lady?"

Olivia handed over her library card; fortunately, all the South Shore libraries belonged to the same Clan and records were interchangeable. "Moira is fourteen. With a passion for cooking. She's planning to study the culinary arts at Johnson & Wales."

"What a good thing it is to discover one's passions early in life!" Mrs. Ritchie didn't seem to be the least put off by Olivia's reluctance to consult her friends. "I discovered my passions when I was about her age. I remember that night, an Esbat of the Flower Moon, as if it were just tomorrow..."

"One thing before you go" Cass Shipton interrupted whatever rapturous anecdote Mrs. Ritchie was about to share. "Well, it's more of a warning. I'm seeing someone unscrupulous hovering around one of your husband's wards. Not the girl, I think. An older boy."

Olivia thought Mrs. Ritchie must have told this woman about Kevin slipping off to Strawberry Hill last month. That's how these so-called clairvoyants worked.

Then Deidre Ryan chimed in. "Much as I'd rather not see the unseen, as it happens, a woman wearing red stockings is hovering around you. I think she wants to tell you something important." Deidre was looking directly over Olivia's shoulder, as if another person had entered the library.

Olivia was getting out of this conclave of weird women *tout de suite.*

"Thank you so much, Mrs. Ritchie. Perhaps another time we'll talk again." Olivia turned to go, clutching Moira's two books.

"And about that break-in," Cass Shipton called after her as she went out the door. "I'm seeing Mary Poppins. Not literally, of course. It's a symbol of some kind."

Mary Poppins? Too much!! Olivia kept going. She could hardly wait to get out of Black Hill and back to sanity. It wasn't until she was on her way home that it occurred to her to wonder how the Shipton woman had known about the break-in.

~

"Dave, have you checked again to see if there are any recent complaints on file against the Slattery clan?" They were in Dave's Bronco on their way to the South Shore Music Circus. Diana Krall was appearing for three days, much to Olivia's delight.

Jamie had a date for the same show (not too surprising, since it was one of few summer events on the Cape to have a certain New York glamor) and had been somewhat mysterious about it. Olivia's plan was to catch up with Jamie and her date at intermission, although Dave had assured her that no one ever found anyone else in that milling press of audience. Having Googled the guy's name, Olivia was eager to size him up in person. It appeared that Karl Albreckt was a German entrepreneur who imported wild abalone from Australia, much of which was re-exported to Japan. A fairly off-the-wall enterprise, but possibly lucrative, knowing Jamie.

The tickets were rather expensive, but Dave had remembered Krall was a favorite of Olivia's. As they drove the dark, coastal road he preferred between Marshfield and Cohasset, he seemed less interested in the starlit ocean than in gazing at her knees in the short green dress, which she knew was *his* favorite. It was a good thing, Olivia thought, when a man still had an eye for his wife's legs. Her first husband, Hank, had noticed every other woman's legs instead. On the other hand, it was also a good thing if a driver kept his eyes on the road.

"I have checked, of course. And there was one report." Dave maneuvered the curvy roads with easy competence, one-handed, because he had reached over to put his hand on Olivia's knee. "A woman in Norwell complained that Slattery knocked on her door one day and claimed to have seen a squirrel coming out of her attic window. Since he happened to have his truck and equipment with him, he offered to get up there and see if he could close up the opening the squirrel was using, and assured her that he would only charge $50, but by the time he was finished, the price had gone up to $500 and she couldn't see that he'd done much of anything. But she wasn't sure, because she was elderly, living alone, and she really hadn't been up in the attic for years. She said his two sons were with him, and she'd felt uneasy about the way they looked at her when she protested that his bill was too much."

"Did someone investigate? You know, Kevin has been helping out with those questionable jobs. Apparently Norah's two brothers disappear from time to time, and when they're not available, the old man grabs Kevin."

"The woman withdrew her complaint." Dave said. He put both hands back on the wheel.

Olivia hoped she wasn't ruining the date mood of the evening. "Obviously, the woman was afraid. Perhaps he threatened her."

"No threats, other than hard looks, according to the woman's report, and no reason given for the withdrawal of charges, other than 'might have been mistaken.' I even checked Slattery for priors, found a similar incident in South Carolina, but again the charges were dropped." Dave's tone had gone grim. "But I'll have a chat with Kevin. I don't want him mixed up in anything shady. Now let's talk about something more pleasant, what do you say?"

"I say *yes*, honey. Sorry."

"No, don't be sorry, Liv. I'm really pleased that you've come to care about the kids. I know it hasn't always been easy. But you've been so wonderful."

Hasn't been easy? Understatement! Still, she basked in the glow of his praise and admiration.

They'd arrived at the big circus tent, and the necessity of finding a place to park took precedence, although Dave always made it look easy. Olivia felt the nagging worry about the Slatterys she'd been carrying fall away, now that she'd handed it to Dave. Just a tiny seed planted. She hoped it wouldn't end up looming over them. Like a sunflower planted in a field of lavender.

Meanwhile, as they were finding their seats, Olivia kept craning her neck to see Jamie and this Albreckt character.

"Give it up and sit down, Liv. You'll never spot them in this crowd. We'll be lucky if we can find them at intermission." Dave was wise to her preoccupation.

But she did see them eventually, right down in the front, facing center stage, best seats in the circular tent-theater. She took out the opera glasses (another impulsive auction purchase) she had tucked into her evening purse. Jamie was wearing a white dress, showing off a lovely tan—how did she manage *that* while spending her days nursing the ailing John Peter Whelan? Her red hair, loose around her shoulders, would be hard to miss. Olivia saw that she was laughing up at a tall, slim guy who was even tanner—with a luminous golden kind of tan only acquired at summer regattas and winter skiing. *Well, at least he isn't doddering*, Olivia thought. Maybe Jamie was going to win the lottery after all.

THE PI WITH BENEFITS CONSIDERS HER OPTIONS

I'd decided to spend a few days at the Harborside Inn, which was ideally located for my surveillance. The restaurant was adequate if you liked "catch of the day" day after day; the accommodations above, however, were tinged with shabbiness. But I'd scored a room overlooking the bird-noisy marsh, directly opposite the Lowenstein farmhouse.

I needed that house to be empty with no menacing mutts to guard it this time. Henry Swett was getting impatient. What did Olivia Lowenstein know, and when did she know it? Could there be someone in a position to make a claim on the Berwind estate? He was already enraged over having to share the loot with his siblings.

Plan B was to get into the Lowenstein woman's computer and copy everything, relevant or not, onto flash drives. While the copying was going on, I'd install hidden spy software to monitor her future searches, a little program which was too sophisticated to be spotted by a routine protection service. Also, listening devices in the Lowenstein land line, if they had one, and in the couple's bedroom and possibly in the kitchen as well. If the Honda van was left at home, I'd attach a GPS tracker under the back bumper. When I got through, Olivia Lowenstein would have no secrets.

I'd begun this assignment, as I always did, by making a thorough background check of the subject through every legal and illegal channel I had at my fingertips. Olivia Andreas Lowenstein had been divorced from a real estate wheeler-dealer and womanizer named Hank Robb when she'd taken up with David Lowenstein, a Plymouth County detective and good-natured sucker who'd given a home to his dead partner's three kids. The couple had met because Olivia was being targeted by a Boston Crime Family, the Benedettos, whose accountant had absconded with a copy of their financial records, which had somehow ended up in Olivia's possession. Her meddling in the affairs of this notorious family had resulted in multiple RICO arrests and some long-term animosity that might come in handy if all else failed. Caesare Benedetto was now a lifetime resident of a maximum security facility in Georgia. Although in failing health, Benedetto's influence could still be felt through the current head of the Benedetto family, Fabio "the Hawk" Falcone, his sister's boy.

Olivia Lowenstein's acquaintance with the criminal element didn't stop there. Her father, Philip Andreas, had been the manager of a prominent Cleveland bank before he'd absconded with the funds from several dormant trust accounts and disappeared off the FBI's radar. I wondered how he'd managed to remain in hiding all these years, with enough money to live quite well. (The amount of Andreas's theft topped a couple of million.) Might be handy information in case I myself ever needed an escape hatch. And I wondered why Andreas had never attempted to contact his only child, as so many thieves-in-retirement had made the mistake of doing. Perhaps he was dead. Or maybe he'd started a new family with some nubile island gal and forgotten all about his eldest daughter.

If I wanted to, I bet I'd be able to find this Andreas, even though he'd eluded the FBI for over twenty years. I have a knack for zeroing in on fugitives, some instinct or intuition into the workings of their minds.

I'd also subjected Detective Lowenstein to a thorough background search, but that guy was as spotless and true as Dick Tracy, except for that one incident with a colleague's wife that was not common knowledge, even among the gossipy community of law enforcement. But his wards were a different story. Their mother was in Federal prison in Danbury, doing a good long stretch, and the father had been mowed down by the same crime family that Olivia had got mixed up with. Good to know. *Knowledge is power,* I reminded myself. Knowledge and my dependable Sig Sauer.

On Saturday, the fourth day of my stay at Harborside, when the very thought of another fried oyster or scallop special made me slightly queasy, my patience finally paid off. I was out on the balcony with my high powered "bird watching" binoculars, studying the farmhouse across the marsh, when a fortuitous exodus took place. First, the detective and his three juvies took off in the Bronco, which I took to be their monthly trip to see Mom in lockup, an all-day affair. Then, Olivia packed up the two dogs into the Honda. Fortunately, she was slow about it—went back into the house for something or other—so I was able to jump into my low-key Dodge, race around the marsh, just in time to catch the Honda heading toward Route 6. I followed the van to its destination, the Happy Tails Spa in Barnstable, although why so far from Marshfield was a mystery. A few minutes after Olivia had dropped off the mutts, I called the groomer, impersonated Olivia, and checked on the appointment schedule. Would there be time for me to visit a friend in Chatham? Oh, yes, the perky receptionist assured me; Sadie and Bruno wouldn't be ready until three that afternoon. Right now they were frisking in the play yard with other dogs until it was their turn to be bathed and clipped.

I continued following my target north to Route 3. Finally the Honda pulled into the parking lot of Cedar Point Inn, where Olivia met up with another woman, a plump redhead. I took a few photos of her and made a note of the mustang convertible's license plate—you never knew what snippet of information might come in handy at some later date. Lunch at the scenic restaurant on Plymouth Bay should be good for a couple of hours. Pausing only long enough to attach a GPS to the Honda, I sped back to Marshfield to break into the empty house and put my well-laid plans into action.

The Dodge was starting to complain about rough usage, I noticed, as I barreled through yellow lights and around narrow corners. Maybe it was time to trade in the old girl for another invisible, non-threatening car, maybe a Buick.

I'd already fixed on an out-of-the way parking spot, down the road from the farmhouse, in a place overlooking the marsh that was much favored by bird-watching crazies. There was one other car there. The driver, an elderly guy, was eating his lunch and observing the snowy egrets snagging theirs. Slapping on my straw hat, I grabbed my binoculars and my paisley bag, ready to wave if he looked up, which he did not. I hurried around the bend, out of his sight, and ducked into the backyard of the farmhouse, to the back door which could not be observed from the road.

Christ! A security system had been installed! Nothing too complicated, though. You'd think a detective could do better. It took me only eleven minutes to dismantle it.

The GPS I'd attached to the Honda in the Cedar Point parking lot informed me that Olivia had not yet left the restaurant to pick up the dogs in Barnstable. So I knew there was plenty of time to complete my work. The contents of Olivia's hard drive were copied onto flash drives which I would peruse that evening. (No rest for the weary PI. Swett would be hassling me for a report, like, *yesterday*.) The Lowensteins didn't own a land line, but I did bug the matrimonial bedroom where so many important conversations might take place. I decided to skip the kitchen, though. All those chattering teenagers—it would be too much!

Just another few minutes to re-arm the security system. I stripped off my latex gloves, tucked them into my paisley handbag, and strolled back to the nondescript Dodge, ready to peer at the marsh through my binoculars and make bird notes if there was anyone watching, but the place where the old guy had parked was empty.

Mission accomplished!

AUGUST 2

Things to Do Today

Appt. new groomer, cancel vet
Lunch with Jamie Cedar Point
Geek Squad of Plymouth—check out flipping images, what is that?
5-year goals inc. PC training, security etc.

It was a long ride to the new place in Barnstable but worth it. At least Olivia was spared having to bathe the dogs herself in the backyard and then beseech the petite Asian vet with gentle hands to clip their nails. When she picked up Sadie and Bruno after lunch, they were clean, clipped, and sweet, redolent of some doggie cologne. There had been no complaints from the dogs about ill-treatment (which would have manifested as distressed panting, low whimpering, and fake coughs) and no complaints from the Happy Tails people about "nervous" behavior—so far. Although the discharge clerk had mentioned that Happy Tails offered a very popular obedience class for older dogs who might be set in their ways.

Between trips to Happy Tails, Olivia had enjoyed the usual raucous lunch with Jamie, even though her friend had diverted all questions about Karl Albreckt as ably as a politician on the hot seat with a TV interviewer. Every time Olivia brought up the German entrepreneur who had squired her to the South Shore Music Circus, Jamie changed the subject to the Berwind baby and related searches.

Olivia hoped the day at Danbury had gone well for Dave, although that might be a tad too optimistic. He'd taken one of his precious vacation days to make the trip on Friday.

There was still an hour or so before Olivia would need to start dinner. The August heat was oppressive in the late afternoon, so she decided to study trading options instead of spending the time outdoors. Sadie immediately trotted into the bedroom for a cool nap. Bruno followed hopefully but no way was he going to be allowed to join Sadie on the king-size bed. That was Sadie's private preserve.

But a moment later, Sadie scampered out of the bedroom again, whining and restless. Olivia put it down to the grooming experience, never a canine favorite. She even had a look at Sadie's paws; no show of blood from inexpert nail clipping. Maybe Sadie was put off by the astringent cologne that wafted from her own fur. Or maybe she just needed to go out. Olivia shooed the two dogs out into the backyard, but not for long. It was too damn hot out there!

Sure enough, Sadie was rolling on the grass, no doubt trying to rid herself of the offending cologne. Bruno nosed her exposed stomach, and she snapped at him crossly. Olivia called them both back inside, smiling at the predictability of their confrontations.

Her smile faded, however, when she sat in the swivel chair at her desk. A person who color-coded her clothes, arranged her books according to the Dewey Decimal System for Smaller Libraries, and alphabetized the herb shelf was also a person who knew how she'd left everything arranged on her desk. Might Danny have been in her office? No, Danny had been on his way to Danbury before Olivia had left the house this morning. And yet the Lalique paperweight had been moved two inches to the left of where Olivia knew she'd left it, holding a few notes that she'd jotted down yesterday about trading options. There was an ink stain the size of a dime on the oak desk, and Olivia had positioned the paperweight to hide it. But now she could see the stain peeking out from beneath the notes. Only a slight alteration. Anyone else might not have noticed, but Olivia's habits bordered on OCD, and her memory was nearly photographic. She could see in her mind's eye exactly the way the desk had looked when she left it this morning. And that stain had not been visible.

The new security system wasn't complicated. It had been engaged when Olivia came home with the dogs; she'd had to turn it off. In leaving the house and in coming home, the alarm seemed to be operating correctly. Now she checked all the downstairs windows, closed because of the AC, and locked as well. No evidence of unlawful entry there. She even went upstairs to the youngsters' bedrooms to check those windows. Sensing some kind of fun game, Bruno jumped up from the cool kitchen floor to follow her, and Sadie also, but with less enthusiasm.

As usual, Kevin's room was as clean and uncluttered as a monk's cell, Danny's a maze of computer equipment and cords, and Moira's a rainbow of discarded shorts and t-shirts. The windows were all closed and locked.

Olivia checked the cellar door, the cellar windows, and the furnace room, beginning to feel foolish. By now there were only a few minutes before it really would be time to assemble the comfort foods she was making for dinner, grilled shrimp, a Greek-style macaroni with béchamel sauce and feta and kefalotyri cheeses, and a chopped vegetable salad, the glory of summer. But first, she would at least read her emails. She hurried into her office, followed by her faithful companions, and turned on her computer.

Sadie stopped in her tracks at the door and howled. Then she rushed forward and appeared to be trying to climb onto the desk. Really, this was too much! The Lalique paperweight, the trading options notes, and a pencil caddy went flying.

"Sadie, you bad girl! Get down this minute!" Olivia hung onto the monitor, which was rocking.

But Sadie ignored Olivia's no-nonsense alpha tone. The pit bull was busy sniffing every inch of the desk, and she didn't like the information she was inhaling. She looked at Olivia and whined, her eyes full of unspoken anxieties, and this time the message got through. Suddenly there was no doubt whatsoever in Olivia's mind. The unknown intruder had come back, somehow had bypassed the new alarm, and spent some time in Olivia's office.

"All right, all right, girl. I get it," Olivia soothed Sadie and pulled the dog off her desk and out of the office, shutting the door firmly. "Let's go get you guys some dinner." There was no change of subject as effective with dogs as the magic word *dinner*.

By the time Dave came home with his depressed tribe of teens, the dogs were mollified and fed, supper was ready, and Olivia was all attention for news of their day in Danbury.

She had decided not to say anything about her (and Sadie's) suspicions. Even later, when they were alone in the bedroom, although tempted to cast all her worries on his comforting shoulders, she held back, not wanting to seem like a crazed conspiracy theorist. She would think matters over on her own and wait until she felt quite sure that her fears had a basis in fact.

This was too sophisticated a break-in to be random mischief—it must have been engineered by the Swetts. Jamie had been right to warn her about making that contact. Not something she'd like to admit to Dave ; she definitely would not say anything tonight. It really had been a hell of a day, with Kevin still poker-faced with his mom and the younger O'Haras needy and whiny. So instead of blurting out the incident of her disturbed desk and Sadie's reaction, she concentrated on giving Dave a soothing massage, which ended in the usual way of intimate massages when Dave turned over and took her into his arms.

Always a sure way to slip the bonds of worry, Olivia thought—making love in the sleeping house with moonlight flooding through east-facing windows lifted them both above earthly cares. Perhaps she was being paranoid. It had been known. At any rate, no way was she going to ruin the blissful mood tonight by spilling her fears. Maybe tomorrow. And maybe not.

~

The next morning, when Olivia turned on her computer to figure out how many damaging searches might have been evident to a professional snoop, the monitor began to play the same crazed pattern of images, just as it had done once before. Stone chapels flipped upward like frames of a movie film played too slowly. The show lasted (Olivia timed it) two minutes exactly.

And another thing—the damned room was too cold again. And yet the AC was still set on a reasonable 72 degrees. When she glanced over at the cushioned rocker in the corner of her office, Olivia thought for a moment she saw a flash of red. And then the damned chair began rocking—how bizarre was that! So with one thing and another, she had just about made up her mind to call Mrs. Mitchell and ask for help, when everything went right out of her head because of Kevin.

A warrant for Cian Slattery had been issued for "fraudulent home repairs involving the elderly." Another fake squirrel-in-the-attic repair scam had not gone so quietly this time. The reclusive old guy whom the Slatterys targeted had once been a State Marshal, and he wasn't about to let these roughnecks intimidate him into paying an outrageous fee.

It was Sunday; detectives on the case hoped to catch Slattery hanging around the camp grounds and not out cruising the county looking for seniors to victimize. After the O'Haras' Danbury excursion; Kevin had taken off for Strawberry Hill both Saturday and Sunday, and so, unfortunately, he was present when the contractor and his two sons were arrested. The arresting officer, a friend of Dave Lowenstein's, had merely asked Kevin to come into the station for questioning that afternoon—with his foster father. But Kevin knew little. He'd been on the first job, but he hadn't seen any squirrel and he hadn't been involved in any overcharging. Cian Slattery and his sons had handled all the money. Kevin had only helped to manage equipment and ladders, and with any unskilled work that needed to be done, for which Cian paid him a minimum wage.

After arraignment, the Slatterys had been unable to make bail immediately, so they were remanded to Plymouth State Correctional Facility to await trial.

In his effort to scrape together bail, Cian Slattery had sold his truck and his daughter's fiddle to other members of the clan who had also come up from South Carolina and were camped at Strawberry Hill. Norah, who was only sixteen, was turned over to DCF. The social worker assigned to her case had denied custody to Norah's aunt Siobhan, who lived in a nearby mobile home, finding her unfit because of numerous prior arrests for shoplifting and drug possession.

~

"Sorry, Kev. That's just not possible." Dave was lingering over a cup of coffee at the dinner table a few days later when Kevin paused in clearing the table to ask if they could give Norah a place to stay before DCF threw her into the foster care system. Dave had already loaned Kevin a rather large sum which he had combined with his own savings to buy back Norah's fiddle. "We don't have room, you know that."

"She's just going to run away. I know it." Kevin, for once, was subdued rather than surly, his concern for Norah more important than posturing.

"Well, don't ask if she can bunk with me! I can't stand that little tramp." Moira, who was wrapping up leftovers in the kitchen, while listening hard to the conversation in the dining room, slapped a roll of plastic wrap on the counter for emphasis.

Kevin looked hopefully at Danny, who was loading glasses onto a tray. "No, I'm not sharing with you, so that Norah can have your room." Danny anticipated the next step in Kevin's argument. "You always mess up my stuff."

"Ha! As if your room could be more of a mess than it is already." Kevin was scornful but also disappointed to have been out-maneuvered by his mind-reading siblings. Kevin had one more card up his sleeve, however. "What about that space up over the garage, Dave? That's like a really good-size room. Liam and I used to practice there before we hooked up with Sean and started using his place."

Moira sauntered out of the kitchen, hands on hips, fourteen going on forty. "Forget it, Kev. That's the 'glory hole' where we keep all our extra stuff. And when Olivia moved in, she put a bunch of boxes up there so you can hardly move around to find anything."

"And there's no bathroom in the garage." Olivia ignored the accusatory tone to point out a more obvious problem.

"Couldn't we put a bathroom up there on the second floor? It's not so hard. I helped Ray Slattery put a lav in a lady's house in one day. Nothing fancy. Just a toilet and sink, you know." Kevin looked down at his hands, which were indeed callused with construction work. "And we've got that outside shower to wash off sand when we get back from the beach. Cold water, but Norah wouldn't mind. That shower will be usable until the end of September."

Olivia put her hand on Kevin's arm. "You're just springing this idea on us, Kevin. Dave will need time to think it over. We'll talk about it later."

"It's still going to be no." Easygoing Dave could be tough and inflexible when he felt strongly enough. And he reacted negatively whenever he felt pushed.

Olivia thought about snooping social workers, the chaperoning challenge, the garage makeover, and worst of all, the claims and scams the Slattery family might come up with in future. It was no light thing to take in a teenager, as no one knew better than Dave. She felt sorry for the Kevin…and for Norah as well. Olivia's own home life had been so unhappy that she'd often sought the warmth and support of Jamie's family circle. And the Andrews had always been there for her. Maybe this was her chance to *pay it forward*.

Still, putting in a damn lav was a bit much. And where would she store those boxes containing her old files?

One possibility was especially troubling to Olivia. If Norah ran away from foster care, what were the chances that Kevin would run with her? And then how would Dave react? She would like to spare him from the hurt and betrayal he might feel if Kevin skipped.

Maybe she could get Dave to at least talk over the idea with her—in the privacy of their own room, away from the family free-for-all. Olivia was sure they could come up with something, if not a garage apartment for Norah.

With any important decision (even whether to marry Dave!) Olivia had always made note of the pros and cons. Now she found herself ticking them off in her head, and there were a great many more items in the "con" list. The thought of that grinning Cian Slattery, for instance. What nasty trouble might he cause for Dave taking in his daughter? On the "pro" side, however, Olivia might be making a friend of Kevin at last. She really knew nothing about Norah personally, though. The girl hardly spoke in Olivia's company. Uncharitable though it might be, Olivia had to consider whether Norah might share the Slatterys' sociopathic ways.

~

Damn! Every time Olivia turned on her computer, she was getting that unsought caravan of images. And always with chills down her back, as if the AC had gone crazy. What was that all about? But, truth be told, the idea of a stone chapel was beginning to trigger a memory of some kind. Where had she seen or read about chapels?

Then, finally it came to her—just as she was waking up from a rather delicious nap. (Olivia did not approve of naps, but the constant perusal of trading options had put her out like a light on this lovely August afternoon when the house was blissfully quiet. Not even a peep from Kevin's Bodhrán.) That article about the demise of St. Rita's Refuge, wasn't there one building left undestroyed—St. Rita's Chapel of Roses on the hill? A shiver went through Olivia when she made this connection. It was almost as if someone were trying to tell her something.

When it came to messages from otherworldly sources, *who ya gonna call?* Olivia called Mrs. Mitchell at the Moon Deer and explained the unexplainable computer phenomena, and the possibility that had occurred to her.

Mrs. Mitchell chuckled quietly. "Perhaps there *is* an uneasy spirit trying to get through to you. That séance—someone spoke through you then. And not the entity you were expecting. We thought there might be two ghosts, as I recall. Entirely possible, you know. Had you thought of going out to Harvard and having a look at that chapel?"

"I'm thinking of it now. Oh, and there's something else. I'm fairly sure that an intruder got in the house the other day, when we were all out—someone who bypassed our security system. Things on my desk weren't in the right place. And Sadie was terribly upset. She kept crawling up onto the desk and sniffing everything."

"Maybe I should talk to Sadie." Mrs. Mitchell took communication with animals for granted, and somehow it did work for her.

"Oh, would you!"

"I think it would be best if I came over to your house when things are quiet. We'll go over the situation where she was spooked. When would it be convenient?"

They made a date, and Olivia breathed a little sigh of relief. Not too deep a sigh, though. If Sadie had sensed an intruder, and it wasn't just Olivia's imagination, she must be in more trouble than she'd bargained for.

~

Mrs. Mitchell took Olivia's concerns quite seriously, as evidenced by her coming over to communicate (or whatever it was she did) with Sadie the very next day. The dogs were delighted to see her, of course, and greeted her like their dearest friend. Olivia knew they valued having someone who really heard or felt the concerns they couldn't put into words. Olivia tried to listen, too, but she didn't understand their language in the visceral way that Mrs. M. did.

As soon as they'd all gathered in the big living room, Mrs. M. crouched down at dog-level and put her arms around both animals. They immediately commenced a long litany of soft doggie noises, even Bruno. The Indian woman listened for several minutes, until they'd quieted, and were satisfied simply to sniff her hands and shoes. Then she got up, adjusted her silver scarf, and sat down on the sofa beside Olivia.

"I believe Sadie is trying to tell us that she's been uneasy ever since a stranger came into this house when she was alone with Bruno. Dogs don't think about time, so I can't tell when this happened. Sadie told that person to leave fast or else. Now that person has been back again, when Sadie was not here to scare her away. This person's odor was strong and familiar. She spent some time in your bedroom and in your 'den'. Sadie would like to knock this person down, maybe give her a warning bite, if she shows up again."

"She?"

"Yes, I'm sure Sadie is trying to tell us it's a woman."

Olivia remembered something weird. Mrs. Ritchie's friend, Cass Shipton, who seemed to know about the first break-in, had warned Olivia about a woman. Mary Poppins, she'd said. A symbol of some kind. Olivia shuddered. Prescience like that made her quite uneasy.

Mrs. Mitchell continued. "And Bruno says his hips are not hurting as much anymore. But he's tired of Sadie bossing him around. He wants me to say that he ought to be allowed on the big bed with Sadie."

Olivia laughed and poured tea for them both. It was ginger tea today, with a slice of crystallized ginger at the bottom of each cup. "Bruno shouldn't hold his breath. Sadie is a feminist's delight. No one ever told her that the male should be the alpha dog."

"So, do you want to tell me about this uneasy spirit that's haunting your computer? Have you seen her?"

"I'm not sure. There was this flash of red near my office rocking chair, and then the chair began to rock by itself. Maybe it was my imagination."

Mrs. Mitchell picked up the ginger slice from the bottom of her cup with long, dark, elegant fingers, her diamond ring glittering, "A rocking chair that suddenly begins to rock is a subtle but sure sign of a presence. Perhaps this spirit once wore red, and that color had a certain significance, almost a bravado."

"I'm getting that *Why me, O Lord* feeling again." But Olivia smiled, because it was so good to talk to someone who didn't question the premise, who made these weird events seem almost normal with her matter-of-fact manner.

"I think this is the other revenant—not Rose. The older woman who came through at our séance. Now it seems she wants you to visit this chapel. I suggest you take many photos while you're there, for two reasons. So you'll remember everything more clearly, and on the off chance that a spirit will materialize in the photo." Mrs. Mitchell nibbled the ginger delicately, with evident pleasure.

"Good idea. Maybe a little photographic evidence will make me feel less eerie."

"And don't go alone. You need someone who can say, *yes, I noticed that, too*, if there are any actual phenomena."

"I'll ask Jamie. You know how level-headed she is, and skeptical."

"Perfect," Mrs. Mitchell agreed. "And also, she's a nurse. It's always good to have a nurse along on any expedition into the unknown."

Olivia would tell Jamie that. The very thought gave her a smile that lasted right through the rest of the day until it was time for Jamie's supper break and Olivia could call her. *Raiders of the Lost Chapel,* she said to herself. Already she was feeling quite up for this adventure.

NANNY BURNS IS PLEASED WITH HERSELF

At last I found a way to get through. That odd machine takes some getting used to—nothing like it in my time, that's for sure—but it is sensitive to energy vibrations. And when you get right down to it, Energy Vibration is just another name for what I am. That's how someone like me, with a Very Good Reason, is able to "haunt" the living.

I needed someone on the Other Side to figure out what became of Hugh's child, and you're a natural channel, dearie, although you may not know it yet. It's my hope and prayer that images of the Rafferty chapel might ring a bell, so to speak. You'd better pay attention, because there'll be no peace until I get you to St. Rita's so that you'll make the connection. We nannies spend our lifetimes contending with other people's spoiled offspring, so we're not liable to take no for an answer.

I know you don't hear all this, but I have to send the fullness of my thoughts out into the Eternal Ether, because Thoughts Are Things, as I've learned from the Guardians. Whatever your heart desires, you have to think about it with your whole body and soul to make it happen. Take that from me, dearie.

Senator Rafferty. It all goes back to him. You'll see. That baby didn't disappear into thin air. Father Damian had him handed over to the Raffertys like so much goods and chattel, a child who should have been raised and loved by the Berwinds, his true family. That George! I don't know exactly where he is now, but I believe he's in the deep, dark hole he deserves. Colder than you-know-what.

The closer I get to the living, the more I realize how peaceful it is not to be part of that world any more. For instance, I can't help feeling that there are dangers hovering around your home, dearie, an aura of encroaching evil. A woman, who looks like butter wouldn't melt in her mouth, is hell bent on keeping me from making things right. You have to watch out for her.

I managed to give that infernal engine she rides around in a few knocks. Best I could do, so far. But I'm learning. It's all a matter of control, as Anya Bharata keeps telling me.

With that villainess on the loose, any time you get that uneasy feeling that someone is after you, you'd better pay attention, dearie. That's your Sixth Sense kicking in—ignore it at your peril.

Now that I've got the hang of Traveling Time, I'll be keeping an eye on your place. I like that glider you've got out back. And the rocking chair in your office is very nice, too. Reminds me of the rocker I used to have in the Berwind nursery all those years ago. Might as well be comfortable while I'm haunting.

Anya Bharata advised me to wear my red stockings. She said a flash of red sometimes penetrates the Veil and catches attention. People who think it's easy to contact the Other Side don't know the half of it. You have to be wily, watchful, and determined, like any good nanny—and I was the best.

AUGUST 9

Things to Do Today

Harvard MA with Jamie—photos!
What about garage? Clean out, in case?
5-yr plan: conversational Greek—why not? 2nd honeymoon, poss.
Ticks search every day! Danny can help
Libr. return Trading Options for Dummies, *borrow* Long-term Stocks: the Road to Security
Dave—DCF contacts?

Jamie was off duty in Dover from Friday through Sunday, when another nurse came in to care for the elderly J. P. Whelan. If it were a "Mike weekend," Jamie's son would be delivered to her condo on Saturday morning. And Dave, of course, worked on Friday. So Olivia and Jamie often got together for lunch at some seaside place on that "free" day. This time, however, Olivia suggested lunch at the Fearless Feeney Tavern in the town of Harvard, after which they would visit the picturesque stone chapel on the grounds of the former St. Rita's Refuge for Women and take many photographs.

Although declaring this excursion was just another skit in Olivia's "theater of the absurd," Jamie was immediately on board for any possible adventure, providing the trip would be made in her sporty silver Mustang convertible.

But this was August, and even Jamie agreed there was no point to broiling in the searing sun. So they drove through the iridescent heat waves with the top up, the AC blasting, and a Country & Western station blaring, Jamie's choice. They joined in on singing "Your Cheating Heart," "Careless Love," and "You Were Always on My Mind" with such gusto that Olivia felt the miasma of worry lifting a little, allowing some mindless amusement to shine through. And that made her realize how much the tragedy of Hugh and Rose had possessed her. She reminded herself that this preoccupation of hers was serious enough to attract some evil intent. Jamie broke into this sobering reverie with a stirring rendition of "The Tennessee Waltz."

"You never liked this stuff in high school." Olivia clutched her seat as they zoomed around corners. "Maybe you should slow down a little so that we can enjoy the music and scenery. Look, that's the Westward Orchards. Gorgeous in spring."

"Yes, and fruitful in fall. But it's August, girlfriend. Just a bunch of trees right now. If you'd been through as many failed marriages and dodgy relationships as I have, you'd begin to see the merits of belting out the blues. And this country music is so explicit, it does my broken heart good." Jamie continued to swerve her Mustang through the hills and dales of Harvard as if the devil were chasing them. Olivia surmised that the romance with Karl was not going well, but she certainly hoped Jamie's disappointment had not progressed to the death wish stage. It was a relief when they arrived at the Tavern and slid to a stop, splattering gravel.

Olivia decided not to pry; Jamie would always tell her the gory details when she was good and ready. After lunch, however, Jamie surprised Olivia by pursuing a more moderate pace to the beautiful grounds where St. Rita's Refuge used to stand. Gone were the Refuge and the Convent. Only St. Rita's Chapel of Roses remained, standing on the hill above the ruins. St. Rita's Church was nearly out of sight down the road.

"All that beef slowed me down," Jamie complained. They had both ordered the Fearless Feeney's Famous Grass-fed Beef Burger with Big Boy Fries and a half pint of Guinness.

"We'll walk it off," Olivia promised, a vow she kept as they trod around the overgrown acres where lilac, forsythia, and rhododendron bushes still thrived in neglect. Olivia wanted to pace through the Refuge's faint outline and its surrounding grounds, just to get a feel of the place.

"Getting any vibes?"

"Oh, shut up. You know I don't believe that places have memories." Olivia was loathe to admit that a chill had run down her neck like an ice cube. "I suppose the bodies are all buried over next to the church. Okay, let's get on with it."

The stone chapel was an exquisite miniature originally crafted by Italian stone masons, its small medieval herb garden meticulously kept. Christmas Rose bushes leaned against the walls on both sides of the carved oak doors; legend had it that the roses bloomed on the Christ Child's birthday every year. The chapel's interior was decorated with murals of St. Rita's life and one extravagant stained glass depiction of her martyrdom, a thorn piercing her forehead.

A young cleric, in charge of admittance, answered the questions of several other tourists. "The thorn remained imbedded in the saint's forehead until she died. The window is most beautiful when the rays of the setting sun shine through the glass, illuminating her glory." He apologized sadly that photographs of the interior were not permitted, but Olivia noticed Jamie dancing around behind the others with her cell phone held at waist height.

"That must have been some decade-long migraine." Jamie eyed the gruesome window with respect.

"Saints have a higher pain threshold, I believe. Now, shush. Listen."

The young cleric, whose name was Brother Pietro, had soulful eyes and a sweet voice. "The original Italian edifice was imported from St. Rita's native province of Cascia, stone by stone, as a gift from the William Alfred Haggerty family to St. Rita's Refuge in 1919. Senator Willie Haggerty was known for his philanthropic gestures, and this magnificent bequest was in celebration of the miraculous birth of the Senator's son and only child, William Martin Haggerty, in 1918. Both parents were beyond the usual age for parenting. Mabel O'Neill Rafferty, who was forty-five, had recited novenas to St. Rita for several years, and her faith was finally rewarded."

There was more, but Olivia didn't hear it. She felt as if that cartoon light bulb had lit up in her head. Was it possible that an intractable mystery from the past could be solved so easily? She tried to remember what had inspired her to make this pilgrimage. Oh, yes—that strange malfunction of her PC. The reoccurring images of stone chapels had triggered a memory of the history of St. Rita's Refuge. Serendipity. Or not. Olivia had experienced the tricks played by a ghost with a grievance before.

"Olivia! Wake up! Are you in a coma, or what?" Jamie peered into Olivia's face and felt her wrist with a nurse's practiced hand. "Let's get out of here. You need some fresh air. This place has a peculiar dustiness, could be an allergen, and your pulse is rather rapid."

Olivia felt herself being coaxed out of the chapel. "Take pictures," she mumbled. "The inscription over the door."

"Yes, dear, I will do that. Now move, please."

With Jamie's coaxing, they were soon at a distance from the chapel. Having deposited Olivia on a stone bench in the herb garden, Jamie was busily taking photos with her phone. After that, she insisted they get into the Mustang and run the AC.

"It's the strangest thing." Olivia allowed herself to be driven away, her mind still a jumble of possibilities.

"Strange is your middle name, Liv."

Seized by a sudden impulse, Olivia cried out, "Oh, my God! We can't leave yet, Jamie. We have to look for Rose's grave. St. Rita's cemetery is right on this road, next to the church. Turn around!"

"Are you crazy? Yes, you have that look in your eye. If you were my patient, I'd be getting a shot ready. What will it prove if we find Rose's grave, exactly?"

"Just do it. I'm not leaving Harvard until we have a look around that cemetery."

Jamie groaned, made a daring U-turn in the middle of the road, and drove in the opposite direction, past the chapel they had just left. Within moments, they were parked in the church lot. When they stepped out of the car, the heat hit them in a sizzling wave, but the cemetery beside the church was filled with great old maple trees that shaded the little avenues, Cypress and Magnolia and Evergreen, a cool invitation.

"I wish I'd brought flowers." Soon Olivia was searching grave after grave, deciphering names on mossy stones in the older part of the cemetery.

"This is like searching the proverbial haystack." Jamie trailed her re-energized friend from row to row.

Olivia was silent, listening to some faint whisper that was probably only her imagination, feeling the pull of a slight breeze, like a hand in her hand. "It's here, I know it."

And—finally—there it was, a leaning, lichen-stained slab in the farthest reaches of the oldest part of the cemetery. *Rose Berwind, 1893-1918.* And beside it, another smaller stone, simply marked *Berwind, 1918.*

"There's your Berwind heir," Jamie said. "Buried beside his ma."

"There's the big lie, you mean. There's nothing in that grave, and if it comes to that, I'll prove it."

"Yeah? Well, don't call on me, Liv. Grave digging is above and beyond."

"I feel as if we should say a prayer or something, don't you?"

"No. But I'm game."

They bowed their heads and contemplated the slender strip of land silently.

"Roses. Damn it, I smell roses, don't you?" Jamie complained. "Maybe some fresh grave downwind?"

"Yes. Roses." Olivia felt her knees buckling—and Jamie's strong hand under her elbow. "It's the heat, I guess."

"Sure it is. We've leaving now, ready or not."

Jamie drove home at a sensible speed, as befitting a vehicle transporting an invalid recovering from shock. And she changed the Sirius radio station to light classical. It was almost four when they arrived back in Marshfield.

"Where's the kava-kava?" Jamie left Olivia on the living room couch and hurried into the kitchen.

Moira looked up, startled at Jamie's entrance. She was sitting at the kitchen table, lovingly turning the pages of her mother's cookbook "That nasty herb stuff? Canister up there." She waved vaguely at a cabinet near the stove.

Jamie made a pot of the calming tea, brought it into the living room on a tray, and insisted that Liv drink hers with lots of honey. "Are you feeling better? Back there at the chapel, you looked as if you'd seen a ghost. Oh, shit. I have got to stop saying that!" She looked around for Moira.

"That's nothing new around here." Moira's raised voice signaled that she could hear quite well from the kitchen.

"Let's go into my room." Olivia took her tea. Jamie detoured to the kitchen, helped herself to a bottle of Stella Artois, and followed.

Hopping off the etched roses duvet with a nonchalant air, Sadie strolled away to find Moira. Olivia sat on the edge of the bed and motioned to Jamie to take the chaise lounge. "I'm all right, really. Just gobsmacked, you might say. A solution to this adoption puzzle has occurred to me. Well, hit me like lightning, really."

"You were mighty quiet on the ride back."

"Thinking. And listening to Debussy. But here's the thing—there's a reason why my PC has been spinning images of little chapels all week. I *had* to go the St. Rita's Chapel of Roses myself. I was *supposed* to make a connection between Haggerty's gift of the chapel in 1919 and the disappearance of Rose's baby in 1918. That damned Father Somebody gave the Berwind baby to Haggerty, and the senator paid him off with the magnificent bequest of that chapel. I don't *know* that—yet—but I'm sure of it. The priest even covered up the adoption with that second, smaller, supposed grave."

"That's quite a stretch of the imagination, especially *your* imagination. Where's the old Liv? The one who only believed half of what she saw and nothing of what she heard?"

"That was before I started keeping company with ghosts." Olivia finished her tea, savoring every drop of the honey at the bottom of the cup.

"Maybe it's a perimenopausal thing. Have you been experiencing any hot flashes?"

Olivia picked up a small green throw pillow and threw it. "I'm younger than you, remember?"

"Yeah, but only by six months. But I guess we've got a few years left before the night sweats and palpitations make us psycho. So what are you going to *do*?"

"Try to verify that the senator's son was adopted. Equally impossible. Then, I want to know if William Martin Haggerty, formerly baby Hugh, had any children who are still living. And grandchildren."

"Listen, Liv. Don't encourage any stray Rafferty to make a claim on the Berwind millions. First of all, a relationship can't be proved. Unless you can find a DNA match, or something physical like that. Second, the Swetts are not going to take kindly to your meddling. You've already had evidence of that."

They were silent for a while. Olivia put her cup on the night table and leaned back on the pillows, her hands behind her head. Jamie finished her beer and gazed out the window at some gulls reflecting the light of the lowering sun on their wings as they scavenged the marsh.

Suddenly, Olivia sat bolt upright. "I know where we can get the DNA!"

Jamie turned back to the room, met Olivia's gaze, now, full of renewed vigor and determination. "Oh, yes? From a couple who lived a hundred years ago?"

"It was right there in front of us all the time!" Olivia sprang off the bed, ready to prove the point, but she was intercepted by Moira, who'd barreled into the bedroom, her frizzy red hair aglow with indignation. Fists planted on her hips, she glared at Olivia. "Liv, you just have to do something about Kevin! He's out in the garage pulling everything out of the glory hole! He just threw a bunch of boxes into my kitchen. Full of *your junk!"*

"I sense a domestic crisis on the horizon. Maybe I'll just mosey back to my neat, quiet, empty town house now."

"No you don't, Jamie! Give me a minute to sort this out. We need to talk."

"Oh, all right. I'll be out on that glider you have in the backyard. It's cooling off now, thank God."

Olivia hurried into the garage to find Kevin, who was cleaning out the second floor with a grim vengeance. Silently, she reviewed the precepts in *How to Talk to Your Teen*. "Kevin, dear. What can I do to help you? You know you can't just unload all this stuff in the kitchen unless you want to make your sister crazy."

"Yeah? Well, where *can* I dump this trash? DCF is coming after Norah on Monday morning. She'll be gone, and if those old ladies have their way, I won't be able to find her." His tone was desperate. Olivia could remember feeling just that way when she was in high school—as if the end of the world were at hand. No one could have convinced her that the world would go right on and become infinitely bigger and better.

"Calm down, dear. There's nothing we can't sort out between us and the rest of the family. My boxes you can cart into my office. I have quite a large storage closet—just pile them in there for now. Things that belong to Moira or Danny you will have to stash in their rooms—neatly. And nothing, absolutely nothing is to be deposited in the kitchen."

"What about a bed? I need a bed for Norah."

Olivia wondered if she was about to let herself in for a load of grief from a DCF social worker. Maybe it would be someone Dave knew and could sweet talk into allowing this "visit" until the Slattery family got sorted out. "Tonight or tomorrow morning, you and Dave will go over to the Home Warehouse to buy whatever is needed for the time being. Don't worry. I'll talk to Dave." This turn of events would not please Dave, but Olivia counted on his generous heart.

Kevin looked at her with an expression in his eyes she had never seen before. Olivia could almost swear it was gratitude. *Chalk one up to Gladys Piffin and her teen-talk book*. It seemed a good moment to float away on her cloud of sainthood and find Jamie.

Jamie was lying back on the glider, gazing at the sky through leafy maples. "Another family catastrophe averted? My hat's off to you, Liv. Better you than me."

"Listen, Jamie. DNA is the answer. And it's right in our hands. We can get DNA from Rose's hair. Remember that lock of hair tied up in a ribbon? In the silver locket? 'To Hugh from his Rose, *I shall but love thee better after death*'? A lab can get DNA off hair, no matter how old, isn't that right?"

Jamie sighed. "Without the hair follicle attached, the chances of getting a profile are little better than nil. Only if the hair shaft hadn't completed its cellular conversion to dead cells. Or you can trace a female hair shaft without a follicle as passed through the female line only. That's mtDNA. Rose didn't have a daughter, though; she had a son. Anyway, I'm not getting a good feeling about this."

"Try anyway. When did you ever get a good feeling about any of my inquiries?"

"True. Hardly ever. Especially when you're relying on spectral evidence. Also, I've been lying here wondering why you're going to all this trouble to upset the Raffertys with the prospect of great wealth. The Raffertys are probably rich enough already. The senator must have left a pretty sizeable estate to his son—political graft being the lucrative business that it is."

Olivia settled into one of the Adirondack chairs with a sigh. "I see your argument. Maybe I'll just look into the surviving Raffertys and see how they're faring."

"No chance of just dropping the whole crusade?"

"Not as long as I'm being haunted by ghosts with an agenda. If there's one thing I've learned, it's that souls of the departed never give up—and they have all eternity to brood over their earthly wrongs."

~

After Jamie left, Olivia got Dave on his cell to report the Norah crisis, then spent some time at her computer, composing a Rafferty family tree. William Alfred Rafferty and his wife Mabel O'Neill Rafferty had only the one son (the stolen Berwind baby) named William Martin Rafferty, born 1918. Photos of the boy's high school graduation from Trinity in New York, Class of '36, showed the senator and his wife looking as proud as a couple of peacocks in full feather.

Olivia studied the grainy reproductions on the Google link. The parents both had light hair; the senator's jaw was square; Mabel's face was soft and round. The son's hair was a mass of dark curls, and his face, as thin as a faun's. The Trinity yearbook cited William "Billy" M. Rafferty: *Thou skill to poet were, thou scorner of the ground.*" Shelley seemed a strange choice for a future lawyer, but the bio note mentioned an interest in aviation. Perhaps that explained the quote from "To a Skylark."

An article on the Raffertys in the Sunday Supplement of *The Boston Globe* showed young Rafferty standing beside his Piper J-5A Cub shortly after graduation from Harvard. A gift from his father? Later articles reported that Billy Rafferty joined the Army Air Force in January 1942, just a month after Pearl Harbor. His name turned up again in an article about Doolittle's daring raid on Tokyo in April of that same year.

After that, nothing, until 1951, when the senator's son married Jennifer Higgins. Just three lines under Marriages, no extravagant wedding spread across the society pages. (*Strange, doesn't fit*, Olivia thought.) There had been no engagement announcement that she could find. An elopement? She delved further and found no record of William Martin Rafferty ever passing the bar and becoming an attorney.

The couple had one son, Gerard Rafferty, born in 1956. And still living!

Both of Gerard's parents, Billy and Jennifer, had died in the 1980s. Well, Olivia could hardly have hoped that the Berwind baby would still be alive and well, so that she could reveal to him his true biological history. If Billy Rafferty had never become an attorney, what *did* he do? She made a note on Saturday's To Do list to find his obit.

In 1990, Gerard had married Stella Razanno. The engagement announcement gave his profession as Professor of English and American Literatures at Middlebury College, where the couple planned to reside. In 1995, a daughter had been born, named Anna Gloria Rafferty. *Anna Gloria—what a lovely name!* Olivia was beginning to feel excited. The hidden drama of the past was unfolding at last.

Olivia wondered if it was common knowledge in the family that Gerard's father had been adopted? Probably not, since the priest at St. Rita's had even gone to the trouble of counterfeiting a grave for Rose's baby. That meant she'd have to convince the Raffertys of the true facts of their heritage. They would probably think she was nuts. Except for the DNA. If a living Rafferty's DNA matched the DNA from Rose's lock of hair, it would prove the case. Otherwise, Olivia was liable to have not one but two ghosts trailing around after her forever. Sweet Rose searching for her son. And that elderly voice, the spirit who called herself Nanny Burns.

There was still the question of finances. Olivia thought about researching the settlement of Senator Rafferty's estate. That project, too, was shelved until tomorrow. Right now it was almost dinner time.

If the Berwind baby a.k.a William Martin Rafferty, "Billy," had died in the eighties, how come Rose and Nanny Burns hadn't got in touch with *him* "beyond the veil" instead of bothering Olivia? Could it be that the two women were stuck in something very like the Catholic notion of limbo, unable to transcend to a higher plane because of their obsession with an infant who should, by rights, have been brought up in the loving bosom of the Berwind family? That Nanny spirit who had come through their séance blamed the whole subversion of justice on "George."

Olivia consulted her Berwind family tree. George Victor Berwind was Hugh's younger brother...who had inherited the whole fortune. Possible motive for Rose's ending up at the Refuge.

And I'm supposed to put everything right? Olivia moaned to herself. *Why pick on someone like me who doesn't even read her daily astrology nonsense?*

These troubling speculations were interrupted by a noisy battle going on in the kitchen, by which Olivia divined that Kevin had revealed his immediate plans for Norah to his siblings. With a sigh, Olivia closed her links and went to calm the hysterics before Dave got home. Moira must be in the midst of dinner preparations. The inviting fragrance of marinara sauce was wafting through the downstairs, another handwritten recipe from Alice O'Hara (Teresa Barbero, in her bank-robbing days.)

"Uncle Dave is *not either* letting that Traveller trash move in with us!" Moira was waving a threatening wooden spoon, stained with tomato, at Kevin, who was lounging against the refrigerator, drinking a glass of milk and eating a slab of marbled spice cake. "That's supposed to be our dessert. And you're going to spoil your dinner, you creep."

"I told you *and told you* that I didn't want you doubling up with me, Kev." Danny was sitting at the kitchen table, his gaze fixed to a hand-held device that appeared to be showing one of the Transformer movies. "The last time you were in my room, you screwed up my Apocalypse VI big time."

Gladys Piffin, help me now, Olivia prayed silently to the teen-talk maven.

"Okay, you guys. Uncle Dave will be home soon, after a very hard week making Plymouth safe for its good citizens, so let's give him a break. I've talked to him on my cell, and he's agreed to help Norah stay clear of DCF for the time being. He's even checked with his contact in at DCF and explained that he will take responsibility for Norah's well-being while we make plans for her future. This is not, repeat *not,* a permanent arrangement. But don't worry, Danny—you will not have to share with Kevin. Norah will rough it upstairs in the garage. And Moira, I've heard you remark on how glad you were to be shut of DCF yourself when Uncle Dave took you in. So let's just treat this as a visit, and be as polite as we always are to guests."

"Where's she going to pee?" Moira was not to be easily mollified.

"Norah will use the first floor lav. She'll have a key to the kitchen door." Olivia frowned slightly. They wouldn't be able to use their brand new door alarm, unless everyone, including Norah, was out of the house. "So, what do you say?"

No one said anything. Kevin finished his fistful of cake, Moira stirred the sauce rather more forcefully than strictly necessary, and Danny returned his attention to the Transformers.

"I'll take that as an okay," Olivia said. "I'm proud of you. She'll be here sometime tomorrow. Do you want me to set the table, Moira?"

"Up to you. Use the pasta dishes, you know the ones with the little Italian flags on them?"

"Flags?"

"I'll get them down for you, Liv." Kevin rinsed his glass and put it in the dishwasher. "Thanks."

~

Kevin hid his genuine relief under an impassive expression, when Dave obligingly agreed to make a trip to Home Warehouse after dinner. Only the two of them, so that there would be room in Dave's Bronco for their purchase of a camp bed. "Yes, a camp bed," Dave said. "This is a temporary arrangement until we can find a Slattery relative who doesn't have a rap sheet to give Norah a home, at least until she's 18 and no longer under the auspices of DCF or subject to her dad's authority, such as it is. After that, Norah can make whatever arrangements she wants, perhaps get a job and a place of her own, maybe even continue her education. I'm checking on the relatives myself. There must be someone decent who'll step up to the plate."

"There's a great-aunt who split with the family, but she lives in South Carolina." Kevin tried to keep the disconsolate note out of his voice.

"You'd miss Norah, I know. And so would the Celtic Storm."

"Yeah. Maybe you can find someone nearer, Dave?"

"I'll check" Dave promised. "The Slattery cousins are legion."

He took the opportunity to have another man-to-man talk with Kevin about safe sex, one that he'd had several times before, much to Kevin's disgust. This time, however, the warnings were specifically in reference to Norah who was now Dave's responsibility. Kevin looked out the window and yawned.

"Okay, okay. I get it, Dave. But here's the thing. You don't know Norah, or you wouldn't worry so much. She's got her own rules."

"I'm glad to hear it."

"Norah's had some trouble with one of her brothers, that Kyle, and she set him straight. She can handle her own affairs."

Kevin decided not to say anything about the little folding knife Norah kept in a sheaf trapped to her bra. She called it a "lady knife." Nor did he repeat any of Kyle's threats to himself, or Norah's warning that Cian might be planning to cash in on the Lowensteins' interest in his daughter.

"She'll be well out of Strawberry Hill, poor kid," Dave said.

"Norah's smart, you know. Genius with the fiddle. Clever with numbers, too."

"Might get her a scholarship. Good job prospects, too. All she has to do is stay out of trouble."

"Like I said, Dave, I get the point."

"Good. You're a clever guy, yourself. I have a world of faith in you."

Kevin scowled in the dark of the car. Trust could be a pain in the ass.

MISSY HYDE ON THE CHASE

It was already Friday morning when I listened to the bug I'd installed, the Lowenstein woman telling her husband that she and her friend Jamie were taking "a day off tomorrow"—which was *today*. They might do some antiquing up through Lexington and Concord. "A day off" is not the same as having lunch together. *They're up to something*, I thought, *and I'm going to find out what.* I hoped they hadn't left yet. In any case, I could follow the GPS on the Honda. I switched off the tape before I had to listen to the usual love-fest in the Lowenstein boudoir. In my profession, I'd had enough of that groping and groaning to last a lifetime.

But the Lowenstein woman didn't take the Honda! And then that redhead drove too damn fast for my dear old Dodge to keep up—I'm definitely trading it in for a nondescript Buick with a souped-up engine. I had to give up the chase just this side of Dedham. I wonder if I ought to stick a GPS on the redhead's Mustang, in case of future expeditions.

Well, I think I got most of the story, later that day, from the useful device I'd installed in the bedroom.

Maybe Olivia Lowenstein is missing out on her true vocation. She seems to be a natural no-holds-barred investigator. What a trail of high-quality snooping I got off her computer! Even without my very special undercover sources, she was able to track down and verify a marriage between Rose Redwood and Hugh Berwind. Although it took place in Canada, not the U.S.. And Rose's last minute switch to her father's surname didn't make the tracking any easier. Most would have given up the chase, but not Lowenstein. Even I wonder how she twigged to Persey.

Maybe Lowenstein had some outside help I didn't know about. The Moon Deer lady? Or someone else? Her *Sent Mail* folder contained a thank you to some branch librarian for her "extraordinary perspicacity." What was that name? Ritchie. How much of the Berwind story has Lowenstein spilled to others in the process of not minding her own business? I hope I don't have to deal with any other small-time minds with big-time information. Still, who's afraid of a little librarian?

It appears that the nosy Lowenstein bitch has made the unlikely connection between Senator Rafferty and a lost Berwind heir. *Just as I did.* I should have realized where Lowenstein and her pal were headed on Friday and simply got there ahead of them. The same chapel of St. Rita where I got my first glimpse of the whole picture. I'd thought at the time there was no need to give Swett an ulcer that would profit me nothing, so I never reported my speculations. Because I pride myself on only reporting facts. Also, there was a danger that Swett, paranoid as he is, might fear that I would blackmail him, threaten to bring forth a new heir, and hold him up for a share of the loot. He couldn't imagine that I might have, like, *a code of ethics*. In Swett's world view, there is indeed no honor among thieves. Nevertheless, in hindsight, I should have filled him in. Broken it to him in small manageable chunks.

Because now a major load of crap is going to hit the fan. I can no longer avoid revealing the whole tangled web to Swett. And Lowenstein's involvement in it.

But first, I needed to verify my information. Unlike the Lowenstein woman, I can't just proceed on any sudden flash of intuition. Swett will expect a well-researched report, not a flight of fancy. So now I wonder where St. Rita's adoption records, if they still exist, might be moldering away. True, the senator's sudden acquisition of a son—a child that Hugh's parents never knew existed—must have been, of necessity, a clandestine operation, but you never know what notes might exists in the margins of original documents.

I have an idea where to look for those records. Fairly easy to check, just a simple break-in. I doubt the place is even alarmed.

Now that I have that spyware installed in Lowenstein's computer, I'll also keep a check on whatever else she sticks her nose into. I can't imagine that her searches will get ahead of mine, but I wouldn't want to find that out the hard way.

When I get all these investigative ducks in a row, Henry Swett III is going to throw a conniption fit, as my sainted grandmother used to say. And he's going to want a solution, which will cost him the big bucks. I haven't quite made up my mind if it would be better to eliminate the remaining Raffertys. There are only the two blood heirs, and Lowenstein will certainly find them. Or should I just get rid of Lowenstein herself? That would certainly be the end of the matter. On the other hand, her husband is a detective with the State Police, and he'd likely be consumed with finding out who and why. When I looked into the guy's background, I noted that he'd never given up on getting his partner's killers. How much more fanatical would he be if it was his wife who got whacked? Unless, of course, I could make it look like an accident. Nothing too obvious—nothing to make forensics suspicious.

I wonder if the farmhouse is powered by *clean, affordable, safe natural gas*? That's a fairly easy event to arrange. I'm not a fan of collateral damage, so I'd choose a day when the rest of the tribe was up in Danbury visiting Ma O'Hara in her orange jumpsuit.

There's one thing still sticking in my craw. Lowenstein had some brilliant idea about DNA that she was about to share with the redhead. But that little O'Hara brat interrupted them, and I never got to hear the end of the story. Where in the name of Christ could she find DNA unless she starts digging up bodies? Hugh Berwind's remains are still in France, but his little wife is right up there in St. Rita's cemetery.

No, Lowenstein may have the tenacity of a rat terrier, but she wouldn't go that far.

AUGUST 10

Things to Do Today

Senator Rafferty—estate disposition?
Billy Rafferty's obit.
Dave—DCF, call in favors?
Danny, promise new game Apocalypse VII
Moira, manners!
Norah, house rules—(what are they?)
Libr. borrow Zen and the Blended Family

Norah arrived the next afternoon, Saturday, with her fiddle case strapped to the bike, a bulging woven bag slung over her shoulder, and a mess of books and shoes in the bike's basket. With her pale yellow hair piled up on her head, wearing a boy's shirt, worn jeans, and scuffed boots, she looked even leaner and more frail than usual. Olivia thought how appearances can be so deceptive. Only the narrow chin revealed an air of determination. But Olivia could sense a core of steel under that delicate frame. This was a girl who knew how to take care of herself, because she'd always had to. *All to the good.*

Olivia showed Norah the bathroom she would be using and gave her a spare key to the back door. She took linens out of the linen closet to carry up to the second floor of the garage. The camp bed was already set up under the eaves. Olivia was touched to see that both dormer windows were sparkling clean, the floor had been mopped, and an old desk of Kevin's had been placed under one window with a folding chair. There was a jar of roses from the garden on an old trunk that would serve as a night table, and another folding chair beside that. While they were at Home Warehouse, Kevin had bought some wooden pegs to hold clothing, and those were now fixed to the wall beside the door.

Norah dropped her bag on the floor and carefully placed her fiddle case on the desk. "Here, let me take those, Mrs. Lowenstein. I'll make up the bed myself."

"Just call me Liv, Norah. Kevin's bringing pillows and a duvet."

Kevin stamped up the stairs with two guest pillows and one from his own room. An old duvet that Moira used for sleepovers was slung over his shoulder. It was Kelly green with white polka dots. He looked at Norah. "It's rough, but it's a place to stay."

"It's lovely, thanks. I'm so glad..." the words trailed off, and Norah smiled brilliantly at Kevin. His face lit up as well with a wide grin; it was as if an arc of visible energy passed between them. Olivia realized that she had rarely seen these two smile, at anyone, even each other.

It won't do to get all sentimental over this arrangement, she warned herself sternly. But she knew it was already too late. She remembered going to the pound to find a good guard dog and being unable to choose between the two mutts in the back cages. And that's how she'd ended up bringing both Sadie and Bruno home.

Still, I never regretted that rescue, whether soft-hearted or soft-headed.

Olivia went back downstairs, only vaguely worried about leaving the young couple alone. Dave had talked to Kevin, he'd assured her. And Kev wouldn't want to do anything to make Norah's present situation untenable and throw her back on the mercies of DCF.

It would be all right.

Somehow this whole summer day had whizzed by, just getting Norah settled and hanging out with Dave in the backyard. Typical August, slightly overcast and humid. A small breeze off the Atlantic gave relief, discouraged gnats, and filled the air with the scent of salt marsh. They drank iced lemon tea while Dave told her about the difficult drug case he was working. Local teens on heroin, especially depressing. An epidemic on the South Shore. Sadly, some of the sellers would surely turn out to be other kids. What he most wanted was to get to the next level, the suppliers.

After dinner, while the whole family, with Norah, watched a night game at Fenway Park on TV, Olivia snuck away to her computer. She'd promised herself a search for Billy Rafferty's obituary. What was it Mrs. Ritchie had advised? Olivia chuckled, remembering: "There's always a great deal to be learned from death, dear. *O sting, where is thy death?*" The librarian did have a zany way with words.

There were four William M. Raffertys listed in the Social Security Death Index. Olivia found none in Massachusetts, one in Vermont, the others in Arizona, Colorado, and Oregon respectively. The Vermont Rafferty had the right birth date. She checked the Boston Globe and several Vermont regional newspapers: Bingo! William Martin Rafferty, a.k.a. Billy Martin (*no Rafferty?*) a well-known poet and essayist (*his nom de plume, then)* had died when his Piper Saratoga crashed into the Atlantic ocean off the coast of Nantucket Island in the spring of 1983, leaving his beloved wife Jenny, their son Gerard "Gerry", and "the many devoted students he had inspired through the years at the Bread Loaf Writers Conference."

Good Lord, a poet and a teacher. There's certainly no money in that, Olivia said to herself. *And it appears as if Gerard followed in his father Billy's footsteps.* It seemed even more important now to track down the disposition of Senator Rafferty's estate.

An article in the *New York Times Review of Books* followed the poet's literary career and included a bibliography. Billy Martin Rafferty, a World War II veteran, won the National Book Award for Poetry in 1944 for his collection *Lost Voices*. He was named a consultant in poetry for the Library of Congress in 1954.The author of this retrospective referred to him as a second-tier poet of discipline and cool observation, whose poems "touched by goodness, cheerfulness, and old-fashioned values, rich in craft and thoughtfulness, may be well treated by readers for generations to come." *Good Lord, talk about damning with faint praise*, Olivia thought.

It was late, and she was drawn by guilt to the cheering family in the living room. The Sox must be winning. She would chase down the senator's estate tomorrow. But before she shut down, she brought up Amazon, intending to order *Lost Voices* and Billy Martin's last book, *Witness: New and Selected Poems.* The first was out of print; she ordered *Witness,* although whether you could learn anything about a person from his poetry was doubtful. Poetry veiled the truth while appearing to reveal all.

~

Sunday, it was agreed, was much too muggy for a picnic on the beach. Dave worked on his wrought iron sculptures in the garage all morning (which avocation had relegated their two cars to the front driveway except in the most extreme weather). He was treated to a lively fiddle concert wafting down from the second floor. It was easy to distinguish Norah's accomplished style from Kevin's screechy attempts to follow. *Poor Dave,* Olivia thought, and took advantage of the time to continue her research. She was almost regretful that it was her day to cook, although it had been difficult enough to wrest half the week's culinary chores away from Moira.

Once filed, a will is in the public domain, as Olivia well knew. First she located the county in which the senator had died, then she viewed the probate court docket online and ordered a copy of the will, making a written request which she faxed to the court. She would be charged for each page of the copy. This was Sunday, so her request would wait until business hours next week when a clerk would process her request and require that she pay the appropriate fee.

Meanwhile, she assuaged her curiosity by bringing up newspaper articles about Senator Rafferty, beginning with his obituary. His death, predictably, left behind his devoted widow, Mabel, and son, William Martin Rafferty, but also his sister, Adeline Rafferty Hines, and her son, John J. Hines. On a whim, she Googled John J. Hines and found him mentioned in an article about Supreme Court Justice Harlan Fiske Stone. A photo showed the justice surrounded by his five young law clerks, who were named underneath the photo, one of them being Hines. Another article cited his unsuccessful run for the office of State Representative, 4th District. A few years later, he became a partner in the firm of Rafferty, Whelan, Byrne, Foley, and Hines.

"Whelan! What luck!" Olivia immediately called Jamie on her cell. "Hey, Jamie…why don't you and Mike come over for supper tonight? We're grilling shish kebabs, and there'll be pasta with fresh tomatoes, olives, and feta, and spinach with pine nuts and raisins."

"Moody picked up Mike this morning, some camping trip ordeal, poor kid. Sure, I'll be there with bells on. Only, just tell me what you're up to. I can hear that little buzz of excitement in your voice. And it has nothing to do with inviting your old friend to the feast."

"I've been doing some research into the Raffertys. I'll make printouts, FYI."

"Okay. And what else?"

"The senator's law firm, Rafferty, Whelan, Byrne, Foley, and Hine. Any relation?"

"To whom?"

"Your Whelan, of course."

"It's a common name, one of the top hundred Irish names. Look it up."

"Still, you could ask the question. I want to know more about Hines, who happened to be the senator's nephew."

Jamie sighed deeply. "What time?"

"Oh, come early. Five-ish. We'll have drinks."

After the call, Olivia printed out some of the articles about Hines. There was something important here, she was sure of it. But right now it was time to marinate the lamb chunks.

She found Moira in the kitchen, inspecting a round tray of baklava suspiciously. "You didn't make this?"

"Believe me, Moira, this will be way better than any pastry I could make."

"I guess. Is Mike coming to dinner?"

Moira seemed to have a talent for hearing conversations not intended for her ears. "Sorry, Mike's going camping with his dad, dear."

"Bummer."

~

August mosquitoes drove the party to dine indoors, leaving only Dave to man the grill, enveloped in Bug-off and surrounded by citronella candles. Otherwise, it was a pleasant family party. After dinner, Norah played a few "old folks" show tunes from *Brigadoon* and *Fiddler on the Roof.* These were followed by songs from the Dropkick Murphys albums: "Never Alone" and "The Wild Rover." Kevin and Norah sang the Irish songs together; Olivia was surprised at Kevin's pleasing tenor voice. Norah's voice, although thinner, accompanied his well; they had obviously practiced their duets.

"They're really good together." Jamie tapped her foot to the rhythm of the Bodhrán and appeared to be feeling quite mellow after pre-dinner martinis and wine with the shish kebabs.

"So, you'll speak to Jack Whelan about the Rafferty-Whelan law firm?"

"Oh, I *suppose* so! What is it you want me to ask?"

"Anything, just anything. Did your patient know that branch of the Whelan family? If so, any gossip that might have been bandied about connected to Rafferty or Hines, specifically how the senator reacted when his son abandoned the law for literature. Matters that cannot be discovered through public records." Olivia offered Jamie a tot of Sambuca in her coffee.

Jamie held out her cup. "Watch out! If you loosen me up with any more booze, you'll have to let me sleep on your sofa."

"Moira has twin beds; you can always bunk with her."

"Only kidding. I'll be fine driving myself home. And I'll talk to Jack Whelan, but the slenator's will should tell you much more."

"Yes, I'm really eager to get my hands on that copy. I'm hoping by Wednesday or Thursday. I'll call you. When the devil is your supper break, anyway?"

"Depends on what kind of a hypochondriacal day we're having. Try at 6:30—that's usually okay."

"And there's something else. A favor I want you to do for me."

Jamie raised an eyebrow that spoke more eloquently than words of the many "favors" she'd done for Olivia in the past, and their consequences.

Olivia went to the decorative little maple desk in the corner of the living room and took a sealed white envelope out of one of its pigeonholes. "Here. Read this later." And to be sure of that, she tucked the envelope into Jamie's handbag loitering on the floor beside her chair. (The envelope contained a few strands of Rose Berwind's hair in a plastic bag and a note begging Jamie to use her "lab contacts" to obtain a DNA report from this miniscule specimen.)

Although Dave didn't appear to have been listening, he stood up now and eyed the two women sternly. He himself had only consumed one bottle of beer with dinner, and much coffee afterward. "No, you won't drive yourself home, Jamie. And neither will Liv drive you. I'll do the driving, and we'll get your car back to you tomorrow."

"Cripes! I have to be in Dover by eight."

"I'll drive the Mustang to your place at seven, and Dave will give me a ride home before he goes to work."

"Really, Liv. Do you have to put up with very much of this cave man stuff?"

Olivia smiled and said nothing. She had been single and responsible for herself for several years between marriages. She knew her own strengths, her freedom of spirit, and being protected didn't offend her at all. In fact, it turned her on.

~

A copy of Senator Rafferty's will arrived over a week later, on Monday morning, with a receipt for the page fee, paid in advance with Olivia's credit card. Olivia disapproved of giving her credit details in order to pay online, but it had become a necessity. Moving with the times, she felt, was vastly overrated.

It was barely ten when she heard the mail carrier stop out front. With her impatient nature, Olivia had always been glad that the Lowenstein home was on an early route. She collected the mail from their box—a stack of catalogs, magazines, and bills—and immediately spotted the Probate Court's return address. Not even waiting until she was back indoors out of the burning morning sun, she'd dropped into a rocking chair on the front porch to tear that envelope open with intuitive eagerness.

The will of William Alfred Rafferty, Esquire, began with the various bequests to household staff and a modest trust fund for the maintenance of St. Rita's Chapel of Roses. His collection of glass flowers to the Peabody Museum. Portraits of his father, mother, and other ancestors to his sister, Adeline Rafferty Hines. His library, *excluding* the law books, to his son William Martin Rafferty. The remainder of the estate (stocks, bonds, savings, and property) was to be divided in equal trusts between his beloved wife, Mabel O'Neill Rafferty, and his nephew, John James Hines, who also got every last law book in that vast dusty Rafferty library. Mabel was granted lifetime tenancy in the Rafferty home in Newton and the summer place in Chatham, with all their attendant furnishings and objets d'art. Upon her death, everything (except Mabel's personal property) would revert to his nephew with the rest of the estate.

Whew! So Billy Rafferty had been cut out of his father's will, with the legal face slap of a few boxes of books, not even the valuable law books at that. A minimal bequest to make the point that the Senator had not overlooked his son but had instead deliberately disinherited him. Olivia thought she knew why. Imagine being childless for years, then finally—miraculously—you were blessed with a son to carry on your name. You were so grateful for that healthy beautiful boy that you endowed the Church (who'd made it all possible) with an imported Italian chapel. You sent your boy to the best schools, groomed him to take your place in the law and politics; he would be your immortality. And your thanks was a young man who threw away that legacy to become a poet, practically a bohemian. Probably the woman he chose for his wife didn't meet Daddy's expectations either. From what Olivia had been able to learn, Jennifer Higgins had been a political activist, an essayist, and part owner of a Vermont book store, with no social significance whatsoever.

Did Mabel go along with all of this? Was she willing to abandon the son she had raised from infancy because of his unorthodox career path? Olivia doubted it. Maybe she would have a look at Mabel's will later.

But right now, she needed to know only one thing: did Billy Rafferty's son share the same DNA as Rose Berwind; was she, in fact, his biological grandmother? Olivia would have to wait for that report, a mission she'd entrusted to Jamie... because Jamie had reliable medical contacts, which seemed a more prudent course than committing an old, fragile specimen to a commercial genomic outfit.

She picked up the rest of the mail off the empty rocking chair where she'd dropped it and gazed out for a moment at her August-exhausted rose garden, making a mental note to do some dead-heading in the afternoon shade. Right now, the heat was so searing that it seemed to shimmy in waves on the paths between rose bushes. As she watched, one of those mirage-like eddys of light seemed to be rising and taking on a misty form. It was that young woman again, the one she and the children had seen before. Danny had said the vision was like a hologram, and so it was. Flowing hair around her head like a halo in the light, a wavering dress, moving through the garden without seeming to touch the ground.

Olivia was transfixed.

Slowly, gradually, the image faded from view, and the garden became just a garden again. Only then did she pull herself together, pick up the rest of the mail, and return to her office, where she dropped everything on the desk. She needed something. A thimbleful of brandy would have been nice, but hardly the way to begin a Monday morning. Olivia went into the kitchen and got herself a glass of lemonade. *Rose.* Rose wanted her to find a baby who'd already lived his long life and died. No way to explain that to a ghost.

But what she could do is to contact Rose's grandson…if only to let him know that the senator who'd taken in his father, Billy, and then cast him off, was not his only family, that a loving spirit was reaching out to him from the past. And then, too, there was the money. Hundreds of millions of dollars. The Berwind legacy.

Olivia wondered what kind of reception Gerard Rafferty would give to the tale she had to tell.

ROSE

Hugh would have loved this garden, all the beautiful roses, his favorite flower. And Hugh would have loved his son. If it weren't for that terrible war, we could have lived such a happy life together. Someone ought to answer for the deaths of all those young men. The politicians, the generals.

There are Guardians here who urge me to move away from this earthly dimension, these worldly concerns…who promise me that I will find Hugh again. That's my dearest wish, but something happened to me when my child was wrested out of my arms. It's true that I no longer belong among the living. But it's also true that I cannot rest in peace. Not yet.

But I'm not alone any more, that's a good thing. I've encountered this strong elderly spirit. Her name is Mary Margaret. She knew and loved my Hugh when he was a child, and she's vowed to help me in my quest. My quest! I wish I were entirely clear on that. All I know is that something or someone is tugging on my soul to make things right.

Mary Margaret says we have been drawn together by a gift she gave to Hugh as a boy, a marquetry case with his name engraved inside, and the locket that I gave Hugh with my picture. Those two gifts from our hearts have met and ignited in the hands of one woman. Her name is Olivia, and Mary Margaret says we can work through her. Olivia is a channel for us.

Mary Margaret says that Hugh's child was stolen away, but there's more. Because she feels the same need to bring light to the dark places of our shared history. She says that when a dreadful wrong happens in life, it's like a pebble thrown into a lake, the ripples go on and on, touching the far banks with dark rivulets. It's up to us, she says, to smooth the waters, to right those wrongs. She will help me.

I must walk in Olivia's garden as often as I can summon the strength. It's terribly difficult, rather like giving birth to yourself. But I must put my quest into her heart. There's no other way to find peace.

AUGUST 20
Things to Do Today

Track down Gerard R.—poss. thru M. College.
Make app.!!!
Chk: Slatterys out on bail?
Don't' forget: O'Haras to St. Timothy's Fair Sat.
Libr. Infamous Family Inheritance Feuds, *also* Safeguard Your Teen

The office secretary at Middlebury College informed Olivia with gentle sympathy that Professor Rafferty was out on long-term medical leave, upon which she could not comment, nor was she allowed to reveal his home address. She could, however, pass on a message, if Mrs. Lowenstein would care to leave one, and possibly Professor Rafferty would get in touch with her.

Mrs. Lowenstein did wish to leave a message. Olivia quickly composed a message that she hoped would sound sufficiently compelling to elicit a response. After she'd done so, however, she began to wonder if "a matter that could benefit you" didn't sound like a cold call to drum up insurance business or some financial scam. The professor's home phone number was unlisted, and faculty addresses were not listed on the Middlebury College website, but these trifling hurdles would never stop Olivia now that she had come this far. She would think of something.

But that afternoon she did receive a return call on her cell, while she was in the walk-in closet she shared with Dave, looking for old clothes to donate to the church rummage sale. The voice was that of a young woman, who introduced herself as Anna Rafferty.

Olivia shot out of the closet and plunked herself down on the chaise lounge where she kept a small moleskin notebook and pen for just such occasions.

"Miss Rafferty! So nice of you to return my call. Miss Rasenberger told me that your father is out on sick leave. I was hoping to have a word. It's very important. Do you think something might be arranged?"

Anna Rafferty sighed. "How important, Mrs. Lowenstein? If you're thinking to sell Dad an annuity or a reverse mortgage, you can save your time and energy. We are not in the market."

"Please do call me Liv. No, it's nothing of that sort at all. I'm an independent records management consultant, but this is not a business matter. I am not selling anything. It's personal. I happen to have come across some information pertaining to your grandfather's family that I thought might be of interest to your father, and I'd like to talk to him about that, not over the phone."

"How important is this information of yours, Mrs. Lowenstein? My father and mother are both in poor health, and, in fact, I've taken a year off from college to care for them. Dad is expected to recover, if all goes well. But, as you see, we don't really have time for the *ancestry.com* kind of thing."

Anna's tone was quite firm. There was nothing for it but to explain right on the phone the nature of Olivia's theories and how they might relate to Gerard Rafferty. It all sounded rather thin, even to Olivia's own ears.

But Anna Rafferty replied, "My grandfather adopted? I'm amazed at your bringing up that possibility. As it happens, that notion is something of a family legend. True or not, I think Dad would be quite interested to hear what you've come up with on that score. I'll talk to him and get back to you. Perhaps you can visit us and tell your tale."

Olivia would be delighted to make an appointment to drive up to Middlebury whenever it was convenient. She did not, however, mention the handwritten will signed by Hugh Delano Berwind. She was saving that to show the Raffertys in person.

When the call was concluded, Olivia was so elated, she practically floated through the house to the kitchen, where she found a scowling Moira making a tuna salad of her own invention for lunch sandwiches, chopping red onion, bell pepper, celery and cilantro with angry energy

Olivia got herself a glass of lemonade from the refrigerator and assessed the storm. "Would you like some help, Moira? Why don't I cut up this cantaloupe to go with the sandwiches:"

"I don't care. Norah's a damn vegetarian, you know. Who asked for that skinny tramp to hang around here, anyway?" Moira demanded.

"Moira, you must not use that language in reference to a guest in our home." Olivia got a cutting board and began work on the cantaloupe. "As I have explained to you before, this is a visit, not a permanent placement."

"Yeah? We'll just see, then. Kevin's sure in no hurry to see the back of her." Moira grabbed jars of capers, hot pepper relish, and mayonnaise out of the refrigerator.

"Uncle Dave is going to find a suitable cousin or aunt to act as Norah's guardian." Olivia began to push melon cubes off the board into a bowl. She added a few blueberries. She'd need something cool after Moira's spicy tuna.

"What about her dad? Hasn't he got out on bail yet."

"Yes, finally. Dave sent me a text to keep an eye out. Norah does not want to be dragged back to Strawberry Hill."

"I wouldn't worry about that one—*our honored guest*—if I were you. She can take care of herself, so I hear." Having spooned in the rest of the ingredients with abandon, Moira began to stir it all together.

Heartburn on a roll, Olivia thought. "What do you mean?"

"That's for me to know and you to find out," Moira said darkly. She began to make the sandwiches. "You can call the troops, if you want,"

On her way to the garage, Olivia got a call back from Anna Rafferty. "Dad is quite intrigued. Had you heard anything about Great-Grandma's will?"

That would be Mabel, the senator's widow. "No, my theories come from some research I did into St. Rita's in Harvard."

"It's a long drive, but if you want to visit us, you can come for lunch on Friday, and we'll talk. Dad's recovering from his last chemo session, and he thinks he'll be well enough by then."

"Sure, that would be wonderful. I have a friend who's been helping me. Would it be too much of an imposition if I brought her along? She can share the driving."

"No, that's okay. I'll just grill some burgers. Nothing fancy. See you about noon?"

Olivia practically danced the rest of the way to the garage. She found Kevin, Norah, and Danny listening to tapes of the Dropkick Murphys. "Lunch is ready. Best not keep Moira waiting."

Norah raised an eyebrow at Kevin; he winked back. *What was that all about?* No self-help book in the world could decode the teen language of silences.

"I'm hungry!" Danny was still open and cheerful. Only eleven, that's why. "I hope it's not tuna again. Can't you get her to stop using all those hot peppers, Aunt Liv?"

MISSY HYDE GETS HER MARCHING ORDERS

So, the Lowenstein woman is making an appointment to see the Raffertys! Lucky for me that she happened to be in the bedroom when the Rafferty girl returned her call. Wish I could have heard both sides of the conversation, but I did get the gist. I just don't know exactly when they plan to meet, but if Lowenstein has anything to do with it, sooner rather than later. Instead of hanging around at the Harborside Inn until I sprout gills, I located the redhead's town house at *The Willows* in Scituate and attached a GPS to her Mustang. That way, whether Lowenstein heads up North on her own, or with that daredevil friend, I can follow with my little Q-bug. If I can position the device outside a window, I'll be able to hear Lowenstein's pitch to Rafferty from wherever I park my Dodge.

Obviously, she intends to float her theory of the adoption to the Raffertys and make trouble for everyone—especially herself.

That spyware I left in her computer turned up her search for Senator Rafferty's will. At first, I couldn't figure why she'd bothered with that, but then it came to me. She wants to know if the money would make any difference in their lives. After all, if the senator had left them wealthy, what would they care about the Berwind connection? She could forget the whole thing and save herself a shitload of grief. So it's clear that this gal has not learned the basics of human nature. No matter how well fixed someone is, they always, *always* want more, especially if that "more" happens to be in the millions.

Speaking of the basics of human nature, I also wonder what's it to Olivia Lowenstein if Rafferty finds out that his grandfather was not his biological relative? What in hell is her motivation for stirring up the past? If her motive isn't money—what is it? That's something I don't get at all. It's as if she herself is haunted by these past events, which is beyond weird. No, that can't be it. Must be the money; she's hoping for a reward, a healthy share of the Berwind fortune.

As far as the Raffetys' financial status is concerned, I already know more than Lowenstein about that. They are very much in need of a financial windfall. Gerard has been fighting leukemia for the past two years, and his wife, Stella, is in the early stages of Alzheimer's. The daughter, Anna, in her third year at the Rhode Island School of Design, has had to leave school and return home because the family cannot afford the round-the-clock home care that has become a necessity. I've seen the police reports of Stella's escapades. By now they would have her fitted up with a GPS, I don't doubt, but their home life is still precarious. For instance, there was that fire when Stella attempted to heat soup for her incapacitated husband.

I didn't have to verify the record of Rose Redford's marriage to Hugh Berwind, because Lowenstein had already done that for me, and all the information was in her computer. But I held off making my report to Swett until I'd confirmed Lowenstein's central theory, the secret adoption of Rose Berwind's baby by the Raffertys. I'd surmised that the adoption records from St. Rita's Refuge, if they had been saved, were probably transferred either into the one building that remained standing, the Chapel of

Roses or, if not there, to St. Rita's church up the road, since the convent was no longer in existence.

Breaking into the chapel was a cinch, and a good guess. Damn dusty place, full of spiders. Must have been hundreds of them, a silvery curtain of the beasts. *Ugh.* I'd covered up carefully the way I usually do, but I still got two bites that continue to itch fearfully; at least a common variety of spider, not deadly like the Northern Black Widow.

Two steel files in the cellar held what was left of the adoption records from the Refuge. Some of the pages were actually singed at the edges. They'd been dumped into the drawers all helter-skelter, but I was able to locate the 1918 folder, and *glory be,* found a handwritten note on Refuge stationery that a girl named Rose Berwind had given birth to a healthy male child, that she had died the same day and the infant was "transferred" privately to the care of Senator Rafferty and his wife. It was signed Sr, Mary Joseph A.A. Those nuns! Nobody could have persuaded one of those officious broads to depart from her routine record-keeping in deference to any great personage, except maybe the Pope.

Although I removed this damning piece of evidence, I did not destroy it. Never know when an original document might come in handy. But I attached a copy to the report I gave to Swett. I included everything I'd learned, *except* that vague mention of DNA—mainly because I can't figure out myself how DNA could be retrieved from the Berwinds at this late date. But I handed the rest to Swett, along with a hefty invoice. Should have demanded hazard pay for those spider bites! Guess I'm just too easy.

As I had anticipated, Swett's got his silk shorts in a twist over this Lowenstein busybody. He wants her prevented from all further interference in the disposition of the Berwind estate by any means necessary. What about the Raffertys? *Maybe*, but Swett seems convinced that the removal of Lowenstein will be sufficient at present. "Whatever it takes," were his last words as he showed me out through the back door to his private study, a concealed little escape hatch he had built into his summer estate in Hingham. The mansion is all new but built to resemble a turn-of-the-century turreted dwelling that Edgar Allan Poe would have appreciated. Just goes to show what a pretentious ass Swett really is.

So there it is—the final solution. And a healthy addition to my off-shore nest egg it will be. But I have to confess, I wish the situation hadn't got this far out of hand. I don't enjoy the prospect, but a gal's got to do what a gal's got to do.

AUGUST 23

Things to Do Today

Jamie: lab results?
To Middlebury: bring fam. tree, photo of inscrip. St. R.;'s chapel, locket, Hugh's case, and copy of handwritten will.
Also, bring something gifty, flowers or cake?
Check plans Norah, Kevin, Moira, and Danny—leave Kev in charge? Or Moira.

This time Olivia insisted on taking the Honda, but she was relieved to have Jamie along, for company and to take a turn at the wheel. It was about as long a day trip as they could drive comfortably; they left at eight to allow four hours, agreeing that they would head home by three at the latest. With Jamie to spell Olivia and pick up their speed, they arrived right on the nose of noon at the Rafferty's place, which turned out to be an old-fashioned Vermont barn converted into a family home.

Anna Gloria Rafferty, olive-skinned, with melting Italian eyes and a lush figure, met Olivia and Jamie at the door and ushered them into the surprisingly contemporary interior with exposed beams, the walls as crowded with art works as an Italian museum. The spacious open area literally took Olivia's breath away, and she could see from Jamie's awed expression, that she was having the same delighted reaction. A balcony encircled the cathedral ceiling and led to bedrooms above the huge first floor which flowed seamlessly from living room to a central kitchen and a dining area that opened to a back garden.

Anna led them into the living room where her parents were ensconced, each on a blue paisley sofa. "Mother…Dad… this is Olivia Lowenstein and her friend, Jamie. My mother, Stella, and my father, Gerry."

"Jamie Finch. Thank you so much, Mrs. Rafferty, for allowing us to visit your amazing home."

"Olivia. And friend Jamie." Mrs. Rafferty, cradled like a papoose in a handmade quilt of many colors, smiled, a lovely smile. She had once been a very beautiful woman, her handsome bone structure and exotic coloring now mirrored in her daughter. Resting on the same couch, nearly encircling the woman protectively, was an alert German Shepherd. The dog eyed the visitors warily.

Gerry Rafferty bounded up and shook hands energetically all around. His faun-like face and curly hair, although solidly gray now, echoed the photos Olivia had seen of his father, Billy Rafferty. "Don't be concerned about Shamus giving you girls the once-over. He's a service dog devoted to watching over my wife, and he takes his job very seriously."

"I can see that," Jamie said. "No sudden moves."

Anna served iced tea in stemmed glasses, and once the preliminaries had been dispensed with, Olivia launched into her speculative tale in more or less chronological order. The locket she had purchased at the first auction, *To Hugh from His Rose.* The marquetry case with its brass plaque, *To my lovely boy Hugh Delano Berwind on his twelfth birthday.* A copy of Hugh and Rose's marriage certificate. The certificate of Rose's death "from complications of childbirth" at St. Rita's Refuge. An article about St. Rita's Refuge as a place where young women without family could give birth, and if they wished, surrender their babies to a better life through adoption. A photo of Rose's grave. A photo of the inscription over the door to the Chapel of Roses. How the priest at the chapel had described the senator's lavish bequest to celebrate the birth of his only child, William Martin, (although Jamie had checked and there were no hospital records of Mabel Rafferty ever having given birth). An article about the Berwind millions and the Swett heirs.

Gerry Rafferty and his daughter listened with attention. Stella gazed out the window and kept smiling. Then while Olivia was in mid-sentence, about to bring out the copy of Hugh's handwritten will, Stella got up and wandered through the kitchen and dining area, out into the garden. Shamus immediately hopped down and followed her.

"It's all right," Anna said softly. "Mom gets restless."

"I see there is a mystery here, but it's hardly been solved yet," Gerry said.

Olivia was just going to explain that there was a slim chance of obtaining DNA from the lock of Rose's hair when Shamus began barking wildly. Gerry Rafferty and his daughter rushed through the garden door, followed by Olivia and Jamie. They found Stella huddled on a teakwood bench while Shamus chased a strange woman down the far garden path. The intruder was wearing a straw hat and a flowered dress, but she ran like an athlete in the home stretch, her paisley handbag flapping at her side.

"Oh, good God, I hope that wasn't one of those Caring Connection people from the church." Anna smiled ruefully and ran after the dog, calling him sharply, while her father sat beside Stella, holding her hand, and speaking to her in a soft, reassuring tone.

"Well, whoever it was, she was moving with enviable speed," Olivia said.

"When last seen." Jamie shaded her eyes with her hand and looked toward the trees where the stranger had disappeared.

"Poor thing. Shamus must have scared her into that amazing sprint."

Jamie did not reply. Her attention caught by something gleaming in the path, she leaned over and picked up a small metal square. Holding it out in her palm, she said, "And what do you suppose this is?"

Anna, who had just returned with the panting Shepherd in tow, examined the item in Jamie's hand. "I've never seen this before. Dad?"

Her dad looked and shook his head. Neither of them made a move to take the object; Jamie slipped it into her pocket.

"What a restful garden you have here. Is that a fish pond?" Jamie moved farther along the path to examine a small pool framed by rocks. "Oh, are those Koi?"

Anna laughed. "No, just ordinary goldfish, the kind that are sold cheap for bigger fish to eat. But if they have a safe, roomy environment, and can winter over, goldfish may become just as vibrant and graceful as Koi."

Shamus positioned himself where Stella could reach his harness and nosed her softly. "Shamus." She said his name, rose from the bench, and followed as he led her back to the sofa in the living room. Everyone followed, and Olivia resumed her story by passing a copy of Hugh's handwritten will to Gerry. While they were reading it, Olivia said she was hoping that some DNA might be obtained from the lock of Rose's hair, although admittedly, it was a slim chance with no follicle attached. She paused, considering what more she could say.

Jamie jumped in. "The thing my friend is not telling you is—do you believe in ghosts?—well, whether you do or not, Olivia has been haunted by two women who apparently cannot rest until Hugh's heir has been made aware of his true family roots."

Olivia looked at her friend in amazement. Was Jamie trying to get them thrown out on their butts?

Unperturbed, Jamie continued: "The money—the stolen inheritance—is secondary. Apparently, ghosts are not into material gain. It's truth and justice they're after."

Gerry looked amused at Olivia's consternation. He relaxed visibly. To his daughter, he said, "Our guests must be getting hungry. Better fire up that grill, dear." Then he went on: "Do these two ghosts have names?"

"You must think I'm crazy. But…yes. One of them is the image of Rose Berwind as she appears in the locket. The other calls herself Nanny Burns. I've seen Rose in my garden. The Burns woman has spoken to us in a séance."

"Let's say I'm giving your story a willing suspension of disbelief. For my own reasons." Gerard Rafferty's smile was not entirely guileless. Olivia realized that he must have an agenda here. This thought was immediately underlined by Anna's reaction.

"A séance!" Anna paused in flipping burgers to clap her hands with delight. "How I wish we could have a séance to bring back your grandmother, Dad, and ask her what the devil she meant."

Olivia and Jamie looked up with avid curiosity, barely masked.

Gerry explained. "That's the real reason I was willing to meet with you to discuss something as personal as my own history. Well, you have to admit, your interest in our family is just a bit outré.

Sorry. But, as it happens, there's a family legend that my father was indeed an adopted child with a mysterious past. Certainly, he was a changeling, if ever there was one, no more suited to the legal and political future that was mapped out for him than a swapped fairy child. A hero and a superb aviator, a beloved poet and teacher, but a complete failure as the heir to carry on Senator Rafferty's legacy. In due time, Grandfather disinherited my father, and they were estranged for the last decades of the old tartar's life. The senator turned then to his nephew Johnny, his sister's boy, to fulfill his dreams of family dynasty."

"I'd be rather glad to find that I'm not related to that tyrant after all," Anna chipped in from the grill. "Almost ready here. Tell them about Great-Grandma."

Gerry smiled at his daughter and continued: "Mabel, my grandmother, felt differently, although forced to hide her devastation at this family rift. But when the senator died, his fortune was all tied up in trust. Although Mabel got a lavish income and lovely homes in which to live for the rest of her life, there was nothing of the senator's fortune that she could bequeath to the son she still adored."

The narrative was interrupted again by Anna, who wanted the whole party to move to an outside picnic area where luncheon awaited them. Anna had arranged the exotic fruits that Olivia brought—Asian pears, persimmons, and pomegranates—as the table's centerpiece.

Shamus deftly guided Stella to the special "peacock" chair where she sat enthroned like a queen; the Shepherd lay at her feet. She looked around the table and smiled brightly. "Hello! My name is Stella. What's yours?"

"I am Olivia, and this is my friend Jamie."

"How do you do." Stella looked down at the table and took up her napkin.

"Mama likes to meet new people." Anna kissed her mother's cheek and poured more tea. Olivia would have killed for a glass of wine, and she didn't doubt that Jamie felt the absence of adult beverages even more keenly.

Gerry continued his narrative as they passed vegetable burgers and salads. "But my grandmother was quietly determined and resourceful. In her will, she left her only son all her 'personal possessions,' which proved to be substantial after all: some very fine jewels the senator had adorned her with over the years, a collection of small Impressionist paintings from her bedroom, most of them birthday gifts, and an extensive private library of first editions, quite valuable. She also bequeathed to Billy her little "nest egg" saved from her various allowances through the years. She'd secretly invested those small sums in quality stocks, and the account topped a hundred thousand at the time of her death. But there was still one more surprise in this will. Mabel had written in her own hand, "I leave everything that is mine to my beloved son, Billy. I could not have loved him more if he were my very own flesh and blood."

Olivia and Jamie looked at each other. Who would have guessed that there'd be confirmation of Olivia's off-the-wall theory from this unimagined quarter?

"Naturally, my Dad was completely shocked," Gerry said, "and none of the family's attorneys could or would shed any light on Mabel's alarming revelation. So Dad hired a private investigator to find out if Mabel had borne a child in 1918 at any hospital in New England, or if she had been attended by any known midwife in that year. She had not."

Before they left that day, much later than they had planned, Gerry readily agreed to provide an inner cheek swab for DNA comparison, in case something could be obtained from the lock of Rose's hair. Jamie took care of that detail with dispatch.

Anna gave them a tour of the Rafferty gallery of art, pointing out her mother's watercolors, which were of extraordinary delicacy.

Once more settled on a blue paisley couch with Shamus, Stella said, with more animation than she had shown all day, "Do you like those? Oh, please do take one!"

"They're exquisite, Mrs. Rafferty. But I wouldn't want to disturb this perfect arrangement."

"Mom no longer paints." Anna's low tone was wistful. Then she pointed out another wall. "The oil portraits and still lifes over there are mine. I was at RISD for three years, but then I was needed here at home. Maybe I'll go back and get my degree later."

"Giving up your senior year must have been hard," Jamie said.

"Family comes first. I love Mom and Dad, and love makes anything easier. And besides—the oncologist believes that Dad is in recession now, so the future is looking better."

~

Olivia and Jamie were way behind schedule when they finally said goodbye to the Raffertys. Olivia called Dave to say she wouldn't be home until nine or so, how was everything?

"A tentative détente is in effect," he said. "Drive carefully, and tell that daredevil friend of yours to keep it under seventy. She hasn't had drinks, has she?"

"Not a drop. The Raffertys appeared to be teetotalling vegetarians."

Jamie, at the wheel, snorted derisively and put her foot down on the gas. "Tell your boss that I'm as sober as a Quaker meeting."

"But we got more than we expected by way of confirmation, honey. I'm over the moon. I'll tell you all about it when I get home. What's Moira making for dinner?"

"Sausage pizzas. She'll save one for you and Jamie."

"Oh, good. What about Norah?"

"Plain cheese. Don't worry. I have the situation well in hand."

A day of exciting disclosures for everyone, and the Raffertys hadn't been at all put out by the notion of ghosts. Olivia congratulated herself on that, and gracefully accepted Jamie's approbation as well.

"Possibly you're not as crazy as I thought," her friend said. "But all that iced tea! Prepare to stop at every gas station."

"Good. Next stop, I'll take the wheel. Dave said to keep it under seventy. "

"Speaking of crazy, what did you make of that woman Shamus chased in the garden?"

"I don't know. Anna thought it might be someone from the church. What was that thing she dropped? You put it in your pocket."

"I looked to me like a Q-bug," Jamie said.

"What's that?"

"World's smallest listening device. Can pick up a whisper at 35 feet. Unlimited range. So I tossed it into the fish pond."

"*Oh, my God!* So...not someone from the Caring Connection, then?"

"Good old Shamus didn't seem to think so," Jamie said. "I sure hope the bitch enjoys listening to the conversation of goldfish."

"How did you know?"

"This investment banker I dated for a while—between husbands—turned out to be a control freak. Set up a little surveillance on me, but I caught on. That Q-bug went down the toilet."

"Sometimes I worry about your taste in boyfriends, Jamie."

"But you admire my defensive instincts?"

"Yes, I'll give you that. You really saved the day back there." Olivia was silent for a few minutes, remembering the bizarre warning she'd received from Mrs. Ritchie's friend.

"Did that woman running out of the garden remind you of Mary Poppins?"

Jamie laughed. "What I could see of her, running for her life. No umbrella though. Are you thinking she might be the same person who broke into your house—twice? Oh, good. We just passed the Massachusetts line. Want to drive for a while?"

"Of course. You don't suppose…"

There was a service area just ahead. Jamie turned into it and pulled up to a self-serve pump before replying. "Yes. You ought to have a tech guy do a bug sweep of your house, just in case. Dave will know someone."

"Dave will be wild if anything is found."

They got out of the car, and Jamie began to fill the tank. "Little did he know when he married you what a life of intrigue and danger awaited him. Will he be angry?"

"Yes, but not at me. Dave never blames me for anything, even when he should."

"Guess you lucked out."

"Yes, and I know it. Want to hit the rest room?"

Jamie groaned. "Yes, of course. I'm swimming in iced tea. Nice family. Very artistic. Extraordinary young woman. Just the kind of people who deserve a financial break. It's not just Dad's cancer. Mom is struggling with Alzheimer's."

"I noticed. So…keep the good thought about that DNA report."

"The Raffertys are going to need a sharp attorney, because the Swetts will surely have a killer team. I'll ask Jack Whelan."

"Thanks, Jamie."

"Oh, that's okay. I'm used to being swept up in your metaphysical missions."

Jamie hung up the gas nozzle, and Olivia took the receipt. They got back in the car with Olivia at the wheel and drove to the fast food court where there were rest rooms.

When they'd returned to the car, Jamie said, "Here's a thought. When you tell Dave all about today's adventures, don't do it in the house. Go outside or take a drive.

"Good point. Although, I think I've had enough driving for today. Sadie said the person who broke in was a woman. Dogs can smell the difference, you know."

"Sadie talks to you?"

"No, she talks to Mrs. Mitchell, and Mrs. M. talks to me."

"Is that so? Okay, then. How many miles to the next martini?"

AUGUST 24

Things to Do Today

Church fair. Kevin dogsit?
Bug sweep today
Jamie: DNA report, when?
Libr. borrow Art of War, *Sun Tzu*

St. Timothy's "Old Home Day" was a sprawling enterprise, half country fair and half carnival, with rides and games of chance run by professionals, alongside competitions for the best apple pie, fruit preserves, and pickles; prize lambs, goats, and rabbits; a book sale in the church's lower floor where classes were held; and an afternoon auction of donated furnishings. Last year the fair had netted the Plymouth church over twenty thousand dollars, and this year was promising to bring in an even greater profit.

Last night, sitting outdoors on the glider, Olivia had told Dave about their surveillance suspicions. A flush of anger had crossed his face at the mere thought of someone skulking around his home—again! He'd banged and thumped around the backyard, swearing roundly and kicking pine cones, but he did not speak crossly to his wife. It was not her fault that someone had a vested interest in her research. Who could have foreseen this hornet's nest?

Dave's loyalty only made her feel guiltier. Jamie had often said that Olivia enjoyed poking a stick into a hornet's nest.

A friend of Dave's, Emil Gorski, from the tech crime unit had agreed to go over the house while they were at the fair. He suggested that they hire someone knowledgeable about spyware to check Olivia's PC as well.

Church fairs were not Olivia's favorite way to spend a summer Saturday, but Dave was determined that his wards should feel themselves as closely connected to St. Timothy's as their father would have wished. Tom O'Hara had been his partner for over a decade, bound by ties of brotherhood that transcended religious beliefs. Although Dave's heritage was Jewish, he was not an observant member of his faith and had readily accepted the role of godfather to Danny, the youngest O'Hara.

Danny was quite thrilled by the races, rides, and other excitements the day offered, and Moira was proud of the cakes she had contributed; she'd even offered to help at the bake sale table. Kevin, at an age when any family activity was unutterably boring, appeared all too pleased to stay home with Norah. They would be needed to keep Sadie and Bruno out of the tech guy's way. Sadie especially was showing a little canine paranoia with strangers these days, a reaction that was especially undesirable in a pit bull terrier. The Lowenstein family knew Sadie was a sweetheart who would never harm a soul and a pushover for a belly rub, but the UPS man and the mail carrier had their doubts.

While Dave and Danny were occupied with shooting ducks for stuffed animal prizes, Olivia wandered away, drawn to the Animal Lovers' booth where a number of personable mutts were being shown off for adoption, sporting colorful neckerchiefs and big doggie smiles. A tall, handsome woman with bronze hair worn in a long braid immediately engaged Olivia in conversation, hoping to find a forever home for one of her charges. Olivia hastily explained that she already had two "rescues" at home, but she just couldn't resist saying "hello" to these cuties. The woman, who introduced herself as Heather Devlin, insisted that there was "always room for one more."

"Devlin"—the name rang a memory bell. It was the same surname as that of her holistic vet. Olivia remembered that Dr. Dick Devlin's wife, heiress of the Plymouth Morgans, was known to be the heart and soul of the no-kill shelter whose booth this was.

Just then, a petite blonde, who'd been sitting at the back of the enclosure sewing, lifted blue eyes from her work and waved. It was the young mother Olivia had met at the Black Hill branch library. *Deidre something.*

"Hello, Olivia Lowenstein! Heather, this is the woman Fiona's been helping with some ancestral research at the library. The one who sees some of the same things I do, *you know*. Did you find the records you were looking for, Olivia?"

Not a discussion that Olivia wished to have in public. "Some of it, thanks. Mrs. Ritchie is amazing." She glanced over to see if Dave and Danny had finished knocking down the ducks yet. Moira had expressed a desire for one of the adorable stuffed bears, preferably the one dressed as a chef.

But as Olivia started to move away, Heather caught hold of her arm, smiling broadly. "Amazing is one word for it. Say, as long as you're here, you may as well pop over to the fortune-telling tent. A friend of ours is reading the Tarot, and she's almost as uncanny as Fiona."

A fortune teller? Oh, please! "Well, to tell the truth, I'm not much into that sort of thing."

Deidre something was practically jumping up and down. "Oh, yes—what a good idea! You must go to Lady Phillipa for a reading! Come along, and I'll introduce you."

She grabbed Olivia's hand as if she were one of the children and headed toward a closed tent at the far end of the carnival midway, her workbag slung over her shoulder. "You'll love this," she assured Olivia. "The reading is only five dollars, and all the money goes to St. Timothy's. Phil does this every year, and it's proved quite popular. Not your average Church carnival attraction, but St. Timothy's doesn't look a gift unicorn in the mouth. Father Matthew says he considers fortune-telling at fairs to be 'all in fun'. Last year the Bishop raised a bit of a fuss, said that such activities were an open door to the demonic influences, but Patty Peacedale, the Presbyterian minister's wife, got her husband Selwyn to have a word with him. Said it would be 'Christian fortune-telling' same as Peacedale sponsors himself at the Gethsemane fair. Have you met Patty? She's helping out at the bake sale. I mean, really—a fair with no fortune teller? Who wants to excommunicate the cash cow? Also, I believe Fiona did a little humming *thing*. Fiona urges us to do good works in the community to improve our image. Ha ha, as if we're all still in danger of being denounced by the Holy Inquisition."

Buoyed onward by this steady stream of chatter, most of which was incomprehensible, Olivia found herself at the door of a tent of many colors. A young couple emerged, looking flushed and pleased. Deidre, although a head shorter, pushed Olivia before her into the candle-lit interior. Cinnamon and sandalwood incense sticks were burning in a small iron cauldron.

"Lady Phillipa," Deidre announced. "I've brought you one of Fiona's protégés who's in need of a reading and some psychic counseling. She's on a quest to unravel a family history, not her own."

Olivia was at that moment upbraiding herself for allowing Deidre to drag her in here, but good manners won, and she sat down opposite the lady behind the crystal ball. *Crystal ball?* Wasn't this supposed to be a Tarot reading?

As if in answer to Olivia's unspoken complaint, Lady Phillipa removed a worn deck of pictorial cards from a red silk drawstring bag and flicked them across the table in a neat line. The Tarot reader had pale skin with winged dark brows, brilliant disturbing eyes, and hair as black as ebony falling straight to her shoulders. A sharp-featured face, but the instant the lady smiled, she became stunningly attractive.

Olivia handed over her five dollars in a daze, and Phillipa swept it into a cash box. She removed the Queen of Wands, pushed the cards into a pack, and directed Olivia to cut them with her left hand, three times into three packs. With the Queen of Wands set at the center, Phillipa swept the three packs into one and began to lay out the cards in a design she called the Celtic Cross, taking them one by one from the top of the deck.

"This card will represent you." Phillipa tapped the queen with a blunt, unpolished nail.

"You don't mind if I stay, do you?" Deidre smiled impishly, revealing two dimples. Not waiting for reply, she curled into a canvas chair in the dark corner. Reaching into her workbag, she took out a small garment and began to sew a seam, almost without looking.

Meanwhile, Phillipa was studying the cards, her chin resting in one hand. "Hmmm. Just look at that," she said.

"Look at what?" Olivia was beginning to feel nervous.

"What's 'above you.' That card is called The Tower."

The card showed a tower being split apart by lightning with a crown toppling and people falling helplessly to the ground below.

"Oh, dear," Deidre whispered from her corner.

Phillipa ignored her and continued. "Let me say first, that a reading is only a ritual for change and growth. It reveals the *possible* future, whose course may be transformed by your own strong intentions or the unexpected influence of a tangential karma."

Olivia sighed. "But the Tower is a danger sign, right?"

"Placed where it is, a shake-up is imminent. The Tower could mean a complete change in your life, or it could be a threat to your home. In this case, I feel it is the latter. And see over here, this young man swinging a weapon? The Page of Swords, reversed, as this one is, suggests that someone is spying on you. And here, the Seven of Swords pictures a person bent on getting away with something valuable. *But...*"

Olivia leaned forward, trying to make sense out of these colorful pieces of cardboard.

"... this other card over here, covering your significator, the Six of Cups, shows helpful spirits from the past guarding you. So many Swords, though—a lot of strife in your immediate future. But here, what's soon to come true, a good Sword, the Knight, a dashing, commanding man to your rescue. It might be your husband, but I don't think so. I believe the Knight is someone from your past, someone about whom you will have mixed feelings. Do you know who that might be? And here, to your home, is the King of Cups. Does your husband have something to do with the law? And this Three of Swords piercing a heart, it's reversed, so that would suggest heartbreak will be averted, but not without a struggle, shown in this Five of Wands.

"Enemies you have, in high and low places, both men and women...but also two strong male figures who will guard you, each in his different way." Phillipa had closed her eyes and looked no more at the Celtic Cross before her. Instead her voice took on an incantatory quality, and she spoke dreamily.

"Not that you are easy to guard. You can be reckless and willful, is that not true? I see that you will be tested in the near future, but you are strong and insightful. Still, it will be necessary for you to trust your own spiritual abilities. As for the eventual outcome, it's The Judgment. Right side up, so in your favor."

Phillipa's eyes opened with an air of surprise. She took a deep breath.

Deidre in the corner clapped her hands. "Super, Phil. Well, trouble, to be sure, Olivia, but now you're aware and can take sensible defensive measures. *Forearmed is forewarned*, as Fiona always says.

Olivia felt that her face had blanched and she might not be in complete command of her voice, so she said nothing.

"Do you have any questions?" Phillipa looked at her closely. "Dee, dear...take out a can of Aranciata from that cooler, will you? I think Olivia needs a sip of something cold and sweet. There are plastic glasses, too."

"One question," Olivia was not proud of herself for asking, but what the hell...she was here, wasn't she? "If I go forward with this matter, will everyone I love be safe?"

"Draw a card from the deck."

Olivia took a sip of the Italian orange soda that Deidre had handed her. She drew the Ten of Pentacles, but another card fell out with it. She tried to slide the second card back, but Phillipa put a hand out to stop her. "This has to count, too," she said. She considered the two cards and smiled.

"The Ten says everyone will be well and happy, even the dogs. You have dogs? Only card in the Ryder deck that pictures family dogs."

Olivia didn't answer. Fortune-tellers tried to elicit information from clients in just this way. The King of Cups was

Dave, of course, but she would not admit that. Still, she felt a sense of relief, even while she berated herself for a fool.

"But this other card, The Moon, is a card of deep secrets, even secret powers. Your own psychic powers will unfold, and you will solve your mystery. But much will still remain hidden. Some things you will never know."

"Maybe I should have stuffed that one back in the deck."

"That's not the way divination works. That extra card flew out of the deck for a reason and therefore must be counted as part of the reading." Phillipa smiled that enigmatic, gorgeous smile that lit up her face—and Olivia's spirits as well.

~

The Lowensteins didn't stay for the auction—but still they left the fair weighed down with purchases. Moira had her Chef Bear (a tribute to Dave's prowess at the shooting gallery) and an armful of old cookbooks. Danny, too, had rummaged through the book sale; he was carrying *Programmer 101, How to Teach Yourself to Write Code,* and *No Bad Dogs,* and a slightly scruffy catcher's mitt from the rummage table. Dave lugged a box containing a set of green leaf side-plates that Olivia had bought, and she carried an apple pie from the bake sale.

Olivia had shaken off the worry brought on by the Tarot reading, and Dave was in a good humor, too—both of them nearly forgetting about Emil Gorski's search. By the time they arrived home, they were tired and merry, stuffed with sausage rolls, funnel cakes, and ice cream. Olivia barely noticed a beat-up Chevy parked on the main road by the marsh. *Some bird-watcher,* she thought. The abundant water bird population was a constant attraction.

But as soon as they got out of Dave's Bronco in the front drive, screams, shouting, and wild barking could be heard from inside the garage (where Dave's art works left no room for parking). He leaned back into the car to grab the remote off the sun visor.

To his credit, Dave put down the box of plates gently on the lawn before opening the garage door and dashing inside. Olivia hastily followed, depositing the apple pie on the porch table. She didn't look back but heard and sensed Moira and Danny dumping their packages and following.

"I knew that dumb blonde would bring trouble," Moira mumbled, as they rushed to see what was causing the commotion, Dave in the lead.

Kevin was at the top of the stairs, holding Norah, who was screaming at her father. Cian Slattery was halfway up the stairs shouting at his daughter, waving a fiddle in midair, and calling her all manner of ugly names that Olivia wished the youngsters weren't hearing. Sadie, upstairs, her big head wedged between Kevin and Norah, growled a low threat. Bruno, at the bottom of the stairs, was barking at Norah's father in a warning manner that prevented him from descending.

"Take the kids out of here." Dave's tone did not leave room for argument. "I'll get this sorted."

Olivia took hold of Bruno's collar and pulled him away. "Moira! Danny! You two, come with me, *right now*." Herding her reluctant charges into the kitchen, she fixed sister and brother with her most no-nonsense gaze. "Stay here with Bruno, and don't go outside until I come for you."

No way was she going to leave Dave alone in the garage with Slattery. She ran back, her heart beating fearfully.

She found Norah's father threatening to smash Norah's fiddle against the wall.

Dave didn't attempt to take the instrument away, although his clenched fists suggested that he would have dearly loved to take action. "If you destroy that valuable instrument, Mr. Slattery, I'll see that your bail is revoked and you're sent back to jail. *Today.*"

"I'd like to know what you're doing with my Norah here," Slattery snarled. "I'll swear out a complaint that you and that gobshite upstairs are using the girl for a skank, if you don't send her home to her da. I know what cops like you are like, pigs!"

"Norah is a ward of the DCF now, and I have their permission to house her until a suitable home can be found. The court has determined that you are not a fit father, and the home you have provided is not suitable or safe."

"I'll kill you, you fucking bastard…" Slattery's eyes were slitted and cold with fury as he started toward Dave, holding up the fiddle as if to break it over his head. Olivia picked up a heavy wrench from the tool bench.

Dave stood and waited, braced to grab Slattery's arm.

But before the men got close enough to swing at each other, Sadie broke through and lunged at Slattery. He cried out and the fiddle went flying into the air. Norah screamed.

With reflexes quicker than she knew she had, Olivia dropped the wrench and leapt forward, catching hold of the instrument before it could crash onto the garage floor.

Using her head like a battering ram, Sadie knocked Slattery down the rest of the stairs. He stumbled, balanced, but fell to his knees when he landed on the concrete floor, crying out in pain. Olivia prayed that nothing was broken.

"You set that damned dog on me, gobshite," he shouted at Kevin. Olivia was not pleased to hear Kevin laugh derisively.

"I'll sue the lot of you. Police brutality!" the injured man screamed. Sadie stood over him, her teeth showing, her growl low, almost soundless. Olivia thought how quickly the big dog could rip out this man's throat. Dave was already reaching to restrain her.

"Uncle Dave didn't touch you, you creep." Moira's voice piped up behind Olivia.

Olivia whirled around, still holding the fiddle as close in her arms as an infant. "Moira! Didn't I tell you to stay in the kitchen!" Then she saw that the girl was holding her cell phone. Moira had been videotaping the whole scene, which rather took the steam out of Olivia's righteous anger.

Dave fixed a strong hand on Sadie's collar. "Moira, you get this dog out of here *right now. And don't come back!* We'll talk about this later."

After Moira hauled Sadie away, tossing a black look at her foster father, Dave reached down to help Slattery to his feet. The man spat at Dave's hand and hauled himself up, painfully, hanging onto the railing for support. He stumbled toward the open garage door.

Before he limped away, Slattery looked back at Dave. "You'll have to pay me, if you want to keep the little slag," he said with an ugly smile. "And it won't be cheap."

Olivia rather wished that Moira was still filming.

No one attempted to stop Slattery as he headed for the Chevy still parked across the road. Exhausted now, the Lowensteins picked up their hastily deposited packages and took them into the kitchen, which smelled deliciously of the pot roast Moira had put into the crock pot that morning.

"That Emil guy left you a note." Moira nodded toward the living room. She and Danny were examining their new/old books at the kitchen table, striving to look uninterested in whatever adult conspiracy was going on. Dave and Olivia hurried to the little maple desk where a bulky sealed envelope was addressed to Dave. He tore it open and tipped the contents onto the desk; a note and two metal objects fell out.

The note said: "Hey, Dave. WTF is going on here? Just the one bug, located behind the headboard of your bed. Some pervert?

Also checked your lady's Honda in the driveway. Magnetic GPS tracker on the back bumper. Everything else downstairs looks clean. But you'd better get Stan the Virus Man to check that computer in her office. You owe me one, buddy. Emil."

Having read the note over his shoulder, Olivia threw herself on the sofa and groaned. It was a commodious sofa of many cushions that embraced her and her troubles with gentle sympathy. She thought she should just stay there and never get up. "Well, here's another nice mess I've gotten you into," she said.

Even in the midst of his consternation, Dave chuckled. "A listening device behind *our bed*?"

"It staggers my mind," Olivia admitted. "But no matter how weird this seems, I don't believe she was after scurrilous stuff. It's this damned Berwind affair."

Dave went into the dining room, then came back with two glasses of Irish whiskey. He sat beside her on the sofa and handed her one. "Tom O'Hara's favorite. I still keep it on hand for emergencies."

"Which this is. And what about that evil Dickensian character, Norah's father?"

"I can handle him. He's on the wrong side of the law, and well he knows it. Why did you say *she*?"

"She?"

"You said '*she* was after.' "

"What if I told you that I've crossed paths with some strange ladies, like the proverbial Wise Women. The one who claimed to be a clairvoyant knew we'd had a break-in, said the intruder was a woman, a Mary Poppins type. Then, when we were visiting the Raffertys, their German Shepherd chased a woman in a straw hat out of the garden. Apparently, she was trying to spy on us with a listening device. A little metal thing she dropped on the path. Jamie picked it up and dumped the thing into a goldfish pond before too much damage was done. She called it a Q-bug. Also, when Mrs. Mitchell had a little talk with Sadie, she said it might have been a woman who broke in."

"Mrs. Mitchell talks with our dog?" Dave sipped thoughtfully and stroked her leg. "You have nice legs. Maybe the first thing about you that caught my attention. You were sitting opposite me on the sofa, and you crossed those long legs."

"I think we should stay on point here, Dave." But Olivia smiled. Then she thought about her Honda, and the smile faded.

"And that bitch has been tailing me!"

"That's the purpose of a GPS pasted to your car, yes. And now I think it's time that you told me the whole story of your involvement with some dangerous people, not the odd bits you've thought you might not alarm me. A Q-bug, was it? Why don't you just start at the beginning."

Olivia sighed. "Why don't we postpone this until later, honey. I think Moira needs me in the kitchen."

Dave laughed. "Moira hasn't needed anyone in the kitchen since she was ten years old. Start talking."

Olivia had the grace to realize this man she loved was entitled to the truth at last. She told him everything, beginning with the locket, the marquetry case, and Rose wafting through the garden. The Berwind inheritance scandal. Her attempts to contact the Swetts. Her epiphany at the Chapel of Roses that led her to Gerard Rafferty and his daughter. The possible DNA match. By the time she'd finished, Moira was calling them to dinner for the third time.

"We'll continue this discussion later. In the privacy of our bedroom, which up until today had not been all that private," Dave said. He kissed her lightly on the forehead, stood, and pulled her up off the sofa. Then he kissed her again, more intently, holding her close, from which Olivia concluded that full disclosure wasn't going to cause a marital rift after all.

"What's the matter with you two?" Moira stood in the living room door with her arms folded across her barely budding chest. The chef's apron tied around her middle hung to her knees. "Didn't you hear me call you?"

Chastened, but still holding hands, Dave and Olivia went into the kitchen. The rest of the family were all in their places at the long oak table. The dogs were clustered around Danny's chair, a position which they calculated would yield the most profit.

"I don't eat meat. Or fish. But I'm not a vegan." Norah passed the platter of pot roast on to Danny.

"Who cares?" Moira said. "Fill up on egg noodles, then. *I'm* not cooking two meals."

Olivia sighed. Moira was a tough cookie, but there was something admirable about her unrelenting fierceness. It would be interesting to see how she turned out, if her bossiness would ever be tempered with diplomacy.

~

Jamie called Monday, on her supper break at Whelan's. "There's good news, and there's bad news."

It was Olivia's turn to cook, according to the schedule she had negotiated with Moira. She was getting ready to broil baby lamb chops to accompany the meatless moussaka she had prepared with Norah in mind. "Lay it on me. Start with the good news."

"Two of Rose's hair strands yielded a limited DNA profile. What there is of it matches Gerard Rafferty's DNA."

"That's very promising, I'd say. And the bad news?"

"My lab guy, who does legal work for a living, says that no way is the match sufficient to establish a direct blood link. Wouldn't stand up in a court of law."

Deep sigh of disappointment. "Well, admittedly, it was a long shot. Maybe if we had other evidence to accompany the report."

"Like what?"

"Proof positive that the senator had adopted Rose's baby. In fact, that alone would do it."

"In your dreams. I do have one other tidbit, though."

"You do? Have you been talking to Jack Whelan?"

"Yes, and the old buzzard just loves to gossip. He says the rift between the senator and his son was common knowledge in the law firm where his uncle Thomas Whelan was a partner. Rafferty, Whelan, Byrne, Foley, and Hines. Uncle Tommy had held forth on the Rafferty scandal one Thanksgiving back in the day when the Whelan family was still getting together for amicable holidays. Jack's brother Geoffrey was not yet the Earl of Ballybane, and Patrick was still a mere parish priest. Then Patrick commented that the senator's son was not a blood relation anyway. Mabel's many novenas in hopes of conceiving had not been blessed by the Lord, and the senator had needed to look elsewhere for an heir, according to Patrick. Not a very priestly observation, Jack said. Uncle Tommy had immediately admonished Patrick to lay off the whiskey."

"Hey, Jamie. That's great work."

"Yeah, I'm getting to be almost as obsessed as you. Not a good sign."

"Just keep Jack talking. Please."

"The family's not close any more. And Tommy Whelan has passed. "

"If the adoption was ever legalized, it must have been the senator's firm that handled it. I wonder…"

MISSY HYDE CONSIDERS A FINAL SOLUTION

All dogs be damned! The Rafferty surveillance did not go well. Should be illegal to harbor an attack monster like that German Shepherd.

Knowing Henry would be pissed if I had no report to give him of Lowenstein's latest gambit, I was forced to invent her conversation with the Raffertys as I was certain it must have gone. She surely told Gerard Rafferty of his real biological parents and encouraged him to pursue his inheritance.

So that's what I told him when Henry and I met at that same Asian restaurant in Somerville the day after my fruitless trip to Vermont. He was livid, of course. Said he depended on me to put a stop to the interfering bitch for good.

Swett literally winced when I told him how much he'd have to pay me for the Lowenstein assignment. The rich are notoriously cheap about paying their help, and Swett is worse than most. Of course I explained that I'll have to get away for a while after I'd done the deed. He'd be on his own. I don't think he really took in all the ramifications of that, too busy fuming over the nuisance of having to deal with Lowenstein. I asked him, what about the Raffertys, but he seemed to think they'd be no threat once Lowenstein was out of the picture. The

Raffertys he would deal with himself, with Weinhardt's usual dirty tricks.

So I've started making my plans. I've already determined that there's a gas range in the kitchen and a gas dryer in the cellar. I could set something up with either appliance, or work directly from the gas meter outside the house. Whatever figures to be best, I'd rather the explosion occurs when Olivia Lowenstein's alone in the house. I'm not a fan of overkill. But I'll make an exception for those friggin' dogs of hers.

I'm too good, that's my trouble. There's a considerable down side, of course, to my soft-heartedness. Lowenstein's husband the State Detective will be left alive and well. And the three juveniles as well. That means the accident has to be completely plausible, the kind of mishap that happens from time to time with gas leaks. Not only must the event itself be above suspicion, but the matter must be concluded ASAP, according to Swett. He has no comprehension of the artistry involved in engineering such an incident.

Luckily, for my line of work, I've always been mechanically inclined, and I rather enjoy a challenge like this. Not as if it's the first time I've fiddled with gas to get rid of a nuisance like Lowenstein. There was a similar busybody in a New Jersey affair. My client that time was a politician with a woman problem. If I were truly unscrupulous, like some I could name, I might have been able to retire on some lucrative sinecure blackmailed out of that sleaze-bag, but I always prefer a lump sum. In cash. It's the cleanest way to do business.

So now I just have to set it all up and wait for the right moment to go boom-boom.

AUGUST 28
Things to Do Today

Market research, catch up!
Libr. return Art of War, *borrow* Native Foods of New England *for Moira*
Call G. Rafferty with update—also, anything in his grandmother's papers?
Wild idea! What if R. threatened to dispute senator's disinheritance?

Olivia at the computer was a lost soul, as intent as if her whole consciousness had departed this realm of flesh and blood for the clean, clear vistas of cyberspace. This was the morning that she was going to concentrate on some timely changes she wanted to make in her portfolio. The day promised to be a peaceful hiatus; Moira and Danny would be at camp for a themed American Indian Day sponsored by Plimoth Plantation. (Moira wanted to study native foods, and Danny fancied himself wearing war paint and waving a tomahawk.) Kevin and Norah had declared their intention to spend the day practicing the Celtic Storm repertoire with Liam and Sean at Sean's house. Sadie was lounging in the master bedroom; Bruno lay at Olivia's feet, snoring lightly.

The stock market was a gratifying arena in which Olivia's practical nature and devotion to detail had proved to be a winning combination—especially now that she'd woken out of her flirtation with options. She tapped and hummed in blissful concentration, sipping a frothy iced coffee from time to time. The big farmhouse, with shades drawn against the August sun, its dark cool rooms scented with new roses and old spices, made Olivia think briefly of an Egyptian queen's tomb. She shook her head and hands to dispel such a whimsical image and picked up a folder of investment notes.

But, in the midst of dismissing that sarcophagal vision, Olivia felt something that broke into her fancies and got her immediate attention—a pinch or a prick in the back of her neck. As she was rubbing the spot—*a bee sting? a pin in the collar of her shirt?*—it seemed that someone was patting her as one would comfort a child. Yet it felt real—not a fleeting impression but a solid hand at her back.

A blast of cold air circled Olivia. The folder she was holding flew from her grasp, and the pages within it fluttered into the air like giant white petals. Jolted from his pleasant nap, Bruno started up and howled in fright. Alerted by Bruno's wail, Sadie jumped off the big bed and rushed into Olivia's office, sniffing the air in a demented fashion. She barked sharply once at Bruno, a direct order. Then both dogs bolted upstairs, Sadie's ears flattened, and Bruno's fur standing up in an odd strip straight down his back.

Olivia thought she heard a soft laugh. *Surely not!*

But the dogs had taken off as if their tails were on fire. At her old house in Scituate, that sort of reaction from Sadie and Bruno had been triggered by an uneasy spirit. Dogs had some senses superior to humans, detecting storms and earthquakes, even epileptic seizures before they happened. The frisson of fear, the unearthly cold that announced the presence of a ghost—dogs felt those vibes acutely. When they sensed a spectral presence, even the most loyal canines would desert their human companions.

So Olivia knew that a supernatural event was really happening right here, right now. A woman's hand *had* patted her back right between the shoulder blades. A woman's laugh *had* followed the undignified flight of the dogs.

The door to the living room swung open on noiseless hinges, beckoning Olivia to follow and investigate. She got up from the desk in a mildly hypnotic state and moved through the door. She imagined that she saw a flash of red just ahead of her.

In the living room, Olivia watched as the front door (the one door that was always kept locked) also eased open. Olivia followed her invisible guide out onto the porch, leaving all the doors open behind her. She looked past her rose garden toward the garage, saw Norah's bike still standing against an outside wall. Hadn't Norah gone with Kevin to practice with their mates? Then the garage's side door slid open as well, a well of darkness. Olivia went down the porch steps, dazzled in the brilliant sunshine. She ducked inside, where the space meant for two cars was filled instead with the impish silhouettes of Dave's wrought iron sculptures. Olivia struggled to adjust her vision to the darkness, to see why the ghost had led her here.

Then she heard Norah's voice. Or rather her cry for help, but half-muffled, as if someone were holding a hand over her mouth. Someone who was upstairs where Norah slept.

Cian, Olivia thought. Quietly, she pulled a baseball bat out of the tub of sports equipment kept in the corner. She tiptoed up the stairs, clutching the bat as if ready for the pitch.

Norah was struggling with a tall, skinny blond man Olivia recognized as her brother Kyle. He was holding one of Norah's arms behind her back; her mouth was covered by his other hand. The boy's shirt Norah liked to wear was ripped open, buttons popped off. With her free hand, she was trying to scratch Kyle's face. He ducked and laughed.

"You dirty little slut," he snarled. "You're giving it away for nothing, aren't you? No more of that, now, *mo rún*. Da wants you home so's you can serve your own dear family like a good girl. *Ouch, you bitch!*" Norah had succeeded in digging a bloody scratch down her brother's left cheek.

Kyle let go of Norah's other hand to put both of his around her throat. Norah screamed.

"Let her go, you damned bully!" Olivia brandished the bat in air.

An ugly sound meant to be laughter emerged from Kyle's mouth. Still holding Norah's throat, he shifted her body around between them as easily as if she were a rag doll.

Olivia put the bat under her arm and used two fingers to whistle. It was a special piercing whistle that Jamie's son Mike had taught her. Then she swung the bat back into striking position.

Norah was struggling but could no longer speak. She brought her knee up against Kyle, but he veered slightly to one side so that the blow fell against his thigh.

Olivia wanted to bring the bat down on his head, but she was afraid of hitting Norah who was now between herself and Kyle, clawing at his hands and struggling to get away.

A dark shadow shot by Olivia, ducked around Norah, and leaped onto Kyle's chest, knocking him back onto the cot with such force that it collapsed on the floor. Sadie stood slavering over Kyle, growling menacingly. Bruno came up right behind her and grabbed Kyle's arm, which was attempting to ward off Sadie.

Freed from her brother's grasp, Norah kicked him in the place she had missed before. With a scream of pain, he rolled into a fetal position, dragging Bruno along.

"That *serves you* right, you bloody bastard!" Norah's voice sounded harsh and hurt after Kyle's rough handling. Still, she reached down and tugged Sadie away by her collar. "Off, Sadie! That's enough, Bruno!"

Olivia let the bat drop, feeling rather foolish to be waving it at nothing.

"Get up and get out of here," she shouted at Kyle Slattery.

"I can't," he moaned.

"*You will*, or I'll have you arrested." Olivia realized right then that her cell phone was still back on her desk. She glanced around for Norah's, and saw that the girl might faint away at any moment. Olivia immediately put her arms around Norah and held her close while Kyle crawled to the door and stumbled down the stairs. A moment later, Olivia heard the sound of a car motor on the marsh road. She wondered if it had been a mistake to let the young man slink away. Well, at least he'd have an aching crotch for his trouble. Norah was no push-over, no matter how weak she might feel after the battle.

~

Olivia helped Norah into yet another boy's shirt—her personal fashion statement that actually accentuated the girl's frail femininity. The bra underneath was rather more substantial than most girls of her slender size would have chosen, those gossamer lacy wisps with their hidden wires.

Kevin had hung a small oval mirror near the door of Norah's room. She looked in it now and fingered her throat.

"I'm afraid your neck will show some bruising," Olivia said. "It's red now but will soon turn purple."

Norah made a face at herself. Then she rummaged around in the trunk that served as her night table and pulled out a red cotton square. This she tied loosely around her neck, cowboy fashion. "I wouldn't want to freak out the kids," she explained.

Looking away, she added softly, "Sure glad you showed up when you did. Thanks, Liv."

In the kitchen, over cups of the hot sweet kava-kava tea that Olivia insisted they drink, she quietly questioned Norah. Why was she at home today? Kevin had said they were both going to Sean Brady's place to practice. Norah said that she'd been feeling tired and restless, and she'd insisted that Kevin go alone. Maybe she'd just needed some space.

Olivia made a mental note to keep an eye on Norah for symptoms of depression that so often go unnoticed in girls. Gently she asked if Norah's brother been abusing her like that at home. Norah said that he'd tried, but she'd made it habit to sleep with a folding "lady knife" under her pillow. "But I felt safe here. I'd left my knife in the desk drawer. Stupid, stupid!"

"Where do you usually keep the knife when it's not under your pillow?" *And especially, where do you keep it when you're at school*, Olivia did not ask. *I wonder if Kevin knows about this?* She leaned down to pat Bruno, who was propped against her leg. Both dogs were under the kitchen table, relaxed but ready. Olivia had praised them and handed out liver treats generously.

"In my boot, if I'm wearing boots. In summer, inside my shirt. Clipped to my bra. It's tricky. I'll show you sometime. Listen, Liv, please don't tell Dave what happened in the garage. I don't think Kyle will try any funny business again. He'll be scared of having his bail revoked."

"Having Kyle's bail revoked would actually be an excellent way to keep you safe. Suppose you did take a swipe at your brother with that knife of yours? You'd be the one in trouble with the law. At the very least, DCF would have you out of here in a flash. Maybe even into youth detention."

"Juvie? That's not happening, Liv. Like, I'd disappear so fast..."

Suddenly the girl's bravado deflated like a pricked balloon, and her blue eyes overflowed with tears. She dashed them away impatiently. "Please, Liv. Kyle is a bastard, but he'd never rat on me. We don't do that. We take care of stuff on our own."

" 'We' meaning the Travellers?"

Norah looked down at her hands, twisting a sodden tissue. "It's the way I was raised. I can't rat on Kyle, either."

Olivia marveled at a code that forbid reporting a physical attack to the law but found such assaults, even including stabbing, a normal way to keep order within the clan. "I'll think about it, Norah. No promises." *What's one more secret kept from Dave?*

"Kevin will put a lock on the door to my room, if I ask him," Norah said.

"He'll be thrilled to be asked. Are you going to tell him about this?"

"*No way*. He'll get all macho, you know, and go after Kyle, and Kyle would hurt him real bad. Kevin would be dead meat."

"Right. Our little secret, then. Good thing that dogs don't talk."

Norah almost smiled. "I had to take a piece of Kyle's sleeve away from Bruno. I put it in the trash. Da makes Kyle wear long sleeves even in summer, to cover his tattoos. He's got a couple of gross Irish Travellers tats. Bad for business, Da says."

Olivia realized that Norah was being almost chatty after their shared ordeal. This was the first time the girl had offered anything more than monosyllabic replies to repeated questions. *Gladys Piffin would be proud.*

NANNY BURNS LENDS A HAND

It takes a strong spirit to pierce the Veil that separates us from those on the Other Side. But then, I've never been one who lacked moral fiber. Being a proper nanny is not for the faint of heart, I don't mind telling you. When I pull on my red stockings in the morning, I know I'll be able to soldier on through any crisis. And then there's my hat pin, too, of course, if a quick jab to the conscience is needed.

It's the nanny's duty to instill civilized values into the children in her charge, especially when their mama preoccupies herself with good works and political causes. My darling boy, Hugh, was always such a credit to my schooling in the nursery, but I have to admit that I failed miserably with George. That's the real reason why I'm still hovering around here, instead of rocking away on the Porch of All Sunsets.

"But why me?" I can hear you wondering. Because you're a natural channel, dearie, and I credit myself with finding you. It was no accident that you just happened to buy Rose's locket and Hugh's "treasure box." Anya Bharata might call that karma, but I believe you were guided to the tragic story of Hugh and Rose. Injustice is like a wrinkle in the fabric of the Universe that sensitive souls like you just can't resist smoothing out.

Olivia is such a nice ladylike name. I have high hopes that you'll keep following my little nudges. The Guardians are warning me not to dilly-dally too long, but I simply can't ascend to a Higher Plane until the wrongs of the past are made right. And Rose, too. She's out there somewhere, and she's not likely to rest until everything is in order again. I've got my work cut out for me there.

And you've got your own hands full, dearie, raising a houseful of Irish children. I'm Irish myself, so I know how unruly those young ones can be. That handsome husband of yours may think he's the guiding influence, but it's always the woman in the home who's in charge. So I really had to give you a warning when that tinker's girl was getting grief from her ruffian brother.

It was like trying to reach through a brick wall, but I managed to touch you at last—to alert you to danger and then to pat your back, the way I've always done with my charges. Comfort and encouragement to do the right thing. Then, just in case they don't get my meaning, a bit of a push in the correct direction.

Open the right doors, and your good intentions will walk right through—that's what I always say.

AUGUST 29

Things to Do Today

Call G. Rafferty today!
  Mabel's papers
  Hines' files
Chk with Dave: Slattery trial date? Likely sentence?
Lock for Norah's room – lend Sadie?
Poss. Black Hill libr.—consult Mrs. R. again?

The aftermath of Kyle's attack had left both Norah and Olivia exhausted. Sensing that the girl, usually a loner, needed the company of an understanding friend, at least for a while, Olivia made them both a light lunch—Greek salad with feta and a side of flatbread cut into thin wedges—which Norah merely picked at. Then, as afternoon began to shade the front of the house, Olivia suggested that Norah help her deadhead the roses; the late summer heat had left them quite dilapidated.

Olivia almost prayed (although she didn't believe in prayer) that no gossamer girl ghost would waft through the bushes—there'd been quite enough shocks to their systems for one day—as she and Norah worked together in comfortable silence.

When Kevin returned on his bike around four, with no clue to the scene that had occurred in his absence, he dragged Norah away to join him for a snack in the kitchen. Olivia had no worry that a sandwich or two would spoil his dinner; there seemed to be no limit to the amount of food he could put away and still remain skinny. Maybe all those calories were going directly to his height; he was almost as tall as Dave now and still growing fast.

Later, Olivia could hear a lilting duet of Irish folk tunes through the open garage window. Norah carried Kevin along in their violin duet, but he was improving at last. Freed from worry about Norah's mental state—music was surely the best of medicines—it seemed a good time to call the Raffertys with her latest brainstorm.

Anna answered the land line number. Her dad was recovering from his latest chemo treatment—they were given a few weeks apart—and was not well enough to talk about the matters they'd discussed, which were stressful to him, Anna said.

"I've had an idea of how we might proceed," Olivia said. But she wondered if that "we" were presumptuous. She was, after all, an intruder into the Rafferty saga. "Something that might establish your dad as an heir to the Berwind legacy. Though I have to warn you that the Swetts would bring out all their legal resources to block any claim."

"Why don't you tell me about it," Anna suggested. "We're at our wits' end here. I mean, the financial picture is pretty bleak. We've even talked about selling the barn, but I'm afraid that would be totally upsetting to Mother. You know our situation."

Olivia thought that "the barn" hardly described the unique Rafferty home, so beautifully designed by that artistic family. "My idea is in two parts. First part: is there any chance that your great-grandmother's personal papers might contain a reference to your grandfather's true parentage? Have you been through everything?"

"All Mabel Rafferty's personal property—anything that wasn't tied to the Rafferty trust for John J. Hines—she left to Grandfather Billy. Mabel always felt he'd been greatly wronged by the trust. The jewelry, the first editions, and such he sold piecemeal over the years as money was needed beyond what his tenure at Middlebury College and pitiful poetry royalties provided. But I believe there were personal papers, letters, diaries, and so forth. I don't know if anyone actually read every scrap."

"What do you think became of all that?" Olivia asked.

"Good question. I'll ask Dad. My guess is that anything left over, having no value for sale, may have been stashed in our attic. Well, we call it the 'attic,' but it's just a big storage closet upstairs. There used to be several boxes all taped up, marked with Mabel's name. I think they may still be there. I'm afraid our family has always been a bunch of pack rats. Dad never throws anything away. He says clutter is the fertile bed of creativity."

"That sounds promising. Do you think you might have a look?"

"I'll do more than have a look," Anna assured her. "If those are Mabel's personal papers, I'll read every damned one. What's the second part?"

"That's the more questionable idea. Am I right in believing that your grandfather never brought suit against the trust that effectively disinherited him?"

"No, he didn't. I think Granddad may have felt too hurt by the senator's inability to accept his literary vocation. Poetry would have been okay with the senator as a hobby, although perhaps a bit too feminine, not macho enough, but Granddad was still expected to follow the family traditions, to excel in law and politics. But Granddad's experiences in the war had utterly changed him. He meant to have an authentic life, his own life. And he'd met the woman he loved and wanted to marry, my grandmother Jenny, who was not socially acceptable to the senator. So Dad just let go of his Rafferty prospects and did his own thing."

"It's ironic that your grandfather had somehow been disinherited from two different family fortunes," Olivia said.

"*Artisti e musicisti sono sempre ai piedi di Cristo*," Anna said. "My mother used to quote that. Artists and musicians are always at the feet of Christ. Meaning so poor and needy that they were dependent on the intervention of Heaven. I think I may be the most practical member of this family. So, is Dad going after Hines your second idea?"

"If your father were to bring suit against the trust, claiming that the senator's own son, your grandfather, ought to have had a share, it's likely that the relative who benefited, Hines, would just love to prove that Billy Rafferty was neither a blood relation nor legally adopted. If there's any such proof at the firm of Rafferty, Whelan, Byrne, Foley, and Hines, I bet John J. would be moved to find it."

"Interesting..." Anna mused. "Only John J. died in 2000. His son, Dwight R. Hines, however, is still an active partner at the firm. Not being adopted, however, is merely a negative. What we would need is some proof positive."

"I forget sometimes how long ago all this happened," Olivia said. "Everyone's dead and gone. But my career has been in records management, so I can tell you that well-kept records are forever. Think of the Egyptian hieroglyphics listing shipments of grain that were bought and sold B.C.E. Who knows what may still lurk in the archives of Rafferty, Whelan *et al*? If we're lucky, a link to Rose Berwind, even a birth certificate."

"We should be so lucky," Anna said. "Seems like a lot of trouble for Dad. I'm not so sure he's up to pursuing a long shot like that."

"Of course, Anna," Olivia said. "I understand completely. I admit to getting some wild ideas from time to time."

"I would wonder at your continuing interest, but it's the ghost, isn't it? The one your friend Jamie mentioned."

Olivia sighed. "A ghost hangs around for a reason. My experience has been that they don't give up easily. Or at all."

Anna promised to give Olivia's proposition some thought. And definitely she would go through Mabel's boxes in the storage closet.

After their phone conversation, Olivia reflected that Anna Gloria Rafferty was quite an estimable young woman, gifted with qualities of curiosity, guts, and determination.

Later, Jamie pointed out to her that Olivia herself fit that description pretty well

~

Olivia had meant to get back to the Black Hill Branch Library, just to see what Mrs. Ritchie might have to suggest now that more of the Berwind story had been discovered. But the last days of August brought a flurry of activity that Olivia, being inexperienced at this family thing, hadn't expected. It was called Getting Ready for School. Fussy Moira and disinterested Danny, having shot up out of their clothes through the summer, now had to be outfitted in suitable and fashionable attire. Having no idea what that might be, Olivia would have to rely on Moira's input. As Olivia saw it, her role was simply to proffer charge cards and veto anything unsuitable or outrageous.

Just at this delicate, busy time, Dave and his friend at DCF had finally located a foster home for Norah of which they both approved, and it was necessary to get her settled, too, before Labor Day. Norah's mother's cousin, Emma Toogood, a woman in her sixties, living alone, would be pleased to share her home in exchange for a little help around the house as increasing vision problems made it difficult to maintain her independence. Cousin Toogood was not a fan of the Travellers, although her own roots were there, and she admired any young person who had the pluck to escape their clannish life.

Norah, however, was reluctant to move away from the safety the Lowenstein home represented. In fact "Shit, shit, no way!" had been her first reaction. But Norah came around to accepting the situation when she learned that she would be driving Emma Toogood's ancient Town Car, and that her mother's cousin was herself a musician who gave piano lessons to supplement her slim income (a pension from her employment in the Norwell Public Schools and her Social Security allotment).

Yet, somehow Olivia felt as if they were setting the frail teenager adrift again. "Your loft room will always be there. If you want to come by for a visit some weekend, we'd all love to see you."

Norah smiled wanly. The unapproachable barrier appeared to be down a bit, so Olivia took the opportunity to give her big warm hug.

Kevin was disconsolate, but on Saturday morning, Norah stoically packed up her few belongings and stashed them into Dave's Bronco for the move to Emma Toogood's little house in Norwell, a two-story, L-shaped dwelling built in the Depression years.

"Hey, dude, it'll soon be too cold for that outdoor shower," she reminded Kevin. "Of course, now I'll be in a different school from you, but Emma promised I can use the Town Car to meet with you guys for Celtic Storm gigs. So that's good. And don't give up the fiddle, Kev. I'll be checking on that."

Then Norah jumped in the Bronco with a little wave. She turned her gaze away as Dave backed out of the driveway.

"Good riddance," Moira muttered. "Now maybe Kev will get his head screwed on right."

"With that the loft space all cleaned up and habitable, you might like to have slumber parties with your girlfriends up there," Olivia suggested to Moira.

Moira's look was utterly scornful. "I don't have *girlfriends,* Liv," she declared in a tone she might have used to disavow nits. "And Danny only has Vinny, because Vinny doesn't have friends either. The Tornitores, you know." Moira raised an eyebrow in a world-weary way that suggested she was all too familiar with the Tornitore family's reputation of being "connected."

"I liked Norah," Danny said. "She didn't say much, though. But Kevin wasn't so mean when she was around."

Not only didn't she say much, Norah seemed to be a girl who left no trace of herself when she moved along. The garage bedroom was clear of any evidence of its occupant, not even a lingering scent. Olivia wondered how such a cool, enigmatic girl had taken hold of Kevin's heart and mind. *A glimmering girl*, she thought.

She questioned Dave about Kevin's crush when they were alone later in the afternoon. "Raging hormones, characteristic of the male teen," was his opinion. "You find Norah reserved and remote, but you're not sensitive to the clues that are arousing Kevin. And then there's her music, of course. Plenty of passion and energy in that fiddle. Obviously, the girl has learned to wear a series of protective masks—think of that abusive bunch she lived with!—and Kevin sees through to the vulnerable girl underneath them. You wore a few masks yourself, back in the day, but they never fooled me, either." The subject seemed to inspire Dave to pull Olivia close and breathe deeply of her neck. He pushed the bedroom door closed.

"Where is everybody?" she asked—wondering, why do men think *the moment's right* when it's so obviously not.

"Danny's upstairs with Vinny playing Diablo III. Moira's doing something with pastry in the kitchen and swearing like a sailor. I guess it's not going well." Dave was pushing her gently back toward the bed.

"And Sadie?"

"Under the kitchen table. She likes raw dough."

"You seem to have thought of everything."

"I try to be alert to opportunity," Dave said.

Olivia heard a short, sharp knock that seemed to come from a space near but not on the wall. "That wasn't opportunity knocking," Olivia said. "*Ghosts, begone!*"

"Relax. It's just the house settling. It's an old house, you know."

"Problem is, I promised Moira and Danny we'd go to Staples for notebooks and things," Olivia reminded him, pushing away. "But maybe opportunity will knock later tonight."

School started on Wednesday the 4th. On the morning of the 5th, Olivia breathed a quiet sigh of liberation as she finished stacking the dishwasher. It was only ten, the whole day stretched before her, full of items of interest to tick off her list. The crisp air, the mellow sunlight, punctuated here and there by a branch of flaming leaves, the chatter of birds massing for the long flight south, even the sweet smell of marsh decay, all called her to be up and out on her own. She closed the dogs in the house with consolation biscuits and headed to Black Hill for a chat with that redoubtable librarian.

This visit was not quite as charmed as the last two; there was a meeting of the quilting society going on downstairs, and the parking lot was full. Upstairs, on the library level, two little girls were sitting on cushions in the children's nook, one of them reading aloud. The other little girl held the resident cat in her lap. Even Omar seemed to be listening to *Goodnight, Moon.*

Mrs. Ritchie greeted Olivia warmly. "I've often wondered about you, my dear. I'm so eager to hear the progress of your research." With the many silver bangles she wore tinkling softly, she indicated the youngsters in the corner. "That's my grandniece. Laura Belle, and Annie Ryan, Deidre's youngest. She reading already, isn't that amazing? Preschool doesn't begin until Monday." Mrs. Ritchie gazed fondly at the charming picture, humming a little to herself. "Shall we have tea?"

Over steaming mugs of lapsang souchong, they settled themselves at Mrs. Ritchie's golden oak desk in the two rolling armchairs. Olivia filled in Mrs. Ritchie on her epiphany at St. Rita's Chapel of Roses that led to her meeting with the Raffertys, the Raffertys' own suspicions that Billy Rafferty had been adopted, the appearance of a straw-hatted woman of evil intent in their garden, the possibility of establishing the Berwind connection at last.

"Gerry Rafferty is Hugh and Rose Berwind's grandson, so I believe. His father, Billy, the Berwind infant given to the Raffertys, was disinherited twice, can you imagine? And the family is in such dire straits, with all their medical challenges. They're even talking about selling their home, a gorgeous restored barn full of Stella's and Anna's art work. I must do something." Olivia felt better just looking into Mrs. Ritchie's kindly gray eyes. Even if the librarian was a wee bit eccentric. Right now, for instance, there were two colored pens (blue and red), a candy-striped stylus, and a pencil topped with a tiny Greek flag stuck into her coronet of braids. They formed a fan like the *pieneta* worn by a Flamenco dancer in her hair.

"I'm concerned about the straw-hatted stranger." Mrs. Ritchie gazed into the middle distance with a tiny frown. "When the ladies and I meet next—the September Esbat, what could be better!—I'll put in a good spell for you. Bane and Baffle, I think."

"Good spell?" Olivia said weakly. "Bane and Baffle?"

"Oh, dearie me. Did I say good spell? I meant a godspell, gospel, of course. Bane and Baffle is like a prayer, really. Don't you worry your pretty head over that."

Olivia was inches taller than Mrs. Ritchie, with the smoothly-toned arms of a long-distance swimmer and strong Athenian features. No one ever really called her "pretty," although Dave often told her that she was beautiful. It was rather heart-warming to be referred to in the diminutive. But totally wrong. Olivia's "pretty head" never shied away from worry over the details.

"Exactly what sort of prayer is Bane and Baffle?"

"It's something like asking the Creator to send that pesky cloud of locusts elsewhere, or the hopping army of frogs, or whatever is plaguing you. Would you like to join us at the Esbat? We do a little dancing, you know, to get our energy going, and then *whoosh!* We release our good prayers right up to the full moon. And Whoever else is Up There. Then we have cakes and ale. Well, not really *cakes and ale*, that's just the old phrase for a merry after-party. Which will be whatever Phil rustles up for us. She's our culinary genius, you know. And the Tarot, too."

Sometimes when Mrs. Ritchie tried to clear matters up, they only became more opaque. *Baffle, indeed*, Olivia thought. Suddenly, the word Tarot resonated in Olivia's brain. "Is Phil by any chance the lady who read fortunes at St. Timothy's Old Home Day fair? The one who looks like the Wicked Queen in Snow White?"

Mrs. Ritchie chuckled. "Yes, she mentioned that Dee had brought you into her tent for a reading. All of us—me and the other ladies—have a sense that there are strong unseen forces circling around you."

"You keep saying 'we', Mrs. Ritchie. How many 'ladies' are in your…uh…club?"

"Five. It's a circle of five, dear. Those unseen forces, now—there are good spirits urging you to right the wrongs of the past, which is usually an impossible quest, but others are malevolent and wish to prevent your intrusion. *Caught between the deep blue sea and the devil.*" Scylla and Charybdis."

Olivia, who knew her Greek mythology, was pleased to recognize the reference. "Sounds about right. How do you suggest I proceed?"

"What you want is proof that Billy Rafferty was, in fact, Rose Berwind's son, given in adoption after her untimely death." Mrs. Ritchie swiveled around to her computer and idly pecked at a few keys. "And no files on earth are locked as securely as Catholic adoption records." She swiveled back and looked directed into Olivia's eyes. "We can do a Finding. At the Esbat. Meanwhile, do you have any protective amulets?"

"As a matter of fact, I do have a bear fetish, a gift from a local shaman," Olivia admitted, feeling more than a little foolish. And yet, that very smooth little sculpture was at this very moment in the pocket of her slacks. It fit in her hand so smoothly, like a lucky coin.

Mrs. Ritchie smiled. "I'm glad you keep Bear close by. Bear is a powerful protector. And when the full moon rises next week, look for some new information coming to light."

"Good research isn't magic, you know," Olivia objected without much conviction. "Isn't there any help you can give me today. Just a clue to follow."

"Google is a wonder, but it's not, alas, the Oracle at Delphi." As Mrs. Ritchie turned back to her computer, the tiny flag in the swizzle stick seemed to wave. She tapped a few keys. "Did you tell me that your séance summoned the spirit of a nanny?"

"Yes. It seemed that she had the care of the two Berwind boys, Hugh and George. I don't know her name, though."

"Mary Margaret Burns," Mrs. Ritchie said.

"How ever did you…?"

"Census, 1938. Listed all the residents of the Berwind mansion in New York, including staff." Mrs. Ritchie kept clicking. "I'm looking at her obituary. Mentions her beloved sister, Sister Mary Joseph."

"Oh, yes, of course." Olivia told Mrs. Ritchie about the traveling Holy Mass card.

"Perhaps Sister Mary Joseph knew something about Rose Berwind. Let's see what our Finding turns up." Mrs. Ritchie swiveled back toward Olivia.

Olivia had at least a dozen more questions, starting with *What the hell is a Finding?* But the little girls, Laura Belle and Annie, the dark and the fair, had finished their story hour and were leaning on Mrs. Ritchie's lap, demanding juice and crackers. Even Omar curled around her ankles insistently. Olivia made her farewells and left the library, vaguely unsatisfied. It seemed as if Mrs. Ritchie had been very little help indeed.

Still, when Olivia got home and let the dogs out for their joyous sprint around the backyard, she glanced at the kitchen calendar. The Harvest Moon, the next full moon, would appear on September 19. Mrs. Ritchie's ladies' club would be meeting to do whatever it was they did by the light of the moon. No matter the source, Olivia would be glad for any information proving that the Berwind infant had been adopted by the Raffertys.

SEPTEMBER 12

Things to Do Today

Lunch with Jamie tomorrow—catch up!
Libr. return Native Foods & A Skeptic's Guide to Ghosts, *pay fine!*
borrow The Bear in Myth and Legend
Check with Anna—anything in Mabel's stuff?
Submit paper Paleography course

Jamie had no more Rafferty gossip to impart to Olivia, but she did have a tidbit about the Swetts.

The Hon. Robyn Gamble, daughter of Lady Jane Gamble, *nee* Swett, had been a guest on the same luxurious private yacht owned by the Wittgenstein family as Jack Whelan's adored grandniece, Harper Whelan, for a summer tour of the Greek Islands. Both girls were in their gorgeous young twenties and cordially despised one another. Harper, who ran in and out of her granduncle's house ("keeping tabs on her inheritance" Jamie said), had regaled her granduncle with vignettes of her cruise. Among them, that the Hon. Robyn claimed her uncle Henry III kept a hit woman in his employ who looked like Mary Poppins.

"Does that sound like the intruder in the Raffertys' garden, or what?" Jamie speared an olive in her perfect martini, and ate it in one bite. "Too bad Shamus didn't have her for lunch."

"Seven degrees of separation!" Olivia declared.

"I'm sorry? Isn't that the name of a movie?"

"Yes, but principally, it's the theory that everyone is only seven or fewer steps away, by way of introduction, from any other person in the world."

"I wonder, then, how near I am to getting an introduction to Colin Firth?" Jamie gazed at the waves off Cedar Point dreamily.

Olivia was not amused. She, too, was staring at the waves, in the cold realization that the person who'd been breaking in to their home was capable of much more than simple surveillance. "Mary Poppins" was a known hit woman. "Oh, God. I'll have to tell Dave. And he's going to be so pissed."

"The Hon. Robyn was royally drunk, so Harper said. She probably exaggerated the hit-woman part for attention. And, besides, you had to suspect that the mean, nasty Henry, who starved his great-aunt for her millions, must have been behind all this strange stuff that's been happening."

"Yes, but sometimes you don't want to know the truth," Olivia said.

"Tell Dave. You'll feel better. The best thing about men is that they're bigger and stronger and insist on standing in front of you when the bullets fly."

"You're a real comfort, Jamie."

Before she could call Anna, the girl called Olivia. "I'm going through every scrap of Great-Grandma Mabel's papers. Rather an interesting project, looking into the lifetime of a direct relative I never knew. No diary, unfortunately, but lots of letters, still in their envelopes. The most relevant from a friend, Beth Hadley, she'd known since they'd been roommates at Mount Holyoke, class of 1902."

Olivia perked up instantly. "Anything about Mabel's son?"

"I'm getting to that. The correspondence continued through the years, less often later. One of the letters referred to Beth's having been a bridesmaid at Mabel's marriage to the senator in 1907. Beth had met a handsome cavalry officer at the wedding, who was calling on her—girl stuff. You know. But in some of the letters after that, she replied to Mabel's concern when she failed to get pregnant. Suggested that it might not be Mabel's fault, would her husband consult a physician?"

"I bet he didn't."

"No further mention of that plan, so probably you're right. But Mabel did consult several specialists herself, who found nothing wrong with her. She also talked to her priest, who recommended a course of novenas of the Holy Rosary dedicated to the Blessed Virgin Mary. Beth favored medical intervention over prayer. I got to like Beth through her letters. Sensible girl. Married her cavalry officer, moved to Austin, Texas, and got pregnant right off the bat."

"Poor Mabel. That must have been a lot to bear."

"Yes, no letters for three more years. Around 1915, Beth wrote to say, enigmatically, that she wished with all her heart that Mabel's new hope would bear fruit. If it would help, Beth would say a novena as well, though she wasn't even a Catholic."

"I think that must have been the plan to adopt, don't you, Anna?"

"I do, definitely, but that word was never mentioned. So far. I still have one more shoe box-full to go. And some photos, maps, charts, and things, possibly grand tours to Europe and what not. But how about you? Any joy yet?"

"What's happening at this end is so incredible that I don't even want to explain. I can tell you more after the full moon."

"*The full moon!* Are you going in for spectral evidence now?"

"I hope you can hold out—financially, that is—until we do get some answers." Olivia was reluctant to explain how deeply she'd strayed from the path of reason to this levelheaded young woman. "And if we do get some evidence, do you have an attorney lined up?"

"I do, and you will absolutely love her. Sonia Perlmutter. She's retired now, but she's always been Dad's lawyer, for wills and stuff. Sonia loves a challenge, so I think we can tempt her away from her farm. She was the chief litigator in several high profile feminist cases."

"That's good, because Swett's attorney is Gretchen Weinhardt."

"The name sounds familiar."

"That's because her clients are usually the super-rich and ruthless."

"Sonia, on the other hand, made her reputation by championing their victims."

"This should be really interesting," Olivia said. But she felt as if she were falling into some awfully deep waters.

The full moon appeared on the 16th. Gazing into the majestic Harvest Moon rising from deep gold to silver over the marshes, Olivia wondered if Mrs. Ritchie and her ladies would actually turn up any new information through their "Finding." But she didn't take time to visit the Black Hill branch library. She was occupied with catching up on her online course in Paleography. Reading Old Handwriting 1500 to 1850, from the University of London, Institute of Historical Research, which proved to be right up Olivia's alley. Perhaps with this new training, she might look forward to working for a museum or college library. Meanwhile, she would keep the good thought.

~

School had been in session for three weeks, the quiet days continuing to bless Olivia with blissful peace, when Norah returned for the weekend. Emma Toogood had gone to Bar Harbor with a friend, another retired teacher, who took over the driving of Emma's Town Car. Norah was nervous about staying alone, for fear the Slatterys had found out where she was living now and would badger her to steal from the old lady. She'd cadged a ride from Sean Brady, part of the Celtic Storm band, in his Chevy truck. His parents, both attorneys who specialized in malpractice suits, had little time but plenty of money to spend on their son.

Unfortunately for Kevin, Dave had planned their regular monthly trip to Danbury for Saturday, and insisted that he go along. Tensions were just beginning to ease between Kevin and his mother, Alice, and Dave didn't want any backsliding. They left early in the morning and planned to be home by six.

Olivia had made an appointment to take Sadie and Bruno to Happy Tails for a grooming session. Happy Tails had emailed an appointment reminder the previous day. When she arrived with the dogs after lunch, the receptionist asked if she wanted them to continue emailing reminders to two email addresses. But Bruno had chosen that very moment to dig in his claws and refuse to be led into the grooming suite, so Olivia was too distracted to question this. She just waved her assent and continued to drag Bruno across the waiting room floor. "Don't embarrass me," she muttered.

Norah had said she'd be fine alone for a few hours in the one place where she felt safe. Danny had loaned her a laptop, and she was going to work on an essay for English Comp and maybe practice her music as well.

"Don't be such a jerk," she'd admonished the brooding Kevin. "She's your mother, no matter how she's got herself banged up with the Feds. I'll still be here tonight and tomorrow. You can show me how you're getting on with the fiddle."

~

Norah was alone in her citadel, clicking through various sources in Google on the history of Irish folk music for her essay, when something at the corner of her consciousness impelled her to look out the garage window. A stranger, a woman, was moving around the house toward the backyard. She looked like a nice enough old broad wearing a straw hat that shaded her face and pink sneakers, yet there was something furtive about the way she moved from one tree shadow to another. It made the back of Norah's neck prickle. Granny would have called that "someone dancing on your grave, girlie." Grannie had been a respected sorceress, and everyone in the family had paid attention to her pronouncements, even Da. Norah paid attention now.

The garage windows faced front to the street and the marsh, and back to the pines, with no good view of the kitchen yard. Norah lost sight of the woman when she moved farther in the direction of the kitchen door. The alarm wasn't even engaged, so that Norah could get into the house to use the facilities. Just in case something funny was going on, Norah decided to slip out the side door of the garage and duck into the house from the dining room side.

In Norah's world, unexpected company was unwelcome, either someone looking for a handout or bringing news you didn't want to hear. Possibly some kind of Bible-thumping Jehovah's Witness, although didn't they usually travel in pairs? She wished Sadie was here, or even Bruno, but she was on her own. Norah moved through the downstairs to the kitchen, peeked out window, and there she was! Some kind of tool in her hand. She was *poking around the gas meter!* And she sure as shit wasn't any kind of gas company employee. The woman seemed to be trying to attach something to the wire that wrapped around the meter. The bitch was up to something all right.

Norah opened the back door and stepped out. "Hey, lady. What the fuck do you think you're doing there?"

That was one surprised woman! She looked at Norah straight on and attempted a reassuring smile, the kind of smile the girl had seen on a number of social workers, none of them meaning her well. Obviously the woman had thought no one was at home, which might have been true if Emma Toogood hadn't picked this weekend to tool around Bar Harbor with her teacher pal.

Still smiling, the woman walked toward her. "Good morning, dear..."

Norah put her hand on the knife in its hidden sheath fixed to her bra.

The woman reached into the paisley handbag over her arm. Norah whipped out her knife and opened it with one fluid motion, holding it underhand in a defensive position.

That was the last thing she remembered.

When Olivia was nearly home with her two neatly groomed, sweet-smelling dogs, Sadie began to fuss and howl. Sadie and especially Bruno loved a car ride—this sort of behavior was very strange indeed. Perhaps some kind of gastrointestinal emergency, Olivia decided. But they were almost home; she hoped Sadie could hold it a few minutes longer.

As soon as she stopped the car in the driveway and opened the back door, both dogs made a bee line for the backyard, quickly outdistancing Olivia. She heard Sadie howling plaintively before she saw Norah lying near the back door. As she knelt down beside the unconscious girl, Olivia's hand was on her iPhone to call 911. But she stopped for a moment when the girl began to rouse. Her eyes fluttered open and she groaned. It was then that Olivia noticed Norah's knife lying nearby. It had been opened, the blade small but sharp and efficient. This was very strange.

"What happened, Norah. Did you fall? Are you ill? I'm calling 911, just lie still."

"That bitch," Norah moaned. "Tasered me."

"*Tasered* you? Bitch? What went on here, Norah?" Olivia felt a cold clutch of fear.

"Not 911. Call Dave," Norah whispered with great difficulty. She began to sit up. Olivia put her arms around the girl to help hold her back and neck straight. "Call Dave!" she said again, this time with stronger urgency.

Sadie was rushing around the yard after some disturbing scent, with Bruno following, uttering occasional sharp barks.

"You need a doctor, Norah." But her finger had already moved to Dave's number, and his phone was ringing. She began talking the moment he said hello in the pleased tone that always greeted her calls. "Dave, something strange just happened here at the house. I found Norah lying in the backyard. She says some woman tasered her. And Sadie is acting oddly, like she did before. When we had that break-in."

"Are you sure she said 'tasered? Jesus! I'll be there as soon as I can. We're way the hell up near Braintree, so I'm going to send the nearest cruiser, and a rescue wagon. Are *you* all right?"

Olivia assured him that she was fine. In fact, she felt the knot in her chest loosening a bit, just knowing Dave would soon be here to take over. "Help is on the way," she told Norah, and it was only a matter of minutes until they heard the sirens.

The two responding officers, a beefy older man and a dark-skinned young woman, having been briefed by Dave about the attack, insisted on searching the house and grounds, but the excited dogs were in defense mode. Olivia had to shove them into the van, firmly shutting the door on their anxious snuffling noses. The rescue wagon rolled in next to the cruiser; the paramedics who jumped out, both women, having been told that a taser may have been involved, immediately checked Norah's heart for any irregularity, her skin for burns, her limbs for muscle damage. She absolutely refused to go to the hospital for observation.

"She's seems fine now," one of the paramedics told Olivia while the other stowed away their equipment "Probably just one jolt, but she hit her head when she fell. That's what knocked her out. It would be better to have her evaluated for a concussion, but she seems quite unwilling. So here's what you need to watch out for…" She proceeded with a list of careful instructions. If there was undue sleepiness, nausea, loss of balance, bring Norah to the hospital immediately.

The rescue wagon rolled out of the driveway, but the two officers stayed until Dave arrived. He didn't bother to carefully park beside her van as he usually did, simply abandoned his Bronco on the roadside and rushed to where Olivia was still keeping an eye on Norah, now sitting in one of their Adirondack chairs. He'd dropped his three very surprised teen-agers at the library with hardly any explanation. Kevin had demanded to know what was going on at the house, was Norah all right?

"She is. There's been another incident, though, and the police are at the house." Dave had looked Kevin straight in the eye. The unspoken message was that Dave was too busy to take any crap right now, and Kevin needed to do exactly as he was told. "Your job is to keep an eye on Moira and Danny until either me or Liv picks you up later."

Kevin had got it. He'd looked away and mumbled, "Yes, *sir*," not without a sarcastic edge.

The male officer informed Dave that the house was all clear, and Dave said he'd take over and make a police report later. The woman gave Dave her card and a sympathetic look. "Give us a call back if you need us."

After they'd cleared out, Dave began questioning Norah. Had she got a good look at the intruder? Did she think she could describe the woman to a police sketch artist? What had Norah seen that caused her to draw her knife?

Learning that the woman had been holding some kind of tool and working on the gas meter sent up an instant alarms. Dave immediately called the gas company to send out a maintenance team; he suspected someone may have tampered with the meter. He was told to stay out of the house until the team arrived.

Olivia could see how the muscles in Dave's neck and shoulders were all tensed up, and his voice as he questioned the two of them was slower and lower than normal. Clearly he was holding himself in strict control when he really wanted to shout and rant. She felt deeply sorry that her own persistent investigations may have brought this danger to his—their—home. But what else could she do? Especially now that she'd met the Raffertys, she just couldn't let go, she thought ruefully. She wanted to call Jamie for a little commiseration and friendly abuse, but that would have to wait until later.

"What should we do?" The question she asked was directed to herself, to Dave, to the blue expanse of sky above them where there might or might not be unseen forces at play.

"I'll be damned if I know," Dave said. "Apparently we need an around-the-clock guard here. Ah, good. Here's the guy."

The guy from Columbia Gas was two guys: the driver, a tall, tanned, strapping technician with a massive tool belt; the other with the clipboard, a slender nerdy fellow who looked about sixteen. Dave began to confer with them in low tones, so Olivia stayed with Norah. She'd wait until Dave was through with the guys from Columbia Gas before going to pick up the family. Maybe this would be a good night to order in pizzas, Olivia thought, and risk Moira's scorn. It was amazing how, in the midst of danger and disaster, someone had better be thinking about *what's for dinner?*

~

On her way to the library, Olivia thought about what the guys from Columbia Gas had said. The wire wrapped around the meter was a guide to the main pipe and should not be touched. There could be no good reason for anyone to fool around with that wire or any other part of the meter, unless… Yes, it was possible to engineer a small gas leak that would accumulate in the house until someone returned home and turned on the stove or something like that.

The question posed by the Happy Tails receptionist, a question she had bypassed at the time, replayed now in Olivia's mind. Was someone else monitoring her appointments? Did that someone know it was the family's Danbury day? What if Norah had not interrupted the woman in the straw hat? What if gas had accumulated in the house while Olivia was out. What if she'd come home and turned on the stove to start dinner?

A slow chill descended on Olivia, moving from her neck right down to her toes.

Olivia didn't approve of talking on her cell while driving, but without thinking about it twice, she called Jamie now. "Where are you?"

"I'm at the *L'Espalier* with a hot date."

"*You are?*"

"No, Liv. It's Mike's weekend, and we're at Burton's Grille having the best burgers on the South Shore. What's going on now?"

Olivia told her.

"Oh, my God, Liv. This must be Swett's work, the bastard. What are we going to do?"

"I don't know, Jamie. Dave may be able to…" But Olivia had arrived at the library. "Listen, I can't talk any more now. Call me tomorrow. Dave will be taking Moira and Danny to church in the morning."

Olivia rounded up the O'Haras and took them home. Moira was annoyed, Danny bewildered, and Kevin in his blackest mood ever. "Norah's fine now," she told him. "She'll be glad to have your company. We have to keep tabs on her for a while." She explained the symptoms they would watch out for. That would give Kevin something to concentrate on besides his anger at having been shelved at the library by Dave.

~

Olivia had almost forgotten about Mrs. Ritchie and was surprised when she called on Sunday morning. "Just one thought, my dear. Well, it's Cass's thought, really. You remember Cass? You met her at the library. She's our clairvoyant, and she did have a fleeting vision at the Esbat."

Olivia groaned silently. *Now what?* "A vision about what?" It was all so incredible. This woman was almost as persistent as she was.

"Cass saw a trunk full of framed photographs. She said there's something there you need. One of the photographs just flew right out of the trunk, you know. In Cass's vision, that is.

It means something, we just don't know what. But *a bird in the bush is worth two in the hand*, if you know what I mean."

Olivia couldn't make sense of that muddled pronouncement, but she thanked the librarian and got off the phone as soon as she could, waiting for Jamie's call. Then she began to think about framed photographs, to see them in her mind's eye. No one knew better than Olivia that they could hold secrets, as she had discovered last year. *A trunk*, Mrs. Ritchie had said?

She called Anna. "Hi, Anna. I just had an idea. Were there any photographs belonging to Mabel up in the attic?"

Anna said yes. In a little painted chest. They hadn't seemed as important as the letters to Anna.

"I think you ought to take every one of them apart. I'm not sure why, but I urge you to do it."

Anna moaned. "Okay, but my poor fingers won't thank you for it. I'll call you if I find anything there, but it sounds like the longest shot ever. What is this, some sort of hunch?"

"You could say that." *Not my hunch, though*, Olivia thought.

MISSY HYDE REVIEWS HER RETIREMENT PLAN

I may not have the great nest egg I'd planned on—it's more of a pullet than an ostrich egg—but a lady always knows when it's time to leave the party. That little banshee who came running at me with a knife got too good a look at my face. Although the taser does tend to rattle the short term memory, I don't think I want to count on that affect. But it's really more than that. I've always had an instinct for getting off the sinking ship in time, which has served me well in the past. After this latest cock-up at Lowenstein's, I could feel my whole life going the way of the Titanic.

The time has come to write off Henry Swett III's murderous agenda. Stress and foreboding make for a troubled gut, and I find myself quite literally sick to my stomach. So I plan to head for my retirement villa on an island untroubled by extradition treaties. (I'll be in interesting company. My research has found a number of notable fugitives in such out-of-the-way places.) I look forward to settling back in a beach chair under the palms, ordering rum drinks, and writing my memoirs. Or threatening to write my memoirs to certain parties who would pay me substantially to run out of ink. Yes!

But I can't quite bring myself to leave Swett high and dry without any reliable resources—did I mention that there really is honor among thieves? So I am going to give Swett a parting gift, a name and a phone number. I might be too soft-hearted myself to wreak significant collateral damage, but there are guys out there who'd stuff their grandmother into a wood chipper for a decent pay-off.

I still have the original document I located (at great risk of spider bites) in the moldy cellar of St. Rita's Chapel. A handwritten note on Refuge stationery that a girl named Rose Berwind had given birth to a healthy male child, that she had died the same day and the infant was "transferred" privately to the care of Senator Rafferty and his wife—signed Sr. Mary Joseph A.A.

Keeping hold of the original is my insurance policy against any trouble with Swett, such as threatening to "out" my services (how would he dare?) or stiffing me on that final bill. Which he might do if he senses that I'm getting away and will no longer be any use to him. As I've often noticed, the very rich are the worst of deadbeats; it's the middle-class who can be relied upon to pay their bills. But it's not as if I'm planning on a farewell bonus. Just what's my due for services rendered.

Not settling accounts with me would be the worst mistake of Henry's misspent life.

SEPTEMBER 23

Things to Do Today

Check /w Anna
Jamie: cancel lunch 27th & foreseeable
Libr. borrow The Sociopath Next Door & The Dangerous Situations Survival Handbook
Check with P.O.—is there another Andreas?
Where is HS yearbook?

With all the anxiety that had settled over the Lowenstein household like a poisonous cloud, Olivia hardly had much worry to spare for the mysterious postcard she'd received the day after the attack on Norah. But it *was* strange. First, because it was addressed to her maiden name, Olivia Andreas, and might never have been delivered if the postal clerk sorting the mail for delivery hadn't glanced only at the address and ignored the absence of "Lowenstein" or "O'Hara." And second, because neither the picture—the statue of Christ the Redeemer looming over Rio de Janeiro harbor—nor the message made sense to Olivia: "Getting in touch. Miss you." Olivia studied the blurry post mark and the stamp. She didn't know anyone in Brazil, or anyone who might miss her, except her mother in Cleveland for whom no amount of attention was ever enough to make up for her lifelong angst.

Still, she pinned the postcard to her office bulletin board to wonder about later. Much later.

Dave had filled out a police report, added to those he'd submitted before when there had been break-ins and illegal surveillance at his house. What he needed now was the identity of the woman described as "a Mary Poppins type" who'd assaulted Norah and may have been trying to blow up his home. The Chief of Detectives gave Dave the go-ahead to consult with the FBI. Dave was armed with a sketch of the woman drawn from details given to a police artist by Norah. The sketch was submitted to face recognition software of known felons and other data bases, but there were no close hits. Dave brought a copy home for Olivia: the face of their enemy.

Norah remembered that the woman had been wearing some kind of gloves, probably latex, which explained why no prints had been retrieved from the gas meter. Any footprints had been obliterated by the men from Columbia Gas.

"Nothing, nothing! Another freaking stone wall," Dave groaned to Olivia in the privacy of their bedroom. He didn't want to frighten the children, but the fact was that they had no way of knowing when and how the woman might strike their family again. It was a terrifying situation. So terrifying, that Norah had not been unhappy at the prospect of returning to her new home with Emma Toogood in time for school on Monday morning.

Olivia thought it rather wonderful that Dave hadn't blamed her by look or word for this precarious state of affairs. He was frustrated, angry, and worried, but he didn't take it out on her or anyone else in the family. He was, in fact, especially tender to her, whispering that he could no longer imagine his world without her and would do anything necessary to protect the life they shared together. But that only made Olivia feel even guiltier.

Dave adjusted their alarm system again and outfitted each of them with "panic buttons" whereby they could instantly connect with the State Police Unit of Plymouth County if there was another incident.

They decided that the house must never be left empty again until the danger had passed. Although just how their old peaceful life might be restored, they had no idea.

Having missed their lunch together on Friday, Jamie came over with Mike on Sunday morning to check on Olivia while Dave and the younger children were at church. Had she really told Dave everything? Yes, yes, Olivia asserted. And he was already investigating all relevant leads.

Dave, Moira, and Danny came home after church (which Dave always sat out at a nearby Starbucks), suddenly filling the rooms with noise and energy. Moira immediately set about making dozens of blueberry pancakes from the batter she'd mixed before church. Olivia and Jamie arranged platters of creamy cheeses, sliced fruit, preserves, and croissants on the big kitchen table.

After brunch, Mike went off with Danny to play ball. Kevin remained in seclusion upstairs. The adults settled in the living room with a fresh pot of coffee. Ignoring Olivia's protests, Jamie told Dave about Robyn Gamble—her hint that "Uncle Henry" employed a hit woman who fit the description of Norah's attacker.

"I'm worried that Swett's so paranoid about his fortune, he's targeting Liv," she said. "It's not Liv's fault, exactly. I mean, you know how blindly obsessed she gets."

"Thanks, pal," Olivia said.

"More tenuous hearsay than evidence," Dave said, "but I'm already looking into this unsavory bastard Henry Swett III. If what you say is true, his association with that woman may have left traces. What other jobs has she handled for him? We already know that Swett must have faked his aunt's will and narrowly escaped jail time. He'd have needed help for that. If Swett is behind these assaults on my family, he's going to be a dead man." Wearing a thunderous scowl, Dave stomped out to the garage to take out his anger on the wrought iron sculpture he was working on. Through the open windows of the living room, Olivia and Jamie could hear his hammer slamming something metal with more than artistic passion.

"Oh, dear," Jamie said. "Don't look at me like that, Liv. Dave needs to be kept aware of who he's looking for, and he has the resources to follow the trail. You don't want to be going in fear for your life forever, do you? It will ruin your skin, which is one of your best features. I've always envied you that Grecian glow."

"Ruin my skin?"

"Yeah, you know, worry lines. Frownies and scowlies.

Olivia was speechless, which was probably a very good thing. They sipped their coffee in silence for a while, listening to Dave banging away, the sounds of Moira running some appliance in the kitchen, Mike tossing a football to Danny in the backyard accompanied by two barking dogs, and faraway upstairs, the mournful beat of Kevin's Bodhrán

"Blindly obsessed, was it?"

"You've often said so yourself," Jamie said. "And, besides, I knew you even before you were Olivia Lowenstein or even Olivia Robb. We've been friends ever since you were that softball champ Olivia Andreas. And I was Ella Jamison Andrews, the chemistry whiz.

They smiled at one another, sharing a kaleidoscope of high school images, different and the same for each of them.

"I was pretty good at math, as well," Olivia said.

"Yes, but I did all your chem. experiments in the interests of not blowing up dear old Garfield High."

"I went looking for our yearbook the other day. Must have misplaced it during the move from Scituate."

"I thought you had those packing cases all codified by number and content in a catalog." Jamie assumed a look of mock surprise.

Olivia sighed. "I've been slipping away from all my reliable good habits. Ever since I've had to cope with those damned ghosts, my whole life has been turned upside-down."

The little maple desk in the corner of the living room rattled. Its drop down leaf flew open, exposing the pigeon holes.

"Best not speak ill of the dead," Jamie said piously. "It's a good thing I don't scare off easily, or I'd be out of this Amityville Horror in a flash."

Olivia's cell phone rang faintly in the distance. She ran to her office to catch the call but she was too late. *Missed Call.* She brought her cell phone back into the living room. She had also unpinned the strange postcard and brought it with her.

"It's Anna's number," she said when she rejoined Jamie.

"So, call her back. Maybe she's found something."

"Of course. Here, look at this postcard while I'm calling. See what you make of it.

~

"I don't believe it myself!" Anna didn't even say hello. Her tone was incredulous.

"*What?* Did you find something? What did you find?" Olivia's questions tumbled out on top of each other.

"I took apart every frame in that trunk. What a merciless job that was! I broke two nails. But worth it, after all."

"For heaven's sake, let's hear it, whatever it is. I'm on tenterhooks!" Olivia's mercurial imagination was running in all directions.

"How did you ever get the idea of looking into those frames?" Anna wondered.

"Never mind that. *What?*"

"It was behind a studio photograph of Granddad. He looked about one year old. I think it may have been a first birthday portrait. A slight, dark little boy with a beautiful smile. Not a whit like those big blond Raffertys. Expensive silver frame, tarnished now of course. The devil to take apart. But behind the photograph there was a document. It appears to be the baptism certificate of 'Infant Berwind' at St. Rita's Refuge, mother's name Rose Berwind. Father's name left blank. Signed by the presiding cleric and witnessed by a nun, probably Rose's nurse."

"Holy Jesus!"

"Exactly. The signatures were Fr. Richard Damian, S.J., and Sr. Mary Joseph Burns, A.A."

"Wow! But…will you be able to prove where you found it? I mean, that's the whole point, confirming a connection between little Billy Rafferty and the infant Berwind."

Anna laughed—or maybe chortled with satisfaction. "When I realized what it might be, I took a bunch of photos with my iPhone—of the document in place. Then, before I even pulled it out of the frame, I ran over next door to get a witness. Because my neighbor is a retired judge, Judge Sparks. Then I removed the certificate from the back of the picture frame, unfolded it, and took more photos."

"Good move. I think you're almost there, Anna.

"I'll talk to Sonia. I think I have enough now to at least broach the subject and just see what she suggests. Maybe she'll simply tell us to forget the whole crazy idea."

"Don't forget to mention that Swett's attorney is Gretchen Weinhardt."

"Okay, why?"

"Sonia Perlmutter has probably heard of a high profile attorney like Weinhardt. Might as well let her know who she'll be up against. You've made her sound like a woman who enjoys a challenge."

"That she is," Anna said.

"Have you finished reading Beth's letters to Mabel?"

"Not yet."

"Do it. You never know."

~

When Olivia got off the phone, Jamie was holding the postcard with a curious expression on her face. But as soon as Olivia relayed the substance of Anna's call, Jamie stuck the postcard under a coaster on the coffee table and switched her attention to this new topic of interest.

"The Raffertys probably had their new baby christened in their own church," Jamie speculated. "They may have shown this baptism certificate to the priest, in confidence."

"Their priest would have known about Mabel's fruitless novenas. They couldn't just appear with an infant son to be christened without any provenance." Olivia picked up the coffee things and put them on a tray. She stuck the postcard in her pocket.

"I wonder how they handled the sudden arrival of a child with no preceding pregnancy. People must have gossiped." Jamie followed Olivia into the kitchen.

"Yes, but not aloud or in print. Senators were sacrosanct in those days," Olivia said. "If the Raffertys were waiting for a suitable infant to become available at the Refuge—which may have taken weeks or even months—Mabel may have gone into a fake confinement somewhere. Anna still has another shoebox of Beth Hadley's letters to read. Might be some sort of hint there."

"Keeping my fingers crossed," Jamie said.

HENRY III DECLINES A DEBT

Believe me, I could write a book on the difficulty of retaining good help these days, Henry grumbled as he reclined in the marble tub with gold faucets, smoking an excellent Cuban cigar. Missy Hyde was only the latest in the caravan of disappointing females he'd had to deal with as he'd traveled the Silk Road of his years. He thought of the invoice she'd presented to him for recent services rendered, including her final attempt to eliminate the Lowenstein nuisance. A botched job by an incompetent contractor. Yes, she had given Henry the name and contact information for her recommended replacement, only the least she could do as she fled the country for some distant hideaway.

Fabio Falcone already had a beef against the target, Missy had assured him, and the job would be done practically at cost. Not by Falcone personally, of course. As *capo dei capi* in Boston, he was way too senior for wet work. But Falcone would give Henry the name of a trusted soldier to finish Missy's inept attempts to rid Henry of the busybody.

Henry considered the adoption record—a marginal scribble, really—that Missy had presented to him with her last report. *The missing Berwind heir, my ass,* Henry scoffed. Let him remain a Rafferty for eternity and not trouble Henry with some ineffectual complaint. Who was that attorney anyway?

Sonia Perlmutter, some retired ambulance chaser. Gretchen Weinhardt would make short work of her. Gretchen had saved Henry's ass once before, when jail time had loomed on the horizon. Henry shuddered. This bath water was getting too damned cold. Standing up abruptly, he stepped out of the tub and lifted a heavy bath sheet from the heated rack. The mirrored room reflected multiple images of Henry. Sucking in an incipient belly, he admired his otherwise trim figure from wavy gray hair, barely thinning at the crown, to his excellent pedicure. He was justifiably proud of his slim, aristocratic feet that modeled his dozens of handmade Ugolini shoes from Florence so beautifully.

Henry donned a cashmere robe and Italian slippers. It was almost time for his massage. Henry had asked the agency to send that same little masseuse he'd had last time, and he was looking forward to her expert ministrations. Should he have given her a larger tip last time, Henry wondered. No, Asian babes weren't spoiled like those Las Vegas blonde bimbos.

As for her final invoice, Missy Hyde could just whistle for that inflated payoff. After all, what could she do to him once she'd fled the jurisdiction to some godforsaken island with three palm trees and a bank? He would take his chances, a safe bet if ever he'd known one.

SEPTEMBER 30

Things to Do Today

Libr. return The Sociopath Next Door, *renew* The Dangerous Situations Survival Handbook
Research Mrs. R & Friends
Review 5-yr plan: poss. add metaphysical studies
Re-up Ancient Docs course
Fresh fish for dinner?

As the days went by, Olivia began feeling particularly housebound. Not only was she reluctant to leave the premises unguarded, she was even more hesitant to leave Moira or Danny on their own at home. Kevin, though—he was savvy enough to watch out for any suspicious activity. When Kevin got home early from school, Olivia would sometimes let herself dash out to the supermarket, post office, or library. It was cooler now, but she left the dogs home anyway. They were a great backup team for Kevin.

The last of September was particularly inviting on the South Shore, the hills alight with brush strokes of russet, ochre, and burnt orange, the air both caressing and energizing. Olivia even reveled in the rich, deep fragrance of dying summer. It was good to be out and about.

After she'd changed books at the Hawthorne library, she decided to take a run over to the Black Hill branch and update Mrs. Ritchie on her progress in the Berwind affair. There was something about the woman's warm inclusive aura that drew confidences even from the most reticent.

Now that school was in session, Monday afternoons at the library were quieter than later days in the week when students began rushing to complete assignments. Olivia arrived in a fortuitous lull between patrons, and Mrs. Ritchie welcomed her with open arms, literally, silver bangles softly tinkling. Not so Omar, who glared from his cushion on the oak catalog files, but refrained from outright hissing.

After assuring the librarian that she had "promising news," Olivia ducked into the tiny kitchen, where she found a bubbling kettle and a tray already set up. She made tea and brought the tray out to the main room. They sat at one of the round oak tables, Mrs. Ritchie maneuvering about in her rolling swivel chair, and Olivia recounted all that she'd researched, learned, and/or set in motion since her last visit.

"I feel that all these small discoveries are leading you straight to your desired goal." Mrs. Ritchie opened the tin of shortbread that drew the devoted attention of Omar. Olivia took one of the rich buttery cookies. Omar got a crumb. "There's no limit to what wonders a woman can work when she releases her intentions to the Divine Cosmos."

"Did I do that? The releasing bit?"

"You're a woman of great psychic power. Surely you know that?"

"I'm not even sure what that means, Mrs. Ritchie. By the way, you get full marks for mentioning the framed photos," Olivia said.

"That was Cass. Always a good idea to listen to Cass. I wish she were here now. I'm worried about you, and I don't quite know why. Cass would see much more."

"I'm quite satisfied with your advice." Olivia realized with a fillip of surprise that this was actually true. She was putting a great deal of stock in the advice of a woman whose conversation was often so filled with digressions and twisted proverbs, it was nearly baffling.

"Well, *don't hatch your chickens before we count them,*" Mrs. Ritchie warned. "You have a number of clues, but I feel they don't quite add up to the solution you seek. There's something else in the wind. I don't know what. I'll hum on it, though."

"Okay." Olivia wondered whether humming on something was similar to praying on it. "Oh, here's something else I almost forgot. I got this strange item in the mail last week." She took the postcard out of her library tote and handed it to Mrs. Ritchie.

The librarian studied it thoughtfully, held it against her soft, plump cheek for a moment, then laid it on the table between them. "No signature. But I believe the handwriting is familiar?"

The handwriting! Olivia felt a slight jolt, like a tiny electric shock. Hadn't she seen this handwriting a long, long time ago? The high "t" cross in "touch," The loopy "y" in "you." At that moment her conscious mind was flooded with memories of unsigned notes she'd received after her graduation from high school and then college. The cashier's checks. She'd never told her mother—or anyone. With her scholarships, her jobs, and those checks, she's been able to avoid the morass of student debt.

"I didn't think so. But maybe. I'll have to consider… compare…" Her voice trailed off into that vague state of mind where thoughts drift out of their logical sequence and start to form nebulous images. This didn't happen often to left-brained Olivia.

She thanked the librarian, not knowing quite what for. They sat in companionable silence for a while. Then, for no special reason, Olivia said, "I can't find my high school yearbook. I must have misplaced it when I moved to Marshfield."

Mrs. Ritchie drew out one of the pencils stuck in her coronet of braids. She reached into the moss green reticule at her feet and found a pad of paper, seemingly without looking. Closing her eyes, she began to doodle on the paper, murmuring "nothing is lost in spirit, nothing is lost in spirit…"

Olivia leaned forward. A trunk was emerging from the pencil marks. It looked somehow familiar. She remembered the trunk that Kevin had set up in the garage bedroom for Norah to use as a night table. A 1930s black hardboard case with the same kind of brass clasps.

"I may have a trunk like that," she said.

Mrs. Ritchie opened her eyes and smiled. "Look inside it, then. Just a hunch. My friends call me The Finder, you know. Just a little knack I have for imagining."

"What do you imagine about the postcard?"

"I think you already know who sent it. A person who is no longer in Brazil."

Olivia felt herself suffused in a wave of heat. *As if my life isn't complicated enough!*

Soon afterward, two mothers with toddlers in tow breezed into the library, disturbing their tête-à-tête with noisy chatter. High time to go home, anyway. Olivia washed out the cups and said goodbye. She was conscious of not wanting to leave Kevin on his own for too long.

As she drove away, she realized that she'd forgotten to show Mrs. Ritchie the police sketch she carried in her handbag. A fog of questions obscured every other thought. *Could it be? Why now? Won't it be dangerous for…? How do I feel about…? Should I tell Dave?* An instant reply to this last unvoiced question rose up from her innermost being.

No!

~

Olivia had always avoided what she thought of as weaknesses attributed to the feminine psyche under the general heading of *hysteric disturbances,* "hyster" being the ancient Greek word for "womb." Lately, however, she'd been dismayed by how often her rational thought processes had been replaced by intuitions, instincts, presentiments, and other vague and baseless suppositions. Driving away from the Black Hill branch library, she felt positively afflicted by a gut feeling that she was being followed or tracked or observed, as if there were unseen eyes watching her every move and invisible ears listening to her private conversations.

She gave herself a mental shake and turned off Route 3 at Exit 6 toward the harbor. As long as she was in Plymouth, she might as well pick up some fresh fish at Wood's on the Town Pier. The slight detour would only take a few minutes, and, besides, the sight of small private yachts and rakish fishing boats moored at the dock, and the lusty, white-capped ocean beyond always lifted her heart. Around the curve of the shoreline, the *Mayflower II* stood as a picturesque monument to local history.

The mound of chunky pink lobster meat in the fish market's showcase was expensive but irresistible. She decided to make lobster mac-and-cheese, a family favorite, for dinner. Since school had started, Moira, busy with soccer practice and homework, had become more flexible and sometimes even welcomed Olivia's intrusion into her kitchen domain. Perhaps the girl was willing to behave like a regular teenager at last and allow Olivia to assume the role of "mom."

Coming out of Wood's with her plastic bag of delectable seafood in hand, she admired the boats and read their names as she walked past. One particular classic beauty caught her attention because of its impeccable restoration, all gleaming dark wood and fresh white paint. Small portholes indicated sleeping quarters aft and an efficient little galley forward. *Calypso.* The name made her smile. Calypso was the island where Odysseus had built his last boat (after losing so many others), the one that would take him home to Ithaca.

She couldn't help but be curious about the owner, but it wasn't mannerly to gawk. She glanced sideways at the figure standing at the helm. The glass panels enclosing the front of the boat were opaque from reflections of the lowering afternoon sun. She could just make out his captain's hat and trim beard in profile. There was something so familiar... Then an odd thing happened. The man seemed to feel her looking at him; he turned and looked back. For some unaccountable reason, she waved at this man she could hardly see through the sun-blinded glass. He lifted his hand in an answering salute. Abruptly she turned and almost ran off the dock. She must take her precious purchase home while it was still chilled. Olivia felt a little chilled herself. All sorts of weird presentiments were assailing her again.

She hurried into her minivan, stowing her package in the small cooler she'd kept there all summer. It still held a few bottles of water. Then she backed up the Honda and nearly raced back to Route 3. It was getting late, and the impromptu menu she'd planned would take a while to assemble.

Even being safely locked into the Honda, speeding north, that uneasy feeling stayed with her, like her own personal storm cloud. Sometimes paranoia is based on an actual danger, Olivia reminded herself. A GPS tracker *had* been removed from her car, spyware from her computer, and a listening device from her bedroom. Nothing hysterical about a healthy respect for an enemy who had shown her hand and might have more tricks up her sleeve. Or *his.* If Olivia were to allow herself to be guided by her so-called sixth sense right this very moment, she would have to admit that the imagined menace now seemed more masculine than feminine. An air of swagger. A macho complacency.

What the hell! She was getting as addle-brained as Mrs. Ritchie. On the other hand, Mrs. Ritchie had often taken a giant leap over logic to land directly on the very thing which was being sought.

All the while Olivia was having this internal dialog, she was also checking in her rear view mirror for a possible trailing car as she drove north on Route 3. The traffic was not too heavy, moving along steadily before the real rush hour would begin. She decided to get off the main route at Exit 10 and take Route 3A through Duxbury to Route 139 to see if she was followed. Two cars took the same exit, one black and one red; she couldn't tell anything more from her rearview mirror, except that neither looked especially new and expensive. Both cars followed her as far at the Harborside Inn, a handsome Georgian building across the street from a sweeping view of the ocean. At its back, where the parking lot was located, one could gaze over the nearby marshland with its graceful rushes and grasses now turning rust, mustard yellow, and brown. Both cars turned into the Inn's driveway and parked in the lot, while Olivia continued around the marsh to home.

A bout of paranoia left one feeling rather stupid, Olivia decided. She resolved to put her fears out of mind and concentrate on making dinner. Sliced tomato salad? Green beans with basil?

~

Two days later, Olivia received another postcard in the mail. The youngsters were all in school, and she was alone with the dogs. She walked back from the mailbox in a daze, Bruno on one side and Sadie on the other, ignoring the rest of the mail in her hand. Collapsing into a rocking chair on the porch, she studied the postcard. Sadie laid her head in Olivia's lap with a concerned look; Bruno settled at her feet. Absently, she gave them each a reassuring pat.

She was transfixed by the picture, not Brazil this time. It was a local touristy postcard showing the *Mayflower II* moored in the downtown historic district. Exactly where she had been on Monday. The other side read, "Watching over you. Trust me."

Same handwriting again! The memory of it had become clearer in her mind since the first postcard. Although it had been many years since she'd seen that distinctive scrawl with its broad lower loops and dramatic "t" crosses, she knew it from countless notes and birthday cards of her early years. *That was her father's hand, for sure.* Could it be, then, that Dad had actually returned to this country? Who else? A wave of anger surged in her gut. This was the man who'd devastated her teen years by absconding with other people's money, leaving her to tough out the scandal and her mother's increasingly aggrieved disposition. Philip Andreas was a thief still wanted by the FBI. *Jesus!* If he had actually returned, she hoped he wouldn't get caught. If only there were some way to tell him to get out of here, to run away, before the FBI (and Dave) found out he was back in their jurisdiction.

From the cryptic lines scrawled on the two postcards, it seemed as if his apparent change of address had something to do with her. Why now? Was he going to ruin everything again? This time there would be a lot more at stake than teenaged embarrassment and a bitter mother. Her life, her love, her family—all were secure and fulfilling at last, and she could not, would not allow her father to wreck the happy, satisfying world she had created with Dave.

Olivia stashed this disturbing postcard with the first one in the marquetry case on her bureau that had held so many other secrets from the past. But out of sight was definitely not out of mind. (She restrained a sudden urge to laugh wildly. Would Mrs. Ritchie have said, *out of mind, out of sight?*)

At least she would be able to confide in Jamie about this newest catastrophe. With Jamie, she could laugh and cry at the same time. There was some comfort in that. But nothing on the phone, because you never could tell who might be listening, as Olivia had learned.

The house must not be left unguarded, so instead of going out together on their usual day, she would invite Jamie here for lunch. Friday was only a couple of days away, and there was that little beacon of hope that Jamie might come up with something. Jamie had a fertile imagination, unrestrained by convention or good sense. Probably just what Olivia needed.

Thinking of Jamie reminded Olivia of the yearbook. She went out to the garage, where Norah's former bedroom was still set up. She climbed up the narrow wooden stairs to the second floor. Kevin's violin was on the desk, and the duvet bore the recent imprint of a resting body. How romantic this room must seem to Kevin, what fantasies it must inspire, although the elusive Norah had left few traces of herself when she moved. Olivia smiled, remembering her own teenage passions. She was just thankful that Kevin preferred to practice Irish fiddle music here (in the presence of Norah's absence) instead of in the house.

Olivia lifted the lamp off the black hardboard trunk beside the cot and opened the brass clasps.

Amazing! Not quite a time machine, but almost. Not only her senior year book, but the three preceding years as well, and a clutter of other school papers. She sank down on the cot and began to go through reports, awards, term papers, classmate portraits. The portraits were in cream-colored cardboard folders. She found her own, with her hair cut short as a boy's, which was how she'd worn it until she met Dave. She touched her soft brown curls, imagining his fingers brushing away errant strands from her forehead. Then she opened Jamie's portrait, which was inscribed, "It's been fun, no matter what. Always remember… Jamie." ("No matter what" meant all the scrapes they'd got in together.) Standing up the portraits, Olivia gazed at herself and Jamie, with some wonder at their naive expressions, their fresh complexions, their confident smiles directed at some point on the studio wall. If only those ingenuous eyes could have seen the future well enough to avoid the pitfalls of marrying Mr. Wrong. Still, it was only the missteps of the past that had brought her to the time and place where she met Dave, who was definitely her Mr. Right. Would they have met anyway? Was their meeting destiny—or chance?

Mrs. Ritchie had told her where to find this lost window to the past. The woman clearly had a gift for some magic art in which Olivia didn't even believe. She'd been meaning to research her somewhat ditsy new mentor. Maybe it was time to see if there were any retrievable history there. She put a checkmark beside the note on her To-Do list.

OCTOBER 3

Things to Do Today

Jamie, lunch, Fri. Shrimp & Artichokes
Wood's Market
Closets, unpack fall, pack summer
Libr. borrow Women Who Think Too Much: How to Break Free of Overthinking and Reclaim Your Life, *renew* The Dangerous Situations Survival Handbook *again.*

Holy Google! The number of hits that came up for Mrs. Ritchie and her friends was staggering. Articles in the *Pilgrim Times* were especially astonishing. They'd been involved in a surprising number of crime stories during the past few years, with several references to criminals they'd had some hand in bringing to justice. Olivia made a note to ask Dave if he'd ever heard of these ladies.

Olivia didn't fancy seeing herself and her own pursuits written up in the *Pilgrim Times* or the *Marshfield Mariner.* She resolved to return to her former autonomy and cease relying on that odd little librarian who was apparently rather well-known locally. *Infamous* was the word.

~

When Olivia scooted out to Wood's Market on the Town Pier to pick up some shrimp for lunch with Jamie on Friday, she wasn't expecting to have her whole world turned upside down.

She could have shopped at the Brant Rock Fish Market, but for some reason she fancied the drive to Plymouth. Would she have avoided all that trauma if she'd settled for local fare? Probably not. That was whole point of W. Somerset Maugham's tale of the "The Appointment in Samarra". Your fate found you, wherever you traveled.

She'd had to wait for Kevin to return home from school, so that the house wouldn't be left unguarded. (And what a drag *that* was getting to be!) Since Kevin preferred to ride his bike to school, he was always home before three, earlier than he would have been if he relied on the school bus. Except on days when Sean picked him up at school, and they went to the Brady house (Sean's parents were rarely home before seven) to practice with the Celtic Storm. Other than that, Kevin was indifferent to after-school activities, even sports. Practicing with the band was his one outside interest, once strictly for his love of Irish music, but now for the chance to be made alternately elated or miserable by Norah. *Poor Kevin.* Olivia thought of how fair-haired, pale Norah glowed when she was enraptured by music—as spellbinding as the nymph Nimue.

But this Thursday, Kevin had come straight home and immediately closed himself in his room. Olivia tapped discreetly on his door and told him she was going to the Plymouth Town Pier and would be home in an hour or so.

Kevin opened the door, looking less sullen than was usual in the old days. In fact, ever since Olivia had helped him rescue Norah from the DCF's well-meaning clutches, his attitude had been much pleasanter. Not warm exactly, but not icy either. Standing right behind Olivia, Sadie and Bruno took the opportunity to rush into Kevin's quarters and sniff about.

"Take your time," Kevin said. "The mutts and I will be hanging out in the backyard. I'll keep an eye out for the sibs, don't worry."

So Olivia took off with a free mind, enjoying the glimpses of the ocean that Route 3A afforded. The waves were quickening in the cooler fall breezes, sparkling dark blue waters and frothy whitecaps. Gulls rising and gliding down wherever a flicker under the water's surface promised a tasty morsel. At this time of day, their wings, gilded by sunlight, flashed like messages at sea. She opened the window and took a deep breath of October on the South Shore.

When her cell phone rang, Olivia deliberated. She really wasn't comfortable talking while driving. Usually she'd let the call go to voice mail, but it occurred to her that the caller might be Kevin and there might be trouble at home. With her right hand, she fished the phone out of her handbag, awkwardly opened it, and said Hello.

"Hello, Livvy. Do you know who this is?"

Was it possible to have a hot flash and a cold chill at the same time? A heart-clutch of joy and a wave of intense anger?

"*Dad?* Is that you, Dad? I don't freaking believe this."

"Yes, Livvy, believe it—it's me, honey. Look in your rear view mirror. I'm right behind you in the black Lincoln. I've been watching the house, waiting for this chance, but you never seemed to leave home."

"*Watching?* Watching from where, exactly."

"From the Harborside Inn parking lot, honey. Gives a clear view of your house, the driveway, the cars. Didn't you know that? Where are you headed right now?"

"Town Pier in Plymouth. What in Christ's name…?"

"Your language, Livvy, certainly has deteriorated. You always used to be so proper, for a teenager. The Town Pier is great. In fact, it's perfect. I'll see you there in a few minutes. We can talk privately on my boat. It's the *Calypso.*"

Olivia (who rarely swore ordinarily) was still cursing when the Lincoln suddenly sped up on a straight stretch and passed her at a speed she didn't want to estimate.

She'd seen her father on that boat! Had she known it was him through that sun-dazzled window? Had he recognized her? Did such wild coincidences actually happen in the real world? A little voice inside Olivia replied, *My real world has been invaded by ghosts, so maybe anything is possible, after all.*

Olivia felt a strange sensation in her legs. They were trembling and shuddering in the weirdest way. Was this what people meant when they said "my knees were knocking?"

~

The Town Pier was crowded, but a car was just pulling out in front of Wood's; she grabbed the space and parked, sitting quite still for a moment to catch her breath and steady her nerves. This was no time for a panic attack. She had to find her father and get him out of her life as fast as possible. Like, yesterday.

She got out of the van and looked around for the Lincoln, but it was nowhere in sight. The *Calypso,* however, was moored in exactly the same slip as before. Was he there? She couldn't see anyone. Fueled by rage and indignation. Olivia marched to the boat and managed to swing herself on board.

"A few days ago—right here—I thought I saw you." *His* voice from the shadow of the cabin "I thought you stopped and waved to me. And it *was* you, Livvy! All grown up. And so beautiful!"

Olivia moved into the interior cabin to confront the man who had been the first to betray her love.

He looked fine. Older, but handsome in a new way. His Aegean profile still strong and proud, his hair gray but thick and wavy, his body stockier but erect. No sign of the degenerate life she had imagined him living, forever on the run, guilt eating away at him. (Apparently not.) She was physically shocked by how glad she was to see him. How much she still loved him. In one moment, he had stepped forward and enveloped her in a big warm hug. He felt so good. He smelled the way her father always smelled, a combination of some spicy soap he used, the tobacco he smoked, and himself.

It took all her strength for Olivia to wrest herself free of this unregenerate thief. "You should never have come back! What were you thinking? Do you want to spend the rest of your life in jail?"

"Sit down, Livvy. We'll talk about my future later. Right now I have to tell you exactly what I *was* thinking, the reason why I've come back, and how I even found you. You're a long way from Cleveland, honey."

That was true. How *had* he found where she was living now? Well, perhaps it hadn't been all that difficult. Olivia herself had traced the century-old marriage of a young couple who'd wed in another country with the girl using a different surname.

"It's been a shock, I know. You'd better have a drink,

a sip of Barbayanni. Best medicine for the nerves." Her father poured them each a small glass of ouzo from a bottle on the polished wooden cabinet. The seats inside the cabin were supple, sleek leather. The whole place smelled of money to Olivia. *Stolen money*. When he'd reached for the bottle, Olivia had thought she'd seen a pistol at his beltline, under the nautical navy blue wool blazer.

Nevertheless, she took the glass he handed her and inhaled the anise aroma. He was right about one thing; she needed this.

"I never planned to come back into your life. I knew I didn't have the right." Philip Andreas sat opposite his daughter and took a measured sip of his drink, his expression sad and apologetic.

What an actor! she scoffed silently. *Let him explain, then. Because it sure is a mystery to me.*

"I won't tell you where I'm living now. What you don't know you can't be persuaded to reveal. But *someone* found my whereabouts, someone who knew my story, and yours. I received a registered letter, addressed to the name on my current passport, the passport to my new life. It was typed, unsigned, and I'll bet, without fingerprints. In fact, I was so sure of that, I never bothered to check. It informed me that my daughter Olivia Andreas, now living in Marshfield, Massachusetts, was in grave danger, due to her own stubborn intrusion into the distribution of an immense fortune, the Berwind estate. That you had come up with a most unwelcome surprise, a possible new heir, entitled to a share of the millions. One of the persons most affected was setting in motion a contract to eliminate this intrusion into his affairs, permanently. Bastard named Swett. The letter suggested that I contact you, warn you, and if it were possible, use my influence to prevent a tragedy."

"*Your* influence?" Olivia drank down the last of her ouzo. Her hand, without consulting her brain, held out the empty glass for a refill. "Who has accepted the contract? What influence could you possibly have on an unknown…" She searched for the right word.

"Unknown hit man." Her father supplied the missing cliché. "Only he's not unknown to me, if my secret correspondent is telling a true tale. I've been given a name, not only of the man who may be assigned to take care of you but also of the boss who controls the contract." He refilled both glasses.

"*Why?* Why would anyone go to the trouble of telling you this, and how does this person know anything at all about me and my activities. And my enemies, if I have any."

"That's the cryptic part." Her father paused, turned, and looked out the window. Was he checking for strangers with evil intentions? For FBI agents coming to arrest him? He turned back to Olivia. "The letter concluded with a few lines that may make sense to you, as they do not to me. It said, 'Tell Olivia that my client stiffed me, so I'm no longer obligated to keep his confidences. And that I'm truly about the girl.' "

Mary Poppins! "She must have had a change of heart." Olivia felt coldly ungrateful for this sorry attempt to make amends. "After breaking into my house twice, bugging my bedroom, putting a tracker on my car, trying to feed drugs to my dogs, and stunning a girl under our protection with a taser."

"A woman, then? I thought as much," her father said. "Probably she told herself that these were merely business assignments for that psycho Swett, nothing personal," her father said. "But now that her employer has failed to honor his end of the bargain, she's taking a woman's revenge."

Olivia snorted. "Irrational and changeable as any woman? I'm told she looks like Mary Poppins, even carries an umbrella."

Philip Andreas started in surprise. "*O Christ!* I think I've seen her. What else do you know about this woman?"

Olivia took out her wallet, removed the police sketch she had folded and tucked in there, and handed it to her father. "The girl living with us—Norah—got a good look at her. I've been carrying this around to show one of the librarians, but now I guess I won't. It's a long story."

Andreas studied the sketch. "At first she barely registered, but then I kept running into a woman who looks like this hanging around the shops, the post office, the bar. I took her for a tourist, one of those spunky spinsters with a taste for out-of-the-way places. *Shit!* Now I'll have to move again."

"As long as you keep going, as far away as possible." That was unkind, but Olivia didn't care. She was beginning to feel weird, like someone no longer tethered to gravity. Maybe the ouzo, but more likely the unreality of a quiet conversation in a luxurious little boat with this familiar stranger whom it would be her husband's duty to arrest on sight.

As if reading her thoughts, Andreas said, "Why the hell did you have to marry a damn state detective, Livvy? Isn't our situation difficult enough? I'll have to see about some things before I can leave here, and I can't have this husband of yours sniffing around. Won't he be duty-bound to turn me over to the FBI?"

"I don't know the answer to that," Olivia said coldly. "Dave is a good man, the best I've ever known. I'm lucky to be married to him. I have to go now. I can't stay away from the house too long—there are children..." She stood up, none too certain of her balance. *This boat sure is rocking,* she thought. A hysterical giggle nearly escaped her.

Her father stood up, too, and held out his strong, familiar hand to steady her. She inhaled his remembered scent again and felt dizzy enough to hang on for a moment.

"Cecelia...your mother...is she all right?" His voice was low, hesitant, guilty.

"How do you suppose she is? The FBI hounded her for years. She lost her job at the State Treasury. A private firm took her on, though. Better money, too. But she's still bitter. She will never forgive you." Olivia could hear bitterness seeping into her own tone.

"I won't try to explain or justify myself. I just couldn't... live that life anymore."

"Please, I don't want to hear it." Olivia steadied herself awkwardly and thrust herself away from him. She would stand on her own two feet just fine.

"I'll call you. Soon."

"You don't have my cell number," she hoped.

"Yes, I do. I called you when you were driving, don't you remember, honey?"

"Oh. Yes. *Right.* I'm not even going to ask."

"Don't be surprised or upset if you see my car when you're driving around town."

"Of course I'll be upset. How long is this going to go on?"

"As long as it takes. If I can negotiate the deal I have in mind, it should all be over soon."

"You know this assailant?"

"I have friends who know his boss."

Olivia looked at her father as if she'd never seen him before. "I know nothing about you."

"All you need to know is that I'm here and I love you."

When she finally got away from the irresistible force field that drew her to this once-loved stranger, driving home a little too fast, she realized that she'd entirely forgotten the shrimp. Well, she could still stop at the Brant Rock market after all.

~

Jamie held the *Mayflower II* postcard in her hand and studied it, back and front, with a bemused expression. "'Trust me'? What an optimist he is! And now, you're telling me that you've actually seen *your father*? *Talked* with him?" Jamie exclaimed. "Where the hell is he? *No, don't tell me.* Just say he's safely hidden from the law."

"I think he's all right, for now." Olivia went on to tell Jamie all about the anonymous message of peril that had brought her father back to the US, the danger to her and perhaps others, the necessity of talking in person and in secret, to impress on her the need for extreme care until he had "negotiated" a solution. Olivia didn't, however, mention Plymouth and the *Calypso*. No sense making her friend legally complicit.

"Incredible, isn't it?" Olivia concluded her story. "Apparently there *is* an odd older woman working for Swett, the same woman who zapped Norah with a taser—and now, lucky for us, she's turned against him and is working out some kind of combination of penance and payback." They were dawdling over the remains of the shrimp and artichoke salad. Olivia poured extra strong coffee into small cups.

"What I really need is another martini," Jamie complained.

"Not unless you want me to drive you home. And besides, we need clear heads today. You have to help me figure out what I should do."

"You won't like my advice. But isn't that what friends are for? Personally, I'm in favor of your spilling the whole worrisome story to Dave. He's entitled to know what you've learned from your father. After all he loves you, and it's only fair that he be given a clue to the dangers that may be surrounding you. And Dave, too, if he happens to be standing nearby. Also, I think if anyone is going to keep you safe, it's Dave you should count on. Your father showing up like some superhero to save the day is all well and good, but who knows when he'll have to go on the run again?" Jamie took a sip of her coffee and made a face. "This is the wake-up cup, all right. I can just feel my brain cells sitting up at attention."

"I know Dad's done some terrible things, but I can't stand the idea of him going to prison. And Dave being the one to send him there." Olivia could feel her voice getting all choked up. *How embarrassing!*

Jamie sipped in silence for a few moments while Olivia got her feelings under control. "I'm not so sure that Dave would want to be responsible for breaking your heart. It could be that you're underestimating your husband. He may be just as capable of going his own lawless way, regardless of consequences, as you are."

"Oh, thanks. That's called autonomy. Marcus Aurelius would approve. But Dave, as you know, is true blue, obsessive about tracking down wanted men. A stickler for 'truth, justice, and the American way.' Dessert?" Olivia took a glass plate of miniature éclairs out of the refrigerator.

"Mmmm. You know I never pass up dessert." Jamie reached for an éclair. "Sure, I know you're a fan of autonomy. Call it what you will, that's what got you into all this trouble."

Olivia thought over her friend's advice, which she had asked for and now viewed with her usual misgivings. "I tell you what. I'll just wait a few days to see what Dad's up to—that negotiation he mentioned—and *then* I'll tell Dave."

Jamie groaned. "I knew you'd say that. You don't happen to have a little handgun, do you? Something small and ladylike that would fit in your handbag?"

"Of course not. You know how adamant I've been about the need for gun control."

"Me, too. I sign every damned petition," Jamie said. "Excuse me for a minute. I have to get something in my car."

Before Olivia could figure what she was up to, Jamie was out to her Mustang and back. She handed Olivia the small revolver she kept locked in her glove compartment and a box of ammunition. "You know how to use this. Your ex taught you at the same time Finch taught me, when they both belonged to that boring gun club on the Cape with all those NRA cowboys."

"No, Jamie. I really can't. There are too many children around this house, and Dave—what would he say, if he found me packing a handgun? I just hope you have a concealed to carry license."

"Of course I do. Remember that I'm much more law-abiding than you, girlfriend." Jamie put the revolver in her handbag. "Okay. I guess I knew you'd say that, but you've got me worried about you. I just want you to be safe."

~

If her father *was* lurking around her, he must be pretty good at remaining invisible, Olivia thought, as she whizzed around on local errands, keeping an eye out for that shiny black Lincoln. Never spotted him once. She hurried home as soon as possible, however, mindful of Kevin holding the fort at the house. But she kept her cell phone within easy reach on the car seat beside her.

A few days later, when she was driving to the Hawthorne library, it rang, giving her such a start, she had to steady herself to prevent lurching off onto a shoulder of the road. "Hello? Who's this?" Looking behind her car, there was no black Lincoln in sight.

"It's me, your father."

"I don't see you."

"Yes, you do. I'm in the gray Buick two cars behind you."

"Oh. I was looking for the Lincoln. You *told* me to look for you in the Lincoln."

"Yes, sorry. It was time for me to rent something different. I don't like to be predictable."

"No worries about that," Olivia said.

"How are you, honey?"

"Worried. About you. About me. About my family. How did you expect me to be? Are you all right? Any FBI types hanging around the pier?"

"The *Calypso* is moored at a different place now, a private marina that belongs to a friend of a friend. But never mind that. There's news. I've reached out to the right people, and that contract has been withdrawn."

Olivia was getting that unreal, untethered feeling again. "Are you sure, Dad?"

"As soon as they pull in their attack dog, it will all be over."

"Not quite over, then. How did you persuade these people, whoever they are, and are you sure they'll honor the deal?" Olivia turned into the Hawthorne Library lot and parked her Honda. The gray Buick did not pull in beside her.

"No question, honey. I've negotiated with this person before. If you make the offer sweet enough, he'll deal."

"Yes? How much was that? And how do you know Swett won't up the ante? By the way, where the Christ are you?"

"You're swearing again. I'm down the road a way. Swett won't raise the stakes because he doesn't know the lady gave him up. And you, you're worth every penny."

"And now what? Are you going back into hiding?"

"Not just yet. *Trust, but verify*, as the Russians say. Love you."

"Dad? Dad?" But Olivia was speaking to a dead line. Her father was gone again. She sat back and closed her eyes, waiting for her heartbeat to slow down to normal. How much of his ill-gotten millions had her father paid to save her, she wondered. *I hope he's still got enough to hide in style somewhere far, far away.*

~

If her dad has paid off this gangster, whoever he was, maybe everything would be all right. No need to tell Dave now about the return of her fugitive father, Olivia decided after thinking it over all afternoon, aided by a glass of cold Chardonnay and a little lie-down on the chaise lounge in her bedroom. When making decisions in the past, she'd always used to jot down pros and cons on a little list, but lately she'd become much more reluctant to commit her thinking process to paper.

Olivia tried to skim through her *Dangerous Situations* library book. *Quicksand. Killer bees.* But the wine had done its relaxing work, and her eyes could not resist closing for a moment. When her cell phone rang, she woke with a start of guilt."

Was it her father? Oh, God, had something gone wrong? "Yes?"

"Hey, Liv, you sound awfully anxious," Anna Gloria said. "Are you all right?"

"Oh. Anna! *No*, I'm not anxious, everything's just fine. I guess I was dozing, and the phone gave me a start. How are you?"

"How am I? Perplexed, confused…but gratified. I have news…good news, Liv."

"Just what I need, some good news. Tell me all."

"The good news is in two parts. First, I read the rest of Beth Hadley's letters. When I got to the 1918 batch, I discovered that they stopped early in the year. They stopped because the last 1918 letter welcomed Mabel Rafferty for the extended visit she had planned to make to Washington, DC, where Beth and her Cavalry officer had moved after he got wounded and assigned to a desk job there. Apparently Mabel spent a few months as a guest of her friend Beth."

"So that's where Mabel spent her fake confinement while she waited for an infant to become available," Olivia said.

"Exactly. The Senator probably sent a telegram, or phoned her if Beth had a phone, to come back immediately when Rose turned up at the Refuge. I think our theory is quite plausible, don't you?"

"Yes, I do." Keeping the phone pressed to her ear, Olivia wandered out to the kitchen and put on a pot of strong coffee. "And the letters after that?"

"Spasmodic. The correspondence fell off as both women got busy with their families. Or it's possible that Mabel was not too comfortable with Beth knowing that she'd never been pregnant. In one of the 1919 letters, Beth admired the photo of Billy that Mabel had sent her. Beth sent a picture of her own family in return, which was still in the envelope. Two boys and a girl. And that's about it."

"Oh. Well, that's no help then." Olivia sat at the kitchen table waiting impatiently for the coffee pot to signal that her much-needed shot of caffeine was ready. "I mean, we know what might have happened, Mabel hiding out so that she could claim to have given birth, but that doesn't prove who the child was."

"But wait. That's not all." Anna sounded positively elated. "Something else, something extraordinary has happened. I got this registered letter in the mail."

Olivia sat up, suddenly as alert clear-headed as if she'd already had that boost of strong coffee. "A registered letter? Typed? Unsigned?"

"Yes, how did you know? I'll read it to you. 'Miss Anna Gloria Rafferty. The enclosed is the original 1918 folder of births and adoptions from the files of St. Rita's Refuge which I retrieved from the cellar of the Chapel of Roses. I believe you will find it useful to your perfectly legitimate claim to a share of the Berwind estate'."

Olivia felt an icy thrill. Mary Poppins had another zinger up her sleeve, then. "And the enclosure?"

"It's just what the letter says it is. A 1918 folder from St. Rita's Refuge. All the records inside bear the Refuge logo. The paper looks old, the records are out of order, and some of the sheets were actually charred at the edges. Naturally, I went through all of them. And I found it!"

The icy thrill got icier. "For God's sake, what? What?"

Anna could barely restrain her excitement. "I found one dated November 15, 1918, which states that a girl named Rose Berwind had given birth to a healthy male child, that she had died the same day. The infant was baptized Hugh Redford Persey Berwind. In the margin, a handwritten note that the infant was "transferred" privately to the care of Senator Rafferty and his wife. It was signed Sr. Mary Joseph A.A."

"Has your attorney seen all this?"

"Not yet. But I've made an appointment. Dad's really sick from the latest chemo, but he's cautiously optimistic. He says that I'm the one who will have to take this forward. He's just not up to it right now."

"You can do this, Anna," Olivia said. Her part was all over now, she could relax, Olivia thought. And maybe the ghost of Rose would "rest in peace," as the saying goes, and leave her in peace, as well. And Swett, too, would have no more reason to bother about her. He'd be too busy fending off the Rafferty claim with his valkyrie attorney. Her father would disappear from her life forever. Dave would have no hard choices to make between love and the law.

Olivia took a big deep breath of relief.

NANNY BURNS GIRDS UP FOR BATTLE

If only I could reach across the Veil and pluck this young woman, Olivia, out of danger. But this is the devilish thing about being what I am, where I am—we're not real in the corporal sense. Only by an immense effort can we even stroke the cheek of a beloved child. It's like trying to squeeze through a wormhole into another time. And anyone who's done that will tell you it's a bruising affair.

But never mind my troubles. This quest all began with a connection—Hugh's marquetry case and Rose's locket—the connection Olivia made. Because of Olivia, the heart's desires of my lovely boy, Hugh, may be fulfilled—that his family will be taken care of, that his Rose will no longer grieve for her stolen child, that the lovers will be reunited in a Better Place.

Which, incidentally, will free me as well. I've rocked long enough on the Porch of All Sunsets. When this business is settled, I'm thinking very seriously of taking that cruise to the Isle of Rebirth. There are no guarantees on which Port of Call you will disembark, though. A body could land anywhere, or even any when.

But I'll jump off that bridge when I come to it. Right now, Olivia is the one I'm concerned about. There's an evil force reaching out, a force that's been unleashed to destroy her. According to the Book of Life, the agent of her death was supposed to be called back and neutralized, but some slight shift in fate prevented it. The Current of Time flows in ever-changing patterns, eddying here, there, and yonder. Even when you believe you can see clear to the bottom, watch out! Events recorded in the Book of Life are variable right up until the moment of Now passes by. Then nothing on earth can lure it back to cancel half a line (as the poet wrote.)

I can see this agent still lurking in the shadows like the bloody Ripper, marking Olivia's routines, her vulnerabilities. He has a plan in that fearsome mind of his. He's not some dog to shake his prey at breakneck speed and be done with her. He's a cat. He likes to play.

And since I have to bear a share of the blame for Olivia's hazardous situation, I'll do what I can to prevent it. But I wonder if it's possible for a ghost nanny to thrash a living, breathing bully boy?

The Guardians warn me that inserting my contrary intentions into the Current of Time, diverting the course of Destined Events, is a willful misuse of my spiritual force. Nothing is prohibited, it's true, but spending my Chi on mundane matters will delay my departure to a Higher Plane.

Nevertheless, I'm about to kick up my red stockings and wade into the fray.

OCTOBER 7

Things to Do Today

No word from P.A.?
Danny: shop for science proj.
Sign up interactive Ancient Docs
Red Sox tickets for Dave's bday
Anna: Perlmutter on board?\

Olivia was unable to keep her promise to take Danny to Computer World after school, but that was the least of her problems.

Because, just about that time, Olivia was tied up with duct tape and stuffed into the trunk of a car, heading God knows where. As far as she could tell, her handbag was gone, the panic button with it. Presumably that madman had tossed the handbag somewhere. If Dave tried to track her cell phone's GPS signal, he'd probably be directed to the store's dumpster or some remote location in the woods.

Stupid! Stupid! She'd been in the Hannaford parking lot, leaning forward to load reusable shopping bags into her van. There was a moment when she might have saved herself. She'd actually *felt* the shadow of someone looming over her back while she was stretched out to adjust the 25-pound bag of dogfood. If only she'd turned—and kicked out, and screamed bloody murder—right then! Instead she'd frozen in sudden terror while an arm, strong as a steel cable, cut off her breath in what she knew was a chokehold. Dave had shown her how to protect her throat from a chokehold by tucking her chin into the crook of the assailant's arm, but a real-life surprise assault was not the same as self-defense play in the bedroom. A few seconds after she'd realized her danger, she had been unconscious.

And now she'd woken up in this stifling trunk, bumping along some dirt road in Hell. Her hands were duct taped together behind her back, and there was duct tape over her mouth. But her feet were free. She could see the inside trunk release lever, and she attempted to kick it open—over and over again without result. Maybe he' done something to disable the lever, Olivia thought. Thinking was hard work with the pain she felt in her throat, in her arms, and across her face where the tape pulled skin taut.

Worst-case advice from *The Survivor's Handbook* replayed in her head: Three Ways to Escape from a Locked Trunk. She'd already tried and failed to release the trunk from the inside. No point in trying to dislodge the back seat of whatever vehicle this was that she was trapped in, because even if she succeeded in crawling through, her attacker would probably just stop the car and finish throttling her. All that was left, then, was to kick out the rear brake light, although her hands weren't free to wave out the hole, if she were even able to make one with her foot. How she wished she was wearing something sturdier than Minnetonka moccasins. L. L. Bean hiking boots would have been nice. Did they make hiking boots with steel toes?

She kept punching at the brake light with her moccasin. The most damage she succeeded in doing (besides bruising her big toe) was to push the brake light halfway free of its setting. What were the chances that some officer would stop this car to write the driver a "fix-it" ticket? Even if the car were stopped, she couldn't scream properly with her mouth taped up. She would have to resort to thumping around, and racking up a few more bruises.

Think! When would Dave begin looking for her? Not until he got home from work and the children started complaining, Danny because she'd "forgotten" to take him shopping for his science project, and Moira, because it was Olivia's turn to cook dinner, and a deal is a deal. Then there was that wild card, her fugitive father. Would he know? Could he do anything? He'd seemed to think he'd handled the matter, got the contract on his daughter cancelled. But what had he said? That whoever got the assignment would have to be reached and informed that there had been a change of plan. Apparently, that part hadn't happened. No one had told this goon to stand down.

Olivia was burning up in the cramped confines of the trunk. *It's like a coffin*, she thought. *Buried, but still alive.* She kept falling in and out of consciousness.

When the vehicle finally jolted to a stop, she came to with a start of pure terror. The trunk flew open. Sunlight blinded her, and a blast of cold air hit her flaming face. Looking up, she almost wished she could pass out again.

A face that might have been handsome if the mouth hadn't been twisted into a malicious sneer. Swarthy skin, tightly curled black hair. Eyes as cold as an Arctic dawn. Strong, rough hands pulled her out of the trunk and stood her on her feet, shaky and disoriented. She shook her head, trying to clear her mind and take in her situation. Not a tall man but as bulky and muscular as a wrestler. Not so very old, either—twenties, maybe. An over-built boy. She could see now that he'd parked his black Chevy sedan at the dead end of a dirt road in the deep woods. When she tried to pull away and drag her feet, the blade of a knife flashed forth in the man's hand. In an instant, she could feel the sharpness of it, her throat stung where the knife had flicked a line across it.

Was this the end? She dared not move or breathe.

"Walk," he ordered her in a surprisingly high-pitched voice, pushing her forward. Ahead she could see there was the kind of small, wooden cabin that hunters use. Was this hunting season? If only someone would wander into this small clearing, holding a rifle, and rescue her? *Yeah? And how likely was that?*

The "hulk" dragged her up three stairs onto a makeshift porch. Holding her bound hands with one of his, he stuck the knife back into a sheath at his belt and unlocked the shiny new padlock that held the door shut. He shoved her in ahead of him so violently that she fell onto the floor, her face pressed into some kind of ragged rug that smelled sickeningly of mildew and mold. Olivia felt the bile surge up from her stomach, but managed not to gag, thinking, *if he goes outside and leaves me alone, I may be able get up and run.*

He hauled her up and tossed her onto a bunk at the far side of the room, *He's a really strong bastard*, she thought. Olivia was tall, broad-shouldered, and no lightweight. But that hopeful idea of running away vanished a moment later when her kidnapper began quickly and efficiently to duct tape her ankles together. *Shit!*

He looked down at her and smiled unpleasantly. "I'll be back, and we'll play, you and me," he whispered, again in that strange squeaky voice. One big, coarse hand pinched her cheek, then stroked her neck, her breast, and her leg. Abruptly, he let her go and strode away out the door. She heard the padlock clicking shut again, and he was gone. She almost felt a sigh of relief. But not quite, since she really couldn't move, except for her head, and turning her neck was quite painful. Nevertheless, she looked around the one-room cabin. *There must be something…*

The windows, she saw now, were shuttered from the outside. What time was it now? Almost six, she thought, probably still bright—it had been a sunny day—but inside this cabin it was as dark and cold as a cave. Still, she peered around, looking for anything she might use to cut through the tape. As her eyes adjusted to the gloom, she saw the sink, a single faucet, a rough sideboard, just planks of wood. A black cook stove that might burn wood. Two frying pans hanging on the wall. A bureau with shelves above. Looked as if it held a few tin plates and cups. A table and two straight chairs. No tools in sight, except an old-fashioned shovel standing by the door, the implications of which made Olivia shudder. *The better to bury a body with.*

Maybe if she could get over to the sink, there might be something under that oilskin skirt she could use to work off the tape on her hands. But how was she going to do that with her feet bound together? *Roll?*

It took several tries to get enough motion going—back and forth, back and forth. Just praying not to break any bones, Olivia made one last mighty effort to throw herself over the edge of the cot and crash to the floor.

Holy crap! The pain in her shoulder brought tears to her eyes. And one ankle seemed to have twisted at an odd strained angle. Well, she'd just have to ignore her body and use her brain. What if she were on her feet instead of lying on the floor. Could she hop?

Pushing herself back toward the bunk, she managed to sit up with her back braced against it. Although her wrists were bound behind her back, her fingers were still free. Grasping the wooden frame of the cot with her fingers, she tried to pull herself upright again and again. And cried, because her fingers just weren't strong enough to lift the whole mass of her body upright. *Give it up, girl.*

At the edge of her worst despair, a strange feeling of calm swept over her body from her aching head to her bound feet. It was as real and physical as being brushed by a soft, warm breeze. Something or someone whispered—in her head? She couldn't be sure. *Don't be scared, dearie. Don't give up, because you will get through this. Remember, you are never alone,* the voice assured her, as if she were a frightened child. If Olivia were religious, she might have felt unaccountably blessed and protected.

With tears running down her face, tears that she couldn't wipe away, not to mention a running nose that she couldn't wipe, Olivia twisted to rub her face on the blanket. Couldn't reach. But then...she noticed something with amazement. All this pushing and pulling seemed to have loosened the tape around her wrists. She wiggled her wrists experimentally.

Yes! They *were* looser! Wasn't there something else in *The Survivor's Handbook* about duct tape? She hadn't really concentrated on that scenario, but just its presence in the handbook must mean that it *was* possible to escape. She twisted her back away from the bed, lifted her arms as high as she could and brought them down sharply. And repeatedly.

Still the tape held, but seemed even a bit looser. Olivia began to wiggle her hands upward and felt one wrist coming unstuck, just a bit, from the tape. Her hand moved upward about a fraction of an inch. Now she began to work the tape in earnest, pulling her hands up from its grip. *Oh, God, this could work.* But would it work before that bastard came back?

Olivia would never know how long it took her, but she did it. Feeling as if she'd broken both shoulders, finally one hand got free to pull the tape off the other. Then her mouth. *Ouch! Damn it to hell!* Then the feet. She stood up at last, very shakily, rubbing her legs to get the circulation going again. She found an ancient chamber pot under the bunk, and she used that with the greatest relief, but her jeans were still damp and disgusting. Just as she stood up again, she heard footsteps outside, and her heart plummeted into her solar plexus.

Olivia stopped thinking. She felt her pains recede and a strange new power surge through her. Dashing across the room, she grabbed that shovel beside the door. Lifted it above her head. Waited for the padlock to click and the door to swing open. She was as tall as her kidnapper. She had the advantage of surprise. She would crush his head like a beetle!

There seemed to be some problem with the padlock. As she waited, salt sweat ran down her forehead and stung her eyes. It sounded as if her returning jailer was twisting that lock with something heavy, like a crowbar. *Why?*

The man on the other side of the door cursed as he opened it, which probably saved him from fatal brain damage. Because in that split second before she brought down the shovel, Olivia realized that the voice she had just heard was not the squeaky tones of her kidnapper, and that the curses were in Greek. *Which was not Greek to her*. She knew those curses and that voice. Olivia hesitated for a fraction of a second. A man stepped through the door. A big gray-haired man with a trim beard, half a head taller than Olivia.

Jesus, it was her father!

~

Philip Andreas jumped away from his daughter, who held a shovel up over her head and clearly had blood in her eye. Slowly the rage and resolution in her expression faded away into incredulity.

"It's *you*! Oh, thank God. But how did you find me?" Olivia's arms slowly lowered and the shovel fell to the floor.

Andreas took her in his arms. "Yes, I do thank God. You're actually here! Are you all right? Did he hurt you?"

"Not yet. But he's coming back. He said that. I was so afraid of what he'd do then. But how did you know what happened?"

Andreas let her go and looked her over. She looked like hell, bruised and dirty, her shirt torn and her jeans stained with motor oil. He made himself smile—a warm, encouraging smile. "When I checked back with the *capo* who held the contract on you, the one who'd accepted my deal and agreed to cancel, he told me that his soldier had fallen off the grid. There was no way to notify him of the change in plan. But this *capo* is greedy, no intention of returning my fee, which was considerable. He'd rather give up his own guy—going off on his own like that indicated a lack of respect, anyway. So he told me where his soldier might have brought you, if you hadn't been dispatched immediately. He knew this cabin. It belongs to his 'boys,' the ones who fancy themselves hunters."

"Oh, my God—he'll see your car! He'll have a gun, and he'll kill us both."

Andreas looked at his daughter's terror-stricken face and felt resolve harden like a fist of ice inside him. This man who had taken his daughter—and was planning to come back to do what? Play with his prey before he murdered her? This sicko bastard must die. Andreas felt the reassuring bulk of the Glock in his belt.

"It's all right, Livvy. I walked in from a different place. I'll get you out of here, and you'll be safe, but we have to leave *now*. Before he comes back." Andreas put his arm around his daughter's shoulders, continuing to talk in a comforting low tone as he hurried her outside into the gathering darkness, striding purposefully into an overgrown path behind the cabin.

"I'll drive you home, and we'll think of something to tell your husband." Andreas felt Olivia pull away from him, saw the flush of anger cross her face. It couldn't be helped. He took hold of her wrist and pulled her along as he explained. "Because here's the thing, Livvy. This cabin belongs to people *who will kill me* if I give it up to the cops. So, you can't reveal to Dave, or anyone, where you were held because, you know, your husband will bring the State Police in and they'll swarm all over this place."

"I *don't know* where we are," Olivia wailed. "I never saw a thing except the inside of the Chevy's trunk while that creep was bringing me here."

"He's gone to ditch that stolen Chevy. His preferred mode of transportation is his Harley, unless he's carrying out a contract. We'll hear him coming back a mile away. You'll know where we are when we get to the car. Middleboro. And the 'creep' is Sonny, the little shit."

"Sonny?"

"Yes. Sonny Abruzzo. One of those wannabes who hang around the social clubs looking for any work the *capo* doesn't want his own made men to handle. But that, too, will be our shared secret." His firm hand propelled Olivia forward.

"He spoke in a strange high voice." Olivia had to push pine branches aside to follow her father through the nearly invisible path.

"Got strung up once by dissatisfied associates, so I hear," Andreas said, without slowing his pace. "Damaged his larynx. Too bad they didn't finish the job."

"You gave me Sonny's name, but what about the boss? The *capo,* as you called him. Boston, I assume. Any relation to Caesare Benedetto?"

Andreas jolted to a stop, causing his daughter to nearly topple over him. He turned abruptly, searching her face as earnestly as if he might be able to read her thoughts. "What do you know about Benedetto?"

"I know that Benedetto is in Federal prison, but such men have a long reach. And I know that he may have found my name among those who put him there."

"His sister's boy runs the business these days." Andreas turned back to the almost-path and urged Olivia along, mumbling as much to himself as to her. "Now I have to wonder how hard Falcone tried to pull Sonny back. No, he told me where to find you. He honored our deal. It will be all right."

His daughter said nothing else, breathless from the effort of following.

Benedetto! How much about my daughter's life I don't know, will never know, Andreas thought.

It took over half an hour for Andreas to reach the gray Buick he had hidden underneath sweeping branches in a pine thicket just off Route 44. He was scratched, out of breath, and achingly weary, not the man he used to be, he reflected sadly. But his daughter was safe; that in itself justified all the trouble and danger of returning to the States.

He seated Olivia, tenderly but hastily, took the wheel and slid the car out of its hiding place back onto Route 44.

She buckled her seat belt and leaned her head back, sighing deeply. "So you were tipped off about the cabin in Middleboro, but that doesn't explain how you actually found the place in those overgrown woods we just trekked through."

"It's near the Rocky Gutter Wildlife Management preserve. Hunting territory. Yes, I was surprised myself. Would you believe it if I told you I felt *guided*, that I headed through those trees as if I was following a GPS tracker straight to you."

"Maybe my resident ghost gave you a push in the right direction," Olivia said wearily.

"Come now, Livvy, even when you were a teen-ager you didn't believe in anything that couldn't be explained scientifically. Including the Church. In fact, you were quite adamant about the Church." Andreas smiled, remembering thirteen-year-old Olivia's resolute practicality. She would spend her Sunday mornings at more profitable pursuits. "Surely, you don't believe in beings you can't see?"

"Yes, I never believed in any of that metaphysical claptrap," Olivia said. "Until I began to have some experiences of the weird myself. It all started when I went to that first auction…" Her voice trailed off sleepily.

But Andreas wasn't paying close attention to Olivia's wandering thoughts. He'd begun to wonder how best to convince his daughter not to tell her detective husband, who must by now be frantic and enraged, details of her abduction that would compromise his relationship with Falcone. Would she care if his life were endangered? Well, one thing was for certain. The sooner he disappeared again—an art at which he considered himself a master—the better for all concerned.

"I'll have to drop you off somewhere close to home. You may be wondering how to avoid telling your Dave about the cabin. Many times, victims of assault are so traumatized that they cannot recall the details," he suggested.

"Yeah? Well, I remember every damned moment," Olivia said angrily. "The Daniel Webster Nature Preserve is close by our house. Maybe that would be a good place. Unless Dave has officers combing the marsh already. But we'd know, because there would be police cars jammed along the road."

Andreas felt a rush of relief as Olivia entered into the spirit of the subterfuge. At least he'd have a sporting chance of getting away. *But not just yet*, he thought. *I'll have to deal with Sonny, first. And give Swett a warning he won't ever forget.*

"Suppose I need to get in touch…"Olivia began.

"I'll call you—when I can, if I can."

They were silent for a long while they headed back to Route 3 and Marshfield. It was now past eight in the evening, mercifully dark, there being only a sliver of moon rising when at last he pulled up in a remote area of the preserve. "How about this?"

"Fine. I can walk from here." His daughter sighed, looked at him with a totally unreadable expression, and touched his cheek before she got out of the Buick. Then she leaned in the open door for a moment. "Thanks, Dad. Take care of yourself. Love you."

That moment was worth everything to him.

~

The alarm had gone out sooner than Olivia could have hoped for.

A young man collecting carts at Hannaford's had noticed the open door of a Honda van and some spilled groceries inside that looked odd. A shopping cart pulled up beside the van held a few more bags in which the employee found frozen foods, including ice cream, already thawing. He'd reported this strange occurrence to the manager, George Biggs, and Biggs hurried out into the lot to ask other shoppers if they had seen what had happened to the driver of the Honda parked in the one shaded row of spaces. No one Biggs collared had noticed anything amiss, and everyone was in a hurry to get home. So Biggs called 911. The dispatcher who took the call decided to trace the van's license number, which took only seconds. Finding the name of the person to whom it was registered took another twenty minutes. The desk officer who received the report of the abandoned vehicle's owner recognized Olivia Lowenstein's name and called Dave, just to check.

Dave raced to Hannaford's, saw for himself how the Honda had been left open and unattended, and tried to call his wife.

After his call had persistently gone to voice mail, Dave moved swiftly into full emergency mode.

A GPS signal from her cell phone located Olivia's handbag in the Donate Books box near the entrance to the parking lot.

Right about then, Dave would have gone crazy if there hadn't been definite procedures to follow in the event of a missing, perhaps abducted, person. Since the missing person was a detective's wife, a great deal of man power, vehicles, trackers, and canines were called into action in a very short time. The full scale search that Dave had initiated was called off when Olivia arrived home with her questionable story of amnesia.

"I'm sorry, honey. I've tried and tried. But I just can't remember anything after what happened in the parking lot. A total blank, I'm afraid," Olivia lied. "It was all too fast and sudden for me to protect myself the way you taught me. Maybe I hit my head when I passed out." She hoped she wasn't overdoing it. "I never even saw his face. All I remember is that arm choking off my breath, then everything went dark. The next thing I knew, I was walking through the familiar woods, and I realized that it was night. I didn't know why I was there or what had happened to me. I just wanted to get home. I seemed to be hurting all over, especially my shoulders. I felt exhausted, as if I'd walked a long way. The thought of home and a hot bath kept me going."

Having taken that longed-for bath, during which she'd perfected her story line, Olivia was now lying on her own bed, wrapped in her green terry robe, with Dave's anxious, insistent, loving face hovering over her. She'd succeeded in dodging his most relentless interrogation until after she'd bathed and been medicated. Whether he believed her or not, she couldn't quite tell.

Moira, Danny, and even Kevin were subdued and anxious, looking in the bedroom door from time to time only to be sent away, either by Dave or Jamie. Olivia had insisted she was merely shaken up and bruised, and she'd flatly refused to get checked out at Jordan Hospital. Jamie was all the nurse she needed.

Jamie had agreed. Immediately after Olivia's call, she'd located a temp to take over Jack Whelan's care in Dover and raced to Marshfield in her silver Mustang. "Good God, what steamroller rolled over you," she'd exclaimed as she'd examined and treated the various cuts, scrapes, and bruises Olivia had acquired in the hours between her abduction in the afternoon and her appearance, fainting on her own doorstep that evening. Kevin had heard her arrive and had helped her inside. She'd used his cell phone to call Dave, and then Jamie.

~

Dave loved Olivia, and he knew her changing moods by heart. He was a naturally observant man who paid attention to details, to nuances, to awkward pauses, to body language, and to eye contact, especially the unblinking honest gaze of someone who is lying. That's what made him an insightful detective, as well as a perceptive husband. And something did not ring true to him in Olivia's tale of being abducted without any memory of what had happened after the initial attack.

He could look into Olivia's eyes and see that she had been badly frightened, and was still frightened—haunted, even—by the memory of a terrifying experience from which she had somehow, by the grace of God, escaped. He could look at her body and see that she had been tied up and banged around. There was even a thin red mark or scratch on her throat.

So Dave asked himself, *why is my wife lying to me? Who or what is she protecting?*

He'd have bet the farm that Jamie knew what he did not, the true story of these last frightening hours. There had been looks and whispers between the two friends, which he had pretended not to notice and tried hard not to resent. Women were like that, capable of the intimate share-all friendships that few men were. But *damn it to hell*, this *was* police business, not some girlish prank. The important thing here was that Olivia should trust *him. He* ought to be her closest friend.

Dave shook off these negative feelings in the interest of having the clear head he would need to investigate his own wife. Perhaps Jamie was the weak link and could be persuaded. Or Olivia would open up eventually. In any case, Dave would bide his time. He would find out what had really happened to Olivia.

~

As soon as Dave had left to liaise with the team who had been searching for his missing wife, Jamie shut the bedroom door and demanded answers. "All right, Liv. What the hell has happened to you? You don't expect me to believe you've blanked out your abduction, do you? It was an abduction, wasn't it? I can see from these marks on your wrists and ankles that you were tied up, possibly with duct tape, and that you struggled to free yourself. And what's this scratch on your neck?"

Olivia grimaced. "Oh, Jamie, it's been the worst experience of my life. I've been scared out of my wits. But I don't dare tell Dave who, what, and where. I just can't."

"And why not? A gal who routinely gets herself in as much trouble as you do is fortunate to have a detective for a husband, I'd say, but only if she tells him what's really going on, however illegal or immoral. So…what *is* going on?"

"I can't tell Dave—and *you* can't tell Dave—because there are people *who will kill my father* if I reveal where I was taken and who took me. You have to *swear*..."

"Of course I swear. When have I ever broken a confidence of yours?"

Olivia reminded her of one or two incidents in their long friendship.

Jamie said, "Oh, that. Ancient history, my dear. Now tell me the whole truth, every detail. Maybe we can figure..."

"No figuring. Just absolute secrecy."

"Okay, okay." Jamie put her hand over her heart and gazed heavenward.

"I'd just finished shopping at Hannaford's and was putting my groceries into the van. I'd sort of noticed the black Chevy parked next to me, and the man getting out of it, but I really didn't pay close attention." Olivia continued her story, punctuated by occasional gasps of horror from Jamie. The chokehold that cut off her breath, becoming conscious locked in the trunk of the Chevy, the sadistic man who'd left her in that remote cabin, threatening to come back to "play." The gruesome possibilities she'd feared. She demonstrated how she'd free herself, and then, *ta da*, how her father had showed up like a superhero just in the nick of time.

"It sounds to me as if you were the Wonder Woman here. But it's good your father showed up. A girl can get hopelessly lost in those Rocky Gutter woods."

"Dad said that the man who attacked me is Sonny Abruzzo, that he works for Benedetto's old mob, now run by Caesare's sister's son."

"Small world." Jamie had once been Caesare Benedetto's private nurse. "I'm surprised that Falcone told your father how to find you. Those mobsters have long memories."

"I think there was a lot of money involved. Money that Dad paid to cancel the contract."

"Well! I guess you have to forgive him for not showing up for your high school graduation, then," Jamie said.

"Yes, I guess you're right. And the least I can do is to protect him as he protected me."

Jamie thought about that for a moment. "Agreed. Whatever he is, and wherever, Philip Andreas will always be your father, and now at least he's redeemed himself—sort of. And there's just no way to tell Dave about Sonny and the cabin without revealing that your most-wanted father is back in town. I bet there'd be a hell of a reward, though."

"I expect so, but I never wanted to know how much."

HENRY III MEETS HIS BÊTE NOIRE

In the luxurious pied-a-terre he'd leased on the new Boston waterfront (his hideaway from the genteel rigors of life on the Upper West Side in Manhattan), Henry James Swett III was fuming. After Missy Hyde had failed him miserably, he'd paid Falcone to rid him of this Marshfield woman. Yet she was still alive and well. When Swett had complained about breach of contract to Falcone, he'd been told to stuff it, that he still owed for his losses at that last high stakes poker game in the North End. Falcone would keep Swett's ten thousand contract fee "on account," and if he didn't shut up, someone would come around to collect the rest.

A total screw-up all around.

And now this shyster Perlmutter had shown up with those fucking original documents that appeared to verify an additional heir to the Berwind fortune. Swett feared it was too late now to stop the civil suit that was bearing down on him like a tsunami. He'd have to confer with his siblings—Lady Jane and that idiot Paul—should they agree to an out-of-court settlement or let the suit drag on for centuries, à la Bleak House? A family consultation was, in itself, almost more of a pain than parting with a share of the Berwind legacy. Almost, but not quite.

But something in his gut was still hungry for payback. He wanted that Lowenstein woman taught a lesson. No woman had ever got the better of him yet, including his two voracious ex-wives. There must be someone else he could hire, someone who could do the job neatly and professionally.

A soothing soak in the Jacuzzi had done nothing to restore his equanimity. Maybe he'd take a long drive while he considered his options. There was a place he knew in Providence where he could find a compliant companion for the things he enjoyed doing, his most secret pleasures. And possibly he would initiate another contact. His bookie has given him a new name and number, this one from Federal Hill. He should have gone the Providence route from the beginning and not depended on Missy Hyde. Any woman who wore pink sneakers could not be trusted to carry out decent wet work. But those Rhode Island guys were really dependable. Swett got dressed and called Syms to bring the Ferrari out of the apartment's cavernous garage.

When Swett strolled out of the ornate front doors ten minutes later, Syms had the car ready at the curb, gleaming and purring. He saluted Swett, pocketed his tip, then headed back to his office in the garage. Swett swung himself into the black and red leather seat, and inserted a tape into the player. *Soultrane* and *Lush Life* would take him all the way to Providence.

What the fuck! The passenger-side door opened and a man slid into the seat beside Swett. He was gray-haired with a neat beard, broad-shouldered, and muscular. And he was holding a Glock aimed at Swett's head. "Drive," he said. "I'll tell you where."

Swett reached for the phone in his blazer pocket.

"I wouldn't do that, if I were you." The Glock was now aimed at Swett's groin. "You and I are going to have a little talk, man to man. I'm not going to kill you, but I might do less damage if you do exactly as I tell you." He reached into Swett's pocket, lifted out the cell phone, and tossed it out the window into a storm drain.

"Who the hell are *you*?" Swett's voice was not as steady as he would have liked.

"I'm your worst nightmare, Swett. Now drive South toward the Cape, you know the way. We'll be getting off Route 3 at Exit 3 to connect with Myles Standish state forest. Nice quiet place this time of year. Don't exceed the speed limit or do anything that will attract the attention of a passing cruiser, if you want to remain operational in the future."

There was something about this man's demeanor that meant business. Swett drove carefully along the prescribed route, his mind working madly. Could this be Falcone's debt collector? No, Swett didn't think so. He knew most of those goons, the big smiles, the cold eyes, the cigars, the diamond pinkie rings. This man was grave, pleasant, polite, and convincing. *So what the fuck did he want?*

Traffic was light, and they made good time. But it was still a long drive, plenty of opportunity for Swett to review his whole life like a drowning man. But when they reached Route 3, his abductor began to explain in the same courteous tone what he wanted from Swett, And Swett vowed, on his life, that he would never bother the Lowenstein woman or any of her family and friends again. On his honor as a gentleman.

When they finally got to Myles Standish, the bearded man directed Swett to park on a godforsaken side road. Swett did not like the look of this. But he clung to the hope that this man meant what he'd said, he was not here to kill Swett. "That's all well and good, Swett. I believe you do understand that Mrs. Lowenstein is never to be troubled by you again, and whatever she is seeking from you, you will comply with in a timely and friendly manner." The man's voice was agreeable but there was a cold, menacing undertone that made Swett shiver. Swett would gladly promise this guy the crown jewels of England if he could just get home safely tonight.

"But the thing is," the calm voice continued, "I know about some of the dirty dealings in your past, Swett, and I fear you have a short memory for promises. So I'm going to leave you something to help you remember that we've had this little talk, and the assurances you've made to me. Think of them as pledged *in blood*. You'd better get out of the car though. It would be a shame to mess up a Ferrari."

~

When Swett regained consciousness, the bleeding had slowed to a trickle, his foot was tightly bandaged, and he was being driven back to his apartment. The pain was killing him, and the shock had left him weak and clammy. The man pulled the Ferrari up to the garage door and used the keychain remote to open it. He drove inside just far enough so that the door remained open, braked, and jumped out. Before he left Swett moaning pitifully, he leaned back in the open door to say one low, powerful word. "*Remember.*" Then he slammed it shut, jogged away down the street, and disappeared.

With his remaining strength, Swett sounded the horn until Syms heard the disturbance and came out of his office. Swett promised Syms a healthy bonus to park the car and get him upstairs in the service elevator to his apartment on the 12th floor, where he called a physician who would make a house call and keep quiet about it—for a generous fee paid in cash. Dr. Cornel Lovejoy's chief practice consisted of prescribing drugs to the rich and infamous. Although his trauma skills might be minimal, he did have a medical license and presumably had gone through medical school. He should be able to dress Swett's injury and administer appropriate antibiotics and maximum pain meds. More importantly, he would not report the matter to the police.

THE SWETT SIBLINGS IN CONFERENCE

Later, Swett gave out the story that he'd been cleaning his pistol when the accident had occurred, amputating the big toe on his right foot. During a slow and painful recovery in the Boston apartment, he'd been approached again by Sonia Perlmutter on the matter of the newly discovered heir—was the Swett family prepared to settle the Rafferty claim and avoid costly and lengthy litigation?

Swett implored his brother and sister to attend a conference in his waterfront apartment. Although not as large as the one he owned in the Dakota, it had a generously proportioned great room. His attorney, Gretchen Weinhardt, would be present, as well as an attorney from Lady's Jane's firm, Hatchett, Hammer, and Cleaves, and Paul's legal representative, Basappa Ramaswami, Esq.

Swett did indeed "*remember*" his ordeal in Myles Standish State Forest, and he was still afraid. An assassin had appeared out of nowhere, a lunatic who did not threaten idly, who had warned Henry not to harm the Lowenstein woman or to stand in the way of whatever cause she championed. Henry's dearest wish now was to get the whole ugly business settled for all time, and his aim in calling this meeting was to gain the cooperation of his siblings on this solution.

Lady Jane screamed blue murder, and murder in every other color. Paul sulked and fingered his worry beads. Henry rested his foot on the raised footrest of his motorized wheelchair and waited for the storm to subside.

When Lady Jane had finally quieted, Henry addressed his siblings and their attorneys in a reasonable, conciliatory tone: "Surely it's in no one's best interest for this suit to drag through the courts for years and years. The Berwind evidence is flimsy and inconclusive at best, but that will not prevent the Raffertys from suing us in civil court."

Invited to discuss the situation informally with the Swetts, Ms. Perlmutter arrived last. A short, heavy woman with iron-streaked hair and a geniality reminiscent of Madame DeFarge in the front row at the guillotine, she sat in an upright side chair with her briefcase close at hand.

After introductions and Lady Jane's cool offer of coffee all around, Ms. Perlmutter distributed multiple copies of the documents attesting to the birth of Hugh and Rose Berwind's son at St. Rita's Refuge and his secret adoption into the Rafferty family. Perlmutter's client, Anna Gloria Rafferty, acting on behalf of her family, was young, strong, and smart—a plaintiff with patience and time on her side.

"Is this all you have? How do you intend to verify this stuff? It could all have been forged. Indeed, it looks specious to me." Lady Jane cast her copies aside dismissively "What do you think, Josef?"

Josef Hammer made a noise in his throat that was perhaps affirmative, and perhaps not.

Henry said that he didn't believe these documents would hold up in court, but the Swetts would like to avoid the ugly publicity of a civil suit and would be open to considering a reasonable settlement.

Ms. Perlmutter said that the documents had been affirmed by the Diocese of Worcester to be genuine. The ink's age had been verified, the paper was identical to other surviving St. Rita's records, the signatures matched by a handwriting expert to the same elsewhere in St. Rita's files. Perlmutter had advised the Raffertys that a fourth heir should be entitled to a fourth of the estate, which when valued might be worth as much as fifty million.

Lady Jane laughed until she coughed and lost her breath. Josef Hammer closed his notebook and zipped up his briefcase. Ramaswami mopped his brow with a large white handkerchief and looked pleadingly from one to another.

Henry nodded at his attorney and sent a warning glance to his simmering sister.

Ms. Weinhardt said that the Swetts were prepared to offer three million to settle this nuisance suit, in return for the Raffertys renouncing all future declarations of Berwind parentage and claims on the Berwind estate.

Henry had calculated that Ms. Perlmutter's share, one million, a sure thing for very little work, would be incentive enough for her to recommend a speedy settlement to her client.

"I will bring your niggardly offer to my client," Perlmutter said. "But I will recommend that she not accept it."

The legal representatives departed soon after, taking with them their heavy, expensive briefcases and all semblance of reason and civility.

"Well, I think that went well," Paul said with a beamish smile.

Lady Jane regarded her brother with a pitiless sigh. "Paul, how can you manage to be so utterly clueless at your age?"

Henry said, "If the Rafferty girl will settle for three mil, we will be well rid of her."

"Henry, you always were an ass, and you still are, but I take your point." Lady Jane studied the pale, beseeching expression on her elder brother's face. "But why does my intuition tell me that that's a little more in this for you? What are you keeping from us?"

"I need to be rid of the Raffertys for good and all. My health will not take any more of this."

"In that case, if the Raffertys agree to three mil, will you be willing to sell the Dakota place to pay the freight?" Lady Jane, a veteran of the divorce courts, knew when her quarry was weakening.

"No!" Paul surprised them both with his vehemence. "You can't put this all on Henry. The karmic repercussions of defrauding our brother would follow us for eternity, Janie. I say, we let those overpaid accountants figure all this out for us, and by the time they get through, it will turn out to be some kind of tax advantage."

"In my opinion, Perlmutter and the Raffertys haven't a leg to stand on." Gesturing her derision, Lady Jane inadvertently hit Henry's wheels. Henry moaned.

"Oh, sorry, Henry. Is it very painful? Do you have enough meds? Who's your doctor?"

"Lovejoy."

"Oh, well, then..." Lady Jane said.

"So we're agreed?" Paul persisted.

"All right, you two wankers, but you'd better hope that the accountants can deal with the financial fallout," Lady Jane said ungraciously. "I don't want my income to be one penny less because of your reluctance to fight the good fight."

"I rather think the Raffertys will jump at the bait," Henry said. "Gretchen did a little background check, and they're in deep trouble, maxed out everywhere, teetering on the brink of bankruptcy, and both parents have huge medical liabilities."

"I'll drink to that," Paul said.

The siblings settled down to toast their fleeting moment of agreement. Lady Jane opened a bottle of Henry's Veuve Clicquot. Paul made himself a pot of decaffeinated green tea.

"One for all, and all for one!" Paul lifted his cup with a gallant smile.

"Never let them see you, Swett." Lady Jane resurrected their teen-age motto.

"Thank Christ this is almost over," Henry declared, and drank deeply.

OCTOBER 18
Things to Do Today

Poss. Wm.-Sonoma w/ Moira
Vinny T for weekend
Check w/ Anna R.
Honda service & sticker—send Kevin?
5-yr plan—pursue new career, ancient docs, no ghostly vibes

Olivia's roses had bloomed on through September, but the rigors of October eves soon blasted the last of the blooms away. On a deceptively sunny afternoon early in October, Olivia ventured outside to sip hot coffee on the front porch and admire the very last rose of summer, a Yankee Lady, hardy rosa rugosa. The rest of the Yankee Ladies had already gone to rose hips, shiny red-gold fruits. She thought about harvesting a colander full of those and making a batch of rose hip jelly. Perhaps a project to share with Moira. It would require the purchase of jars, covers, a jelly strainer, a candy thermometer, and heaven knows what else. There was nothing Moira enjoyed more than a trip to a kitchen equipment store, even though almost everything could be bought online. There were probably some old-time recipes for rose hip jelly in the box lot of collectible cookbooks she'd brought for Moira at that auction last June.

How different this last six months would have been if she'd never won the bid on Hugh Berwind's marquetry case that fateful evening and found his handwritten will under its lining! Well, for one thing, she wouldn't have been haunted (again!) by ghosts seeking justice, wouldn't have put the whole family in danger pursuing the wrongs of the past, wouldn't have met the Raffertys and taken up their cause, wouldn't have been kidnapped by that sleazebag Sonny, wouldn't have been contacted by her enigmatic father, and, not least, wouldn't be in this quandary about what to tell Dave.

I really should think seriously about that. But the effort of concentrating slipped away into a light trance as she rocked in the comfortable rocker and gazed at the spoils of October. Arbors over the front gate and elsewhere in the garden were no longer blazing with roses, and the brisk air was fragrant only with the moist odor of sweet decay. But many of the rose bushes, particularly the English hedging roses, were still green-leafed and would be until the first killing frost. As she gazed at the wrought iron bench, a white misty column seemed to rise and move dreamily through the paths between bushes, trailing wisps of vapor like long sleeves. A shiver of breeze moaned through garden. Olivia smelled the fragrance of roses that weren't there anymore. *Rose! Would she never be at peace?*

Olivia's cell phone rang, shattering her spellbound mood.

"It's me," her father said.

"Yes. Is everything all right?"

"That's what I called to tell you. I'm fairly confident that you will never be troubled by Swett and any of his hired thugs again. I thought that you would want to know that you can take a deep breath and go on with your peaceful life as it used to be, and your family as well."

"Oh my God, what did you do?"

"Only as much as I had to. I expect to leave within the week, so you will be able to tell your detective that you have remembered a little more about your ambush. But I would rather you didn't mention Rocky Gutter, though. After all, Falcone did honor our deal, and it would be a shame to have the FBI tracking through those woods, spooking his merry men and scaring off the deer."

"So…I won't see you again?" Olivia admitted to herself that she felt a shiver of loss.

"Who can predict what the future may bring? But no, probably not. Providing you can stay out of trouble."

"Doubtful." Actually, Olivia had vowed to stay out of trouble forever, but she was curious to know how her father would respond to a whiff of future dangers.

"Not much chance I'll get a tip from an anonymous well-wisher very time someone's gunning for you. But if you do ever need me, put a classified ad in the *Cleveland Plain Dealer*. For sale: Greek Orthodox Icon St. Ariadne of Phrygia."

"You read the *Cleveland Plain Dealer*? St. Ariadne? What should I use for a contact number?"

"No, not personally. Someone reads it for me. Too complicated to explain. Legend has it that St. Ariadne successfully hid from her pursuers in the mountains of Phrygia. Use any name and phone number that isn't yours."

"Dad! Be careful. Find a good place and stay safe."

"I love you, Livvy." And he hung up before she could reply.

~

On Saturday morning, Anna Gloria called to say that she'd had an offer of settlement from the Swetts, which she and her dad had decided to accept, if only to put all this ugly business behind them. Olivia was thrilled; she just hoped it was enough, but it seemed ill-mannered to ask. Anna wondered if it would be okay to stop by on Saturday afternoon; she would be on her way to visit an artists' colony in Truro. She wanted to see again the marquetry case that had belonged to her great-grandfather who died in World War I. The original copy of Hugh Delano Berwind's handwritten will was in the hands of the Rafferty's attorney now, but Anna wanted to hold the case that had contained it one more time.

"Of course you may. And it would be wonderful to see you." *Perfect solution!* Olivia was thinking. She would give Anna the marquetry case and the locket. Not only did they belong in spirit to the Raffertys, but there was always the hope that the Berwind ghosts would go along with them. Would she have to warn Anna of that possibility? *Oh, I suppose so.*

Anna arrived in a Hyundai Elantra that looked new. "Venetian Red, don't you love it? Only a year old. It's my going-back-to-RISD celebration car." She pronounced it *RIZ DEE.*

Dave popped out of the garage to meet the visitor, allowing her to admire his sculptures before returned to his latest creation, St. Joan on horseback.

"Those are really fine," Anna said. "Your husband ought to think about having his own show someday."

"Dave relegates his art work to hobby status, but I'll suggest it," Olivia said. "Has your Dad bought a new car, too?"

"Dad's still hanging on to his old van for the time being. Like he doesn't believe in the settlement. We've been church mice for so long…"

"I understand caution. Your dad should look at a Mercedes, though. I have a feeling your mother would love it." Olivia couldn't believe she heard herself say, *I have a feeling…* If this kept up, she'd end up as daft and ditzy as the ladies at the library.

"You're right about that. My mom adores understated luxury. And Dad would do anything to bring back her smile. They love each other so much." Anna, who had been beaming with excitement, suddenly looked near tears.

They were standing in the kitchen while Olivia made up a tea tray. Olivia put down the cups and took Anna into her arms. She could almost feel her warm affection for this young woman flowing from her heart to Anna's. *What was this now? Amateur Reiki?*

Sashaying into the kitchen, accompanied by Sadie, Moira broke the mood with a scornful look at the tray. "You ought to put on some of those oatmeal cookies I made yesterday. Chocolate chips and raisins. Better than that stuff." She flipped scornfully though the store-bought gingersnaps Olivia had arranged on a glass plate.

"Anna, this is my…my step-daughter Moira. Moira, this is Miss Anna Gloria Rafferty. She's a student at the Rhode Island School of Design."

"Yeah. Nice to meet you, Miss Rafferty. I hear the culinary program at RISD is pretty good. I'm going to Johnson & Wales, maybe. What do you think?"

"I'm glad to meet you, too. And this little girl is… Sadie?" Anna's outstretched hand seemed to fascinate Sadie. Possibly lingering traces of Shamus, Olivia thought.

"You should visit them both and feel the vibes for yourself. Let me know if you schedule a trip to RISD, and I'll show you around," Anna said. "Providence is a super culinary city."

"Yeah, maybe. Thanks."

While Moira was arranging her oatmeal cookies on top of the gingersnaps, Danny trooped into the room with a wide grin and his pal Vinny T, who was staying for the weekend. Bruno trotted along behind the boys, tongue handing out of one side of his mouth, tail madly waving. Suddenly the kitchen seemed quite crowded.

After Olivia introduced Anna to the boys, they instantly grew quieter, stopped pushing each other, and were mannerly, an affect the exotic girl would probably have on males of any age. Even Dave had stood taller when introduced to Anna.

Then Danny blurted out, "We need some sandwiches and stuff, Aunt Liv. We're going hiking in Daniel Webster." Danny appeared to be excited over a hike in the local nature preserve. Usually he was indifferent to outdoor activities in favor of hunching over his computers, and he had few school friends. So this was good. Even though Danny's best bud's dad was "connected"—*Cadillac Tom Tornitore*. Dave did not believe in interfering in teen friendships, but he was keeping a close eye on this one.

"I'll make their lunches, Liv," Moira offered. She began sliding gingersnaps off Liv's glass plate into a small baggie. "Ham and cheese, okay? Vinny likes roasted peppers, too, right?"

"If you end up at the beach, don't throw sticks in the water for Bruno. It's too cold now," Olivia warned. "And take your phone." All the O'Haras had GPS tracking devices in their cell phones.

Full of joy and Saturday energy, the boys slammed out into the garage to find Dave. Olivia left the picnic fixings in Moira's competent hands and whisked Anna into her office, where she'd already brought the Berwind marquetry case, carefully protected by white tissue in an open cardboard box, ready to transfer to the legitimate hands of Hugh's great-granddaughter. Anna touched it reverently, opened the top to read the inscription inside, ran a finger over the newly polished brass. "Was it his mother who gave Hugh this, do you think?"

"No, I believe it was his old nurse, Nanny Burns, who loved him very much. She still worked for the Berwind family and was sorry to be parted with her 'lovely boy' as he went off to Phillips Exeter." Olivia did not add that she'd heard this herself from the ghost of the old nurse.

It was another unusually warm day, so Olivia brought her guest onto the front porch, insuring a private chat on a busy Saturday. Talking quietly, they drank their scalding tea. The bushes surrounding the bench were still green-leafed, with a sprinkling of yellow. They'd be gone soon enough, though. Olivia sighed.

"Sonia met with the three Swett heirs and their attorneys," Anna said. "Henry Swett has an apartment on the Boston Waterfront. Very ritzy."

"It should be. The Berwind estate was worth 200 million when the Swetts got their hands on it."

"I can't even imagine a sum like that," Anna said. "Still, money can't buy brains. Sonia said Henry was in a wheelchair. Apparently, he'd had an accident while cleaning his gun. Shot off his own big toe."

Olivia thought about that. How many times was "an accident while cleaning his gun" the euphemism for something else? To prevent an incident from becoming public knowledge.

Anna continued blithely, "With the Swett settlement in process—it's three million, Liv!—we've been able to hire some full time nursing help. Your friend Jamie gave us some good recommendations, and I believe we've found ourselves a treasure. With someone to watch over Mom—and Dad, too, when he needs it—I feel as if a heavy cloak has been lifted off my shoulders, although I never thought of it as heavy while I was wearing it. Dad's last tests were good. He may be in remission. But caring for Mom alone is just too much stress. Most of the time, though, he soldiers on, even cooks many of their meals. He's been doing some writing, too. A history subject that has always interested him. World War I. Anyway, now that I'm free to return to RISD, even though it's midterm, the future seems to be opening up for me. I'll be able to graduate next year, and there's a gallery in New York that's expressed an interest in my work. We'll see. Fingers crossed."

Olivia breathed a quiet sigh of gratitude. People who'd never been wealthy could get by quite well on the two million the Raffertys would end up with, after Perlmutter took her slice. "All excellent news. And there's something else I want you to take with you." Olivia reached into her pocket and took out the locket. "I think your great-grandmother would want you to have this."

Anna opened the locket with her fingernail and gazed at the portrait. "She was so beautiful," she sighed. "Thank you."

"I bought the locket and the marquetry case at two different auctions, strangely enough. Maybe it's my imagination, but once connected in my possession, their joined energy drew me into your family's past," Olivia said. "I ought to warn you that these two keepsakes might be haunted."

"I wouldn't mind," Anna said. "They're family, after all." Impulsively, she hugged Olivia warmly and kissed her on both cheeks in the Italian style. "You have been our blessed angel. I will never forget your goodness in finding our true family roots."

Later, as Olivia watched Anna walk gracefully down the garden path to her car, carrying her family treasures, the last of the afternoon sun seemed to follow her, burnishing the long dark hair, lingering on the lush figure. Olivia blinked, then blinked again. Yes, she thought she saw a misty figure rise from the bench and follow the girl, melting into the last of the sunlight as Anna swung herself into the driver's seat of the Hyundai.

Rose, Olivia thought. *She's touched her great-granddaughter, she's seen that Anna's all right, better than all right, glowing with her loving nature, her talent, and her new freedom. Now Rose can leave this earthly plane of existence, and maybe find Hugh somewhere in that other dimension*. Olivia liked to believe that love continues forever.

~

Jamie stopped by Sunday evening, right after her ex had picked up Mike. Everyone was watching the Red Sox game in the living room amid noisy cheers and catcalls. With a meaningful glance and a slight inclination of her head, Jamie indicated that she and Olivia should talk elsewhere. "Let's go into my office," Olivia suggested.

"And bring wine," Jamie said. They detoured to the kitchen to fill glasses with the open bottle of Merlot in the refrigerator.

Jamie sat in the sometimes-haunted rocker, her feet on the footstool, Olivia in the small green wing chair. She thought Jamie wanted to hear all the latest from Anna. Well, yes, but that wasn't all. She'd brought a copy of the *Boston Globe*, dated October 16, folded to highlight a small item on page 3.

> *Fatal Motorcycle Accident in Allston. Santino Abruzzo, 37, of Medford, was killed instantly yesterday when his 2012 Harley-Davidson motorcycle crashed into parked front-end loader at the Purgatory Road construction site. Police were called to the area about 1:45 a.m. said Officer Steven Garfield, a police spokesman. Nearby residents who were awakened by the crash complained that it took the police nine minutes to arrive at the site. Abruzzo had been decapitated by*

> *the shovel and was pronounced dead at the scene. The cause of the accident is under investigation.*

"Good God! Santino. Sonny?" Olivia said.

"...will trouble you no more." Jamie finished the sentence. "I tracked down the obituary. Santino was 'Sonny' to his family and friends. Leaves a mother and two sisters. It could be a coincidence, but...do you suppose?"

"I refuse to suppose," Olivia said. Still, she folded the article and put it under the Lalique paperweight on her desk.

"Has *he* got away?"

"Yes."

"That's good then. Superheroes should always get lost after danger has been averted and the villains foiled."

"We don't know..."

"Sure, we don't," Jamie said.

~

Troubled by her own shifting world view, whose former solidity seemed to be shape-changing like Salvatore Dali's pocket-watch in "The Persistence of Memory," Olivia had been avoiding the Black Hill branch library and Mrs. Ritchie. The librarian would only jar Olivia's tenuous hold on her old universe. But after Anna's visit, it occurred to Olivia that she really owed her the last chapter of the Berwind story. It was Mrs. Ritchie who had sent her to St. Rita's in the first place.

After all the fears of recent months, Olivia felt a heady sense of freedom when she took off for south Plymouth on Monday afternoon. She was no longer weighed down by the responsibility of protecting their home and family from unknown dangers. Her father's assurance that she would be troubled no more, while worrisome for other reasons, was somehow convincing. And for sure, she knew that her personal nightmare, Sonny, could never threaten her again. However the accident had happened, she would choose to believe that Sonny had misjudged his speed, his vehicle, and the dark road with its hazardous construction site.

When she drove into the library parking lot, there were a very few cars, as was usually the case. Not for the first time, Olivia worried that someday the underuse of this branch might come to the attention of those who allocate library funds, and the decision would be made to close its doors. Some of today's visitors were not even library patrons; Olivia remembered that the green Rav4 and blue Mazda wagon parked there today belonged to ladies of Mrs. Ritchie's circle. She wondered if she'd get a chance to speak to Mrs. Ritchie at all.

But as it turned out, she was welcomed like an old friend, not only by Mrs. Ritchie, but also by the petite blonde who was called Dee Ryan, and the other woman with the entrancing smile, Cass something.

She found the three women sitting together at one of the round tables, their heads together as if conferring. *Or plotting something*? A line from Macbeth came to mind, *when shall we three meet again?*—but Olivia brushed it away. Really, the ladies *were* a bit strange but it wouldn't do to become overly fanciful about the ordinary housewives of Plymouth.

"Ah, Olivia! You're alone at last," the blonde cried with a mischievous twinkle in her eyes, two dimples in evidence.

"Alone?"

"Well, yes. I mean, without those pesky ghosts hanging around you."

That was true. Olivia could feel it, too, surely part of her newfound sense of freedom. But she hesitated to go there with this young woman whom she hardly knew.

Mrs. Ritchie rescued her from replying. "Oh, don't mind, Dee. Her ability to see beyond the Veil is sometimes discomforting."

"That's an understatement," Dee said wryly. "I usually say nothing of this to the mundanes, Olivia. The witch laws may have been repealed—nevertheless, I err on the side of caution. But Fiona has sort of adopted your pursuit of justice for the dead…"

The mundanes? What or who? "Thank you," Olivia said, although not sure for what. "Actually, I'm here today just to tell Mrs. Ritchie that the issue of the unknown Berwind heir has reached a happy resolution. The Swetts, inheritors of the entire Berwind fortune, have agreed to a settlement, which to them may seem paltry, but to the Raffertys is like winning the lottery just as you're about to have your household goods repossessed. So, in a sense, everyone's happy."

"Even your unseen companions?" Dee asked.

"I believe they're following their hearts—and their hearts belong to a lovely, talented young woman, Anna Gloria, who is the last of Hugh Delano Berwind's direct family line. I know they'd want me to thank you especially, Mrs. Ritchie."

"You're free of them, then," Mrs. Ritchie's friend, Cass, said. She'd been sitting quietly, seemingly fascinated by the little dragonfly Tiffany lamp on the librarian's desk, but now she turned the full force of her remarkable green eyes toward Olivia. "But there's something I'm seeing that I believe you want to know."

Not looking away, Olivia waited for whatever would come next.

"I'm seeing a traveler—someone you care about very deeply. He is getting off a plane in Madagascar. I think he's being met by a vintage Rolls. The driver is relieved to see him again." Cass sat back and closed her eyes. "That's about it, but I think it will mean something to you. I mean, to know that this particular man has landed safely."

Olivia felt tears sting her eyes. Even if this clairvoyant pronouncement was bogus, it was totally comforting. She would Google Madagascar as soon as she got home, hoping to find that the country had no extradition treaty with the US. *Be safe, Dad*.

Dee went into the tiny kitchen and came back with a glass of something she handed to Cass. "Water and ginger syrup," she said. "Helps with the nausea."

Having had about as much metaphysical stuff as she could manage to stomach herself, Olivia left soon after. She was warmly hugged by Mrs. Ritchie, and soothed by the soft tinkle of her many silver bangles. "You must be a guest at one of our full moon Esbats, dear. I think you'll find it quite inspiring. *If horses were wishes, a-riding we would go.*"

~

The studied disinterest of teenagers that Kevin affected at all times dropped off him in an instant when he saw the old Toyota that Dave had bought him. A private sale from one of Dave's colleagues, the Corolla was slate gray with a few dents and scrapes, but a smile of pure joy illuminated the boy's face. Olivia couldn't help smiling herself. *He'll remember this as the best gift ever—his ticket to freedom, to impressing Norah,* she thought. What a chance Dave was taking on Kevin's good sense—what a fine, generous man she'd married! Sometimes she really wondered how good-hearted Dave had ever been drawn to policing—it would make more sense if he'd entered the clerical life.

The thought of that made Olivia smile even more. *Well, maybe not. Way too sexy!*

She was still wrapped in her amused, grateful private mood, when they went to their room later. *Maybe now is the time*, she thought as she slipped into bed. Not for nothing was she wearing a silky new nightgown.

"Dave, I think I've remembered a little more about—what happened to me—you know, that time at Hannaford's."

Dave looked down at his wife without comment. Really, he could be infuriatingly inscrutable at times. Nevertheless, she went ahead with her prepared, edited version of the abduction. She even thought she knew the thug's name. Santino Abruzzo. She'd seen that name printed on something inside the cabin where that Neanderthal had brought her. The only part of her ordeal that remained too blurry to recall was the cabin's location. Dave sat down beside her on the bed and took her in his arms. *So far, so good,* she congratulated herself.

"Liv, sweetheart. There's a little more to this story than you're telling me, isn't there?" Dave said. "Your father's the real reason you've had this traumatic amnesia, right? I believe you're protecting him. You thought I'd give him up to the FBI if I knew he was back in the States. He is or was back in the States, right?"

Olivia had rarely been left speechless in her lifetime, but this was one of those times. She buried her face in Dave's shoulder, hiding her embarrassment, her fear.

His embrace tightened. Reassuring. "It took me a while to work this out, you know. But I started with the premise that the Liv I know and love has a brilliant mind, and she takes pride in remembering details. This is a woman who can kill in stock trading through sheer data analysis. Who will find the most obscure fact hidden in some moldy old records. And now she's telling me that she can't remember what happened after she was subdued and abducted from a supermarket parking lot? Give me a break!"

"I don't know what you mean," Olivia mumbled, still without revealing her red face and chagrined expression.

"So I began to consider motive. What would motivate Liv to lie to me, the one person who was most intent on avenging her, who wanted more than anything in the world to take down the creep who had frightened and abused his wife? And then I had this thought. Is there anyone in Liv's life, in her past even, who she might try to protect, even from her husband? *Especially* from her husband, the detective, a man sworn to uphold the law and apprehend criminals? *Bingo!*" Dave unclenched Olivia's hold on his shoulder and looked her in the eye. "He's gone now, isn't he? Your father, wanted by the FBI for grand larceny. *That's* why you've suddenly 'remembered' a few more details."

Olivia looked into those soft, kind brown eyes that always drew her in, and had ever since she'd first met Dave. "All right. I confess. No wonder you decided to become a detective. When you can't find the actual evidence, you just push ahead on suspicion and intuition, right?"

"Right. Now let's hear the truth. All of it."

If Cass the clairvoyant is worth her salt, Dad is safe in Madagascar now. So Olivia told Dave all she remembered, including the part her father had played in her rescue, leaving out only the Rocky Gutter site. Dave would probably figure that out, too, she worried. Still, she claimed she'd been totally lost in the woods somewhere, that her father had found her and driven her as close to home as he dared.

"I can't say I'm sorry not to have been caught on the horns of *that* dilemma—whether to give up your father or not," Dave said.

"And would you have?"

"We'll never know now, will we?"

Dave was smiling, though. And what she saw in his face was that this was a man she could trust above all others, the one who would never hurt or betray her. At this moment, she believed Dave wouldn't have made himself a hero in the eyes of the FBI at the expense of his wife's pain and misery. He knew all too well what his foster-children went through with their mother locked up in Federal prison. Dave was on her side, always. *Good to know!*

She reached up to kiss that warm, generous mouth, and the kiss just kept on growing more intense until they were both swept up into their own private, timeless world, a place they shared with no one else. Its laws were particular to themselves, and its first commandment was to be true to their love. Everything else came second.

In November, a large flat package arrived by UPS. The delivery man propped it by the front door, shrouded in plastic against the cold drizzle. Olivia was grateful that Sadie and Bruno were indoors at the time. Strange packages made them nervous, and rightly so.

She opened it on the kitchen table and felt a flush of surprise and pleasure. In a style reminiscent of the Impressionists, but totally her own nonetheless, Anna had created a rose garden with shimmering images of a girl in a white dress and a man in uniform. The two figures seemed to be made of a bright soft energy that blended into the garden. Olivia could not be sure where their images ended and the leaves began. The note said, "This is the way I envision Hugh and Rose, together and at peace at last. I wanted you to have a reminder of how grateful they must be, as we are, for your bringing the truth to light. Love, Anna Gloria."

Made in the USA
Columbia, SC
10 July 2018